分類主題
ESSENTIAL
實用搭配詞
Collocation

MP3下載引導頁面

https://globalv.com.tw/mp3-download-9789864544233/

掃描QR碼進入網頁並註冊後,按「全書音檔下載請按此」連結,可一次性下載音檔壓縮檔,或點選檔名線上播放。
全MP3一次下載為zip壓縮檔,部分智慧型手機需安裝解壓縮程式方可開啟,iOS系統請升級至iOS 13以上。
此為大型檔案,建議使用WIFI連線下載,以免占用流量,並請確認連線狀況,以利下載順暢。

Introduction
前言 ≡

說得自然，寫得道地：搭配詞的力量

WHAT IS COLLOCATION?
什麼是搭配詞？

「a tall boy」和「a tall building」這兩種表達方式都是正確的。然而，以「a high building」與「a high boy」來說，只有「a high building」是正確的表達，沒有「a high boy」這種說法。換句話說，building 這個單字既可以與形容詞 high 也可以與 tall 搭配使用，而 boy 則僅與 tall 搭配使用。

像這樣，某些特定單字與其他單字經常一起使用的情況，稱為「連語」或「搭配詞（collocation）」。以字源的觀點來說，在 collocation 這個字彙中，col 表示「一起」，locate 表示「出現，被發現」，因此可以理解為「一起出現的詞語」。以下再看一些搭配詞組的例子：

- a heavy smoker：老菸槍（經常吸菸的人）。表示 smoker 這個單字常與形容詞 heavy 搭配使用。

- get approval from...：獲得…的許可。表示 approval 這個名詞經常

與動詞 get 和介系詞 from 一起使用。get 後面通常會接名詞，當它接名詞 approval 之後，後面常常會再接介系詞 from，用來表達「獲得…的認可」。

- attitudes towards...：attitude 常與介系詞 towards 搭配使用，表示「對於…的態度」。
- closely related with...：表示「與…密切相關」，副詞 closely 修飾分詞 related，表達「關係密切的」的意思。

WHY COLLOCATION?
為什麼要學搭配詞呢？

那麼，為什麼我們要學習「不同字詞搭配在一起」的單字學習法，而不是單純記憶單字本身呢？背單字已經很困難了，為什麼還要額外學習搭配詞呢？接下來將從三個方面進行說明，請牢記重點。

學習搭配詞的三個原因！

第一，對於語言的四大技能（聽、說、讀、寫）有極大的幫助。

第二，語言習得的過程並非學習「單一字彙」，而是學習語言的「組塊」。

第三，「語言的組塊」（搭配詞）常常沒有明顯的規則（意即，母語人士習慣這樣說）

首先，學習搭配詞對於口說和寫作有極大的幫助。舉個例子，你應該熟悉動詞 give 吧！這個單字的含義多樣化。但是，僅僅知道 give 有很多種意思，就能真正掌握這個動詞了嗎？當然不是。具體來說，我們必須了解 give 在實際生活中是如何運用的，也就是說，只有真正掌握「give 的搭配詞」，才能說自己真正了解 give 這個動詞。例如，從「give someone a gift（給某人禮物）」這樣的日常簡單表達，到「give one's word（做出承諾）」這樣稍微複雜的用語，只有當你對這些用法瞭若指掌時，才能說自己真正掌握了 give 這個動詞。因此，平時學習並熟記與 give 相關的搭配詞，才能在口說和寫作中將這個動詞運用得恰到好處。

當我們熟悉大量的搭配詞時，不只在英文閱讀上能明顯提升速度與理解力，也能增加閱讀時的信心。同樣地，在聽力方面，對常見搭配詞的掌握也能減少逐字理解的負擔，讓理解更快速、自然。例如，當你閱讀或聽到「surf the net」這個短語時，即使你知道 surf 是「衝浪」，net 是「網路」，但如果不了解這兩個單字的結合意思是「上網，瀏覽網頁」，那麼你就得再花時間去理解兩個字結合起來的意思。而這些零散的時間積累起來，就會成為學習者之間閱讀和聽力能力有差距的根源。因此，如果你已具備一定的詞彙基礎，並希望提升多益（TOEIC）、托福（TOEFL）…等考試的成績，學習搭配詞是不可或缺的過程。

第二，學習語言的過程其實就是學習「搭配詞」的過程。回想我們兒時學習說話的過程，與其說是逐字逐詞地學習，不如說是透過特定情

境中的語言輸入，將多個詞彙結合在一起的學習過程。一開始，孩子可能學會像「媽媽」、「爸爸」、「水」這類的單字，但不久之後，他們會整體吸收像「喝水吧」、「和媽媽一起玩吧」這樣的表達方式。也就是說，他們會接觸到像「喝水」、「和⋯一起玩」⋯這樣的搭配詞。因此，跨越單字學習的範圍，進入搭配詞的學習領域是很重要的。

最後，有個重點：英文裡的搭配詞很多都難以用文字的邏輯來解釋，因此通常必須特別去記憶。例如，英文裡的「警告」是 warning，那麼「發出警告」的「發出」應該搭配哪個動詞呢？許多人可能會回答「make warnings」，但其實在英語中，「provide warnings」的使用頻率遠高於「make warnings」。換句話說，儘管「make warnings」在語法或語意上並沒有特別不妥之處，但「provide warnings」顯得更加自然。因此，對於某些特定的表達，與其依賴邏輯，不如透過記憶來學習和掌握這些搭配詞。

Now, COLLOCATION!
現在，開始來學搭配詞吧！

雖然我們經常在背單字，或翻閱單字書，但很多人可能連一句完整的英文都無法順利說出口，也無法正確寫出一個完整的英文句子，或者，雖然認識一些單字，但一聽到英文廣播就腦袋一片空白，閱讀文

章時還得費盡心力花上許多時間勉強讀懂了一些內容。《分類主題 實用搭配詞》這本書，就是希望帶大家再次檢視自己的英文單字學習方式。透過搭配詞的訓練，我們想強調的是一種不同於以往的字彙學習模式，也期待和大家一起分享在英文學習路上成長與進步的喜悅。

《分類主題 實用搭配詞》，推薦給這樣的你！

- 看著影集英文字幕時，單字幾乎都認識，但關掉字幕直接聽時，卻又聽不懂了？推薦你《分類主題 實用搭配詞》。
- 想大幅提升閱讀速度嗎？推薦你《分類主題 實用搭配詞》。
- 單字認識得不少，但開口說不出話來嗎？推薦你《分類主題 實用搭配詞》。
- TOEIC 分數尚可，但寫作能力卻一塌糊塗嗎？推薦你《分類主題 實用搭配詞》。

透過學習搭配詞，徹底突破以往純單字記憶學習的局限吧！

目錄

Introduction 説得自然，寫得道地：搭配詞的力量 2

| Part One | Collocations with 10 Essential Verbs 與 10 個核心動詞有關的搭配詞 |

DAY 01 **DO** ① 14
DAY 02 **DO** ② 18
DAY 03 **DO** ③ 22
DAY 04 **FIND** ① 27
DAY 05 **FIND** ② 31
DAY 06 **FIND** ③ 35
DAY 07 **GET** ① 40
DAY 08 **GET** ② 44
DAY 09 **GET** ③ 48
DAY 10 **GIVE** ① 52
DAY 11 **GIVE** ② 57
DAY 12 **GIVE** ③ 62
DAY 13 **HAVE** ① 67
DAY 14 **HAVE** ② 71
DAY 15 **HAVE** ③ 75
DAY 16 **HOLD** ① 79
DAY 17 **HOLD** ② 84
DAY 18 **HOLD** ③ 88
DAY 19 **KEEP** ① 92

DAY 20 **KEEP** ②	96
DAY 21 **KEEP** ③	100
DAY 22 **MAKE** ①	105
DAY 23 **MAKE** ②	110
DAY 24 **MAKE** ③	115
DAY 25 **SHOW** ①	120
DAY 26 **SHOW** ②	125
DAY 27 **SHOW** ③	130
DAY 28 **TAKE** ①	135
DAY 29 **TAKE** ②	139
DAY 30 **TAKE** ③	143
DAYS 01-30 **Final Check-up**	148

Part Two | **Collocations on Essential Subjects**
關鍵分類主題的搭配詞：名詞

DAY 31 **Business and Economy**（商業與經濟）	154
DAY 32 **Finance**（金融）	162
DAY 33 **Work and Office**（工作與辦公室）	171
DAY 34 **Information**（資訊）	180
DAY 35 **The Internet**（網際網路）	189
DAY 36 **Press and Media**（新聞與媒體）	197
DAY 37 **Opinion**（意見）	206
DAY 38 **Family and Social Relationships**（家庭與社會關係）	216
DAY 39 **Social Concerns**（社會議題）	225

Contents

DAY 40 **Customs and Habits**（習俗與習慣）................................... 233
DAY 41 **War and Peace**（戰爭與和平）.. 242
DAY 42 **Politics and Institution**（政治與制度）.............................. 251
DAY 43 **Liberty and Responsibility**（自由與責任）........................ 260
DAY 44 **Law**（法律）.. 269
DAY 45 **Food**（食物）.. 278
DAY 46 **Health**（健康）... 287
DAY 47 **Clothing**（服裝）.. 295
DAY 48 **Weather**（天氣）... 304
DAY 49 **Sports**（運動）... 313
DAY 50 **Travel and Transportation**（旅行與交通）........................ 321
DAY 51 **Language**（語言）... 329
DAY 52 **Study and Academic Work**（學習與學術工作）.............. 340
DAY 53 **Art**（藝術）.. 349
DAY 54 **Feelings**（情感）.. 357
DAY 55 **Interest and Concern**（興趣與關注事項）........................ 366
DAY 56 **Values and Ideals**（價值與理想）..................................... 375
DAY 57 **Signs and Symbols**（標誌與象徵）................................... 385
DAY 58 **Direction and Movement**（方向與移動）......................... 394
DAY 59 **Danger**（危險）.. 404
DAY 60 **Aid and Cooperation**（援助與合作）................................ 412
DAYS 31-60 **Final Check-up** 422

Answer Key 解答與翻譯 426
Index 索引 470

本書特色與使用說明

1 使用手機掃描每個單元右上方 QR 碼，練習每一個搭配詞及其例句的發音及語調，同時訓練聽說的能力。

2 在開始當天的訓練課程之前，務必事先閱讀並掌握該課的學習重點。

3 本課會出現的搭配詞都在這裡一目瞭然，幫助你快速掌握這些關鍵的常見用法與詞語搭配。

4 每一個搭配詞都有一個實用例句，透過句子讓你更容易理解並記住此搭配用法，也能幫助你在寫作或口說時靈活運用。

5 到了驗收學習成果的時候了。這裡的練習題幫助你檢視對搭配詞的理解程度，透過實際填空題加深記憶並強化應用能力。

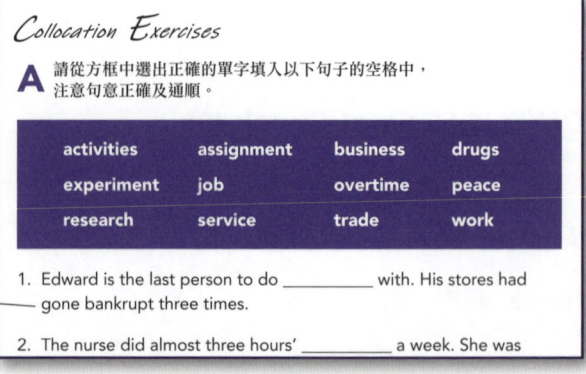

6

從 Day 31 開始的課程有不同的練習題！這些練習設計更貼近實際語境,不再只是單字填空,而是要思考動詞與名詞的正確搭配,培養真正的語感與應用能力,同時提升句子結構與理解力。

Collocation Exercises

A 請將 List 1 的動詞與 List 2 的名詞做適當的連結,且符合完整句意。

List 1	List 2
exceeded	a long recession
launched	a new product
maintain	warfare expenditures
plunged into	our budget
reduce	the insurance

1. Do you think we _____ _____ ? I think we will soon come out of it.
2. We _____ _____ in the market. To our sadness, nobody seems to recognize it.
3. The high official agreed upon the plan to _____ _____ .

B 在以下句子空格處中選出適當的字詞。

6. The government is divided on the issue: The prime minister insists on increasing _____ while the minister of finance and economy says we need to decrease it.
   (a) the asset   (b) the economy
   (c) the budget   (d) the warfare

7. Every salesman has to be aware of _____ . The marketplace is getting more and more saturated with similar products.
   (a) the competition   (b) the component
   (c) the study   (d) the virtue

7

相信大家對於這樣的選擇題應該不陌生,因為像這種語境型選擇題正是 TOEIC、GEPT 等英語檢定考試的常見題型。透過練習不僅能強化字彙與語感,還能幫助你在應試時更快掌握句意、排除干擾選項,提高答題正確率。

8

Answer Key
解答篇

DAY 01　DO ①

1. business, 愛德華是最不值得一起做生意的人。他的店已破產 3 次了。
2. overtime, 那位護士一個星期幾乎要加 3 個小時的班。她回到家時總是筋疲力盡。
3. research, 他正在進行跨國企業的研究。他說自己的發現將讓世人驚訝。
4. job, 儘管她身體孱弱, 她仍然完成了一件了不起的工作。我們真的深受感動。
5. activities, 在一些學校裡, 學生們必須參加課外活動才能畢業。
6. experiment, 即使已經與同學一起做了實驗, 你們也必須提交自己的話所撰寫的個人報告。
7. service, 目前, 僅男性必須服兵役。然而, 女性正主張平等, 這麼說來, 女性也該服兵役嗎？
8. assignment, 你不要自己寫作業。那不是你的作業 — 那是你孩子的作業。
9. trade, 研究全球經濟是一回事。實際從事貿易工作又是另一回事。
10. work, 他們正在尋找承包新購物商場建設工程的一些公司。
11. We are doing research on Korean traditional dance.
12. He did his assignment while smoking.
13. The state requires all men to do three years' military service.
14. I don't think he did a great job. He was just lucky.

每一課的練習題都附有解答及翻譯, 幫助你即時確認學習成效, 同時透過中文說明更清楚理解句子的意思與語境。這樣的設計特別適合自學者, 也能有效應用在準備像是 TOEIC、GEPT 等英語檢定考試上。

9

最後附上前面所有課程中出現過的搭配詞索引, 讓你能快速查找、複習曾學過的內容。遇到不熟悉的用法或寫作卡關時, 只要翻到索引頁, 就能迅速找到正確搭配詞, 大大提升學習效率與實用性。

Index
搭配詞索引

A

abandon an ideal	379
abolish censorship	202
abuse a privilege	229
accelerate progress	397
accept a fact	185
accept a treaty	246
accept advice	418
accept criticism	341
accept responsibility	262
access information	181
access the net	192
administer an affair	252
admit charges	262
adopt a policy	252
adopt a position	212
adopt a practice	237
adopt a tone	336
advise caution	406
aggravate a symptom	291
agree on a treaty	247
agree to a treaty	247
alleviate pain	291
alleviate poverty	229

Part One

Collocations with 10 Essential Verbs
與 10 個核心動詞有關的搭配詞

Collocations with

DAY 01

Day-01.mp3

DO ①

動詞 do 在英文裡具有「做某事」如此廣泛的意義。正如「做」這個字在中文裡有非常多的用法一樣，英文的 do 也能與許多名詞搭配使用，形成多種搭配詞組。例如，do research 表示「進行研究」，而 do overtime 則表示「加班」。

Collocation at a Glance

Verb + Noun	Meaning	Verb + Noun	Meaning
do an activity	做活動	**do** a trade	進行交易
do an assignment	完成作業／任務	**do** an experiment	做實驗
do business	做生意	**do** overtime	加班
do a job	完成一份工作	**do** service	提供（公眾的）服務
do work	工作，做事	**do** research	進行研究

Collocation in Use

do an activity 做活動

There are several *activities* we can *do* in our English class.
我們的英文課上有一些活動可以進行。

do an assignment 完成作業／任務

He *did the assignment* while drinking, so it has many typos.
他邊喝酒邊完成作業，因此裡面有很多錯別字。

do business 做生意

She is the last person to *do business* with.
她是最不值得一起做生意的人。

do a job 完成一份工作

You *did a* great *job*.
你做得很好。

do work 工作，做事

I *did* a lot of *work* yesterday.
我昨天做了很多工作。

do a trade 進行交易

They had to bribe the gangsters to *do the trade*.
他們必須賄賂這些流氓來進行這筆交易。

do an experiment 做實驗

We have *done the experiment* with our classmates.
我們已經和同學們一起做過了這項實驗。

do overtime 加班

She *did* almost three hours' *overtime* a week.
她每週加班將近三個小時。

do service 提供（公眾的）服務

The government required all men to *do* two years' military *service*.
政府要求所有男性服兩年兵役。

do research 進行研究

He is *doing research* on intercultural communication.
他正在進行跨文化交流的研究。

DAY 01

Collocation Exercises

A 請從方框中選出正確的單字填入以下句子的空格中，注意句意正確及通順。

activities	assignment	business	drugs
experiment	job	overtime	peace
research	service	trade	work

1. Edward is the last person to do _____ with. His stores had gone bankrupt three times.

2. The nurse did almost three hours' _____ a week. She was always exhausted when she came home.

3. He is doing _____ on multinational corporations. He says his findings will surprise the world.

4. In spite of her physical handicaps, she did a great _____. We were really moved.

5. In some schools, students need to do extracurricular _____ for graduation.

6. Even though you have done the _____ with your classmates, you must turn in your own individual report expressed in your own words.

7. At this time, only men should do military _____. However women are advocating for equality, so then, should women also do military _____?

8. Don't do the _____ yourself. It's not your homework--it's your child's.

9. To study the global economy is one thing. To do the actual _____ is another.

10. They are looking for some companies to do the construction _____ for the new shopping mall.

B 請將以下句子翻譯成英文。

11. 我們正在研究韓國的傳統舞蹈。
_____

12. 他一邊抽菸一邊做作業。
_____

13. 那個國家要求所有男性服三年兵役。
_____

14. 我不認為他做得很好。他只是運氣好而已。
_____

15. 與其同一時間做很多事情,你不如專注於一件事。
_____

Collocations with DO ②

DAY 02

Day-02.mp3

如先前提到，動詞 do （做某事）有非常廣泛的意思，自然地，在日常生活中許多表達用語都會出現動詞 do。例如，do hair 表示「弄頭髮」，do laundry 表示「洗衣服」，do food 表示「做食物」等。

Collocation at a Glance

Verb + Noun	Meaning	Verb + Noun	Meaning
do an article	寫文章	**do** hair	整理頭髮
do the dishes	洗碗	**do** the laundry	洗衣服
do drugs	使用毒品	**do** a favor	施予恩惠
do exercise	做運動	**do** nails	修剪指甲
do food	做食物	**do** something/ anything	做某事／做任何事

Collocation in Use

do an article 寫文章

Thanks for *doing an article* on the new trend of kilt wearing.
感謝您撰寫有關蘇格蘭裙服新趨勢的文章。

do the dishes 洗碗

Doing the dishes is not a woman's job any more.
洗碗已經不再只是女性的工作了。

do drugs 使用毒品

Doing drugs may be popular, but it can carry life-long consequences.
吸毒雖然常見，但它可能對一生造成影響。

do exercise 做運動

Apart from watching films, we can also *do exercise* to release stress.
為了減輕壓力，我們除了看電影，還可以做運動。

do food 做食物

John is *doing* the *food* to celebrate your new business.
約翰正在為慶祝你展開新事業而準備食物。

do hair 整理頭髮

Wow, she's awesome! I love the way she *does hair*.
哇，她真棒！我喜歡她整理頭髮的方式。

do the laundry 洗衣服

I'm not the only one who *does the laundry*, vacuuming, and walking the dog.
洗衣服、吸塵和遛狗的，不是只有我一個人。

do a favor 施予恩惠

Would you *do* me *a favor* and water my plants while I'm gone?
能否幫個忙，我不在的時候幫我澆花好嗎？

do nails 修剪指甲

If you want to express your femininity, *do* your *nails* and wear a little lipstick.
如果你想展現自己的女性魅力，可以修剪指甲並塗上一點口紅。

do something/anything 做某事／做任何事

I can't *do anything* without my little sister following me.
要是我的小妹沒跟在我身邊，我什麼都做不了。

DAY 02

Collocation Exercises

 請從方框中選出正確的單字填入以下句子的空格中，注意句意正確及通順。

article	dishes	drugs	exercise
favor	food	hair	homework
laundry	nails	puzzle	something

1. It would be good to do _____ other than yoga.

2. One of the best ways for addicts to stop doing _____ is to seek counseling and therapy.

3. We called a catering service to do the _____ for the party.

4. I am planning to do a(n) _____ about Korean culture.

5. For a much more fashionable look, do your _____ in a red color.

6. My father always does _____ that irritates me.

7. I like the way she does _____ because the styles are always unique.

8. She may forget to add the soap when she does the _____.

9. I cannot thank him enough. He did such a great _____ to me when I was in need of help.

10. As he did the food for me, I volunteered to do the _____. It was a "nice division of labor" because I am a terrible cook.

B 請將以下句子翻譯成英文。

11. 旅行出發前後,都請做好指甲修護。

12. 我喜歡他處理事情時那種沉著的方式。

13. 如果你想表達自己,可以試著寫一篇文章。

14. 他在兩個兒子死於一場嚴重的車禍後開始吸食毒品。

15. 很多當老公的會說他們「幫老婆洗衣服」。但事實上這是他們自己的工作。

Collocations with

DO ③

DAY 03

Day-03.mp3

動詞 do 除了在 DAY2 中探討日常生活中使用的具體表達外,還可以用於表示抽象的活動。例如,do a calculation 表示「算一下,算一算」,do sum 表示「算出總和」,do thinking 則表示「進行思考」…等意思。

Collocation at a Glance

Verb + Noun	Meaning	Verb + Noun	Meaning
do arrangement	做安排,進行擺設	do reverse	反過來做
do a calculation	算一下,算一算	do sum	算出總合
do evil	做壞事	do thinking	進行思考
do honor	成為榮耀	do translation	做翻譯
do injustice	不公平對待	do the trick	達成結果,有效果

Collocation in Use

do arrangement 做安排,進行擺設

Every week I would bring a bunch of flowers home to *do* an *arrangement* for my mother.
我每週都會帶一束花回家,為我母親做插花。

do a calculation 算一下，算一算

Jennifer *did a* quick *calculation* and determined that John could jump about eight times faster than Drake.
珍妮佛迅速地算了一下，確定約翰跳躍的速度大約是德雷克的 8 倍。

do evil 做壞事

If you *do evil*, it might return to you in the form of disasters, diseases, or wars.
如果你做壞事，可能會以災難、疾病或戰爭的形式報應到你身上。

do honor 成為榮耀

Such a noble achievement *does* great *honor* to this young officer.
如此偉大的成就成為這位年輕官員的極大榮耀。

do injustice 不公平對待

A nation has no right to *do injustice* to another country.
一個國家無權不公正地對待另一個國家。

do reverse 反過來做

"Buy low and sell high" is a rule for successful investment. Yet so many people *do* the *reverse*.
「低買高賣」是成功投資的法則。但許多人卻反其道而行。

do sum 算出總合

I am able to *do* this *sum*, either in my head or with pencil and paper.
無論是心算還是用紙筆來算，我都能算出總合。

do thinking 進行思考

Ask questions of your students that make them *do* the *thinking* and talking.
提出能讓你的學生們思考及交談的問題。

do translation 做翻譯

For the time being, he *does translation* of game manuals from French to English.
目前，他正在做將法文遊戲手冊翻譯成英文的工作。

do the trick 達成結果，有效果

Twenty minutes of exercise every day may *do the trick* to help you lose weight.
每天 20 分鐘的運動可能有助你減重的效果。

Collocation Exercises

A 請從方框中選出正確的單字填入以下句子的空格中，注意句意正確及通順。

arithmetic	arrangement	calculation	damage
evil	honor	injustice	reverse
sum	thinking	translation	trick

1. It does us great _____ to have the President here for our graduation.

2. Enter the first gate and then the second gate. Do the _____ when leaving.

3. To separate education from culture is to do _____ to ethnic minorities.

4. One of my friends does _____ from French to English for his job.

5. Can you do this _____ in your head? I want you to add all the numbers from 1 to 100.

6. If you want to win the game, offence alone won't do the _____.

7. If you do _____ to somebody, you will get that back.

8. We can also do the _____ of the music we created for you.

9. He asked me whether we could make our students do the critical _____. He has been interested in how we can let the students take different perspectives rather than just accept the given content.

10. Although he is not so good at doing a(n) _____, he is a gifted child at mathematics.

B 請將以下句子翻譯成英文。

11. 無論是出於理智或情感，我都有作惡的可能。

    _____

12. 鼓勵學生思考以及表達是教師的本分。

    _____

13. 如果你想跑得比你弟弟快，這本書可能有用。

    _____

14. 仍有許多機構對殘疾人士有不公平的對待。

　　_____

15. 何不反向操作試試看？我想問題會更容易解決。

　　_____

Collocations with

FIND ①

DAY 04

Day-04.mp3

從今天開始，我們來詳細了解與動詞 find 有關的搭配詞。find 通常的意思是「發現」或「找到」，且其受詞可能為人事物。例如，find a culprit 意為「找到一名罪犯」，find a recruit 指「找一名新進員工」，而 find a replacement 則表示「找一位接替者」。

Collocation at a Glance

Verb + Noun	Meaning	Verb + Noun	Meaning
find an ally	找到一位盟友	**find** a recruit	招募一名新成員
find an alternative	找到一個替代方案	**find** a replacement	找到一個替代方法／接替者
find a culprit	發現一名罪犯	**find** a sponsor	尋找贊助商
find a mate	找到一位伴侶	**find** a survivor	發現一名倖存者
find an occupation	找到一份工作	**find** a volunteer	尋找一名志工

Collocation in Use

find an ally 找到一位盟友

If you cannot *find an ally*, you should make one.
如果你無法找到盟友，你就應該創造一個。

find an alternative 找到一個替代方案

He couldn't *find an alternative*. He was at a cul-de-sac.
他找不到替代方案。他陷入了四面楚歌的困境。

find a culprit 發現一名罪犯

The culprit was found in New York.
那名罪犯在紐約被發現了。

find a mate 找到一位伴侶

Some birds use noise to find a mate.
某些鳥類會利用聲音來尋找伴侶。

find an occupation 找到一份工作

As the economy slows down, it is hard to find a decent occupation.
由於經濟景氣低迷,要找到一份還不錯的工作變得困難。

find a recruit 招募一名新成員

The company had no difficulty in finding recruits.
那家公司在招募新進員工方面沒有遇到困難。

find a replacement 找到一個替代方法/接替者

We need to find a replacement for him.
我們必須找到一位接替他的人選。

find a sponsor 尋找贊助商

He finally found the greatest sponsor of his life.
他終於為自己的人生找到了最好的贊助者。

find a survivor 發現一名倖存者

The reporter found 7 tsunami survivors in the village.
記者在那個村落中發現了 7 名海嘯倖存者。

find a volunteer 尋找一名志工

Nowadays it is very hard to find volunteers.
如今要找到志工很困難。

Collocation Exercises

 A 請從方框中選出正確的單字填入以下句子的空格中，注意句意正確及通順。

ally	alternative	culprit	mate
occupation	recruits	replacement	rookies
sponsor	survivors	ticket	volunteer

1. He was 33 years old and thought he was old enough to find a soul _____.

2. We must find a(n) _____ now or we have no option but to follow the boss's directions.

3. Listen! You have too many enemies out there. If you cannot find a(n) _____, you should make one.

4. We placed an advertisement in the local newspaper to find a(n) _____ for the NGO activities.

5. You must show your ability to find a(n) _____ in that company.

6. The painter found a wealthy _____ and was able to open her own exhibition in the prestigious Metropolitan Museum.

7. They found 20 _____ in the fire accident.

8. We need to find a(n) _____ for him. He's going to quit next week.

9. Fingerprints on the phone in the room offered the police a crucial clue to finding the _____.

10. It is getting more and more difficult to find _____ for the special force. Most young people prefer doing administrative jobs to working in the field.

B 請將以下句子翻譯成英文。

11. 他擁有自然科學領域的博士學位,因此在研究產業中找到一份工作並非難事。

12. 總統必須在下個星期前找到一位替代總理的人選。

13. 該公司試圖尋找一個汽車召回問題的替代方案。

14. 警方未能找到罪犯。事實上,他就藏身在警局內的廁所裡。

15. 人事部門最重要的職責之一就是招募新進員工。

Collocations with FIND ②

DAY 05

Day-05.mp3

今天我們要將搭配詞的學習重點擺在 find 後面接表達「情感」或「心理狀態」的抽象名詞。例如，「find comfort」意思是「尋找慰藉」，「find inspiration」意為「獲得靈感」，「find the nerve」則是「鼓起勇氣」的意思。

Collocation at a Glance

Verb + Noun	Meaning	Verb + Noun	Meaning
find comfort	尋找慰藉	**find** the nerve	鼓起勇氣
find courage	找到勇氣	**find** peace	平復心情
find forgiveness	尋求寬恕	**find** relief	找到解脫
find happiness	找到幸福	**find** salvation	尋求救贖
find inspiration	尋找靈感	**find** satisfaction	找到滿足感

Collocation in Use

find comfort 尋找慰藉

I *found comfort* in listening to music rather than in talking with people.
我尋找慰藉的方式是聆聽音樂，而非與他人交談。

find courage 找到勇氣

He will *find courage* in the voice of his wife.
他將在他妻子的聲音中找到勇氣。

find forgiveness 尋求寬恕

Can he *find forgiveness* from his daughter?
他能夠取得他女兒的原諒嗎？

find happiness 找到幸福

I *found* true *happiness* in sharing my life with family.
我在與家人分享我的生活時找到真正的幸福。

find inspiration 尋找靈感

He used to *find* his musical *inspiration* from the traditional fair.
他經常在傳統集市中尋找音樂的靈感。

find the nerve 鼓起勇氣

The boy *found the nerve* to talk back to the tall girl.
那男孩鼓起勇氣反駁了那高個子的女孩。

find peace 平復心情

Do you think we can *find peace* in prayer?
你認為我們能從祈禱中找到內心的平靜嗎？

find relief 找到解脫

She couldn't *find relief* in watching the old video of her son.
她無法藉由觀看她兒子過去的影片找到解脫。

find salvation 尋求救贖

Some people seem to *find salvation* in art.
有些人似乎會在藝術當中尋求救贖。

find satisfaction 找到滿足感

He is the type of person who *finds satisfaction* in group harmony rather than in personal achievement.
他是那種從群體和諧，而非個人成就中找到滿足感的人。

FIND ② 033

Collocation Exercises

A 請從方框中選出正確的單字填入以下句子的空格中，注意句意正確及通順。

comfort	courage	difficulty	forgiveness
friends	happiness	inspiration	nerve
peace	relief	salvation	satisfaction

1. "Some people seem to find _____ in money and fame. But what man has created cannot save us," said the minister.

2. At that moment, the story of David and Goliath flashed in his mind. He found the _____ to stand up to the older students who were teasing him. The result? Of course, he was beaten up.

3. A variety of welfare policies are designed to help people find _____ and achieve self-actualization.

4. He is the type of person who finds _____ in "doing perfect" rather than "doing good."

5. Whenever I was in difficulty, I found _____ in religion. But she said it was just a self-deception.

6. What is the best way to overcome fear? It is to find _____ within yourself.

7. She couldn't find _____ in looking at the pictures of her son. He was gone forever and no one was able to bring him back.

8. This world is full of agonies but we can find _____ in meditation and inspirational dialogues.

9. He found _____ for his fantasy novel from the ancient myths.

10. The offender could not find _____ from the deceased victim, which made him suffer from a sense of guilt for a long time.

B 請將以下句子翻譯成英文。

11. 他曾經從韓國的藝術中尋找他的音樂靈感。

12. 她無法在賺錢中找到真正的快樂。

13. 那位母親試圖在看著已故女兒的照片時尋求慰藉。

14. 那名男子沒能鼓起勇氣反駁他的老闆。

15. 在樂透中比在政治中尋求救贖更好。

Collocations with FIND ③

DAY 06
Day-06.mp3

今天要學習的是 find 後面接與「資訊」或「邏輯」相關名詞的搭配用法。比如，「find discrepancy」表示「找出差異點」、「find a precedent」表示「尋找先例」，以及「find a pretext」表示「尋找藉口」這樣的用法。

Collocation at a Glance

Verb + Noun	Meaning	Verb + Noun	Meaning
find a clue	找線索	find information	找資料
find (a) discrepancy	發現差異點	find meaning	尋求意義
find evidence	找證據	find a precedent	找到先例
find an explanation	尋求一個解釋	find a pretext	找個藉口
find a flaw	找到缺陷	find a relationship	找關係

Collocation in Use

find a clue 找線索

The police could not *find any clues* and the case has been wrapped in mystery.
警方無法找到任何線索，且這起案件籠罩在謎團之中

find (a) discrepancy 尋求差異點

You must explain *the discrepancy* I have *found* between the two files.
你必須對我在這兩個檔案中發現的差異做個解釋。

find evidence 找證據

The boy *found* some *evidence* against the plaintiff.
那個男孩找到了對原告不利的一些證據。

find an explanation 尋求一個解釋

She couldn't *find a* reasonable *explanation* for it.
她無法為此找到一個合理的解釋。

find a flaw 找到缺陷

No *flaw* was *found* in his solution to the equation. It was perfect.
他對於這個方程式的解答中，未被發現任何缺陷。它是完美的。

find information 找資料

The spy failed in *finding* confidential *information* from the government.
那名間諜未能從政府那邊獲取機密資訊。

find meaning 尋求意義

You cannot *find* the *meaning* of your life by gambling.
你無法藉由賭博找到你人生的意義。

find a precedent 找到先例

We could not *find any precedent* for this kind of project.
我們無法找到任何此類專案的先例。

find a pretext 找個藉口

She couldn't *find a* plausible *pretext* for being late.
她無法找到一個合理的藉口來解釋遲到的原因。

find a relationship 找關係

He is doing a project to *find the relationship* between love and hormones.
他正在進行一個專案，目的是尋找愛情與荷爾蒙之間的關係。

Collocation Exercises

A 請從方框中選出正確的單字填入以下句子的空格中，注意句意正確及通順。

cause	clue	discrepancy	explanation
evidence	flaw	information	lessons
meaning	precedent	pretext	relationship

1. The state tried to find a(n) _____ for searching the home, but it was absolutely absurd.

2. Even cutting-edge technology cannot find a proper _____ for the miraculous construction of the pyramids in Egypt.

3. Can you explain the _____ I have found between the two documents? The two must be identical but they are different.

4. Don't try to find the _____ in other people without examining your own first.

5. We could not find a(n) _____ for this kind of project. That means we must start from scratch.

6. Do you want to find _____ in life? Then you must read a lot, travel often, and do work that inspires you.

7. The spy succeeded in finding confidential _____ from the secret agency.

8. The thief was so cautious that the detective could not find any _____ that he committed the crime.

9. The doctoral student found crucial _____ against his advisor's hypothesis. However, he did not publish it.

10. His research shows that we can find a strong _____ between one's cultural background and his way of developing a topic in writing.

B 請將以下句子翻譯成英文。

11. 這名駭客無法找出這兩個檔案之間的任何差異。

12. 人類數千年來一直試圖在哲學和宗教方面尋找生命的意義。

13. 美國為攻打伊拉克，找到了一個他們認為合理的藉口 — 大規模毀滅性武器（WMD）。

14. 他在書中找到了一個重要的線索。有一些字母被做了記號。

15. 由於我們無法找到類似的先例，我們必須從頭開始。

Collocations with GET ①

DAY 07

Day-07.mp3

從今天開始，學習英文裡含義最廣泛的動詞之一，get 的搭配詞用法。動詞 get 通常表示「獲得（得到）」的意思。例如：get an approval 意為「獲得批准」，get a guarantee 意為「獲得保證」，get a chance 意為「獲得機會」。

Collocation at a Glance

Verb + Noun	Meaning	Verb + Noun	Meaning
get access	獲得存取權限	**get** an edge	取得優勢
get an apology	得到一句道歉	**get** exposure	獲得曝光
get (an) approval	獲得批准	**get** a guarantee	獲得保證
get a benefit	獲得利益	**get** the last word	擁有最後決定權
get a chance	有機會	**get** a sentence	被判刑

Collocation in Use

get access 獲得存取權限

He failed to *get access* to classified information.
他未能獲得存取機密資訊的權限。

get an apology 得到一句道歉

I never *got an apology* from my mother for what she did.
我從未因為母親的作為而得到一句她的道歉。

get (an) approval 獲得批准

The project has not yet *got the approval* from the board of management.
該專案尚未獲得管理階層的批准。

get a benefit 獲得利益

Everybody wants to *get a benefit* from their business.
每個人都希望從自己的事業中獲利。

get a chance 有機會

I *got a chance* to meet with the basketball coach.
我有機會與籃球隊的教練見面。

get an edge 取得優勢

The argument was heated and no one *got an edge* over the other.
辯論十分激烈,沒有人能從對方那裡取得優勢。

get exposure 獲得曝光

You can succeed if you utilize an effective, yet inexpensive way to *get exposure* for your business.
如果你利用一種既有效又不昂貴的方式來讓你的公司獲得曝光,就有可能成功。

get a guarantee 獲得保證

He won't *get a guarantee* of perfect health even though the operation was successful.
即使手術成功,他也無法獲得健康無虞的保證。

get the last word 擁有最後決定權

She always *got the last word* in every single argument.
她在每一場爭論中總是擁有最後的決定權。

get a sentence 被判刑

He *got a sentence* of life in prison for the murder charge.
他因謀殺罪被判處無期徒刑。

DAY 07

Collocation Exercises

A 請從方框中選出正確的單字填入以下句子的空格中，注意句意正確及通順。

access	apology	approval	benefit
chance	edge	experience	exposure
guarantee	last word	reputation	sentence

1. The obstinate man never let the others get the _____ and the argument failed to get an agreement.

2. How long will it take to get the _____ once I submit a complete and accurate application?

3. The dead boy's parents got the driver's _____.

4. You only get one _____ to make a first impression.

5. If you want to get a(n) _____ with the dietary approach to losing weight, you may have to be acutely aware of your food combinations.

6. You cannot get _____ to restricted web communities until the administrators grant you admission to them.

7. He got a(n) _____ of 5 years for shooting someone.

8. An increasing number of job seekers are visiting plastic surgeons in a quest to get a(n) _____ on competitors for jobs in a still-tough economy.

9. You need to get enough _____ to different genres of writing to become a proficient writer.

10. After he got a(n) _____ of promotion from his manager, he decided to stay with the company.

B 請將以下句子翻譯成英文。

11. 目前，在中東的恐怖分子活動被媒體大肆報導。

    _____

12. 雖然你無法保證一定會贏，但你應該站在正義的一方奮戰。

    _____

13. 經過長期的戰爭之後，該國逐漸取得對敵人的優勢。

    _____

14. 他獲准進入機密圖書館，但他卻是個文盲。

    _____

15. 他雖然獲得了上司的批准，但因為沒有錢，無法請假離開。

    _____

Collocations with
GET ②

DAY 08

Day-08.mp3

今天我們來看看動詞 get 後面接與「知識」或「感覺」有關的抽象名詞，而這時 get 通常是指「掌握」、「理解」等意思。例如，get a grasp 表示「理解」，get the hang of 表示「掌握～的訣竅」，get a point 則表示「抓住重點」，諸如此類用法。

Collocation at a Glance

Verb + Noun	Meaning	Verb + Noun	Meaning
get an answer	得到答案，答對	**get** an impression	有印象，似乎覺得
get the feeling	有感覺	**get** the joke	聽懂／理解笑話
get a grasp	掌握住，可以理解	**get** a perspective	得到一個觀點／取得見解
get the hang of	掌握…的訣竅	**get** a point	抓到重點
get an idea	有個主意／想法	**get** (a) taste	嘗試／試吃；體會

Collocation in Use

get an answer 得到答案，答對

You *got* all the *answers* right.
你全都答對了。

get the feeling 有感覺

Under circumstances in Orwellian societies, you'll *get the feeling* you're being watched.
在奧威爾式社會的環境中，你會有種被監視的感覺。

get a grasp 掌握住，可以理解

I can help you *get a grasp* of campus life.
我可以幫助你了解校園生活。

get the hang of 掌握…的訣竅

Once you *get the hang of* playing the trumpet, you'll like it.
一旦你掌握了吹喇叭的訣竅，你就會喜歡上它。

get an idea 有個主意 / 想法

Where did you *get the idea* that I'll be moving to England?
你從哪裡得到我會搬到英國的這個想法？

get an impression 有印象，似乎覺得

I *got the impression* that she was trying to set me up on a blind date.
我似乎覺得她試圖安排我參加一場相親。

get the joke 理解笑話

The man who laughed last probably did not *get the joke*.
最後笑的那個男人可能根本沒聽懂這個笑話。

get a perspective 得到一個觀點 / 取得見解

I've *got a* new *perspective* on my school.
我對我的學校有了新的觀點。

get a point 抓到重點

You almost *got the point*, but still missed something.
你幾乎抓住了重點，但還是漏掉了一件事。

get (a) taste 嘗試 / 試吃；體會

Through several years of experience, he *got a taste* of life in rural areas.
經過數年的經驗，他體會到鄉村生活的滋味。

DAY 08

Collocation Exercises

A 請從方框中選出正確的單字填入以下句子的空格中，注意句意正確及通順。

answer	direction	feeling	grasp
hang	impression	idea	joke
perspective	point	reason	taste

1. You obviously don't get the _____. How long does it take to understand the simplest of things?

2. When I looked into your eyes for the first time, I got the _____ at once that we already had met before.

3. Participatory observation and close analysis of conversation might be the best way to truly get a(n) _____ for the people and the culture.

4. There's always one person who doesn't get the _____ while all the others fall out laughing.

5. Where did you get the _____ that I'll be moving soon?

6. I don't think you got the _____. Before jumping to the conclusion, pause and think twice about whether it makes sense.

7. A neat and readable resume can make the employers get the _____ that you are serious about finding a job.

8. When I got the _____ of the bass at age 14, I started playing with groups all over the country.

9. His evasive answers made it hard to get a full _____ of this situation.

10. If you get a fresh _____ on your writing process, you can break "writer's block" more easily.

B 請將以下句子翻譯成英文。

11. 我發現這是一本能讓人精通英文的優良讀物。

12. 當你步入成熟階段時，會對人生有不同的觀點。

13. 第一次見到她時，我的印象是她是一個善良的人。

14. 掌握打鼓訣竅的過程雖然辛苦，但也充滿樂趣。

15. 他總說自己抓到了重點，但卻一錯再錯。

Collocations with GET ③

DAY 09

Day-09.mp3

當我們要表示「獲得結果」或「得到分數」時，常使用 get 這個動詞。例如，「get a grade」表示「獲得一項成績」，「get a promotion」表示「獲得升遷」，「get a result」表示「有了結果」，「get a score」表示「得到分數」。此外，「get a name」有「得到名聲，成名」的意思，這一點值得注意。

Collocation at a Glance

Verb + Noun	Meaning	Verb + Noun	Meaning
get a grade	得到一項成績	**get** a name	搏得名聲
get hiccups	打嗝	**get** a promotion	獲得升遷
get a job	獲得一份工作	**get** a result	有了結果
get leave	獲准休假	**get** a score	得到分數
get a liking	產生好感	**get** a shot	拍照

Collocation in Use

get a grade 得到一項成績

I deserved to *get a* good *grade* on the test because I studied weeks in advance!
我提前幾週就開始準備，因此這項考試理應獲得好成績。

get hiccups 打嗝

The child *gets hiccups* very easily.
那個孩子非常容易打嗝。

get a job 獲得一份工作

I *got a job* as an assistant.
我找到了一份助理的工作。

get leave 獲准休假

My brother recently *got* paternity *leave* when his child was born.
我哥哥最近在孩子出生時休了育嬰假。

get a liking 產生好感

He *got a liking* for literature.
他對文學產生了好感。

get a name 搏得名聲

She *got a name* for herself by singing on Broadway.
她在百老匯演唱而為自己搏得了名聲。

get a promotion 獲得升遷

I *got a promotion* to group manager in my department.
我榮獲升遷為我部門的組長。

get a result 有了結果

He took the TOEIC test several times, but always *got* the same *result*.
他考了幾次的多益，但結果總是相同。

get a score 得到分數

I wonder how I *got this score*. Probably there are some problems in the evaluating process.
我想知道自己為什麼拿到這樣的分數。可能是評分過程出了一些問題。

get a shot 拍照

I used my camera phone and *got a shot* of the actress as she was leaving the restaurant.
那位女演員離開餐廳時我用手機拍下了她的照片。

DAY 09

Collocation Exercises

A 請從方框中選出正確的單字填入以下句子的空格中，注意句意正確及通順。

grades	hiccups	job	leave
liking	loans	name	promotion
perspective	results	score	shots

1. Someone put a frog in my jacket pocket. As soon as I found it, I was so surprised that I got _____ for an hour.

2. We made a lot of efforts on the product and got good _____. We made big money.

3. He dared to get out his camera and got some _____ of the storm as it moved toward him.

4. Some students obviously get some good _____ for turning in work that isn't as good as other students'.

5. Working experience, a positive attitude, and good communication skills enable you to get a permanent, full-time _____.

6. Have you still got some _____ left? Then, how about going on a fishing trip with me?

7. She's actually starting to get a(n) _____ for me this time. The present really worked.

8. I worked as hard as the others but never got a(n) _____. I'm going to look for another job.

9. For an extra fee, you can get your writing _____ with the comments attached.

10. The politician desires to get his _____ in the papers.

B 請將以下句子翻譯成英文。

11. 那位導演因執導這部熱門電影而聲名大噪。
    _____

12. 他取得這項考試的最高分。
    _____

13. 她拒絕請病假並且繼續工作。
    _____

14. 在總理面前打嗝確實令人尷尬。
    _____

15. 他因未獲晉升而感到沮喪。
    _____

Collocations with

GIVE ①

DAY 10

Day-10.mp3

今天開始要學習的是 give 的搭配詞。give 可用於描述抽象性的舉止或作為，例如 give a hand（提供協助），也可用於描述具體的行為，例如 give a look（看一眼）或 give the eye（拋媚眼）。

Collocation at a Glance

Verb + Noun	Meaning	Verb + Noun	Meaning
give birth	生產，生育	**give** the eye	拋媚眼
give a boost	給了一劑強心針	**give** a hand	給予協助
give chase	追逐，追求	**give** a look	看一眼，呈現
give a cue	提供線索，使有跡可循	**give** a ring	打電話
give details	提供細節	**give** a view	提供觀點

Collocation in Use

give birth 生產，生育

I *gave birth* to my first baby on the bedroom floor in my apartment.
我在我公寓臥室的地板上生下我第一個孩子。

give a boost 給了一劑強心針

This product will encourage customers to buy more music, thus *giving a boost* to the industry.
這項產品將鼓勵顧客購買更多音樂，進而促進這項產業的繁榮。

give chase 追逐,追求

At that moment, he was *giving chase* to a suspected criminal.
當時,他正追捕一名疑犯。

give a cue 提供線索,使有跡可循

A baby *gives a cue* to the mother when it wants to be fed or comforted.
嬰兒在想被餵食或需要安慰時,會讓母親有跡象可循。

give details 提供細節

If your appeal is based on a medical need, please *give* any *details* that you think are relevant to your claim.
如果您的訴求是基於醫療上的需要,請提供您認為與您的訴求相關的詳細說明。

give the eye 拋媚眼

I noticed he was *giving* her *the eye* as she walked by in a revealing dress.
我注意到當她正穿著暴露的衣服走過時,他對她拋了媚眼。

give a hand 給予協助

I *gave* them *a hand* moving a few of the larger items.
我幫他們搬了幾件較大的物品。

give a look 看一眼,呈現

The photo collection *gives a look* into California's nature.
這組照片展現了加州的自然風光。

give a ring 打電話

By buying several calling cards, he could often *give* me *a ring* during his business trip abroad.
他買了數張電話卡,如此他在國外出差時便能經常打電話給我。

DAY 10

give a view 提供觀點

Jason's journals *give a view* of American society.
傑森的日誌提供一個美國社會的觀點。

Collocation Exercises

A 請從方框中選出正確的單字填入以下句子的空格中，注意句意正確及通順。

birth	boost	chase	cry
cue	details	eye	hand
hint	look	ring	view

1. The article about the 1987 election seems to arouse the greatest interest, largely because it gives a(n) _____ into previously little known political events.

2. The patrol boat gave _____ and a 3000 km race ensued, with the two boats sometimes less than 1000 meters apart.

3. The beautiful woman simply grinned and waved as passers-by gave her the _____.

4. Use a light bulb just bright enough for you to read by. A bright light gives a(n) _____ to your brain that it is time to wake up.

5. This Saturday they moved in, so I said hello and gave them a(n) _____ moving a few of the larger items.

6. This page gives _____ of the badminton leagues we play in.

7. I'll give you a _____ when I get back to the office.

8. The woman gave _____ to quintuplets by using fertility drugs.

9. A good deed can give a big _____ to your reputation.

10. This telescope will give a better _____ of landscapes than any other ones.

B 請將以下句子翻譯成英文。

11. 自從那位美國女子搬進來後，我丈夫就一直對她拋媚眼。

12. 這篇文章似乎在暗示女性，使用精子銀行是解決不孕問題的最佳方法。

13. 一名不幸的年輕男子追求著我那美麗但善變的孫女。

14. 他藉由成立一支鄉村交響樂團來活絡當地社區。

15. 他根據自己對關鍵期的看法，詳細說明了人生初期的語言教育。

_____

Collocations with

DAY 11

Day-11.mp3

GIVE ②

give 這個動詞常用來表示傳遞某事物。例如，「說明」這個動作，可以理解為「向人傳達意思」，因此可以用「give an account」這樣的搭配詞來表達。而「指示」則包含「傳達指令」的意思，因此可用「give an instruction」來表達。

Collocation at a Glance

Verb + Noun	Meaning	Verb + Noun	Meaning
give an alibi	提出不在場證明	**give** an example	舉例說明
give an account	說明	**give** an instruction	給予指示，提供使用說明
give comfort	給予慰藉	**give** odds	有勝算，有（獲勝的）機率
give a demonstration	示範，展示	**give** a total of	總計為，總共是
give evidence	作證	**give** voice	賦予發言權，讓…（某人）發聲

Collocation in Use

give an alibi 提出不在場證明

She *gave an alibi* that she had been in the London Park Hotel at that time.
她提出了不在場證明，聲稱當時自己在倫敦公園飯店。

give an account 說明

It is difficult for me to write about it, but I can *give* you *an account* by phone.
要我寫下來很困難，但我可以打電話來向你說明。

give comfort 給予慰藉

The church commended the dead to God, buried them, and *gave comfort* to the bereaved ones.
教會將往生者託付給上帝、安葬他們，並給予遺屬慰藉。

give a demonstration 示範，展示

The Chairman introduced Mr. Jackson who *gave a demonstration* of a product named Big Mouth.
主席介紹了傑克森先生，他展示了一款名為 Big Mouth 的產品。

give evidence 作證

Before you *give evidence*, you will be asked to take an oath.
在提供證詞之前，你將被要求進行宣誓。

give an example 舉例說明

I explained the concept and *gave an example* of a way to use it in our school.
我解釋了這個概念，並舉例說明一個運用在我們學校的方法。

give an instruction 給予指示，提供使用說明

This manual *gives* you *instructions* on how to play the graphic software.
這本手冊針對如何使用此繪圖軟體提供使用說明。

give odds 有勝算，有（獲勝的）機率

Past experiences *give odds* for her winning as pretty slim.
從過去的經驗來看，她獲勝的機率相當低。

GIVE ② 059

give a total of ... 總計為，總共是

There are perhaps 6-10 fleets *giving a total of* 1500 to 3000 ships.
大約有 6 到 10 支艦隊，且共有 1,500 到 3,000 艘船。

give voice 賦予發言權，讓…（某人）發聲

Give voice to a child who may be in danger.
讓可能身處險境的孩子能夠有發言權。

Collocation Exercises

A 請從方框中選出正確的單字填入以下句子的空格中，注意句意正確及通順。

account	alibi	comfort	demonstration
evidence	example	explanation	instruction
odds	outline	total	voice

1. Since he cannot give a(n) _____ without exposing his secret identity, Clark is forced to go to jail until the mess can be straightened out.

2. The accused was required to give a(n) _____, but he kept silent.

3. I even gave _____ of approximately 20:1. In other words, they lose a dollar if he stays in office; I pay them twenty if he leaves on time.

4. It's been ten years. All that time I never once found the courage to give _____ to the words that for so long I had held in my heart.

5. He gave a(n) _____ of the successful work of the Brain Injury Council, whose membership is mostly made up of people with brain injuries and their families.

6. After burying him, the pastor gave _____ to the visitors.

7. The catalogue for 1900-1910 gives a(n) _____ of 302 registrations.

8. This report by Amnesty International gives _____ that the National Security Law infringes on human rights.

9. During the driving practice, I was given the _____ to drive at a steady speed.

10. Can you give me a(n) _____ on how to put these together?

B 請將以下句子翻譯成英文。

11. 我甚至無法連鼓起勇氣安慰那些腦部受傷的人。

12. 跟我說明一下你為什麼被迫給他們 20 美元。

13. 她指示她的學生們大聲朗讀課本。

14. 我們應該讓那些在惡劣環境中受苦的移工有發言權。

　　_____

15. 那個男孩提出自己當時在家念書的不在場證明，但他的衣服卻髒得不成樣子。

　　_____

Collocations with GIVE ③

DAY 12

Day-12.mp3

在 give 後面加上「活動」類的名詞，可以構成「舉辦某項活動」這樣的搭配用語。例如，give an audition 可用來表示「舉辦一場試鏡會」，give a party 則表示「舉行一場派對」。此外，give way (to something) 這個搭配用語也經常出現，意指「對⋯（某事物）讓步」。

Collocation at a Glance

Verb + Noun	Meaning	Verb + Noun	Meaning
give access	給予使用權限	**give** a party	舉辦派對
give an audition	進行試鏡	**give** a rebate	提供退款回饋金
give (a) dimension	增添層次（或深度、廣度等）	**give** a start	開始，啟動
give a discount	給予折扣	**give** a wave	（揮手）道別
give first-aid	進行急救	**give** way	讓路，被取代

Collocation in Use

give access 給予使用權限

Public authorities may *give access* to an official document.
公家機關可能給予一份官方文件的閱覽權限。

give an audition 進行試鏡

I am going to take the speakers to one of our studios and *give* them *an audition*.
我打算把那些講者帶去我們的一間錄音室讓他們試鏡。

give (a) dimension 增添層次（或深度、廣度等）

I think male vocals can *give a dimension* to the song that will really enhance the melody.
我認為男音可以為這首歌增添某種層次，並可使旋律更加豐富。

give a discount 給予折扣

We can *give* you *a discount* if you pay the full amount in cash.
如果您以現金一次付清，我們可以給您折扣。

give first-aid 進行急救

Please *give* them *first-aid* until an ambulance arrives.
請先為他們進行急救，直到救護車抵達。

give a party 舉辦派對

If you are *giving a party*, you might expect guests to bring a great gift.
如果您要舉辦派對，您也許會期待客人帶來一份很棒的禮物。

give a rebate 提供退款回饋金

Our company will *give* you *a rebate* ranging from $75 to $125 on the purchase of a new dishwasher.
本公司將在您購買新款洗碗機時提供 75 至 125 美元的回饋金。

give a start 開始，啟動

If it is economically reasonable, the government will *give a start* to this project.
若符合經濟效益，政府將啟動這項專案。

give a wave（揮手）道別

She *gave* me *a* small good-bye *wave* and then disappeared around the corner.
她輕輕地向我揮手道別，然後在轉角處消失了。

give way 讓路，被取代

Silent movies *gave way* to talkies, as ice boxes gave way to refrigerators.
無聲電影讓位於有聲電影，就像冰箱取代了冰櫃一樣。

Collocation Exercises

A 請從方框中選出正確的單字填入以下句子的空格中，注意句意正確及通順。

access	audition	background	dimension
discount	first-aid	groan	party
rebate	start	wave	way

1. I would like to give a big _____ and enjoy eating some of the unusual food that people ate in those days.

2. We offer a prompt payment incentive; we will give you a(n) _____ if you pay the full amount on or before the date the first installment is due.

3. Since the last century, the proud tradition of American television journalism has been giving _____ to an entertainment-driven industry.

4. This web site gives _____ to the Library of Congress and to a variety of other services and information.

GIVE ③   065

5. Polluted cities can give a(n) _____ to the residents who buy hybrid (gasoline-electric) cars and turn in a conventional gasoline car for recycling.

6. Brian asked me if I would take the speakers to one of our studios and give them a(n) _____ .

7. Although everybody is obliged by law to give _____ to an injured person, it is not a rare sight that cars pass the scene of a road accident without even stopping.

8. When I saw him looking so sheepish in his car, I couldn't help slowing down to give him a(n) _____ and a smile.

9. Many Koreans share the belief that early English education will give their children a head _____ to academic and social achievements.

10. The special features in DVDs give an interesting extra _____ to the movie watching.

B 請將以下句子翻譯成英文。

11. 一旦我帶他們到我其中一間錄音室時，我就要舉辦一場盛大的派對。

_____

12. 感謝你讓我開始進行網站翻譯的工作。

_____

13. 當我經過坐在車子裡的他時,他正讓路給另一輛車通過。

14. 她開心地向我揮揮手,但她眼中卻泛著淚水。

15. 劇組為 200 人舉辦了一場試鏡,但最終沒有錄用任何人。

Collocations with

HAVE ①

DAY 13

Day-13.mp3

如果只知道 have 這個動詞是「有，擁有」的意思，那麼你肯定會經常遇到許多難題。今天要學的是，「have + 受詞」可理解為「做某件事」。例如，have an argument 意為「爭論」，have an agreement 意思是「達成協議」，have a check 則表示「進行檢查」。

Collocation at a Glance

Verb + Noun	Meaning	Verb + Noun	Meaning
have an abortion	進行墮胎手術	**have** a baby	懷孕，懷上孩子
have an affair	有婚外情，搞外遇	**have** a chat	閒聊
have an agreement	達成協議，取得共識	**have** a check	做檢查，進行確認
have an argument	爭論，爭吵	**have** a check-up	進行健康檢查
have an arrangement	有約定，簽訂協議	**have** a go	嘗試，試試看

Collocation in Use

have an abortion 進行墮胎手術

Nowadays, so many Koreans are deciding to *have an abortion*.
如今，有許多韓國人決定進行墮胎手術。

have an affair 有婚外情，搞外遇

She's *having an affair* with one of her students.
她正與自己其中一個學生有婚外情。

have an agreement 達成協議，取得共識

None of the candidates *has an agreement* to save the economy.
沒有任何候選人在拯救經濟這方面有所共識。

have an argument 爭論，爭吵

I got totally exhausted after *having an argument* with her.
和她爭論了一番之後，我感到完全筋疲力盡。

have an arrangement 有約定，簽訂協議

The company *has an arrangement* with the bank for three years' low interest loans.
該公司與這家銀行簽訂為期三年的低利貸款協議。

have a baby 懷孕，懷上孩子

Mary was confused how she could *have a baby* because she was not yet married to Joseph.
瑪利亞對於自己是如何懷孕的感到困惑，因為她尚未與約瑟結婚。

have a chat 閒聊

We *had a* lively *chat* with each other.
我們彼此聊得很起勁。

have a check 做檢查，進行確認

Have a check before the luggage is put on the plane.
在行李進行托運之前，請先進行確認。

have a check-up 進行健康檢查

You should *have a* physical *check-up* for military service.
你應該去做服兵役所需要的體檢。

have a go 嘗試，試試看

I want to *have a go* at sky-diving.
我想嘗試跳傘。

HAVE ①

Collocation Exercises

A 請從方框中選出正確的單字填入以下句子的空格中，注意句意正確及通順。

abortions	affair	agreement	argument
arrangement	baby	chat	check
check-ups	comment	go	support

1. Both sides had a(n) _____ about who should pay the legal fees.

2. Part of taking care of yourself is having regular _____ to see if your body is healthy.

3. Her husband strenuously denied that he had a(n) _____ with one of her friends.

4. I don't want to have a(n) _____ with an irrational opponent who always precludes negotiations.

5. We already have three children but we are trying to have another _____.

6. Come and have a(n) _____! If you make it yourself, you'll be more proud of it.

7. I had a(n) _____ in the office yesterday with my boss about the progress of the project.

8. Before you make a decision, have a quick _____ over your car to make sure it has not been stolen or damaged.

9. The couple were divorced, but they had a(n) _____ to meet together regularly for the sake of their children.

10. An increasing number of women began to speak out that they had _____ and share their stories within the support group.

B 請將以下句子翻譯成英文。

11. 管理單位宣布已與工會達成一項確保福利服務的協議。

12. 有些女性在決定要墮胎時會經歷情感上的一番掙扎。

13. 討論會的小組成員針對目前核能問題展開了一段冗長的爭論。

14. 醫生建議他做身體檢查，但他卻置之不理。

15. 他們只是簡短聊了幾句，卻對彼此產生了好感。

Collocations with HAVE ②

DAY 14

Day-14.mp3

have 的後面也常接表示「（人的）情感或傾向」的名詞。例如，have affection 可用來表示「有愛慕之意」或「有感情」，have an attitude 是指「抱持某種態度」，have a bent 則表示「具有某項天賦或才能」。此外，have access to 的意思是「擁有…的使用權或存取權」。

Collocation at a Glance

Verb + Noun	Meaning	Verb + Noun	Meaning
have (an) access	擁有…的使用權或存取權	**have** an attitude	抱持某種態度
have (an) addiction	有成癮（症狀）	**have** a benefit	獲得好處，享受福利
have an advantage	具有優勢	**have** a bent	具有天賦（或才能）
have affection	有感情	**have** a choice	擁有選擇權
have (an) assurance	有信心，深信不疑	**have** a clue	掌握線索

Collocation in Use

have (an) access 擁有…的使用權或存取權

The programmer *has access* to the classified database.
那位程式設計師擁有存取機密資料庫的權限。

have (an) addiction 有成癮（症狀）

She *has an addiction* to coffee and cookies.
她對咖啡和餅乾有成癮的狀況。

have an advantage 具有優勢

The product *has the advantage* of being easy to carry.
這項產品具有便攜的優勢。

have affection 有感情

I *have* deep *affection* for my first grandchild.
我對我的第一個金孫懷有深厚的情感。

have (an) assurance 有信心,深信不疑

I *had* complete *assurance* that the university would grant me admission.
我(當時)很有自信這所大學會錄取我。

have an attitude 抱持某種態度

Most people *have a* negative *attitude* to aging.
大多數人對於老化抱持負面的態度。

have a benefit 獲得好處,享受福利

Many Koreans *have the benefit* of having high-speed internet access, and use it every day.
許多韓國人享受著高速上網的便利,並且每天都在使用。

have a bent 具有天賦(或才能)

Some of the most famous intellectuals *have a bent* for political satire.
一些很有名的知識分子非常擅於諷刺政治。

have a choice 擁有選擇權

She *had* no *choice* but to accept the invitation.
她別無選擇,只能接受邀請。

have a clue 掌握線索

The police *had* no *clue* how the robbers broke into the mansion without being noticed by security guards.
對於劫匪如何在不被警衛發現的情況下闖入豪宅,警方毫無頭緒。

HAVE ② 073

Collocation Exercises

A 請從方框中選出正確的單字填入以下句子的空格中，注意句意正確及通順。

access	addiction	advantage	affection
appointment	assurance	attitude	benefit
bent	blessing	choice	clue

1. The professor has a strong negative _____ towards an unhealthy social environment.

2. He obviously has great _____ for his pet.

3. When I won a prize in a photography contest, I realized that I had an artistic _____.

4. As the police raids were conducted in four directions simultaneously, the criminals had no _____ other than to give in.

5. The shopping mall has an immense _____ from the dense population of the area.

6. They don't have any _____ where to find the appropriate remedy for the virus-infected computer.

7. The country does not have any firm _____ that no attack will be carried out against its regime.

8. The company has a competitive _____ over the rival company.

9. Some politicians seem to have a serious _____ to power.

10. Millions of people with HIV/AIDS in poor countries still do not have _____ to potentially life-saving drugs.

B 請將以下句子翻譯成英文。

11. 這家商業顧問公司有獨特的管道可獲取最新的金融資訊。

12. 一旦你對網路成癮，它就會主宰你的生活。

13. 這個網站的優勢在於任何使用者都能進入。

14. 她對家人的感情比對社交活動更加深厚。

15. 擁有積極的態度是成功的關鍵。

Collocations with HAVE ③

DAY 15

Day-15.mp3

今天的學習重點是，接在動詞 have 後面，且與邏輯或抽象概念有關名詞的搭配用法。例如：have an agenda 意為「有議程」或「懷有特定意圖」，have a connection 指「有關聯」或「存在聯繫」，have an insight 表示「具有洞察力」，have a comment 則意指「有意見，做了個評論」。

Collocation at a Glance

Verb + Noun	Meaning	Verb + Noun	Meaning
have an agenda	有議程	**have** a difference	存在差異
have cause	有（正當）理由	**have** a difficulty	遇到困難
have a comment	有意見，有話要說	**have** an effect	有效果，產生影響
have a connection	有（人脈）關係	**have** an urge	有一股衝動
have credibility	具有公信力	**have** an insight	有洞察力，有深刻的見解

Collocation in Use

have an agenda 有議程

I *have a* specific *agenda* for the meeting.
我有一份明確的會議議程。

have cause 有（正當）理由

No one *had cause* to doubt her sincerity and dedication.
沒有人有理由懷疑她的真誠與奉獻。

have a comment 有意見，有話要說

Do you *have any comment* on these matters? If so, send your opinion to me.
您對這些問題有任何評論嗎？如果有，請將您的意見發送給我。

have a connection 有（人脈）關係

He is believed to *have connections* with politicians who occupy top international positions.
據信他與擔任國際高層職位的政客有人脈關係。

have credibility 具有公信力

The broadcasting system used to *have* great *credibility*, but it lost it because of false reports.
這個廣播系統曾經擁有極高的公信力，但後來因播報假新聞而失去信譽。

have a difference 存在差異

Both candidates might *have a difference* of philosophy in this campaign, but they appear to be the same to me.
兩位候選人在這次選戰或許有些理念上的不同，但對我來說，他們都一樣。

have a difficulty 遇到困難

This program can help you if you *have difficulties* with literacy skills.
如果您有識字方面的困難，這個程式或許對您有幫助。

have an effect 有效果，產生影響

The treatment certainly *had an effect*.
這個治療當然有效果。

have an urge 有一股衝動

Though she knew her disability, she *had an urge* to see the world.
儘管她知道自己的殘疾，但仍有想要去看看這個世界的一股衝動。

have an insight 有洞察力，有深刻的見解

She *has an insight* into living a healthy life.
她對於健康生活有深刻的見解。

Collocation Exercises

A 請從方框中選出正確的單字填入以下句子的空格中，注意句意正確及通順。

agenda	appearance	cause	comment
connections	credibility	differences	difficulties
effect	insight	promise	urge

1. If you want to communicate well with others, you should have a(n) _____ into what other people are thinking and feeling.

2. The Kyoto Protocol had a significant _____ on global warming.

3. If you really want to have _____ as a teacher to teenagers, the key is to have something they need, want, and can use.

4. Any student who has _____ with their school assignments should be encouraged not to lose their interest in learning.

5. I had a strong _____ to look out the window after I heard a loud noise.

6. You have no _____ to cower in fear. You're doing the right thing.

7. The union had a(n) _____ on the issues of access to health care service.

8. The arrested men are alleged to have _____ to a terrorist network.

9. Police will have no further _____ until they've got all the paperwork done.

10. Even identical twins may have some physical _____; they may have _____ in their environment.

B 請將以下句子翻譯成英文。

11. 兩位選手意見分歧很大，但他們仍彼此合作良好。

12. 如果您有任何意見，請發送電郵到這個位址。

13. 我有一股衝動想握住她的手。

14. 這次會議有太多的議題，因此與會者無法專注於一項議題。

15. 簡潔性和可及性是一個網站具有可信度的要件之一。

Collocations with HOLD ①

DAY 16
Day-16.mp3

今天我們的學習重點是與動詞「hold」相關的搭配詞用法，特別在與政治與社會相關領域中。例如 hold a conference 意思是「召開會議（或記者會）」；hold an election 意思是「舉行選舉」；hold a summit 表示「舉行高峰會（首腦會談）」；hold power 則用來表達「掌握權力」或「維持政權」。

Collocation at a Glance

Verb + Noun	Meaning	Verb + Noun	Meaning
hold an auction	舉行拍賣會	**hold** talks	舉行會談
hold a conference	召開會議	**hold** the balance	保持平衡
hold an election	舉辦選舉	**hold** the key	掌握關鍵（因素）
hold a meeting	召開會議	**hold** the reins	掌控局勢
hold a summit	舉行高峰會（首腦會談）	**hold** power	掌握權力

Collocation in Use

hold an auction 舉行拍賣會

The museum *held an auction* on March 1st to sell works of art.
該博物館於 3 月 1 日舉行了一場販售藝術品的拍賣會。

DAY 16

hold a conference 召開會議

The group *held a conference* to present the results of the research project.
該團體召開一場展示研究計畫成果的會議。

hold an election 舉辦選舉

The committee was supposed to *hold an election*, but no one volunteered to chair the committee.
該委員會理應舉辦一場選舉，但沒有人自願擔綱委員會的主席。

hold a meeting 召開會議

The representatives proposed to *hold a meeting* to discuss the relief issue.
代表們提議召開會議討論紓困的議題。

hold a summit 舉行高峰會（首腦會談）

Both organizations have planned to *hold a summit* next month.
兩組織已計劃下個月舉行一場高峰會。

hold talks 舉行會談

The student association asked the principal to *hold* formal *talks* about the exam schedule.
學生會要求校長針對考試行程召開正式的會談。

hold the balance 保持平衡

It is hard to *hold the balance* between unconditional love and conditional commitment.
在無條件的愛與有條件的承諾之間保持平衡並不容易。

hold the key 掌握關鍵（因素）

Who do you think *holds the key* to strengthen the defense of our team?
你認為誰掌握了強化我們球隊防守力的關鍵？

HOLD ①

hold the reins 掌控局勢

The vice president actually *holds the reins* of power in the group.
副總裁實際上掌控著該集團內部的決策權。

hold power 掌握權力

The generals *held power* over the nation through a bloody coup d'Etat.
那些將軍透過血腥政變掌握了國家的統治權。

Collocation Exercises

A 請從方框中選出正確的單字填入以下句子的空格中，注意句意正確及通順。

auction	balance	conference	election
key	lease	meeting	power
promise	reins	summit	talks

1. The regime broke the promise to hold a free _____ and quelled the civil movements opposing the dictatorship.

2. Even after the law becomes effective, it holds no _____ over us for 3 years.

3. The committee has agreed to hold a(n) _____ to decide procedural issues on that matter.

4. Minor parties and independents hold the _____ of power in the Congress.

5. What policies hold the _____ to pulling this country out of recession?

6. The countries held secret multilateral _____ on the current nuclear threats.

7. The Department of Education announced last week that it would hold a(n) _____ discussing teenage sex education.

8. Do you think it can be justified that a few politicians who held the _____ of government led the country into a war?

9. Whales Friends is to hold a fundraising _____ , which will have a lot of cool things to bid on.

10. A report from the government says that the two Koreas could hold a(n) _____ within two months.

B 請將以下句子翻譯成英文。

11. 你認為兩韓何時會再度舉行高峰會？

   _____

12. 每年一次，該校會舉辦拍賣會來為其獎學基金募款。

   _____

13. 曾幾何時，許多妻子對她們的先生握有掌控權。

   _____

14. 這個非政府組織舉辦一場策劃環保運動的「綠色會議」。

   _____

15. 學校要求教師（應該）於嚴格與寬容之間保持平衡。

Collocations with HOLD ②

DAY 17

Day-17.mp3

hold 最常見的意思是「擁有，持有」。例如，hold office 意指「任職，身居要職」，也就是「身居某種職位」的意思；hold a patent 表示「擁有一項專利」，hold a share 則意指「持有股份」。此外，hold a view 常用來表達「抱持某種觀點」。

Collocation at a Glance

Verb + Noun	Meaning	Verb + Noun	Meaning
hold an inquiry	進行調查	**hold** a rank	獲得高階職位（或某種地位）
hold office	任職，身居要職	**hold** a record	保持紀錄
hold a patent	擁有專利權	**hold** a share	擁有某種分量
hold a position	任職，擔任職務	**hold** a value	抱持某種價值觀
hold promise	有前景／希望／可能	**hold** a view	抱持某種觀點

Collocation in Use

hold an inquiry 進行調查

Some students complained of cheating, and requested the school to *hold an inquiry*.
一些學生投訴作弊情事，並要求校方進行調查。

hold office 任職，身居要職

The mayor *holds office* for a two-year term.
市長的任期為兩年。

hold a patent 擁有專利權

The company *holds the patent* on the software.
該公司持有這個軟體的專利權。

hold a position 任職，擔任職務

What *position* did you *hold* just prior to this one?
您在擔任這個職位之前，曾經身居何職？

hold promise 有前景／希望／可能

This drug *holds promise* for treating heart disease.
這種藥物可望用來治療心臟病。

hold a rank 獲得高階職位（或某種地位）

The officer is going to *hold a rank* of commander in a year.
這位軍官將於一年後晉升為指揮官。

hold a record 保持紀錄

Who *holds the record* for most goals scored in a K-League season?
誰保持著 K 聯盟單一賽季進球最多的紀錄？

hold a share 擁有某種分量

The company *holds a* huge *share* of the domestic market.
該公司在國內市場擁有龐大的市占率。

hold a value 抱持某種價值觀

The values you *hold* might hurt another person's feelings.
你所堅持的價值觀可能傷害到他人的感受。

hold a view 抱持某種觀點

Some people *hold a* skeptical *view* toward therapists.
有些人對於治療師抱持懷疑的看法。

DAY 17

Collocation Exercises

A 請從方框中選出正確的單字填入以下句子的空格中，注意句意正確及通順。

inquiry	office	opinion	patent
position	promise	rank	record
sales	share	values	views

1. Those who hold different _____ on these matters must back up their opinions with convincing arguments.

2. The innovators claimed to hold the _____ for the technology, and they were granted the rights for it.

3. The Education Discussion Forum introduced its panel of four members who all hold the _____ of Distinguished Professors.

4. In Korea, a president holds _____ for a term of 5 years and is not eligible for re-election as president.

5. Further investment is needed to hold the company's _____ of an increasingly competitive market.

6. New hybrid vehicles hold _____ for improving fuel efficiency.

7. The army steadfastly refused to hold a(n) _____ into the suspicious death.

8. Capitalists hold no other _____ than the maximization of profits.

9. In all the flowers that are used to make perfumes, red roses have been regarded as holding the first _____.

10. I'd like to introduce a superman who holds the _____ for selling 125 cars a month.

B 請將以下句子翻譯成英文。

11. 100 公尺短跑的世界紀錄保持人是誰？
    _____

12. 這名女子擔任該黨發言人的職務。
    _____

13. 這種新的學習策略可能有助於提升學業成績。
    _____

14. 這家新創公司擁有幹細胞技術的專利權。
    _____

15. 一些支持在家上課的人對學校教育抱持不以為然的看法。
    _____

Collocations with

HOLD ③

DAY 18

Day-18.mp3

要注意的是，hold 除了可表示「擁有，持有」之外，它還有「阻止，抑制」這樣完全不同的意思。例如，hold one's breath 表示「屏住呼吸」，hold fire 意指「停止射擊，不採取行動」，hold one's tongue 則表示「閉嘴，不說話」。此外，hold a tune（保持音準）雖然含義與上述詞組略有不同，但也是一個實用的搭配用法。

Collocation at a Glance

Verb + Noun	Meaning	Verb + Noun	Meaning
hold one's breath	（因緊張而）屏住呼吸	**hold** hostage	劫持人質
hold fire	停止射擊，按兵不動	**hold** moisture	保持水分
hold line	（電話中）請別掛電話	**hold** territory	守護領土
hold tongue	閉嘴，別說話	**hold** attention	抓住注意力
hold hands	手牽手	**hold** a tune	保持音準

Collocation in Use

hold one's breath （因緊張而）屏住呼吸

The sudden military raids left the village dwellers little option but to *hold their breath*.
突如其來的軍事突襲行動讓村民們幾乎別無選擇，只能屏息以對。

hold fire 停止射擊，按兵不動

The hunter *held fire* until the bear came into his sight.
獵人一直按兵不動，直到熊進入他的視線範圍。

hold line （電話中）請別掛電話

Hold the line. I'll answer the phone in a minute.
請不要掛斷電話。我馬上回來接電話。

hold tongue 閉嘴，別說話

Hold your *tongue* and listen to what I have to say.
閉上嘴巴，聽我把我話說完。

hold hands 手牽手

The couple was *holding hands* while walking on the moonlit street.
那對情侶手牽著手，走在月光照耀的街道上。

hold hostage 劫持人質

The man claimed that he was *held hostage* in a UFO.
那名男子聲稱自己曾被劫持在一架 UFO 內。

hold moisture 保持水分

Sandy soils do not *hold* much *moisture*.
沙質土壤無法保留太多水分。

hold territory 守護領土

The tribes strived to *hold* their *territory* against the intruders.
這個部族為守護自己的領土而努力抵禦入侵者。

hold attention 抓住注意力

The lecture could not *hold* the *attention* of most students.
這場演講無法抓住多數學生的注意力。

hold a tune 保持音準

She really can't *hold a tune*, but I enjoy going to karaoke with her.
她確實五音不全，但我還是很喜歡跟她一起去唱卡拉 OK。

DAY 18

Collocation Exercises

A 請從方框中選出正確的單字填入以下句子的空格中，注意句意正確及通順。

attention	breath	delivery	fire
hands	hostage	line	moisture
movement	territory	tongue	tune

1. Hold your _____ whatever you may see or hear. It's important that this room remain completely quiet.

2. The police were ordered to hold their _____ as the criminals advanced toward them.

3. We're looking for a new member to join our band who has a good ear for music and can hold a(n) _____.

4. Heating air will increase its capacity to hold _____, and lower its relative humidity.

5. The country was suspected to have attempted to hold _____ rather than achieve the spread of freedom and liberty.

6. Will you hold the _____, please? I'll see if the manager is in.

7. The speaker's announcement held the _____ of the large audience for over 15 minutes.

8. Eight laborers held _____ by insurgents last week were freed and handed over to their countries.

9. What if the monster doesn't show up itself? Do we just sit here holding our _____?

10. When Mary held her _____ out to him, he hesitated for a while and finally stripped off his gloves.

B 請將以下句子翻譯成英文。

11. 我們在恐懼中屏住了呼吸。

12. 年輕男子牽著他女友的手後，思考著接下來怎麼辦。

13. 這部電影整整兩個小時把觀眾的注意力完全抓牢。

14. 這名上士命令他的人停火，但沒有人聽見他的聲音。

15. 那個男孩表演了一個魔術且成功吸引了女孩的注意。

Collocations with KEEP ①

DAY 19

Day-19.mp3

keep 不僅有「保有，維持」的意思，也常用來表示「遵守，堅守」。例如，keep an engagement 和 keep a promise 意為「遵守約定」，keep a resolution 則表示「堅定決心」。此外，keep faith in someone/something 指的是「對某人或某事保持信念」。

Collocation at a Glance

Verb + Noun	Meaning	Verb + Noun	Meaning
keep an account	作帳，記錄帳目	**keep** a promise	遵守承諾
keep a diary	寫日記	**keep** a record	留下紀錄
keep an engagement	履行約定／承諾	**keep** a resolution	堅定決心
keep faith	保持信念（或信心）	**keep** statistics	持續記錄統計數據
keep a file	保存檔案	**keep** value	保值

Collocation in Use

keep an account 作帳，記錄帳目

He should *keep an account* of all expenditures.
他應該記錄所有支出的帳目。

keep a diary 寫日記

Some people find it useful to *keep a diary*.
有些人發現寫日記是有用處的。

keep an engagement 履行約定／承諾

They *keep the engagement* made by the government.
他們履行了政府說過的承諾。

keep faith 保持信念（或信心）

We are challenged to *keep faith* in our relationships.
我們面臨著對彼此關係保持信心的挑戰。

keep a file 保存檔案

The CIA *keeps files* on the armistice agreement.
CIA 保存了與停戰協定有關的檔案。

keep a promise 遵守承諾

The Prime Minister has yet to *keep his promise* to reduce taxes.
首相尚未履行他減稅的承諾。

keep a record 留下紀錄

The manufacturers should *keep a record* of all ingredients.
製造商應該保所有成分的紀錄資料。

keep a resolution 堅定決心

I have managed to *keep* my New Year's *Resolution* to study harder.
我一直努力堅持自己「要更加用功」的新年決意。

keep statistics 持續記錄統計數據

My baseball team *keeps statistics* on players' performances.
我的棒球隊一直都有統計球員表現的紀錄。

keep value 保值

Even 10 years from now, the ring will *keep* its *value* because of its high-quality diamond.
即使從現在起再過 10 年，這戒指仍將因其優質的鑽石保有它的價值。

DAY 19

Collocation Exercises

A 請從方框中選出正確的單字填入以下句子的空格中，注意句意正確及通順。

account	assessment	diary	engagement
faith	files	promise	record
resolutions	secret	statistics	value

1. The president wants to keep _____ on his people legitimately by using The Patriot Act and terrorism as a means to justify his actions.

2. Atheism is spreading all over the world. Because of this, many people are challenged to keep their _____ in God.

3. The company had put forth every possible effort to keep the _____. However, they failed to do it, and went bankrupt.

4. A product with good durability and design will keep its _____. It won't need to be discarded or replaced with a new one.

5. In order to monitor the population growth of a nation, it is necessary to keep _____ on all births that occur.

6. There's no rule that you have to keep a(n) _____ every day or every week, but some people find it useful.

7. He should keep a(n) _____ of all receipts and expenditures and make out a financial report at the end of each quarter.

8. The manufacturers keep a(n) _____ of the supplier or importer of all ingredients, however small the quantity may be.

9. I believe that people's faith in democracy can make a certain politician keep his or her _____.

10. Many people fail to keep New Year's workout _____ but every promise you make yourself is worth keeping.

B 請將以下句子翻譯成英文。

11. 總統應信守承諾並釋放被監禁的環保運動人士。

12. 寫日記能讓我們反省日常生活（的種種）。

13. 他仍然堅定戒菸的決心。

14. 這位牧師選擇死亡來作為堅定其基督教信仰的一個理由。

15. 記錄所有會議內容是有必要的，這是為了確保明確的溝通。

Collocations with KEEP ②

DAY 20

Day-20.mp3

keep 並非指一個瞬間的動作,而是一個表示持續做某動作,或進行某種活動的動詞。因此,它經常被譯為「保持,維持」。例如:keep a balance 意思是「維持平衡」、keep a distance 意思是「保持距離」、keep a shape 意思是「保持特定形狀」。

Collocation at a Glance

Verb + Noun	Meaning	Verb + Noun	Meaning
keep a balance	保持平衡	**keep** perspective	保持正面觀點
keep control	持續掌握/掌控	**keep** a secret	保守秘密
keep a distance	保持距離	**keep** a shape	維持形狀
keep pace	保持步調一致	**keep** sight	保持在視線內,牢牢記住
keep peace	維護和平	**keep** an eye	保持注意

Collocation in Use

keep a balance 保持平衡

I *keep a balance* between the simple and the complicated.
我在簡單與複雜之間保持平衡。

keep control 持續掌握/掌控

In spite of offensive comments, the prime minister *kept control* of her temper.
儘管承受著攻擊性的言論,首相仍將她的脾氣控制住。

keep a distance 保持距離

The detective *keeps his distance* from the prime suspect.
這名警探與主要嫌疑人保持距離。

keep pace 保持步調一致

Physicians *keep pace* with new technologies.
醫生們隨時在吸取新的技術。

keep peace 維護和平

What the UN does in this region is to *keep peace*.
聯合國在這個地區的工作就是維護和平。

keep perspective 保持正面觀點

This book helps me *keep perspective* on linguistics.
這本書有助於我保持對語言學的正面觀點。

keep a secret 保守秘密

The telltale story of this newspaper failed his effort to *keep a secret* until his death.
這家報社的爆料內容使得他無法將秘密帶進墳墓。

keep a shape 維持形狀

The book cover is coated to *keep the shape*.
書本封面經過塗層處理，以維持形狀。

keep sight 保持在視線內，牢牢記住

You have to *keep sight* of your goal when you carry out research.
進行研究時，你必須始終看清楚自己的目標。

keep an eye 保持注意

Keep an eye on my camera. I'll be right back.
看好我的照相機。我馬上就會來。

DAY 20

Collocation Exercises

A 請從方框中選出正確的單字填入以下句子的空格中，注意句意正確及通順。

balance	confidence	control	distance
eye	name	pace	peace
perspective	secret	shape	sight

1. What the UN has to do in this region is to keep _____ between conflicting parties which had agreed to cease fire. They should settle their differences through conversation rather than war.

2. The detective on the trail of a murderer kept his _____ from a seductive woman who he thought would be the prime suspect.

3. A batterer begins and continues his behavior because violence is an effective method for gaining and keeping _____ over another person.

4. Businesses must keep _____ with population shifts and changing needs. Otherwise, they can't survive.

5. Her face suddenly blushed as if she could no longer keep a(n) _____. She felt the urge to disclose everything.

6. You have to keep _____ of your goal and remember that even the longest journey starts with just one small step.

7. It's important to keep _____ when we look at our own past and want to learn from things which we consider our shadow.

8. It is crucial to keep the _____ of animals and plants in the environment.

9. Your shirt seems like a new one. How does it keep its _____ in the glove compartment of a car?

10. Don't worry. I just had a few cameras installed up the ceiling, which are keeping a(n) _____ on customers 24 hours a day.

B 請將以下句子翻譯成英文。

11. 這個盒子太過脆弱，無法保持這蛋糕的形狀。

12. 政府掌控著股市的起落。

13. 你可以幫我顧一下孩子，直到我回來嗎？

14. 她和這位年輕的老闆保持距離，以避免同事們的關注。

15. 保守秘密遠比製造秘密困難得多。

Collocations with
KEEP ③

DAY 21

Day-21.mp3

在職場或家庭中，與人維持關係相當重要。keep company with someone 的意思是「與某人維持友誼」，keep contact with someone 則表示「與某人保持聯絡」。此外，keep house 指的是「料理家務，照顧家裡」，而 keep a pet 則表示「飼養寵物」。這些用法都值得牢記。

Collocation at a Glance

Verb + Noun	Meaning	Verb + Noun	Meaning
keep change	把零錢留著，不必找零	**keep** house	料理家務
keep company with	與…（某人）有來往	**keep** a pet	養寵物
keep contact with	與…（某人）保持聯絡	**keep** one's temper	克制脾氣
keep a grip	緊緊抓住，取得掌控權	**keep** track of	持續追蹤（進度）
keep one's hand in	經常練習（以免技藝荒廢）	**keep** (a) watch	密切關注

Collocation in Use

keep change 把零錢留著，不必找零

I *keep change* in my car for homeless people.
我車上備有零錢，以便給無家可歸的人。

keep company with 與…（某人）有來往

Thomas is proud to *keep company with* famous artists.
湯瑪斯對於自己能夠與知名藝術家來往而引以為傲。

keep contact with 與…（某人）保持聯絡

We can *keep contact with* close relatives or friends via e-mail.
我們可以透過電子郵件與近親或友人保持聯絡。

keep a grip 緊緊抓住，取得掌控權

The boss was able to *keep a grip* on his employees through effective incentives.
那位老闆透過有效的獎勵措施才能夠留住他的員工。

keep one's hand in 經常練習（以免技藝荒廢）

James says he tried to *keep his hand in* drama.
詹姆斯表示，他試著保持對於戲劇的熱忱。

keep house 料理家務

I *kept house* for my parents who visited for a long time.
我為長時間來訪的父母料理家務。

keep a pet 養寵物

Keeping a pet is not allowed in this apartment.
這棟公寓禁止飼養寵物。

keep one's temper 克制脾氣

When he's drunk, Frank needs to *keep his temper*.
法蘭克在喝醉酒時必須控制好脾氣才行。

keep track of 持續追蹤（進度）

The police *keep track of* illegal distribution of MP3 files.
警方持續追蹤 MP3 檔案的非法流通情況。

keep (a) watch 密切關注

The researcher *keeps a* close *watch* on the statistical procedure.
這名研究人員密切關注統計流程。

Collocation Exercises

A 請從方框中選出正確的單字填入以下句子的空格中，
注意句意正確及通順。

change	company	contact	grip
hand	hour	house	job
temper	track	pets	watch

1. When he has a discussion, he usually speaks loudly, ending up causing a quarrel. He needs to keep his _____.

2. He really loves drama. Although known best as a CEO, Carter tried to keep his _____ in the performing arts.

3. Our friends and those with whom we keep _____ on a regular basis influence our lives. So we endeavor to have good relationships with them.

4. It is a free spreadsheet that lets you keep _____ of your income, taxes, and purchases.

5. The notion is changing that it is the wife's duty to keep _____. The husband needs to make practical efforts to achieve a truly equal relationship.

6. With the computer and the Internet, we can easily check the news headlines, and also keep _____ with close relatives or friends.

7. Always keep careful _____ over children near swift water—at all times.

8. The Ministry of Education has a plan to educate existing teachers so they would be able to use more interventions and strategies to keep a(n) _____ on their students.

9. I heard that in some countries leaving coins behind is considered very impolite, so I usually keep the _____.

10. Does keeping _____ do harm to animals' rights to freedom or vice versa?

B 請將以下句子翻譯成英文。

11. 飼養寵物可以減輕老年人的孤獨感。

___

12. 儘管在國外留學，他仍與其家鄉的朋友保持聯絡。

___

13. 這是五千韓元，不用找了。

___

14. 我覺得他必須控制好自己的脾氣。你不這麼認為嗎？

___

15. 我覺得一旦校友結婚了，就很難與他們保持聯絡。

_____

Collocations with MAKE ①

DAY 22

Day-22.mp3

今天開始，我們要來學習以動詞 make 作為核心字彙的搭配詞。由 make 本身的含義來說，它經常出現在與經濟活動相關的搭配用語中。例如，make a deposit/withdrawal 指的是「存款／提款」，make an investment 表示「投資」，而 make a purchase 則表示「購買」。

Collocation at a Glance

Verb + Noun	Meaning	Verb + Noun	Meaning
make an apology	道歉	**make** (a) payment	支付款項
make a deposit/withdrawal	存款／提款	**make** a profit	獲取利潤
make (an) improvement	改善，改進	**make** a purchase	購買，購物
make an investment	投資	**make** a recommendation	提出建議／推薦
make an offer	提出（價格、工作機會等的）建議	**make** a response	做出回應

Collocation in Use

make an apology 道歉

You don't need to *make an apology*. It's not your fault.
你不需要道歉。這不是你的錯。

make a deposit/withdrawal 存款／提款

The sponsor is required to *make a deposit* of 30 percent of the profits.
贊助人被要求存入收益的 30%。

make (an) improvement 改善，改進

She is working hard to *make improvements* in her work.
她正在努力提升自己的工作效能。

make an investment 投資

He *made an investment* in the company.
他投資了那家公司。

make an offer 提出（價格、工作機會等的）建議

You are expected to *make a* reasonable *offer*.
您預計將提出合理的報價。

make (a) payment 支付款項

The tenant failed to *make a payment* within 24 hours.
這位房客未能在 24 小時內支付款項。

make a profit 獲取利潤

The software company *makes a* huge *profit* from the new system.
該軟體公司透過這部新的系統獲得了巨額利潤。

make a purchase 購買，購物

She *made a* good *purchase* for her boyfriend's birthday.
她為男友買了一份很棒的生日禮物。

make a recommendation 提出建議／推薦

You can *make a recommendation* based on your analysis.
您可以根據您的分析提出建議。

make a response 做出回應

I am not ready to *make a response* at this time.
我現在還沒準備好做出回應。

Collocation Exercises

A 請從方框中選出正確的單字填入以下句子的空格中，注意句意正確及通順。

apology	arrangement	improvement	investment
offer	payment	profit	purchase
recommendation	response	speech	withdrawal

1. Richard made a(n) _____ for his girlfriend. But she was disappointed with what he bought.

2. Even though the government is oppressing, people are struggling to make a(n) _____ in the democracy.

3. In case the banks are closed on the holiday, he should make a(n) _____ from the account.

4. She always makes a pertinent _____ to her clients. They believe in her ability.

5. Nowadays, the stock value of this electronic company is increasing. People should hurry to make their _____ before the share prices go up.

6. If he didn't commit such a stupid fault, I think that he would not need to make a(n) _____.

DAY 22

7. In your final paper, you can make a(n) _____ based on your analysis and opinion.

8. The company allows people to sell and make a(n) _____ from their free software, but does not allow them to restrict the right of others to distribute it.

9. This internet site no longer requires visitors to make _____ just in credit card. You can also transfer money from your savings account.

10. We hope that you would make a(n) _____ for our letter without hesitation. Then, we may make a snap decision for this issue which would have fatal consequences.

B 請將以下句子翻譯成英文。

11. 他必須在一週內支付租金。

12. 她沒有對他的求婚做出回應。

13. 在安置新的配備之後，該公司獲得不錯的利潤。

14. 他向她誠摯道歉，但她認為那是假的。

15. 那位攝影師推薦了各種數位相機和鏡頭。

_____

Collocations with MAKE ②

DAY 23

Day-23.mp3

相較於其他核心動詞，make 可以帶出更多搭配詞。今天，我們將重點擺在語言相關的搭配詞，例如 make a speech（發表演說）、make conversation with someone（與某人交談）、make a statement（發表聲明）等。

Collocation at a Glance

Verb + Noun	Meaning	Verb + Noun	Meaning
make an appointment	預約，掛號	**make** (a) noise	吵鬧，製造噪音
make a call	打電話	**make** a reference	提及，引用
make contact	聯繫	**make** a reservation	預約
make (a) conversation	交談，對話	**make** a speech	發表演說（或正式演講）
make a mess	弄亂，弄得亂七八糟	**make** a statement	發表聲明，提出說明

Collocation in Use

make an appointment 預約，掛號

You can *make an appointment* in person.
你可以親自預約。

make a call 打電話

He *made a call* to her using his friend's cellular phone.
他用他朋友的手機打電話給她。

make contact 聯繫

Students are required to *make contact* with their professor.
學生們被要求與他們的教授聯繫。

make (a) conversation 交談，對話

A young guy is trying to *make conversation* with a beautiful girl.
一名年輕男子正試圖與一位美麗的女孩攀談。

make a mess 弄亂，弄得亂七八糟

You always *make a mess*.
你總是弄得一團亂。

make (a) noise 吵鬧，製造噪音

The baby *made noise* all day long.
那嬰兒整天吵鬧不止。

make a reference 提及，引用

The revolutionist *made a reference* to Marx's works.
那位革命家提到了馬克思的著作。

make a reservation 預約

Breakfast will be provided to those who *make a reservation*.
早餐將提供給有預約的人。

make a speech 發表演説（或正式演講）

The company *made a speech* in front of CEOs from all over the world.
該公司（代表）在來自世界各國的執行長面前發表談話。

DAY 23

make a statement 發表聲明，提出說明

The New York Times *made a statement* about the president's scandal.
《紐約時報》對總統的醜聞發表了一份聲明。

Collocation Exercises

A 請從方框中選出正確的單字填入以下句子的空格中，注意句意正確及通順。

appointment	call	contact	conversation
fight	mess	noise	reference
reservation	speech	statement	success

1. The teacher should be compassionate and have the ability to make a(n) _____ with his or her students.

2. The government made a(n) _____ that the president was assassinated by a high-ranking official who had considerable complaints about the current political situation.

3. To make a(n) _____ at an available time, call us at the phone number below. Otherwise, you may visit our office in person.

4. If you want to make an international _____, you need to press "0" before dialing the number.

5. It took 2 hours to clean up what my son made a(n) _____ of. I'm really exhausted.

6. The White House said the president would make a(n) _____ on the war today in Texas.

MAKE ②   113

7. Unless you are in a particularly bad situation, the bear will run away when you make a(n) _____.

8. The revolutionist made a(n) _____ to The Communist Manifesto by Marx to emphasize the progress of history.

9. I regret to say that you'd better make _____ with other universities which may fulfill your academic expectation.

10. The hotel recommends that you should make a(n) _____ in advance. If not, you may have to wait for a long time or, at the worst, find another hotel.

B 請將以下句子翻譯成英文。

11. 在預約之前，請先確認會議室的排程。

_____

12. 學生必須在課程開始時與教授聯繫。

_____

13. 競選期間，這位總統候選人發表了一場關於減稅的演說。

_____

14. 東南亞國協領導人就亞洲的未來發表了一份聲明。

_____

15. 那孩子總是把房間弄得亂七八糟,但他的父母認為這是他有創造力的表現。

Collocations with MAKE ③

DAY 24

Day-24.mp3

當 make 後面接「與行為有關」的字詞時，有「進行某項特定行為」的意思。例如，make an arrest 意為「逮捕」、make an assessment 意為「進行評估」、make haste 意為「趕緊，加快速度」。此外，make a point 也有「明確表達觀點」的意思，這一點值得記住。

Collocation at a Glance

Verb + Noun	Meaning	Verb + Noun	Meaning
make an assessment	進行評估	**make** an error	犯錯
make an arrest	逮捕	**make** haste	趕緊，加快速度
make a contribution	有貢獻，做出貢獻	**make** a point	明確表達觀點
make a difference	有差別，有影響	**make** a start	出發，開始
make a discovery	有所發現	**make** a visit	進行訪問

Collocation in Use

make an assessment 進行評估

An assessment has to be *made* on the proposal to clean up the environment.
對於這項清潔環境的提議，必須進行評估。

make an arrest 逮捕

The police *made an arrest* of the murderer at Seoul Station.
警方在首爾車站逮捕了那名殺人犯。

make a contribution 有貢獻，做出貢獻

The engineer *made a contribution* to the development of the new computer.
那位工程師在這新型電腦的開發上有所貢獻。

make a difference 有差別，有影響

Gender *makes* no *difference* in language proficiency.
性別對於語言能力沒有影響。

make a discovery 有所發現

Newton *made a discovery* about the law of gravity.
牛頓發現了萬有引力定律。

make an error 犯了錯誤

He *made an error* in filling out the application form.
他在填寫申請表時出了個錯誤。

make haste 趕緊，加快速度

Make haste or the opportunity will pass you by!
快點，否則機會就和你擦肩而過！

make a point 明確表達觀點

The English teacher *made a point* about the importance of grammar.
英文老師明確指出文法的重要性。

make a start 出發，開始

The sprinter *made a* good *start*.
那位短跑選手起跑順利。

make a visit 進行訪問

On the way home, she *made a visit* to Mike's office.
回家途中,她順道去了一趟麥克的辦公室。

Collocation Exercises

A 請從方框中選出正確的單字填入以下句子的空格中,注意句意正確及通順。

arrest	assessment	contributions	endeavor
error	difference	discovery	haste
name	point	start	visit

1. The LCD market made a good _____ in the beginning of the year, but the price has decreased since February.

2. All the people made _____ to rebuilding the town, which had been destroyed during the civil war.

3. I believe that my physical disability makes no _____ in breaking the world record. I will not get frustrated like I did in the past.

4. Please let us know in advance if you would like to make a(n) _____. Then, we will provide you with better counseling.

5. Her gesture to make a(n) _____ was effective to draw the audience's attention. Everyone nodded their heads.

6. During the interview, he was so nervous that he made an unconscious _____ in defending his wrong behavior.

7. He is trying to make an epoch-making _____ of the technology to transplant a stem cell, which is expected to one day provide a cure for debilitating diseases.

8. Environmental organizations insist that an extensive _____ has to be made of the National Park before tunneling work starts.

9. Police have made a(n) _____ in the murder of a young man who was killed inside a bar. Witnesses said that he was stabbed during a fight over a spilled drink.

10. Samsung is making _____ to resolve electronic equipment losses by a stoppage of power supply. But it has not found the origin which caused the shutdown of power.

B 請將以下句子翻譯成英文。

11. 檢方在疑犯逃往國外之前將其逮捕。

12. 政府要求大使加速進行最終協商。

13. 她花了一週的時間對所有學生的論文進行評量。

14. 我應該從事什麼樣的工作才能為韓國的社會做出貢獻？

15. 標語上寫著:「你的態度決定你的行動。你的行動帶來改變。」

Collocations with SHOW ①

DAY 25
Day-25.mp3

今天開始，我們要來學習 show 這個動詞與各種名詞結合的意義。例如，show 後面接像 film 這種有具體含義的單字時，意思是「上映，放映」。那麼，「show someone the door」是什麼意思呢？雖然可以直譯為「給某人看看這扇門」，但實際上它隱含的意思是「趕走，請某人離開」。

Collocation at a Glance

Verb + Noun	Meaning	Verb + Noun	Meaning
show ability	展現能力	**show** leadership	展現領導力
show deference	表達敬意	**show** a passport	出示護照
show the door	趕走，請某人離開	**show** a profit	有獲利，產生收益
show (a) film	放映電影	**show** teeth	露出牙齒
show goodwill	表達善意	**show** the way	指引方向，帶路

Collocation in Use

show ability 展現能力

It is very important that they *showed the ability* to think freely and that they made their own decisions.
他們展現出獨立思考的能力並做出自己的決定，這一點非常重要。

show deference 表達敬意

The employees have always *shown deference* to the founder of their company.
員工們經常對他們公司的創辦人展現敬意。

show the door 趕走，請某人離開

"Allow me to *show* you *the door* on your way out!" he said angrily to the woman.
他憤怒地對那名女子說，「我要請你出去！」。

show (a) film 放映電影

They *showed the film* to the British audience, whose reaction was quite mixed.
他們放映了這部電影給英國觀眾們看，而他們的反應相當分歧。

show goodwill 表達善意

Israel agreed to free 200 Palestinian prisoners, partly to *show goodwill* ahead of the elections.
以色列同意釋放 200 名巴勒斯坦囚犯，部分原因是想在選舉前展現善意。

show leadership 展現領導力

School authorities have *shown* their *leadership* in pedagogical areas such as defining the shape of curriculum.
學校當局一直在教育學領域中展現其領導力，例如規劃課程架構。

show a passport 出示護照

At the entrance to the security area you must *show* your *passport* and boarding pass.
在進入安檢區時，您必須出示護照和登機證。

show a profit 有獲利，產生收益

If the company *shows a profit*, we should invest. If it shows a loss, let's reconsider our decision.
如果這家公司有獲利，我們理應投資。如果它是虧損的，我們得重新考慮我們的決定。

show teeth 露出牙齒

She grinned, *showing teeth* like small white pearls.
她露齒一笑時，也露出了潔白如珠的牙齒。

show the way 指引方向，帶路

The movie, *The Love*, has *showed* me *the way* to get in touch with my true feelings.
電影《愛》指引了我觸及內心真實情感的道路。

Collocation Exercises

A 請從方框中選出正確的單字填入以下句子的空格中，注意句意正確及通順。

ability	deference	door	film
goodwill	leadership	loyalty	passport
profit	sign	teeth	way

1. It is said that the Romans were brutal in war but they showed _____ towards all who sided with them.

2. In the 80's, TV networks started requiring that their news divisions show a(n) _____, which placed them in the hands of the advertisers.

3. The Classic Competition in Seoul, where Michael showed his _____ at playing piano in front of many guests, was really successful.

4. The hardest thing is that there is no one there to show you the _____ to figure out problems. You have to do it on your own.

5. Our company has decided to show the _____ to workers who smoke, even if it's on their own time.

6. When we visited the production studio, they showed the _____ on a large screen.

7. The governor continues to show his _____ and commitment to our community.

8. The dog may growl, snarl, show _____, or bark.

9. The fact that the region's most powerful players--including China, India, and the United States--show _____ to ASEAN by participating in these forums demonstrates that ASEAN still matters.

10. A customs officer will ask you to show your _____ and your bag will be scanned.

B 請將以下句子翻譯成英文。

11. 最棘手的事情是，沒有人在教育學領域展現其領導力。

_____

12. 學校當局請抗議校方管理政策的學生們離開了。

_____

13. 每次微笑時，我總是被要求露齒而笑。

_____

14. 她在喜劇方面展現了出色的才能,很快就成為了百萬富翁。

15. 向國旗表達敬意並不代表我們支持現任政府。

Collocations with SHOW ②

DAY 26

Day-26.mp3

show 後面常接與「情感」有關的詞語。例如,「show affection」意思是「表達愛意」,「show concern」表示「表達關心／擔憂」,「show partiality」表示「表現出偏袒／不公平的態度」,而「show unease」則表示「流露不安的情緒」。

Collocation at a Glance

Verb + Noun	Meaning	Verb + Noun	Meaning
show affection	表達愛意	show hand	攤牌,表明意圖
show concern	表現關心／關切	show mercy	表示寬容,手下留情
show diplomacy	展現外交手腕	show partiality	表現偏袒
show faith	展現信任	show respect	表達敬意
show a flair	展現卓越才華	show unease	流露不安

Collocation in Use

show affection 表達愛意

They kiss and embrace to *show affection*.
他們以親吻和擁抱來表達愛意。

show concern 表現關心／關切

Good doctors *show concern* for their patients.
好的醫生會對他們的病人表示關心。

DAY 26

show diplomacy 展現外交手腕

She *showed diplomacy* and ability for managing difficult political situations.
她展現了外交手腕以及管理艱難政治情勢的能力。

show faith 展現信任

The manager *showed faith* in me by picking me straight away.
經理立刻就選中了我，展現出對我的信任。

show a flair 展現卓越才華

The best politicians *show a flair* for interacting with many different types of people.
最優秀的政治家擅長與許多不同類型的人互動。

show hand 攤牌，表明意圖

Because I am in discussion with a number of people, I won't *show* my *hand* on that issue.
由於我還在和一些人討論當中，因此我還不會對那問題展現立場。

show mercy 表示寬容，手下留情

The kidnapper *showed mercy* to Nick and sent him home.
那名綁匪對尼克手下留情，將他送回家。

show partiality 表現偏袒

He never *showed partiality* and remained indifferent in debates.
他從不表現偏私，且在辯論會中始終保持中立。

show respect 表達敬意

To *show* your *respect* for family and friends, send this beautiful arrangement of pink flowers.
若要向家人和朋友表達敬意，可以送上這束美麗的粉色花卉。

show unease 流露不安

Many voters *showed unease* and a deep skepticism about the plan.
許多選民對此計劃流露出不安的情緒與強烈的懷疑。

Collocation Exercises

A 請從方框中選出正確的單字填入以下句子的空格中，注意句意正確及通順。

ability	affection	concern	diplomacy
faith	flair	hand	impatience
mercy	partiality	respect	unease

1. All products submitted to the competition are taste tested by a panel of judges who do not show _____ towards a particular brand.

2. Your parents have shown _____ in you. Giving you a new car shows that they value you enough to give you more responsibility.

3. Courts tolerate peaceful, communicative demonstrations, but show considerable _____ when demonstrations threaten "order."

4. This is a one hour multiple-choice written test with puzzles; however, it is enjoyable for students who show a(n) _____ for mathematics.

5. He must be a great poker player because he never shows his _____. He keeps his emotions below the surface and stays calm.

6. Please show _____ with others in the chat room. Anyone using foul language or engaging in disrespectful conduct will be asked to leave.

7. I was inspired with his potential and the way he showed his _____ toward his audience when he was on stage.

8. He was willing to show _____ to someone else who also didn't deserve it.

9. The National Police shows _____ over the recent increase in malicious crimes such as murders, rapes, and human traffics.

10. A woman needs her husband to show _____ to her in the way he speaks to her and of her--to always speak highly of her to others, and to never belittle her.

B 請將以下句子翻譯成英文。

11. 他向擁有解謎才能的學生們發表了一場令人印象深刻的演說。

12. 公民們對於新政府的成立表達關切。

13. 你不能這麼快就表明立場，否則會透露出太多的資訊。

14. 那位護士展現出慈悲心，將這名乞丐帶了回家並為他治療。

　　_____

15. 當兒子說要辭掉工作並自行創業時，母親面露不安的表情。

　　_____

Collocations with SHOW ③

DAY 27

Day-27.mp3

當我們想表達某種情況或現象呈現「特定意義」時，常會用到 show 這個動詞。例如，show a pattern 意為「呈現特定模式」，show a sign 表示「顯現某種跡象」，show a tendency 則指「展現某種傾向」。此外，show vestige 有「可見殘跡」的意思，這一點也值得記住。

Collocation at a Glance

Verb + Noun	Meaning	Verb + Noun	Meaning
show approval	表示認同／支持	**show** proof	顯示證據
show a bias	顯現偏見	**show** a sign	呈現某種跡象
show (a) change	產生變化	**show** a tendency	展現某種傾向
show a pattern	呈現特定模式	**show** a vestige	顯示一絲跡象
show promise	展現前景或可能性	**show** the world	讓全世界看見／知道

Collocation in Use

show approval 表示認同／支持

It was a lively atmosphere. All the people *showed approval* for the service and decor of the club.
氣氛熱鬧非凡。所有人都對俱樂部的服務和裝潢表示認可。

show a bias 顯現偏見

When people use sexist language they are actually *showing a bias*, even if they are unaware of it.
當人們使用性別歧視的語言時,即使當下沒有意識到,實際上也顯現出偏見的態度。

show (a) change 產生變化

Air transportation lost jobs while truck transportation *showed* no *change*.
航空運輸業流失（或減少）了工作機會,而貨運業則沒有任何變化。

show a pattern 呈現特定模式

The plant workers *show a pattern* of lung and some other cancer, which is several times higher than that found in the rest of the state.
工廠工人呈現出肺癌及一些其他癌症的特定模式,其發病率高出該州其他地區的數倍。

show promise 展現前景或可能性

This vaccine *shows promise* for AIDS patients.
這種疫苗讓愛滋病患者看到希望。

show proof 顯示證據

This photo *shows proof* of a lion roaming the campus.
這張照片顯示有獅子在校園內遊蕩的證據。

show a sign 呈現某種跡象

The house *shows signs* of being extremely neglected.
這房子呈現出極度被忽視的跡象。

show a tendency 展現某種傾向

Results from the pretest *show a tendency* to believe that drugs are very simple to obtain.
前測結果顯示,人們普遍傾向於認為毒品的取得非常容易。

show a vestige 展現一絲跡象

A physician must *show* no *vestige* of uncertainty or fear, no matter how nearly overwhelmed he or she might be.
醫生不能展現出一絲一豪的不確定或恐懼感，無論他們可能多麼地感到崩潰。

show the world 讓全世界看見／知道

I'm here to *show the world* that anything is possible.
我在這裡就是要讓所有人知道任何事情都可能發生。

Collocation Exercises

A 請從方框中選出正確的單字填入以下句子的空格中，注意句意正確及通順。

approval	bias	change	exhibition
interest	pattern	promise	proof
sign	symbol	tendency	world

1. He showed _____ as a rookie, but his potential didn't seem to be fulfilled as injuries forced him to sit out for a while.

2. A recent survey of working families in Ohio showed a(n) _____ against black people.

3. The dean showed _____ for the new system to pay by the use of a hand stamp, rather than an original signature.

4. The group is showing a(n) _____ to want to be together as a whole and not split into separate parts.

5. Unfortunately, my personal hope that the writer would show a(n) _____ of maturity quickly ended after reading the first paragraph.

6. Now it's Christmas time and it's a good chance to show the _____ how generous you are.

7. The HIV/AIDS study conducted by Mr. Mandela shows a(n) _____ in sexual behavior.

8. Please be aware that you need to show _____ of English language proficiency to be admitted to the university.

9. This movie shows a typical _____ of psychoanalysis. Mental conflicts and abnormal behaviors of the hero are originated from babyhood relationships between him and his parents.

10. Park Ji-sung showed the _____ that he completely recovered from the leg injury by scoring the golden goal in the last match over Chelsea.

B 請將以下句子翻譯成英文。

11. 他讓全世界看見他的潛能是可以實現的。

　　_____

12. 人們有時會對年長者或身心障礙者有所偏見。

　　_____

13. 他的畫作展現出一種扭曲「真實」的模式。

　　_____

14. 這項統計顯示年輕人對於政治越來越冷漠的趨勢。

15. 他的陳述證明了他是這起犯罪的共犯之一。

Collocations with TAKE ①

DAY 28

Day-28.mp3

今天開始，我們要來學習與 take 有關的搭配詞。與 get 或 have 一樣，take 也是涵義極廣的動詞之一。例如，它可以與表示時間的名詞結合，形成「休息一下」（take a break）、「暫停一下」（take a second）…等各種搭配用法。讓我們一起學習這些不同的搭配詞吧！

Collocation at a Glance

Verb + Noun	Meaning	Verb + Noun	Meaning
take a break	休息一下	take an order	接獲訂單
take a chance	冒險一試	take a picture	拍照
take a course	選一門課程，確定路線	take a pill	服藥
take the day off	放一天假	take a second	稍作停頓
take a message	接收訊息，（幫您）留言	take a test	參加考試

Collocation in Use

take a break 休息一下

You need to *take a break*.
你需要休息一下。

take a chance 冒險一試

You'll never know if you can succeed if you don't *take a chance*.
如果你不冒險一試，就永遠不會知道自己能否成功。

take a course 選一門課程，確定路線

She *took an* introductory *course* in the law school.
她在法學院修了一個入門的課程。

take the day off 放一天假

All the employees will *take the day off* on New Year's Day.
所有員工將在元旦放假一天。

take a message 接收訊息，（幫您）留言

He's not here now. Can I *take a message*?
他現在不在。要幫您留言嗎？

take an order 接獲訂單

The bookstore *took* a lot of *orders* for books about the popular new diet.
那間書店接獲大筆關於新流行減肥法的書籍訂單。

take a picture 拍照

The Milky Way is so big that we cannot *take a picture* of it without a powerful telescope.
銀河系太過龐大，沒有強大的望遠鏡我們無法拍攝其全貌。

take a pill 服藥

You need to *take* this *pill* at least 30 minutes prior to breakfast.
你必須在早餐前至少 30 分鐘服用這顆藥。

take a second 稍作停頓

He needed to *take a second* to reorganize his thoughts.
他需要稍作停頓來重整其思緒。

take a test 參加考試

Before I *take a test*, I usually study at least two weeks in advance.
我通常在考試之前會預先花至少兩週的時間來念書。

Collocation Exercises

A 請從方框中選出正確的單字填入以下句子的空格中，注意句意正確及通順。

break	chance	course	day off
message	order	part	pill
picture	orders	second	test

1. More than 100 employees will take the _____ to donate their skills and time to nonprofit organizations.

2. Let me take a(n) _____ for someone who is unavailable or out of the office.

3. You need to take a(n) _____ and stretch to get your blood flowing. Sitting down for long hours without a break can be harmful.

4. I hope that my husband can simply take a(n) _____ each day and gradually regain the function of his liver.

5. I took a(n) _____ of the landscape around my school with a digital camera.

6. A student who has never taken an introduction to economics should take this _____.

7. I advise you to take a(n) _____ to collect your thoughts before the interview begins.

8. If you aren't able to take a(n) _____ on the day it is scheduled, it is your responsibility to arrange for a make-up test in advance.

DAY 28

9. He knew she would turn down his dinner invitation, but he took a(n) _____ anyway.

10. This Chinese restaurant takes delivery _____ even via text message.

B 請將以下句子翻譯成英文。

11. 我鼓起勇氣邀請了最漂亮、最受歡迎的女孩一起參加舞會。

12. 我不在時,請秘書接收訊息。

13. 服務生幫我們點了餐,但之後卻沒再回來送餐。

14. 醫生囑咐我父親每天服藥兩次,但他卻只是每天喝酒。

15. 因為感冒了,我請了一天假。我整天都在睡覺。

Collocations with TAKE ②

DAY 29
Day-29.mp3

今天我們將學習重點擺在 take 與表示身體動作的名詞結合時的搭配用法。例如，take a breath 意為「呼吸」、take a jump 意為「跳躍」、take note 則表示「注意，留意」等。

Collocation at a Glance

Verb + Noun	Meaning	Verb + Noun	Meaning
take a breath	吸一口氣，喘口氣	**take** a look	看一下
take delight in	樂於…（做某事）	**take** note	關注，留意
take effort to	努力…（做某事）	**take** a shape	成形，呈現某種形狀
take an interest in	對…產生興趣	**take** the trouble to	不辭辛勞地去做…
take a jump	躍升，暴漲	**take** a turn	輪流（做某事）

Collocation in Use

take a breath 吸一口氣，喘口氣

He *takes a* deep *breath* before the job interview.
他在開始這場工作面試前深深吸了一口氣。

take delight in 樂於…（做某事）

I often *take delight in* small things.
我常常在小事情中獲得喜悅。

take effort to 努力去…（做某事）

She *took effort to* express her feelings to him.
她努力向他表達自己的感受。

take an interest in 對…產生興趣

The government has *taken an interest in* weapons development.
政府有意進行武器的開發。

take a jump 躍升，暴漲

Mike could have *taken a jump* to the presidency.
麥克本來可躍升至總裁大位。

take a look 看一下

I *took a look* at the statistical output.
我看了一下統計的結果。

take note 關注，留意

He *takes note* of recent advances in human rights.
他有在關注最近的人權進展。

take a shape 成形，呈現某種形狀

This cake *takes a shape* of a triangle.
這個蛋糕呈現三角形狀。

take the trouble to 不辭辛勞地去做…

Almost 20 years ago, people didn't *take the trouble to* read a classic novel.
將近二十年前，人們還不願費心地去閱讀一本經典小說。

take a turn 輪流（做某事）

Each student should *take a turn* as the discussion leader.
每個學生都應輪流擔任討論會的領導者。

Collocation Exercises

A 請從方框中選出正確的單字填入以下句子的空格中，注意句意正確及通順。

breath	delight	effort	interest
jump	look	note	place
shape	trouble	turns	vote

1. Poor readers don't want to take the _____ to infer the author's intention from the content. So their scores on a reading proficiency test are lower than expected.

2. The X-generation takes _____ in destroying the old way of doing things. The older generation sometimes can't understand their behavior.

3. I think that an ambitious woman can take a(n) _____ up to the highest position in this company, if she's very capable and intelligent.

4. While I took a close _____ at the security system of my company, I found some defects.

5. A Korean person takes _____ to express their emotions in subtle ways. But an American is more direct and goes straight to the point.

6. If you were to connect each point, the resulting line would take the _____ shown in Figure 7, which should look familiar to you.

7. When a dolphin needs to take a(n) _____, it comes up to the surface of the water.

8. I hope that people around the nation will take more _____ in the environmental movement.

9. Please take _____ that you need to register online for further information.

10. It was a long trip and we took _____ driving.

B 請將以下句子翻譯成英文。

11. 他承認自己忽略了人權的最新進展。

_____

12. 這項活動要求每一位學生輪流擔任課堂討論的主導人。

_____

13. 他深深吸了一口氣後，朝著她跑了過去。

_____

14. 我樂於參與公民運動。然而，我的父母希望我去賺錢。

_____

15. 我的朋友特地開車送我到車站，讓我及時回到家。

_____

Collocations with TAKE ③

DAY 30

Day-30.mp3

take 的後面可以接抽象名詞。例如，take advantage of 意為「利用…」，take charge 意為「承擔責任」，而 take issue with something 則表示「反對某事」或「對某事提出異議，針對某事進行辯論」。此外，take a point of view 可用來表達「採取某種觀點」，這些都是很常見的表達用語。

Collocation at a Glance

Verb + Noun	Meaning	Verb + Noun	Meaning
take (an) action	採取行動	take part in	參與…
take advantage of	善加利用…	take the place of	取代…（某人或物）
take aim	瞄準，針對	take a point of view	採取某種觀點
take care	小心，當心	take (an) issue	提出異議，爭論
take charge	負起責任，掌控	take a risk	承擔風險

Collocation in Use

take (an) action 採取行動

He *took* instant *action* when the hostage was killed.
當人質被殺時，他採取了立即的行動。

take advantage of 善加利用⋯

She *took advantage of* the opportunity presented to African Americans.
她善加利用這個賦予非裔美國人的機會。

take aim 瞄準，針對

The author *took aim* at corrupt politicians in his new book.
這位作家在他的新書中處處針對著腐敗的政客。

take care 小心，當心

The state should *take care* of people's life and property.
國家應該照顧到人民的生命與財產。

take charge 負起責任，掌控

You need to *take charge* of your health.
你需要好好管理自己的健康。

take part in 參與⋯

I agreed to *take part in* this research.
我同意參與這項研究。

take the place of 取代⋯（某人或物）

This device is designed to *take the place of* other machines.
這款裝置設計用來取代其他機器設備。

take a point of view 採取某種觀點

He *took the point of view* of the oppressed.
他接受了受壓迫者的觀點。

take (an) issue 提出異議，爭論

I want to *take issue* with your statement.
我想對於你的陳述提出異議。

take a risk 承擔風險

At that time I loved traveling, and I was young enough to *take a risk*.
當時我熱愛旅行，而且我夠年輕，可以勇於冒險。

Collocation Exercises

A 請從方框中選出正確的單字填入以下句子的空格中，注意句意正確及通順。

action	advantage	aim	booking
care	charge	issue	part
place	point of view	ride	risk

1. Information and communication technology is not only taking the _____ of traditional teaching methodology, but also is changing the relationship between teachers and students.

2. People assume that it is reasonable that the state would take _____ of them from cradle to grave.

3. The authors take _____ at several myths about statistics, which they introduce in the preface. But the content is not easy to follow without knowing the scientific and social context.

4. It might be advantageous to take instant _____ when the machinery breaks down.

5. Considering your age, it is the time to take _____ of your health by eating better food and exercising more.

6. If the president does not take a(n) _____ with this project, then your plan will be passed.

7. They take the _____ of financial managers who would like to interact with very efficient capital markets.

8. The engineers are reluctant to take the _____ of developing new technology because nobody is willing to give financial support.

9. Take full _____ of dictionaries in English vocabulary learning. Especially dictionaries for second language acquirers are beneficial.

10. Thirty-two students took _____ in the MBA writing workshop which focused on the importance of essays in the MBA admission process.

B 請將以下句子翻譯成英文。

11. 一旦註冊後，你就能善加利用線上學習的功能。

12. 傑出的科學家們將參與這場會議並發表演說。

13. 他冒著極大的風險，試圖將她從失火的大樓中救出。

14. 這位右派教授對政府的社會主義勞動政策提出異議。

15. 地方政府應針對日益嚴重的高齡化問題採取立即的行動。

Days 01-30

Final Check-up

（1-5）請從方框中選出適合填入下方句子括弧內的動詞形式。

do(did)	get(got)	show(showed)	find(found)
give(gave)	make(made)	hold(held)	keep(kept)
take(took)	have(had)	ride	risk

1 There are several activities we can (　　) in our English class.

She is the last person to (　　) business with.

Apart from watching films, we can also (　　) exercise to release stress.

A nation has no right to (　　) injustice to another country.

2 The museum is going to (　　) an auction on March 1st to sell works of art.

The hunter would (　　) fire until the bear came into his sight.

Sandy soils do not (　　) much moisture.

The lecture could not (　　) the attention of most students.

3 I (　　) a chance to meet with the basketball coach.

She (　　) a name for herself by singing on Broadway.

I (　　) a promotion to group manager in my department.

I used my camera phone and (　　) a shot of the actress.

4 You need to (　　) a break.

All the employees will (　　) the day off on New Year's Day.

I often ( ) delight in small things.

I loved traveling, and I was young enough to (　　) a risk.

5 We (　　) a lively chat with each other.

She (　　) no choice but to accept the invitation.

The treatment certainly ( ) an effect.

Though she knew her disability, she (　　) an urge to see the world.

（6-10）請將 (A) 和 (B) 正確配對，以完成句子。

(A)	(B)
6. This page gives 7. The software company makes 8. The thief was so cautious that the detective could not find 9. The Prime Minister has yet to keep 10. A recent survey of working families in Ohio showed	(a) details of the badminton leagues we play in. (b) a bias against black people. (c) his promise to reduce taxes. (d) a huge profit from the new system. (e) any clue that he committed the crime.

（11-15）請從下方選出適當的單字填入括弧內，使句子通順完整。

effort	point	share	track	views

11. Those who hold different _____ on these matters must back up their opinions with convincing arguments.

12. You obviously don't get the _____. How long does it take to understand the simplest of things?

13. The police keep _____ of illegal distribution of MP3 files. But Internet users continue developing new expedients to avoid their oversight.

14. A Korean person takes _____ to express their emotions in subtle ways. But an American is more direct and goes straight to the point.

15. Further investment is needed to hold the company's _____ of an increasingly competitive market.

（16-20）請根據以下中文翻譯，在空格中填入適當的搭配字詞。

16. Who _____ _____ _____ _____ for the 100m sprint?
（誰是 100 公尺短跑的世界紀錄保持人？）

17. Will you _____ _____ _____ _____ my kids until I get back?（在我回來之前，你可以幫忙照顧我的孩子嗎？）

18. It took her one week to _____ _____ _____ _____ of all the students' essays.（她花了一個星期才批改完所有學生的論文。）

19. During my absence, ask the secretary to _____ _____ _____ _____.（我不在的時候，請秘書接收訊息。）

20. The president has to _____ _____ _____ _____ the prime minister by next week.（總統必須在下週前找到可以接替總理的人選。）

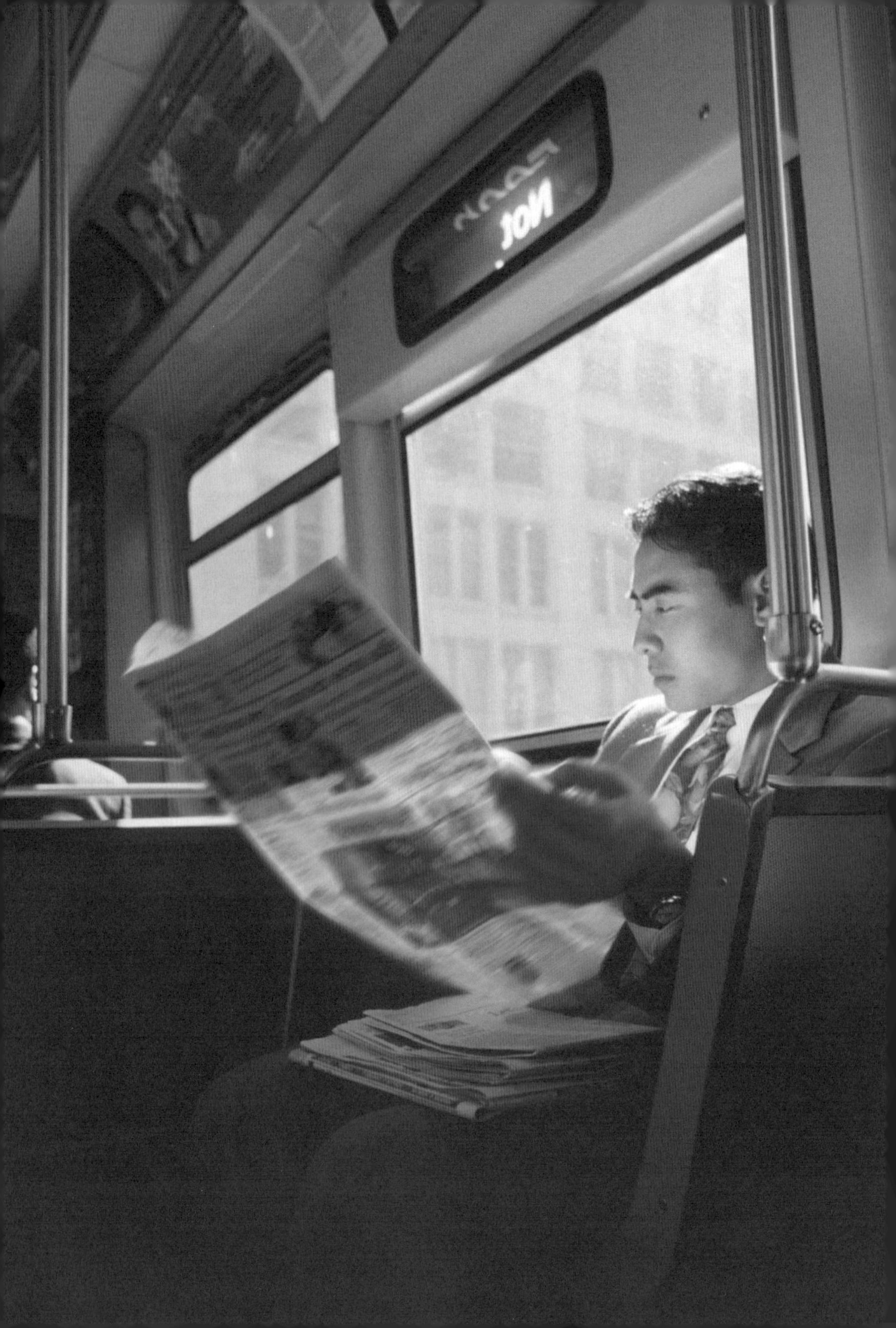

Part Two
Collocations on Essential Subjects
核心主題分類:名詞的搭配詞

Collocations on

DAY 31

Day-31.mp3

Business and Economy

從今天開始，我們將以名詞為中心，按照主題分類來學習搭配詞。首先，我們要先認識一些商業與經濟相關的核心詞彙，例如 revenue（收入）、recession（經濟衰退）、products（產品）等，然後學習其搭配用法。例如：increase/lose revenue（增加／減損營收）、cause/beat a recession（引發／對抗經濟衰退）、develop/promote products（開發／推廣產品）、acquire/issue shares（收購／發行股份）⋯等。我們將仔細學習 30 個關鍵的表達用語。

Collocation at a Glance

Verb + Noun	Meaning	Verb + Noun	Meaning
earn **revenue**	賺取收入	face **competition**	面臨競爭
increase **revenue**	提高營收	fight off **competition**	擊退競爭對手
lose **revenue**	減損營收	acquire **shares**	收購股份
promote **a product**	促銷產品	hold **shares**	持有股份
develop **a product**	開發產品	issue **shares**	發行股份
launch **a product**	推出產品	trade **shares**	交易股份
cause **a recession**	導致經濟衰退	balance **a budget**	平衡預算
beat **a recession**	對抗經濟衰退	approve **a budget**	批准預算
plunge into **a recession**	陷入經濟衰退／經營困頓	cut **a budget**	刪減預算

Business and Economy

set **a price**	設定價格	have **an asset**	擁有資產
increase **a price**	提高價格	acquire **an asset**	取得資產
cut **a price**	降低價格	transfer **an asset**	轉讓資產
provide **insurance**	提供保險	reduce **expenditure**	減少支出
claim **insurance**	申請理賠	incur **expenditure**	產生支出
maintain **insurance**	維持保單有效，續保	meet **expenditure**	應付開銷

Collocation in Use

earn revenue 賺取收入

The agency *earns* public *revenue* for schools.
該機構為學校賺取公共資金。

increase revenue 提高營收

Good customer service can *increase revenue*.
良好的客戶服務可以提高營收。

lose revenue 減損營收

The business may *lose revenue* due to falls in sale prices.
該企業可能因銷售價格下滑而出現盈虧。

promote a product 促銷產品

Sometimes new *products* need to be *promoted* with a press release.
有時，新產品需要透過新聞的發佈來促銷。

develop a product 開發產品

Don't hesitate to invest in *developing* innovative *products*.
不要猶豫投資創新產品的開發。

launch a product 推出產品

They successfully *launched products* on the web.
他們成功地在網路上推出了產品。

cause a recession 導致經濟衰退

Higher oil prices may *cause a recession*.
較高的油價可能導致經濟衰退。

beat a recession 對抗經濟衰退

Small companies are struggling to *beat the recession*.
小公司正奮力對抗經濟衰退中。

plunge into a recession 陷入經濟衰退／經營困頓

The country *plunged into a recession* before recovering.
該國在復甦之前陷入了經濟衰退。

face competition 面臨競爭

Facing cut-throat *competition* in the market, the company is at risk.
面對市場上的激烈競爭，該公司正處於搖搖欲墜狀態。

fight off competition 擊退競爭對手

You must *fight off competition* to get better results.
要獲得更好的結果，你必須擊退競爭對手。

acquire shares 收購股份

GM has *acquired* a large amount of *shares* in a foreign company.
GM 已收購一家外國公司的大量股份。

hold shares 持有股份

Name any company which *holds shares* of more than 10% of total capital.
請指出一家持有超過其總資本 10% 股份的公司。

issue shares 發行股份

Investors are *issued shares* on an annual basis.
投資人每年都會獲得發行中的股份。

Business and Economy 157

trade shares 交易股份

Many people *trade shares* on the NASDAQ stock exchange, but it's not always the best answer.
許多人在納斯達克交易所買賣股票，但這並非一直都是最明智之舉。

balance a budget 平衡預算

A reduction in spending will *balance the budget*.
減少支出可以讓預算平衡。

approve a budget 批准預算

It's better to decide now whether to *approve the budget* or vote it down.
現在最好就決定要不要批准預算或否決它。

cut a budget 刪減預算

Why did they *cut the budget* by a total of $10,000?
他們為什麼刪減了總計 1 萬美元的預算？

set a price 提高價格

We *set a price* lower than the current trading price.
生產成本的上升將推高價格。

increase a price 訂定價格

Arise in production costs will *increase prices*.
我們訂定的價格低於目前的交易價格。

cut a price 降低價格

The company has been *cutting prices* to boost sales since 1998.
該公司自 1998 年就一直以削價方式來提升銷售量。

provide insurance 提供保險

The employee wanted them to *provide insurance* for a specific period.
那名員工希望他們提供一定期間的保險。

claim insurance 申請保險理賠

Anyone who has membership is entitled to *claim insurance* for car theft.
任何擁有會員資格的人都有權申請汽車失竊的保險理賠。

maintain insurance 維持保單有效，續保

You'd better *maintain insurance* against loss or damage.
你最好保有遺失或損害的理賠保險。

have an asset 擁有資產

There are few who *have assets* below $10,000.
資產低於 1 萬美元的人寥寥無幾。

acquire an asset 取得資產

Call "Your Plan" today to *acquire assets* from your own income.
立即打電話給「Your Plan」，並用您自己的收入來獲取資產。

transfer an asset 轉讓資產

Mr. Donald *transferred* billions of *assets* to his children last year.
唐納德先生去年將數十億資產轉讓給他的子女。

reduce expenditure 減少支出

One cannot be rich unless he or she *reduces* unnecessary *expenditure*.
不減少不必要的支出，就無法致富。

incur expenditure 產生支出

That investigation can *incur expenditure* for official purposes.
那項調查可能會產生公務方面的支出費用。

meet expenditure 應付開銷

I wonder if we should make loans to *meet expenditure*.
我在考慮是否應該貸款來應付開銷。

Business and Economy

Collocation Exercises

A 請將 List 1 的動詞與 List 2 的名詞做適當的連結,且符合完整句意。

List 1	List 2
exceeded	a long recession
launched	a new product
maintain	warfare expenditures
plunged into	our budget
reduce	the insurance

1. Do you think we _____ _____ ? I think we will soon come out of it.

2. We _____ _____ in the market. To our sadness, nobody seems to recognizeit.

3. The high official agreed upon the plan to _____ _____ .

4. Expenditures _____ _____ . We had $500 but we spent $20,000.

5. He wanted to _____ _____ , but he had no money available.

DAY 31

B 在以下句子空格處中選出適當的字詞。

6. The government is divided on the issue: The prime minister insists on increasing _____ while the minister of finance and economy says we need to decrease it.
   (a) the asset
   (b) the economy
   (c) the budget
   (d) the warfare

7. Every salesman has to be aware of _____. The marketplace is getting more and more saturated with similar products.
   (a) the competition
   (b) the component
   (c) the study
   (d) the virtue

8. He _____ half of his assets into his son's name to evade a succession tax.
   (a) accumulated
   (b) froze
   (c) owned
   (d) transferred

9. You need to consider the influence of _____ new shares. It has a huge impact on the company's investor relations.
   (a) issuing
   (b) backing
   (c) entering
   (d) serving

10. _____ price is not a panacea for the sales downturn: It may give the impression to the customers that your product is not top quality.
    (a) Delivering
    (b) Enhancing
    (c) Cutting
    (d) Supporting

C 請將以下句子翻譯為英文。

11. 這個非政府組織試圖在沒有獲得援助的情況下平衡其預算。

12. 該公司發行了兩種類別的股票。

13. 由於非法拷貝泛濫，DVD 市場已損失大量營收。

14. 就在我叔叔買進 3,000 股時，該公司隨即破產。

15. 那名詐欺犯請領了保險金。結果後來發現他是自殘的。

Collocations on Finance

DAY 32

Day-32.mp3

account（帳戶）、interest（利息）、loan（貸款）等詞彙經常出現在與 finance（財務）相關的內容中。此外，像是 open/close an account、give/get a refund、make/waste money、claim/draw a pension 等固定搭配的表達方式，也值得學習並加以活用。今天就來將仔細學習與財務這個主題有關的 38 個搭配用語。

Collocation at a Glance

Verb + Noun	Meaning	Verb + Noun	Meaning
close **an account**	解除帳戶	incur **a fee**	產生費用，需支付費用
hold **an account**	持有帳戶	reimburse **a fee**	退還／報銷費用
open **an account**	開立帳戶	declare **bankruptcy**	宣告破產
give **a refund**	給予退款	escape (from) **bankruptcy**	擺脫破產窘境
make **a refund**	申請退款	face **bankruptcy**	面臨破產（危機）
offer **a refund**	提供退款	go into **bankruptcy**	破產
get **a refund**	取得退款	deposit **money**	（在銀行）存款
demand **a refund**	要求退款	make **money**	賺錢
charge **a fee**	收取費用	save **money**	存錢，省錢
cover **a fee**	負擔費用	waste **money**	浪費錢

Finance

withdraw **money**	提款	draw **a pension**	領取退休金
apply for **a loan**	申請貸款	get **a pension**	拿到退休金
arrange **a loan**	申辦貸款	qualify for **a pension**	符合退休金請領資格
take out **a loan**	取得貸款	make **a deposit**	（到銀行）存款
charge **interest**	收取利息	pay **a deposit**	支付訂金／保證金
control **interest**	控制／干預利率	attract **investment**	吸引投資
earn **interest**	（常指投資方面）獲得利息收益	encourage **investment**	鼓勵投資
make **interest**	賺利息	make **an investment**	進行投資
claim **a pension**	申請退休金	promote **investment**	促進投資

Collocation in Use

close an account 解除帳戶

Before you *close* your *account*, make sure you withdraw all your money.
在您解除帳戶之前，請確保您已經提領完您全部的錢。

hold an account 持有帳戶

What if I don't have enough money to *hold an account*?
如果我沒有足夠的錢來持有一個帳戶，這怎麼辦？

open an account 開立帳戶

Can I *open an account*?
我可以開立一個帳戶嗎？

give a refund 給予退款

I need a receipt to *give* you *a refund*.
我需要收據才能為您退款。

make a refund 申請退款

I don't think we can still *make a* full *refund* after 2 weeks.
我不認為我們兩週後還能申請全額退款。

offer a refund 提供退款

We don't *offer* any *refunds* or exchanges at all.
我們完全不提供任何退換貨服務。

get a refund 取得退款

You can *get a refund* on all the products.
您可以針對所有商品申請退款。

demand a refund 要求退款

It's my right to *demand a refund*.
要求退款是我的權利。

charge a fee 收取費用

You'll be *charged a fee* for the exam.
您將得支付考試的（報名）費用。

cover a fee 負擔費用

Will this money be enough to *cover* your *fees*?
這筆錢足夠讓你負擔費用嗎？

incur a fee 產生費用，需支付費用

Some customers may *incur an* additional *fee*.
某些顧客可能得支付額外的費用。

reimburse a fee 退還／報銷費用

We'll *reimburse the fee* up to $50.
我們最多可報銷 50 美元的費用。

declare bankruptcy 宣告破產

Corporations can *declare bankruptcy*.
公司可以宣告破產。

escape (from) bankruptcy 擺脫破產

Here's an update on the best strategy to *escape bankruptcy*.
這是最佳擺脫破產策略的最新資訊。

face bankruptcy 面臨破產（危機）

Small businesses are *facing bankruptcy*.
中小企業正面臨破產危機。

go into bankruptcy 破產

When his plan failed, he *went into bankruptcy*.
當他的計劃失敗時，他破產了。

deposit money （在銀行）存款

The *money* will be *deposited*.
這筆錢將存入帳戶。

make money 賺錢

It's not easy to *make money*.
賺錢並不容易。

save money 存錢，省錢

I *saved* all my *money*.
我把我所有的錢都存起來了。

waste money 浪費錢

Don't *waste* time and *money*.
別浪費時間和金錢。

withdraw money 提款

He planned to *withdraw* his *money*.
他打算提取自己的錢。

apply for a loan 申請貸款

You are entitled to *apply for a loan* from a local bank.
你有資格向本地銀行申請貸款。

arrange a loan 申辦貸款

How do I *arrange a loan* for the students?
我要如何為學生申請貸款？

DAY 32

take out a loan 取得貸款

Take out a loan to repay your debts.
去辦一筆貸款來償還你的債務吧。

charge interest 收取利息

How much *interest* do they *charge*?
他們收取多少利息？

control interest 控制／干預利率

The government doesn't *control interest* rates.
政府不會干預利率。

earn interest （常指投資方面）獲得利息收益

What is the quickest way to *earn interest* as an investor?
作為投資人賺利息的最快方式是什麼？

make interest 賺利息

You can *make* more *interest* if you keep your account balance above $5,000.
如果你的帳戶餘額保持在 5,000 美元以上，你可以賺得更多利息。

claim a pension 申請退休金

Mr. Big is not entitled to *claim a* retirement *pension*.
比格先生還沒有資格申請退休金。

draw a pension 領取退休金

You can *draw* your *pension* at the age of 60.
你可以在 60 歲時領取你的退休金。

get a pension 拿到退休金

It's important to *get* my *pension* if I am laid off.
如果我被解雇，拿到退休金這件事就很重要了。

qualify for a pension 符合退休金請領資格

To *qualify for a* disability *pension*, you must have a medical disability.
要符合領取殘障補助金的資格，你必須有醫療證明的殘疾。

make a deposit 存款

I just *made a deposit* of the paycheck in your account.
我剛剛把薪水存入了你的帳戶。

pay a deposit 支付訂金／保證金

You are required to *pay a deposit* on the apartment.
你得支付這間公寓的押金。

attract investment 吸引投資

The company needs to *attract* a little more *investment*.
這家公司必須吸引更多資金投入。

encourage investment 鼓勵投資

The government is considering a policy to *encourage investment*.
政府正在考慮一項促進投資的政策。

make an investment 進行投資

Don't *make a* risky *investment*.
不要做高風險的投資。

promote investment 促進投資

The party started a campaign to *promote investment* in rural areas.
該政黨發動一場促進鄉間區域投資的活動

DAY 32

Collocation Exercises

A 請將 List 1 的動詞與 List 2 的名詞做適當的連結，且符合完整句意。

List 1	List 2
attract	a secret account
charge	sudden bankruptcy
declared	high fees
opened	new investment
qualify for	disability payments

1. I cannot forget the day when my CEO _____ _____ .

2. You don't _____ _____ for the disabled. Insomnia is not regarded as a disability.

3. The corrupt official _____ _____ abroad to hide his dirty money.

4. Don't withdraw cash from your credit card banks _____ _____ for doing so.

5. His business plan failed to _____ _____ and he left the company.

B 在以下句子空格處中選出適當的字詞。

6. You would incur _____ if you exceeded your transfer limit.
   (a) an additional fee   (b) an annual audit
   (c) a considerable asset   (d) a potential saving

7. The thief was arrested while applying for _____ at the local bank.
   (a) a grant   (b) a loan
   (c) a refund   (d) a salary

8. She's pulling in a lot of money. She makes _____ of $15,000 into her account every month.
   (a) a bid   (b) a deposit
   (c) a money   (d) a stock

9. The Federal Reserve Board has the authority to _____ interest so that the economy can maintain its stability.
   (a) fluctuate   (b) control
   (c) endorse   (d) invest

10. Note that you cannot _____ a refund for electronic goods unless you have the receipt.
    (a) see   (b) put
    (c) get   (d) spend

DAY 32

C 請將以下句子翻譯為英文。

11. 您須提交您的收據才能取得退款。

12. 似乎購物是她人生的目標。她總是揮霍金錢。

13. 在他女朋友被該銀行解雇後,他關閉了自己的帳戶。

14. 他在當地的福利中心領取養老金。

15. 我們試圖擺脫破產的命運。

Collocations on

DAY 33

Day-33.mp3

Work and Office

今天我們將學習重點擺在職場上的一些核心字彙，例如 meeting（會議）、contract（合約）、office（辦公室），同時將進一步探討日常實用的搭配字詞，如 have/lose a contract、decrease/increase a salary、deserve/win a promotion、ask for/give a confirmation 等。這裡提供 40 個精選的表達用語，絕對值得您學習！

Collocation at a Glance

Verb + Noun	Meaning	Verb + Noun	Meaning
attend a meeting	參加／出席會議	have a confirmation	進行確認
call a meeting	召集會議，開會	need a confirmation	需要確認
cancel a meeting	取消會議	get the bottom line	掌握重點
postpone a meeting	將會議延期	understand the bottom line	理解重點
have a meeting	開會	deserve a promotion	應獲得晉升
assist a manager	協助經理	get a promotion	獲得晉升
promote someone to manager	晉升某人為經理	win a promotion	成功晉升
ask for a confirmation	請求確認	want a promotion	想獲得晉升
get a confirmation	取得確認	get passed over for a promotion	晉升未果
give someone a confirmation	給予某人確認	manage a factory	經營工廠

DAY 33

open a factory	開設工廠	sign a contract	簽署合約
run a factory	經營工廠	win a contract	成功取得合約
set up a factory	設立工廠	give a presentation	進行發表會
shut down a factory	關閉工廠	make a presentation	做展示
manage an office	管理辦公室	attend a presentation	參加發表會
run an office	經營辦公室	decrease a salary	減薪
supervise an office	監管辦公室	earn a salary	領薪，掙薪水
have a contract	簽訂合約	increase a salary	加薪
lose a contract	失去合約	propose a salary	提出薪資方案
negotiate a contract	洽談合約	receive a salary	拿到薪水

Collocation in Use

attend a meeting 參加／出席會議

The president is not able to *attend the meeting*.
總裁沒辦法出席這場會議。

call a meeting 召集會議，開會

I'm going to *call a meeting* to discuss some hot issues.
我打算開個會討論一些熱門的議題。

cancel a meeting 取消會議

I was shocked he *canceled* that important *meeting* due to the CEO's schedule.
我對於他因 CEO 的行程而取消了那場重要會議這件事感到震驚。

postpone a meeting 將會議延期

If he is unable to attend the meeting, we can *postpone the meeting* to a more convenient date.
如果他無法參加會議，我們可以將會議延後至一個更方便的日期。

have a meeting 開會

We've got to *have an* informal *meeting*.
我們必須開一場非正式的會議。

assist a manager 協助經理

Would you *assist a manager* as a secretary?
你願意擔任秘書來協助經理嗎？

promote someone to manager 晉升某人為經理

It is about time that I *promoted her to* the position of marketing *manager*.
現在該是我讓她晉升行銷經理職位的時候了。

ask for a confirmation 請求確認

The press corps *asked for a confirmation* of the agenda.
新聞記者團要求確認議程內容。

get a confirmation 取得確認

Both of the parties are trying to *get a confirmation* from the president.
雙方都在試圖取得總裁的確認。

give someone a confirmation 給予某人確認

My assistant will *give you a confirmation* on the meeting schedule.
我的助理會給您確認會議行程。

have a confirmation 進行確認

I'll contact the office to *have a* final *confirmation*.
我會聯繫辦公室做最後確認。

need a confirmation 需要確認

Do you really *need a confirmation* for the dinner menu?
你真的需要確認晚餐菜單嗎？

get the bottom line 掌握重點

I tried to *get the bottom line* from his words.
我試著從他的話中掌握重點。

understand the bottom line 理解重點

Did you *understand the bottom line*?
你理解重點了嗎？

deserve a promotion 應獲得晉升

Do you think he *deserves a promotion*?
你覺得他應獲得晉升嗎？

get a promotion 獲得晉升

I *got an* unexpected *promotion*.
我意外地獲得了晉升。

win a promotion 成功晉升

No one's working harder to *win a promotion* than he is.
沒有人比他更努力爭取到晉升機會。

want a promotion 想獲得晉升

Do you really *want a promotion*? Then show your competence to the CEO.
你真的想獲得晉升嗎？那就向 CEO 展現你的實力吧。

get passed over for a promotion 晉升未果

He was depressed because he *got passed over for this promotion*.
他因為這次晉升未果而感到沮喪。

manage a factory 管理工廠

Ms. Shon has been *managing our factory* successfully.
孫女士一直成功管理著我們的工廠。

open a factory 開設工廠

I plan to *open a* small *factory*.
我計劃開一家小工廠。

run a factory 經營工廠

A manager must be hired to *run a factory*.
必須聘請一名經理來經營工廠。

set up a factory 設立工廠

The company aims to *set up a* semiconductor *factory* near Seoul.
該公司計劃在首爾附近設立一家半導體工廠。

shut down a factory 關閉工廠

During the IMF crisis, many people had to *shut down* their *factories* due to economic downturn.
在 IMF 危機期間，許多人因經濟衰退而不得不將他們的工廠關閉。

manage an office 管理辦公室

I realized that there are many difficulties in *managing a* huge *office*.
我了解要管理一個大型辦公室有許多困難。

run an office 經營辦公室

It takes 3,000 dollars a month to *run this office*.
經營這間辦公室每個月要花 3,000 美元。

supervise an office 監管辦公室

He will *supervise the office* from next month.
他自下個月起將負責監管這間辦公室。

have a contract 簽訂合約

It's not easy to *have a contract* with a multinational corporation.
與跨國公司簽訂合約並不容易。

lose a contract 失去合約

Never miss or *lose an* important *contract*.
千萬別錯過或失去一份重要的合約。

negotiate a contract 洽談合約

We are always ready to *negotiate a contract* with the right dealer.
我們隨時準備與合適的經銷商洽談合約。

sign a contract 簽署合約

I need her to *sign a contract* for the project.
我需要她簽署這項專案的合約。

win a contract 成功取得合約

Who *won the contract* in that tough competition?
是誰在那激烈的競爭中,成功拿下這份合約?

give a presentation 進行發表會

Last night we were *given an* impressive *presentation*.
昨晚我們進行了一場精采的發表會。

make a presentation 做展示

There's going to be a seminar about how to *make a* successful *presentation*.
將會有一場如何成功地做展示的研討會。

attend a presentation 參加發表會

Will you *attend his presentation* on the outlook of the IT industry?
你會去參加他關於 IT 產業前景的發表會嗎?

decrease a salary 減薪

The company *decreased his salary* on the grounds that he was lazy.
公司以他懶惰為由給予減薪。

earn a salary 領薪,掙薪水

"It's hard to *earn a* decent *salary*," said the husband.
丈夫表示,「要掙得一份優渥的薪水很難。」

increase a salary 加薪

There is no possibility for the company to *increase salaries*.
該公司沒有加薪的可能性。

propose a salary 提出薪資方案

The other company *proposed a* very competitive *salary*.
另一家公司提出了一份極具競爭力的薪資方案。

receive a salary 拿到薪水

Many workers in developing countries *receive a* low *salary*.
許多開發中國家的工人薪資偏低。

Collocation Exercises

A 請將 List 1 的動詞與 List 2 的名詞做適當的連結,且符合完整句意。

List 1	List 2
give	a presentation
have	the bottom line
run	the construction contract
understand	a meeting
win	the office

1. First of all, consider whether the meeting is really necessary. To _____ _____ just for the sake of it is a waste of time and resource.

2. I couldn't make him _____ _____ . He was a complete idiot when it came to accounting.

3. The team is certain to _____ _____ . It is worth 2 billion dollars.

4. Do I really have to _____ _____ ? I thought an informal e-mail would do.

5. He says he can _____ _____ via e-mail and the remote conferencing system. However, managing an office requires face-to-face contact and personal communication.

B 在以下句子空格處中選出適當的字詞。

6. The headhunter proposed a pretty _____ to me, but I didn't like the job.
   (a) competitive salary
   (b) high cost
   (c) minimum wage
   (d) tough task

7. Two companies were able to _____ by exchanging the exclusive MOU.
   (a) abandon the contract
   (b) break the news
   (c) complete the deal
   (d) weaken mutual trust

8. The board of directors _____ him to senior manager in the marketing division. That means now he is responsible for both domestic and overseas marketing.
   (a) allocated
   (b) condemned
   (c) degraded
   (d) promoted

9. The receptionist from the tourist company _____ me the confirmation that I could take the flight. However, it was cancelled due to the heavy snowfall.
   (a) cut
   (b) informed
   (c) gave
   (d) put

10. To _____ a company is just a starting point. Running it is another story.
    (a) educate (b) finish
    (c) open   (d) walk

C 請將以下句子翻譯為英文。

11. 由於工人罷工,總裁將這間工廠關掉了。
    _____

12. 老闆向我確認了這項預訂。
    _____

13. 這場會議已取消,且他被大幅減薪了。
    _____

14. 你必須擬定一份書面合約並在上面簽字。
    _____

15. 我承認她應得到快速的升遷。
    _____

Collocations on Information

DAY 34

Day-34.mp3

information（資訊）、update（更新／最新訊息）、privacy（隱私）、access（存取）等，對於生活在資訊化時代的我們而言，都是相當熟悉的單字。讓我們一起來學習運用如 break/invent a code、accept/select a fact、send/show details、have/deny access 等搭配用法吧！同時會讓英文寫作更加精煉流暢。以下是本書精選的 38 個常見的表達用語。

Collocation at a Glance

Verb + Noun	Meaning	Verb + Noun	Meaning
need **information**	需要資訊	edit **a document**	編輯文件
gather **information**	蒐集資訊	save **a document**	儲存文件
access **information**	存取資訊	present **a report**	提交報告
exchange **information**	交換資訊	issue **a report**	發出／發佈報告
give **an update**	告知最新資訊／消息	release **a report**	發佈／公開報告
provide **an update**	提供／發布更新	break **a code**	破解密碼
get **an update**	得知最新資訊／消息	crack **a code**	解開密碼
receive **an update**	收到最新資訊／消息	use **a code**	使用密碼
open **a document**	開啟文件	invent **a code**	創造密碼
create **a document**	建立文件	respect **privacy**	尊重隱私

Information

disturb **privacy**	干擾隱私	check **details**	確認細節
violate **privacy**	侵犯隱私	have **a tip**	有訣竅
have **access**	有存取權／接近的機會	give **a tip**	給建議／訣竅
gain **access**	獲得存取權，得以進入	take **a tip**	討教，學習訣竅
deny **access**	拒絕存取	use **a tip**	運用訣竅
restrict **access**	限制存取	know **a fact**	了解事實
send **details**	寄發詳細資訊	select **a fact**	選擇真實資訊
discuss **details**	討論細節	accept **a fact**	接受事實
show **details**	顯示細節	interpret **a fact**	解釋事實

Collocation in Use

need information 需要資訊

Before we send you the item you ordered, we *need* some *information* from you.
在寄送您訂購的物品之前，我們需要您提供一些資訊。

gather information 蒐集資訊

Gather as much *information* as you can.
請盡可能蒐集更多資訊。

access information 存取資訊

There was no choice but to *access information* through the FBI.
別無選擇，只能透過 FBI 來存取資訊。

exchange information 交換資訊

We *exchanged information* in a civil way.
我們以文明的方式交換了資訊。

give an update 告知最新資訊／消息

Give Bill a call and *give* him *an update*.
打電話給比爾，告知他最新資訊。

provide an update 提供／發布更新

Please select a web site which at least *provides a* bi-monthly *update*.
請選擇一個至少每兩個月更新一次的網站。

get an update 得知最新資訊／消息

You didn't *get* the latest *update*?
你還沒收到最新的資訊嗎？

receive an update 收到最新資訊／消息

The CEO *receives an update* on the progress.
執行長會收到有關進度的最新資訊。

open a document 開啟文件

Open and print the attached *document*.
打開並列印附加的文件。

create a document 建立文件

The student *created a* great design *document*.
這名學生建立了一份出色的設計文件。

edit a document 編輯文件

Let him check out and *edit this document*.
讓他查看並編輯這份文件。

save a document 儲存文件

Don't forget to *save* the current *document*.
別忘了儲存目前的文件。

present a report 提交報告

You'll have to *present a* brief *report*.
你將得提交一份簡短的報告。

issue a report 發出／發佈報告

The UN *issues reports* throughout the year.
聯合國這一整年都會發佈報告。

release a report 發佈／公開報告

The government refused to *release a* secret *report*.
政府拒絕公開一份機密報告。

break a code 破解密碼

If you *break that code*, you can figure out the answers.
如果你破解了那組密碼，就能找出答案。

crack a code 解開密碼

I can't believe you *cracked my code*!
我不敢相信你居然解開了我的密碼！

use a code 使用密碼

Use my access *code*.
使用我的通行密碼。

invent a code 創造密碼

Who *invented* Morse *Code*?
是誰發明了摩斯密碼？

respect privacy 尊重隱私

I just miss all those people who *respect my privacy*.
我只是懷念所有尊重我隱私的人。

disturb privacy 干擾隱私

The apartment is not noisy and doesn't *disturb the privacy* of people's homes.
這間公寓沒有吵雜聲，不會干擾住戶的隱私。

violate privacy 侵犯隱私

You should make a promise not to *violate privacy*.
你應該承諾不侵犯隱私。

have access 有存取權／接近的機會

I *have* no *access* to him.
我沒有接近他的機會。

gain access 獲得存取權，得以進入

He was accused of illegally having *gained access* to the facility.
他被指控非法進入該設施。

deny access 拒絕存取

It *denied* further *access*.
它拒絕了進一步的存取。

restrict access 限制存取

The server automatically *restricts access* based on IP address.
伺服器會根據 IP 位置自動限制存取權限。

send details 寄發詳細資訊

Tell him to *send* back a few *details*.
告訴他回傳一些詳細的資訊。

discuss details 討論細節

We can *discuss the details* over dinner.
我們可以在晚餐時討論細節。

show details 顯示細節

A photo *showing details* of Seoul needs to be included.
必須包含一張可以看見首爾市詳細特色的照片。

check details 確認細節

I'll *check* every design *detail*.
我會確認設計上的每一處細節。

have a tip 有訣竅

Old-timers *have a tip* on how to climb the corporate ladder.
老員工有個教你如何在公司步步高升的訣竅。

give a tip 給建議／訣竅

Maybe you can *give* me some *tips*.
也許你可以給我一些訣竅。

take a tip 討教，學習訣竅

I was told to *take a tip* from an old man
有人告訴我應該找老人家討教。

use a tip 運用訣竅

See how to do it faster *using* these *tips*.
看看如何運用這些訣竅來才能做得更快。

know a fact 了解事實

It doesn't matter that you don't even *know* all the *facts*.
即使你不了解所有事實也無所謂。

select a fact 選擇真實資訊

Select the facts about Canada.
選擇有關加拿大的真實資訊。

accept a fact 接受事實

It can be hard for you to *accept the fact* that we're just friends now.
要你接受「我們現在只是朋友」的事實可能有困難。

interpret a fact 解釋事實

It's no use attempting to *interpret the facts*.
試圖解釋這些事實是沒有意義的。

Collocation Exercises

A 請將 List 1 的動詞與 List 2 的名詞做適當的連結，且符合完整句意。

List 1	List 2
are denied	its special report
released	my privacy
respect	a safety tip
save	access
take	your document

1. "I wish you'd stop interfering and _____ _____ ," she said with a look of annoyance.

2. Journalists without a valid license _____ _____ to confidential information.

3. In order not to lose what you've written so far, _____ _____ as often as possible.

4. The authority _____ _____ based on the police investigation into the crime.

5. Please _____ _____ from me; put the chemicals back on the shelves and step away from them.

B 在以下句子空格處中選出適當的字詞。

6. This internet portal site _____ a regular news update on current activities.
   (a) calls
   (b) provides
   (c) reveals
   (d) works

7. Scientists are _____ worldwide information on any signs that the earth is getting warmer.
   (a) facing
   (b) gathering
   (c) making
   (d) taking

8. Different ways of _____ the facts can lead to a totally different conclusion.
   (a) accumulating
   (b) denying
   (c) interpreting
   (d) preserving

9. Security programmers feel ashamed when their _____ is cracked. On the other hand, hackers are proud of breaking into security systems.
   (a) setup
   (b) installation
   (c) code
   (d) virus

10. Let's stop talking about abstract themes and _____ some details.
    (a) avert
    (b) discuss
    (c) skip
    (d) weave

DAY 34

C 請將以下句子翻譯為英文。

11. 只有情報來源擁有破解這道密碼的程式。

12. 如果你對這項提案感興趣，我會在一週之後寄給你進一步細節。

13. 情報機構因竊聽民眾通訊而嚴重侵犯了隱私。

14. 政府將發布一份關於自由貿易協定（FTA）的協商報告。

15. 他給了我一些如何增加網站訪客流量的建議。

Collocations on

DAY 35

Day-35.mp3

The Internet

常見與網路科技相關的字詞，如 website（網站）、net（通訊網）、e-mail（電子郵件）、blog（部落格）…等，還有與電腦相關的搭配用語，例如 clean/spread viruses、boot/hack a system、control/filter spam、install/patch a program…等，在此也為您做了個統整。只要學會這 34 個搭配詞彙，像是寫電子郵件時，就能感到輕鬆自如！

Collocation at a Glance

Verb + Noun	Meaning	Verb + Noun	Meaning
log in to a **web site**	登入某個網站	install a **system**	安裝系統
log out from a **web site**	從某個網站登出	upgrade a **system**	升級系統
go **online**	連接網路，上網	enter a **password**	輸入密碼
spend time **online**	上網消磨時間	forget a **password**	忘記密碼
stay **online**	保持連線	reset a **password**	重設密碼
clean **viruses**	清除病毒	retype a **password**	重新輸入密碼
scan for **viruses**	掃描病毒	create a **blog (of one's own)**	建立（自己的）部落格
spread **viruses**	散佈病毒	start a **blog (of one's own)**	開始經營（自己的）部落格
boot a **system**	啟動系統	control **spam (mail)**	管制垃圾郵件
hack a **system**	入侵／駭入系統	fight **spam (mail)**	抵制／對抗垃圾郵件

DAY 35

filter **spam** (mail)	過濾垃圾郵件	uninstall **a program**	解除安裝程式
access **the net**	連接網路	delete **an e-mail**	刪除電子郵件
hook up to **the net**	接上網路	forward **an e-mail**	轉寄電子郵件
surf **the net**	上網瀏覽	receive **an e-mail**	接收電子郵件
download **a program**	下載程式	reply to **an e-mail**	回覆電子郵件
install **a program**	安裝程式	send **an e-mail**	寄送電子郵件
patch **a program**	修補程式	open **an e-mail**	開啟電子郵件

Collocation in Use

log in to a web site 登入某個網站

It's an indication that you have failed in *logging in to the website*.
這表示你未能成功登入那個網站。

log out from a web site 從某個網站登出

So many people forget to *log out from an* Internet banking *web site*.
很多人都會忘了登出網銀。

go online 連接網路，上網

Do I always have to *go online* to check my e-mails?
我一定要連上網路後才能查看我的電子郵件嗎？

spend time online 上網消磨時間

These days many children *spend time online* doing nothing productive.
現在許多小孩只是上網消磨時間，卻沒有做任何有效益的事情。

stay online 保持連線

He doesn't like to *stay online* chatting with a friend.
他不喜歡在網路上和朋友聊天。

clean viruses 清除病毒

Did you *clean* the latest worm *viruses* from your hard drive?
你是否已經清除你硬碟中最新的蠕蟲病毒了？

scan for viruses 掃描病毒

Use this software to *scan for viruses* on your computer.
用這軟體來掃描你電腦裡的病毒。

spread viruses 散佈病毒

Agroup of hackers are charged with *spreading* computer *viruses* intentionally.
一群駭客被指控故意散佈電腦病毒。

boot a system 啟動系統

I cannot *boot the* operating *system*.
我無法啟動作業系統。

hack a system 入侵／駭入系統

We need you to attempt to *hack a* confidential *system*.
我們需要你試著駭入一個機密系統。

install a system 安裝系統

Try *installing a* Linux *system*.
試著安裝 Linux 系統。

upgrade a system 升級系統

Would you *upgrade your system* to the latest version of Windows now?
現在你要將你的系統升級到最新版本的 Windows 嗎？

enter a password 輸入密碼

Enter your password to log in to the website.
輸入你的密碼來登入這個網站。

forget a password 忘記密碼

What shall I do? I *forgot my password*.
我該怎麼辦？我忘記我的密碼了。

reset a password 重設密碼

Reset your password on a regular basis.
請定期重設你的密碼。

retype a password 重新輸入密碼

Retype your password to confirm the password change.
重新輸入你的密碼來確認密碼變更。

create a blog (of one's own) 缺翻譯

An elderly person might have difficulty in *creating his or her own blog*.
年長者可能在建立自己的部落格時遇到困難。

start a blog (of one's own) 開始經營（自己的）部落格

When did you *start your own blog*?
你是從什麼時候開始經營自己的部落格的？

control spam (mail) 管制垃圾郵件

The government issued a new policy to *control spam mail*.
政府發布了一項新政策來管制垃圾郵件。

fight spam (mail) 抵制／對抗垃圾郵件

The network team has been *fighting spam mail* to enhance communication efficiency in the company.
網路團隊一直在對抗垃圾郵件，以提升公司內部的通訊效率。

filter spam (mail) 過濾垃圾郵件

We are scheduled to introduce new software to *filter spam mail*.
我們預計將引進新的軟體來過濾垃圾郵件。

access the net 連接網路

Not all the people in the world can *access the net*.
並非全世界所有人都可以上網。

hook up to the net 接上網路

Let's *hook up to the net* to read the latest news.
我們把網路連上,來看看最新的新聞吧。

surf the net 上網瀏覽

Surfing the net for hours is not a good habit.
長時間泡在網路上不是個好習慣。

download a program 下載程式

Download a graphic *program*.
下載一個繪圖程式。

install a program 安裝程式

Did you *install an* anti-virus *program* on your computer?
你是否已在自己的電腦上安裝了防毒程式?

patch a program 修補程式

Patch a program to enhance its functionality.
修補程式來提升它的功能性。

uninstall a program 解除安裝程式

Why don't you *uninstall the program* to get more disk space?
為什麼不解除安裝這個程式來釋放更多的磁碟空間呢?

delete an e-mail 刪除電子郵件

Please click the button to *delete the e-mail*.
請點擊這個按鈕來刪除這封電子郵件。

forward an e-mail 轉寄電子郵件

I usually *forward an e-mail* to my colleagues.
我通常會把電子郵件轉寄給我同事。

DAY 35

receive an e-mail 接收電子郵件

What are you going to do if you *receive an* unexpected *e-mail* from your ex-girlfriend?
如果你意外地收到前女友寄來的電子郵件,你打算怎麼辦?

reply to an e-mail 回覆電子郵件

Please *reply to this e-mail* as soon as possible.
請盡快回覆這封電子郵件。

send an e-mail 寄送電子郵件

Don't forget to *send an e-mail* to your client.
別忘了給你的客戶發一封電子郵件。

open an e-mail 開啟電子郵件

Don't *open an e-mail* that says: "You've won money!" It's a virus!
不要打開一封標題為「你中了獎!」的電子郵件。那是病毒!

Collocation Exercises

A 請將 List 1 的動詞與 List 2 的名詞做適當的連結,且符合完整句意。

List 1	List 2
download	the program
filter	the spam mail
hacked	the net
scan for	the system
surf	viruses

1. His hobby is to _____ . He knows all the useful websites.

2. I have to _____ . I cannot watch the video clip on my computer.

3. There's something wrong with the system. Somebody must have _____ .

4. There is so much junk mail nowadays. We need to purchase software to _____ .

5. He explained how antivirus software worked to _____ _____ on their computers.

B 在以下句子空格處中選出適當的字詞。

6. Will you please _____ the mail to me? I didn't receive the mail due to problems with my mail server.
   (a) filter　　　　　　　　(b) forward
   (c) receive　　　　　　　(d) reply

7. I have difficulty in _____ a blog of my own. I'm computer illiterate. Could you give me some tips?
   (a) naming　　　　　　　(b) sending
   (c) showing　　　　　　 (d) starting

8. Please _____ your password in the Confirm text box.
   (a) draw　　　　　　　　(b) forget
   (c) memorize　　　　　　(d) retype

9. Can we leave comments on your blog without _____ the website?
   (a) breaking into　　　　(b) browsing around
   (c) logging in to　　　　 (d) turning down

10. It is not good for your health to _____ online for too long. Try to reduce your web surfing and increase the time for outdoor activities.
    (a) behave
    (b) cover
    (c) manage
    (d) stay

C 請將以下句子翻譯為英文。

11. 你一天花多少時間上網？

12. 你必須養成「登出網站」的習慣。

13. 我忘記我的密碼了，所以我沒辦法進入這個網站。

14. 已提供有關解除安裝此程式的說明。

15. 只要打開電子郵件並閱讀訊息即可。

Collocations on

DAY 36

Day-36.mp3

Press and Media

像 scoop（獨家消息，新聞搶先報）、headline（標題）、editorial（社論）、conference（會議）等單字，都是與大眾媒體相關的重要核心詞彙。此外，若學會 host/watch a show、carry/run an editorial、abolish/tighten censorship、issue/publish a journal…等搭配詞，將能大大提升閱讀理解能力。這裡總共整理了 42 個表達用語。

Collocation at a Glance

Verb + Noun	Meaning	Verb + Noun	Meaning
announce news	發佈新聞，宣布消息	publish a journal/magazine	出版期刊／雜誌
hear news	聽到消息	read a journal/magazine	閱讀期刊／雜誌
leak news	洩露消息	subscribe to a journal/magazine	訂閱期刊／雜誌
receive news	接收新聞，收到消息	carry a headline	刊登頭版新聞
get a scoop	取得獨家內幕消息／新聞	grab a headline	登上頭版／成為焦點新聞
submit a scoop	提交獨家消息	hit a headline	登上／成為頭條新聞
have a scoop	擁有獨家消息／新聞	make a headline	登上媒體頭版
work on a scoop	進行獨家新聞作業	scan a headline	瀏覽頭版新聞標題
find a scoop	發現獨家消息／新聞	draft a manifesto	草擬一份正式聲明
issue a journal/magazine	發行期刊／雜誌	draw up a manifesto	擬定一份正式聲明

DAY 36

launch a manifesto	發佈正式聲明	write an editorial	撰寫社論
sign a manifesto	在聲明書上簽字	attend a conference	參加會議
support a manifesto	支持一項聲明	call a conference	召開會議
cite/quote a source	引用／引述消息來源	convene a conference	召集會議
name a source	指出消息來源	go to a conference	去參加會議
reveal a source	揭露消息來源	organize a conference	籌辦會議
host a show	主持節目	abolish censorship	廢除審查制度
see a show	觀看節目	impose censorship	進行審查
watch a show	觀賞節目	pass censorship	通過審查
carry an editorial	刊登社論	relax censorship	放寬審查
run an editorial	發表社論	tighten censorship	加強審查

Collocation in Use

announce news 發佈新聞，宣布消息

Now we have *announced* ten big *news* items.
我們現在已經宣布了十條重大新聞了。

hear news 聽到消息

Have you *heard* the good *news*?
你聽到這個好消息了嗎？

leak news 洩露消息

Who *leaked the news* out to them?
誰把這消息洩露給他們了？

receive news 接收新聞，收到消息

Every morning I *receive news* by e-mail.
每天早上我都會收到電子郵件新聞。

get a scoop 取得獨家內幕消息／新聞

Go *get the scoop* of a lifetime from that celebrity!
去從那位名人那裡挖一條獨家內幕消息吧！

submit a scoop 提交獨家消息

Click here to *submit your scoop*!
點擊這裡提交您的獨家消息吧！

have a scoop 擁有獨家消息／新聞

I *have a scoop* for you.
我有個獨家內幕要告訴你。

work on a scoop 進行獨家新聞作業

He's *working on the scoop* of the century.
他正在處理本世紀的獨家大新聞。

find a scoop 發現獨家消息／新聞

John has *found the* inside *scoop* on his girlfriend.
約翰發現了關於他女友的內幕消息。

issue a journal/magazine 發行期刊／雜誌

It makes no money to *issue a* monthly *journal*.
發行月刊是賺不了錢的。

publish a journal/magazine 出版期刊／雜誌

What about *publishing a* technology *magazine*?
出版一本科技雜誌如何？

read a journal/magazine 閱讀期刊／雜誌

He makes his living from *reading a magazine* to a blind man.
他靠為一位盲人朗讀雜誌來謀生。

subscribe to a journal/magazine 訂閱期刊／雜誌

Don't miss this chance to *subscribe to the journal* for $10 a month.
別錯過這個機會，訂閱這份期刊每月只需 10 美元。

carry a headline 刊登頭版新聞

The newspaper *carries headlines* from many different sources.
這份報紙刊載了許多不同來源的頭條新聞。

grab a headline 登上頭版／成為焦點新聞

Do you know the scandal that *grabbed the headlines*?
你知道那件躍上媒體頭版的醜聞嗎？

hit a headline 登上／成為頭條新聞

That single news item *hit the* world *headlines*.
那條新聞登上國際頭版了。

make a headline 登上媒體頭版

It's surely enough news to *make a headline*.
這肯定是一個足以成為頭條的新聞。

scan a headline 瀏覽頭版新聞標題

You can *scan the headlines* to find the most recent information.
你可以瀏覽頭版新聞標題來獲取最新資訊。

draft a manifesto 草擬一份正式聲明

What you have to do next is *draft an* election *manifesto*.
你接下來要做的就是草擬一份競選宣言。

draw up a manifesto 擬定一份正式聲明

The NGO finally succeeded in *drawing up a manifesto* against nuclear arms.
這個非政府組織（NGO）終於成功地擬定了一份反核武聲明。

launch a manifesto 發佈正式聲明

This is a good time to *launch a manifesto*.
現在是發佈正式聲明的好時機。

sign a manifesto 在聲明書上簽字

Get him to *sign the manifesto*.
讓他在這份聲明書上簽名。

support a manifesto 支持一項聲明

It's not easy to ignore *a manifesto supported* by 90% of the people.
要忽視一份獲得 90% 人民支持的聲明可不容易。

cite/quote a source 引用／引述消息來源

When you *cite* online *sources*, just refer to this provided form.
當你要引用網路上的資源時，只要參考提供的這份表格。

name a source 指出消息來源

The man continually refuses to *name the source*.
那名男子一直拒絕透露消息來源。

reveal a source 揭露消息來源

The ruling party is being forced to *reveal the source*.
執政黨正被迫公開消息來源。

host a show 主持節目

Who's going to *host the show*?
誰將主持這個節目？

see a show 觀看節目

Let's go to *see a show*.
我們一起去看場表演吧。

watch a show 觀賞節目

I just *watched the show* you previously recorded.
我剛剛看了你之前錄製的節目。

carry an editorial 刊登社論

The morning paper *carries an editorial*.
早報刊登了一篇社論。

run an editorial 發表社論

He *runs an editorial* in a national newspaper.
他在一份全國性報紙上發表了社論。

write an editorial 撰寫社論

Every time the professor is asked to *write an editorial*, he says no.
每次教授被要求撰寫社論時,他都會拒絕。

attend a conference 參加會議

We will have to *attend a* women's *conference*.
我們將必須參加一場婦女會議。

call a conference 召開會議

A conference will be *called* to discuss human rights.
將召開一場討論人權問題的會議。

convene a conference 召集會議

The government offered to *convene a conference* to discuss the strike.
政府提議召集會議來討論罷工問題。

go to a conference 去參加會議

The President *went to a* press *conference*.
總統前去參加一場記者會。

organize a conference 籌辦會議

It is a difficult and demanding task to *organize a conference*.
籌辦一場會議是一項困難且具挑戰性的任務。

abolish censorship 廢除審查制度

It's too early to *abolish censorship* in our country.
現在就廢除我們國家的審查制度還為時過早。

impose censorship 進行審查

We think they are trying to *impose censorship* on the Internet.
我們認為他們正試圖進行網路審查。

pass censorship 通過審查

Our movie failed to *pass censorship*.
我們的電影未能通過審查。

relax censorship 放寬審查

Maybe it's possible to *relax censorship* of foreign films.
也許可以考慮放寬外國電影審查制度。

tighten censorship 加強審查

There can be a protest against *tightening censorship* of the press.
強化新聞審查這件事可能帶來抗爭行動。

Collocation Exercises

A 請將 List 1 的動詞與 List 2 的名詞做適當的連結，且符合完整句意。

List 1	List 2
carries	religious censorship
convene	a diplomatic conference
draw up	an editorial
grab	headlines
pass	the Communist Manifesto

1. Egyptian TV shows will soon have to _____ _____ . The Minister of Information has decreed that TV dramas must respect the values of Egyptian society.

2. Marx and Engels decided to _____ _____ to proclaim their revolutionary ideas to the world.

DAY 36

3. While extremely catastrophic events _____ _____ in the press, more common weather shifts such as those that pose risks to weather-dependent businesses go virtually unnoticed.

4. The International Herald Tribune today _____ _____ from the New York Times assessing the Russian Federation's on-going financial difficulties.

5. A number of States have now requested that the Director General _____ _____ to consider the proposed amendments.

B 在以下句子空格處中選出適當的字詞。

6. Click on the "_____ a Scoop" button to send your own story to us.
   (a) Hold (b) Open
   (c) Remove (d) Submit

7. He _____ the news that his company would be acquired within 2 weeks.
   (a) applied (b) improved
   (c) leaked (d) created

8. I used to _____ to several sports magazines, but I spend money on photography books now.
   (a) issue (b) publish
   (c) read (d) subscribe

9. It is a typical plagiarism case to use phrases without _____ their sources.
   (a) digging (b) citing
   (c) emphasizing (d) inferring

10. He has been _____ the show for 20 years. Now his broadcasting is as natural as his talk with his friends at a bar.
    (a) avoiding   (b) combating
    (c) hosting   (d) imagining

C 請將以下句子翻譯為英文。

11. 魔術師在自己家中舉辦這場魔術表演。

12. 那位記者喝了三瓶燒酒後,透露了他的獨家消息的來源。

13. 他確實想要向該雜誌社投稿一則獨家新聞並讓自己成名。

14. 我收到了一則戲劇性的消息:烏龜在賽跑中打敗了兔子。

15. 他們開始發行一本關於如何賺大錢的雜誌。

Collocations on Opinion

DAY 37

Day-37.mp3

今天我們要來看看與想法和意見等名詞相關的搭配詞，例如個人的 opinion（意見）或 view（觀點）、position（立場），以及 bias（偏見）。例如，have/open a debate、make/reach a decision、voice/express opposition、have/handle a complaint…等，這些都是在描述辯論過程時可以使用的搭配詞。讓我們來學習從中精選的 46 個表達用語吧！

Collocation at a Glance

Verb + Noun	Meaning	Verb + Noun	Meaning
have a debate	進行辯論	confirm opposition	確認反對立場
encourage a debate	鼓勵辯論	declare opposition	宣布反對立場
lose a debate	贏得辯論	voice opposition	發出反對聲浪
win a debate	輸了辯論	express opposition	表達反對立場
open a debate	開啟辯論	achieve a consensus	達成共識
make a decision	做出決定	break a consensus	打破共識
reach a decision	達成決定	reach a consensus	達成共識
announce a decision	宣佈決定	have a bias	抱持偏見
reconsider a decision	重新考慮決定	display a bias	表現出偏見
reverse a decision	推翻決定	show a bias	顯現偏袒／偏見

Opinion

avoid a bias	避免偏見	raise an objection	提出反對意見
correct a bias	糾正偏見／偏好	state an objection	陳述反對意見
have an opinion	持有某種意見	meet an objection	面對反對意見
hold an opinion	堅持某種看法	withdraw an objection	撤回反對立場
express an opinion	表達意見	have a complaint	有所抱怨
state an opinion	陳述意見	voice a complaint	表達不滿
change an opinion	改變意見	handle a complaint	處理抱怨
have views	持有觀點	listen to a complaint	傾聽抱怨
hold views	抱持觀點	resolve a complaint	解決抱怨／訴事件
express views	表達觀點	adopt a position	採取某種立場
support views	支持觀點	take a position	採取某種立場
challenge views	質疑觀點	defend a position	捍衛立場
make an objection	提出反對意見	change one's position	改變某人的立場

Collocation in Use

have a debate 進行辯論

We've *had a* heated *debate*.
我們已進行過一場激烈的辯論。

encourage a debate 鼓勵辯論

His class *encourages* different *debates* among students.
他的課程鼓勵學生們進行不同的辯論。

lose/win a debate 贏得／輸了辯論

There's something more important than *winning* or *losing a* political *debate*.
有些事情比政治辯論中的勝負更為重要。

open a debate 開啟辯論

Some people annually *open a debate* about the existence of UFOs.
每年都會有一些人發起關於幽浮是否存在的辯論。

make a decision 做出決定

It's time to *make an* important *decision*.
是時候做出一個重要的決定了。

reach a decision 達成決定

Did you *reach a* final *decision*?
你（們）是否已有了最終的決定？

announce a decision 宣佈決定

I'm so sorry to *announce an* unexpected *decision*.
我很抱歉要宣布一個大家意料之外的決定。

reconsider a decision 重新考慮決定

Never stop forcing the agency to *reconsider* previous *decisions*.
務必繼續對該機構施壓，使其重新考慮之前的決定。

reverse a decision 推翻決定

I'd rather *reverse the decision*.
我寧願推翻這項決定。

confirm opposition 確認反對立場

The UN *confirms* its *opposition* to racism again.
聯合國重申其反種族主義的立場。

declare opposition 宣布反對立場

The citizens *declared* strong *opposition* to that discrimination.
公民們宣布強烈反對那樣的歧視行為。

voice opposition 發出反對聲浪

Many people gathered to *voice opposition* to presidential impeachment.
許多人聚集起來，對於總統彈劾一事發出反對聲浪。

express opposition 表達反對立場

Foreign leaders *express opposition* to attempts against the Olympic torch relay.
外國領袖們對於試圖阻撓奧運聖火傳遞的行為表達反對立場。

achieve a consensus 達成共識

One of the most important aims is to *achieve a consensus* among different countries.
其中一個最重要的目標是讓不同國家之間達成一項共識。

break a consensus 打破共識

It is not right to *break the consensus*.
打破共識是不對的。

reach a consensus 達成共識

After *reaching a consensus*, we will launch a project.
在達成共識後，我們將發動一項計畫。

have a bias 抱持偏見

Even foreigners *have a bias* about immigrant workers.
甚至外國人也對移工抱持偏見。

display a bias 表現出偏見

Ensure that you do not *display a bias* due to race or gender.
確保你不會因種族或性別而表現出偏見態度。

show a bias 顯現偏袒／偏見

Very often he *shows a bias* for lawyers.
他常常對律師表現偏袒的態度。

avoid a bias 避免偏見

Avoiding a cultural *bias* is essential in writing.
在寫作中避免文化偏見是必需的。

correct a bias 糾正偏見／偏好

The project's goal is to *correct* children's *bias* toward TV with media literacy education.
這項計畫的目標是透過媒體素養教育來糾正孩子對於電視的偏好。

have an opinion 持有某種意見

Do you *have a* negative *opinion* about genetically modified food?
你對基因改造食品有負面看法嗎？

hold an opinion 堅持某種看法

Who else *holds a* positive *opinion* for tax cuts?
還有誰對減稅堅持正面看法？

express an opinion 表達意見

The participant *expressed* her *opinion* that there is no "holy war."
那位參與者表達她的「無聖戰」觀點。

state an opinion 陳述意見

State a reasonable *opinion*.
提出一個合理的看法。

change an opinion 改變意見

I can't understand him because he *changed* his *opinion* without any particular reason.
我無法理解他，因為他在沒有任何特別的理由之下改變了他的看法。

have views 持有觀點

Every student *has* different *views* on the problem.
每位學生對這個問題都有不同的看法。

hold views 抱持觀點

She's the person who *holds* romantic *views* on love.
她是一個對愛情抱持浪漫觀點的人。

express views 表達觀點

Now I'm going to tell you about why I *expressed* positive *views* on the idea.
現在我來告訴你，為什麼我會對這想法表達正面觀點。

support views 支持觀點

I think this journalist *supports* leftist *views* on social welfare.
我認為這位記者支持關於社會福利的左派觀點。

challenge views 質疑觀點

Who dares to *challenge* the CEO's *views* on the business strategy?
誰敢質疑執行長對於經營策略的看法？

make an objection 提出反對意見

Every citizen has the right to *make an objection* to the government's policy
每位公民都有權對政府的政策提出反對意見。

raise an objection 提出反對意見

It was then that she *raised an objection* to the decision to hire a new CEO.
就在那時，她對聘任新執行長的決定提出反對意見。

state an objection 陳述反對意見

Just feel free to *state* any *objection* to a policy.
隨時歡迎你對政策陳述任何反對意見。

meet an objection 面對反對意見

The team *met an* unexpected *objection*.
該團隊遇到預料之外的反對意見。

withdraw an objection 撤回反對立場

We strongly urge you to *withdraw your objection* to affirmative action.
我們強烈呼籲你撤回對平權行動的反對立場。

have a complaint 有所抱怨

Nobody *has a complaint* about the company's dress code.
沒有人對公司的服裝規定有任何抱怨。

voice a complaint 表達不滿

I called and eagerly *voiced* my *complaints*.
我打了電話，並急切地表達了我的不滿。

handle a complaint 處理抱怨

He can *handle* workers' *complaints* effectively.
他能夠有效地處理員工的抱怨。

listen to a complaint 傾聽抱怨

We are open to *listen to* students' *complaints* on a regular basis.
我們樂意定期傾聽學生們的抱怨。

resolve a complaint 解決抱怨／申訴事件

I guess the supervisor is in charge of *resolving* residents' *complaints*.
我猜主管負責解決居民的投訴。

adopt a position 採取某種立場

The professor has no choice but to *adopt a* socio-political *position* on the issue.
這位教授別無選擇，只能在這個問題上採取社會政治的立場。

take a position 採取某種立場

Take a neutral *position*.
採取中立的立場。

defend a position 捍衛立場

Well, he managed to *defend his position*.
嗯，他成功地捍衛了自己的立場。

change one's position 改變某人的立場

He seems to *change his position* on tax cuts.
他似乎在減稅問題上改變了自己的立場。

Opinion

Collocation Exercises

A 請將 List 1 的動詞與 List 2 的名詞做適當的連結，且符合完整句意。

List 1	List 2
defend	students' diverse complaints
express	a general consensus
handle	their opinion
reached	their opposition
voiced	your political position

1. Students _____ _____ to the dean's pledges. They were also against his conservative views on college administration.

2. One of a teacher's qualifications is the ability to _____ _____ on school education.

3. Shy people are reluctant to _____ _____ in public. However, some of them are really good at private communication.

4. It seems that they have _____ _____ . However, they have different opinions about the details.

5. _____ _____ as far as it defends human rights. It would be helpful to have effective relationships with activists working locally.

DAY 37

B 在以下句子空格處中選出適當的字詞。

6. We should knock down our rivals as soon as we _____ a debate.
   (a) challenge   (b) change
   (c) open   (d) revise

7. We don't _____ your political views but we respect your freedom of speech.
   (a) hear   (b) lose
   (c) open   (d) support

8. The role of cultural education is crucial in helping our children _____ a racial bias.
   (a) create   (b) avoid
   (c) stand for   (d) support

9. How can you _____ the decision? It was a product of long-term negotiations between two parties.
   (a) enhance   (b) implement
   (c) proliferate   (d) reverse

10. He seems to _____ his objection to the privatization of the factory; his strategists have reached the conclusion that he needs to endorse the government's new policy on private sectors.
    (a) coauthor   (b) keep
    (c) withdraw   (d) zigzag

C 請將以下句子翻譯為英文。

11. 老年人不會改變他們的看法。年輕人則沒有任何意見。

12. 我們需要主席的確認才能推翻這個決定。

13. 該政黨決定撤回反對立場,並支持該候選人。

14. 他似乎已經改正自己對於黑色人種的偏見。

15. 那位政治家公開表示他反對該黨的經濟政策。

Collocations on Family and Social Relationships

DAY 38

Day-38.mp3

今天要探討的是與 family（家庭）有關的核心字彙，例如 relatives（親戚）、marriage（婚姻）、solidarity（團結在一起）… 等常見搭配用法。這裡整理了 38 個非常實用的搭配詞表達用語，例如：annul/propose a marriage、build/develop a relationship、demonstrate/express solidarity、bring up/feed a family…等。

Collocation at a Glance

Verb + Noun	Meaning	Verb + Noun	Meaning
have **relatives**	有（一些）親戚	move up/down **a hierarchy**	升階／降階
look after **relatives**	照顧親人	bring up **a family**	養育家庭
lose **relatives**	失去親人	feed **a family**	養家糊口
support **relatives**	接待親戚	have **a family**	有一個家庭
attack **an enemy**	攻擊敵人／軍	raise **a family**	養育家庭
defeat **an enemy**	擊敗敵軍／人	ask for **a divorce**	要求離婚
fight (against) **an enemy**	與敵人對抗／戰鬥	go through **a divorce**	經歷離婚（過程）
make **an enemy**	樹立敵人	seek **a divorce**	尋求離婚（協助）
create **a hierarchy**	建立階級制度	want **a divorce**	想要離婚
establish **a hierarchy**	確立階級關係	break (off) **an alliance**	解除同盟

Family and Social Relationships

form **an alliance**	結成同盟	lead **a team**	帶領團隊
have **an alliance**	有同盟關係	annul **a marriage**	宣告婚姻無效
demonstrate **solidarity**	展現團結	have **a marriage**	擁有婚姻關係
express **solidarity**	表達團結	propose **marriage**	求婚
promote **solidarity**	促進團結	build **a relationship**	建立關係
show **solidarity**	展現團結	damage **a relationship**	壞了關係
build **a team**	成立團隊	destroy **a relationship**	破壞關係
form **a team**	組建團隊	develop **a relationship**	發展關係
launch **a team**	創立團隊	improve **a relationship**	改善關係

Collocation in Use

have relatives 有（一些）親戚

I *have relatives* living abroad.
我有居住在國外的親戚。

look after relatives 照顧親人

She's been *looking after* her older *relatives*.
她一直在照顧她年長的親戚。

lose relatives 失去親人

Most residents *lost* their *relatives* during the hurricane season.
大多數居民在颶風季節期間失去了他們的親人。

support relatives 接待親戚

There's no one to *support relatives* during their visit here.
這裡沒有人可以在親戚來訪時接待他／她們。

attack an enemy 攻擊敵人／軍

Attack any *enemies* we encounter.
對我們遇到的任何敵軍發動攻擊。

defeat an enemy 擊敗敵軍／人

The general ordered us to *defeat* and disarm *the enemy*.
將軍命令我們要戰勝敵軍並解除其武裝。

fight (against) an enemy 與敵人對抗／戰鬥

It's a kind of tragedy for both parties to have no common *enemy* they have to *fight against*.
對於兩黨來說沒有共同的敵人需要去對抗，這真的是一種悲劇。

make an enemy 樹立敵人

The anti-war movement *made enemies* of conservative groups.
反戰運動使保守派團體視之為敵人。

create a hierarchy 建立階級制度

Your job is to *create a hierarchy* and order in an organization.
你的工作是在一個組織裡建立階級制度和秩序。

establish a hierarchy 確立階級關係

Grooming is one of the ways of *establishing a hierarchy* between animals.
梳理毛髮是在動物之間建立階級的方式之一。

move up/down a hierarchy 升階／降階

A person may *move up and down* the social *hierarchy*.
一個人在社會階級制度中可能會往上升或往下降。

bring up a family 養育家庭

Young men should learn how to *bring up a family*.
年輕人應該學習如何養家。

feed a family 養家糊口

He earns enough to *feed* his *family*.
他賺的錢足以讓他養家糊口。

have a family 有一個家庭

Joe *has a family* of four.
Joe 的家裡有四個人。

raise a family 養育家庭

I want to get married and *raise a family* on a single income.
我想結婚,並單靠一份收入來養家。

ask for a divorce 要求離婚

Brad seemed to *ask for a divorce* for an acceptable reason.
布萊德似乎有正當的理由來要求離婚。

go through a divorce 經歷離婚(過程)

She *went through a divorce* unprepared.
她在毫無準備的情況下離了婚。

seek a divorce 尋求離婚(協助)

Anyone in trouble can get help in *seeking a divorce* from their partner.
任何遇到困難無法和其伴侶辦理離婚者均可尋求協助。

want a divorce 想要離婚

They both agreed that they *wanted a divorce*.
他們雙方都同意要離婚。

break (off) an alliance 解除同盟

No one expected they would *break* the military *alliance* with the country.
沒有人預料到他們會與那個國家解除軍事同盟。

form an alliance 結成同盟

The two countries *formed a* strategic *alliance* for defense.
兩國組成了一個防禦性的戰略聯盟。

have an alliance 有同盟關係

GM *had alliances* with many business partners.
通用汽車與許多商業夥伴建立過聯盟關係。

demonstrate solidarity 展現團結

This performance *demonstrates solidarity* with human rights activists.
這場表演展現出對人權活動者的團結支持（＝表達聲援人權活動者）。

express solidarity 表達團結

The lawyers *expressed* their *solidarity* with the victims.
律師們表示支持受害者並與其站在一起。

promote solidarity 促進團結

There's a need to *promote solidarity* across borders.
有必要促進跨界的團結合作。

show solidarity 展現團結

International visitors *show* international *solidarity* against racism.
國際訪客展現出反種族主義的國際團結。

build a team 成立團隊

A sales *team* was *built* for the holiday season.
為因應假期旺季成立了一個銷售團隊。

form a team 組建團隊

According to the manual, we must *form a team* of three to five members.
根據手冊規定，我們必須組建一支三到五名成員的團隊。

launch a team 創立團隊

Water Lands *launched a team* of lifeguards into the sea to rescue people.
水上樂園派出了一組救生員下海救人。

lead a team 帶領團隊

He's the one who *led* the national soccer *team* to the top seed.
他是帶領國家足球隊奪得第一種子位置的人。

annul a marriage 宣告婚姻無效

I strongly asked a court to *annul the marriage*.
我強烈要求法院宣告這樁婚姻無效。

have a marriage 擁有婚姻關係

The same-sex couple couldn't *have an* open *marriage*.
這對同性伴侶無法擁有公開的婚姻關係。

propose marriage 求婚

I'm going to *propose marriage* to my sweetheart under the sea.
我打算在海裡向我的愛人求婚。

build a relationship 建立關係

Nothing is more important than *building* good *relationships* with customers.
沒有什麼比與顧客建立良好關係更重要。

damage a relationship 壞了關係

Don't let your jealousy *damage our relationship*.
別讓你的嫉妒心壞了我們之間的關係。

destroy a relationship 破壞關係

Learn how not to *destroy a* trustful *relationship* with friends.
學習如何不去破壞與朋友之間的信任關係。

develop a relationship 發展關係

A classroom is defined as the place teachers and students *develop an* ongoing *relationship*.
教室被定義為老師與學們建立持續關係的地方。

improve a relationship 改善關係

That single book helped *improve* and boost *relationships* in my life.
就是那本書幫助我改善並增進我生活中的人際關係。

Collocation Exercises

A 請將 List 1 的動詞與 List 2 的名詞做適當的連結，且符合完整句意。

List 1	List 2
bring up	a long-term relationship
build	a divorce
have	a childless marriage
launch	a multidisciplinary team
seek	a family of 6 boys

1. We must _____ _____ with them. They have strategic importance to us.

2. Don't _____ _____ as an exit from your current unhappiness.

3. She wanted to _____ _____ , but her husband continuously insisted that their married life would be much happier with children.

4. Psychologists and neuroscientists in the university plan to _____ _____ to do research on language acquisition.

Family and Social Relationships   223

5. I really respect my mother. She had to _____ _____ by herself but made no complaint.

B 在以下句子空格處中選出適當的字詞。

6. She had no _____ at all. She was an orphan.
   (a) employees   (b) parents
   (c) seniors   (d) staff

7. NGOs and government expressed _____ in addressing problems of global warming. They organized a joint rally.
   (a) complete contradiction   (b) individual participation
   (c) political prejudice   (d) social solidarity

8. He moved up _____ very quickly. It seemed that the only goal in his life was to be a CEO of the company.
   (a) the board   (b) the building
   (c) the hierarchy   (d) the lineage

9. If you overcome your desires, you are braver than somebody else who _____ his or her enemies; for the hardest victory is over self.
   (a) attacks   (b) forgives
   (c) hides   (d) treats

10. _____ a divorce could mean "a death" as the emotions experienced are very similar to losing someone close.
    (a) Falling about   (b) Looking through
    (c) Going through   (d) Putting through

C 請將以下句子翻譯為英文。

11. 她要求丈夫快點離婚，但他拒絕了。

12. 伊拉克戰爭促進了中東國家之間的團結。

13. 他們共組了一個對抗黑手黨的聯盟，但黑手黨根本不在乎他們做了什麼。

14. 學生和教師們組成了一個專案團隊來解決這個問題。

15. 改善與你的同儕和家人之間的關係。

Collocations on Social Concerns

DAY 39

Day-39.mp3

aid（協助）和 welfare（福利）是為了解決 conflict（衝突）和 problem（問題）的一種方式。今天，讓我們要來學習 36 個實用的搭配詞組，包括：claim/retain right(s)、cause/handle a conflict、alleviate/reduce poverty、abuse/exercise a privilege…等。

Collocation at a Glance

Verb + Noun	Meaning	Verb + Noun	Meaning
call for **aid**	請求援助	break down (a) **prejudice**	打破偏見
provide **aid**	提供援助	have (a) **prejudice**	抱有偏見
receive **aid**	獲得援助	overcome (a) **prejudice**	克服偏見
withdraw **aid**	撤回援助	find **an opportunity**	找到機會
improve **welfare**	改善福利	give **an opportunity**	提供機會
promote **welfare**	增進福利	grasp **an opportunity**	抓住機會
cause (a) **conflict**	引發衝突	seize **an opportunity**	把握機會
handle (a) **conflict**	處理衝突	compromise **security**	危害安全
provoke (a) **conflict**	挑起衝突	ensure **security**	確保安全
settle (a) **conflict**	解決衝突	improve **security**	改善安全（措施）

DAY 39

tighten (up) **security**	加強安全（措施）	reduce **poverty**	降低貧困（率）
claim **right(s)**	主張權利	abuse **a privilege**	濫用特權
protect **right(s)**	保護權利	exercise **a privilege**	行使特權
respect **right(s)**	尊重權利	grant **a privilege**	授予特權
retain **right(s)**	保有權利	approach **a problem**	解決問題
alleviate **poverty**	減輕貧困	cause **a problem**	引發問題
eliminate **poverty**	消除貧困	face **a problem**	面對問題
eradicate **poverty**	根絕貧困	pose **a problem**	造成問題

Collocation in Use

call for aid 請求援助

We need to *call for* more *aid* to Somalia right now.
我們必須呼籲立即給予索馬利亞更多援助。

provide aid 提供援助

The Food Bank promised to *provide aid* with no questions asked.
「食品銀行」二話不說即承諾提供援助。

receive aid 獲得援助

We need to *receive* financial *aid*.
我們需要獲得財務援助。

withdraw aid 撤回援助

The institution *withdrew the aid* without notification.
該機構在未通知的情況下撤回了援助。

improve welfare 改善福利

These pamphlets are about strategies to *improve* animal *welfare*.
這些小冊子是關於增進動物福利的策略。

promote welfare 增進福利

He was awarded for trying to *promote* child *welfare*.
他因為努力促進兒童福利而獲得獎勵。

Social Concerns

cause (a) conflict 引發衝突

His death *caused conflict* within the family.
他的死在家庭內部引起了衝突。

handle (a) conflict 處理衝突

We welcome anyone who can *handle conflicts* successfully without fighting.
我們歡迎任何能在不打鬥的情況下成功處理衝突事件的人。

provoke (a) conflict 挑起衝突

Refrain from words that might *provoke a conflict*.
請避免使用可能挑起衝突的言語。

settle (a) conflict 解決衝突

Please send someone to *settle the conflict*.
請派人來解決這場衝突。

break down (a) prejudice 打破偏見

We've got to have a talk to *break down the prejudice* and distrust.
我們必須進行一次談話，以打破（彼此的）偏見和不信任。

have (a) prejudice 抱有偏見

Everybody *has* some bias or *prejudice*.
每個人多少都會有一些成見或偏見。

overcome (a) prejudice 克服偏見

Parents are responsible for helping their children *overcome prejudice*.
父母有責任幫助他們的孩子克服偏見。

find an opportunity 找到機會

He managed to *find the opportunity*.
他試著找到了機會。

DAY 39

give an opportunity 提供機會

The king *gave* him *the opportunity* to save his neck.
國王給了他一個保命的機會。

grasp an opportunity 抓住機會

Just *grasp an opportunity* and turn it into success.
只要抓住機會,並將其轉化為成功。

seize an opportunity 把握機會

Wait and try to *seize an opportunity* to gain access.
耐心等待,並試圖把握機會來取得成功。

compromise security 危害安全

HTML could *compromise security*.
HTML 可能有危安之虞。

ensure security 確保安全

This is my duty to *ensure the security*.
確保安全是我的職責。

improve security 改善安全(措施)

Soon they will *improve security* for the gate.
很快地他們就會改善大門的安全措施。

tighten (up) security 加強安全(措施)

We've *tightened our security*.
我們已經加強了我們的安全防護。

claim right(s) 主張權利

It's ridiculous that we have to pay in order to *claim our rights* as students.
我們必須付費才能主張我們作為學生的權利,這太荒謬了。

Social Concerns

protect right(s) 保護權利

The army was sent to *protect our rights*.
軍隊被派去保護我們的權利。

respect right(s) 尊重權利

Our company *respects* your *right* to privacy.
我們公司尊重您的隱私權。

retain right(s) 保有權利

I don't know who *retains the copyright*.
我不知道誰是這個著作權的持有人。

alleviate poverty 減輕貧困

Many countries have been trying to *alleviate* global *poverty*.
許多國家一直在努力減輕全球的貧困問題。

eliminate poverty 消除貧困

The government set a plan to *eliminate poverty* in 7 years.
政府制定了一個 7 年內消滅貧困的計畫。

eradicate poverty 根絕貧困

It is important to *eradicate* child *poverty*.
根除兒童貧困是很重要的。

reduce poverty 降低貧困（率）

The Minister said he would *reduce poverty* by 10% in 2 years.
部長表示，他將在兩年內將貧困率降低 10%。

abuse a privilege 濫用特權

Never *abuse the privilege* in any way.
無論如何都不能濫用特權。

exercise a privilege 行使特權

He could get away from it by *exercising the privilege* of the rich.
他可能藉由行使富人的特權來脫罪。

grant a privilege 授予特權

The committee *granted* some groups *privileges*.
委員會將特權給了一些團體。

approach a problem 解決問題

I don't like to *approach* the prison *problems* that way.
我不喜歡用那樣的方式來解決監獄問題。

cause a problem 引發問題

That could have *caused* severe *problems*.
那可能已經導致嚴重的問題。

face a problem 面對問題

What is the greatest *problem* we *face*?
我們面對的最大問題是什麼？

pose a problem 造成問題

Squatters *pose a problem* for landowners.
違規佔地者對地主構成了問題。

Collocation Exercises

A 請將 List 1 的動詞與 List 2 的名詞做適當的連結，且符合完整句意。

List 1	List 2
ensure	equal opportunity
gives	the unfair prejudice
overcome	urban poverty
reduce	equal rights
respects	national security

Social Concerns   231

1. It is very hard to _____ _____ some Western people have against Asians.

2. Society says it _____ _____ to all. But I think this world is so unequal.

3. Feminist education does not focus just on woman empowerment. Rather it _____ _____ of men and women.

4. His idea to _____ _____ was ridiculous. He argued that we all have to move to a rural area.

5. We must _____ _____ on the Korean peninsula. It is a basis for reunification.

B 在以下句子空格處中選出適當的字詞。

6. The International Red Cross _____ emergency aid from the United Nations.
   (a) called for   (b) held
   (c) improved   (d) ran into

7. The government _____ security against possible threats during the president's visit.
   (a) found   (b) gave
   (c) settled   (d) tightened

8. The world's oil supply sometimes _____ military conflicts in the Middle East.
   (a) causes   (b) claims
   (c) faces   (d) grasps

9. The USA's efforts to _____ the conflict are not going to make a big difference with the situation we see in Iraq.
   (a) encourage   (b) settle
   (c) involve   (d) bring

10. Anybody interested in broadcasting on TV can apply for this competition; so _____ the opportunity to express yourself in front of the camera!
    (a) give   (b) change
    (c) seize   (d) cease

C 請將以下句子翻譯為英文。

11. 他們在當地發起一場促進兒童福利的活動。

12. 一些大使濫用他們所擁有的外交特權。

13. 他們以一種新的方式來處理這個問題。

14. 我們應該隨時隨地保護人權。

15. 女王賜予那位騎士相當大的特權。

Collocations on Customs and Habits

DAY 40
Day-40.mp3

今天將針對「custom（習俗）、convention（慣例）、culture（文化）、habit（習慣）⋯」等相關字詞，來探討各種搭配詞。像是 create/foster a culture、follow/maintain a custom、cherish/establish a tradition、adopt/prohibit a practice ⋯等表達方式，都是可以靈活搭配運用的。我們在此將學習 40 個這搭配用語。

Collocation at a Glance

Verb + Noun	Meaning	Verb + Noun	Meaning
cause (an) addiction	導致成癮	foster (a) culture	孕育文化
cure (an) addiction	治癒成癮（症）	produce (a) culture	生產文化
have (an) addiction	有成癮性	follow a custom	遵循習俗
overcome (an) addiction	克服成癮	maintain a custom	維持習俗
treat (an) addiction	治療成癮（症）	observe a custom	遵守習俗
break with convention	打破傳統／慣例	preserve a custom	保存習俗
follow convention	遵循傳統／慣例	respect a custom	尊重習俗
observe convention	遵守傳統／慣例	become a fashion (trend)	成為潮流
create (a) culture	創造文化	follow a fashion (trend)	跟隨潮流
develop (a) culture	發展文化	introduce a fashion (trend)	介紹／引入潮流

set a **fashion (trend)**	創造潮流	establish **a routine**	建立常規
acquire **a habit**	養成習慣	follow **a routine**	遵循常規
break **a habit**	改掉習慣	challenge **a stereotype**	挑戰刻板印象
develop **a habit**	養成習慣	create **a stereotype**	建立刻板印象
make **a habit**	成為習慣	reinforce **a stereotype**	強化刻板印象
adopt **a practice**	採納做法	reject **a stereotype**	拒絕刻板印象
follow **a practice**	遵循做法	cherish **a tradition**	珍惜傳統
prohibit **a practice**	禁止做法	establish **a tradition**	建立傳統
break (with) **(a) routine**	打破常規	follow **a tradition**	遵循傳統
change **a routine**	改變常規	maintain **a tradition**	保有傳統

Collocation in Use

cause (an) addiction 導致成癮

Placing a computer in a child's own room can *cause an* Internet *addiction*.
將電腦放在孩子自己的房間可能會導致網路成癮症。

cure (an) addiction 治癒成癮（症）

Visit our center to *cure* your alcohol *addiction*.
來我們的中心治療你的酒癮。

have (an) addiction 有成癮性

Everyone *has an addiction* to something.
每個人都對某種事物有成癮性。

overcome (an) addiction 克服成癮

The singer has struggled to *overcome* a drug *addiction* since he was 27 years old and has a long criminal history record relating to his addiction.
這名歌手自 27 歲起就一直努力於克服毒癮，並且長期以來都有著與毒癮相關的犯罪紀錄。

treat (an) addiction 治療成癮（症）

This is *an addiction* that is hard to *treat*.
這是一種難以治療的成癮症。

break with convention 打破傳統／慣例

It's very hard to *break with* old *conventions*.
很難打破舊有的慣例。

follow convention 遵循傳統／慣例

Following a traditional *convention* is not always correct.
遵循傳統慣例並非一直都是正確的。

observe convention 遵守傳統／慣例

He had the courage to refuse to *observe convention*.
他有勇氣拒絕遵循傳統。

create (a) culture 創造文化

Teenagers are *creating* their own *culture*.
青少年正在創造自己的文化。

develop (a) culture 發展文化

He is said to have *developed a culture* of recognition and praise.
據說他培養了認同與讚美的文化。

foster (a) culture 孕育文化

Here we *foster* Asian *culture*.
我們在這裡孕育了亞洲文化。

produce (a) culture 生產文化

The magazine *produces* underground *cultures*.
這本雜誌產出了地下文化。

follow a custom 遵循習俗

Don't force people to *follow a* particular *custom*.
不要強迫別人遵循某種特定習俗。

maintain a custom 維持習俗

Many traditional groups *maintain* native *customs*.
許多傳統團體維持著本土的習俗。

observe a custom 遵守習俗

Parents should teach their children to *observe* traditional *customs*.
父母應該教導他們的孩子遵守傳統習俗。

preserve a custom 保存習俗

The objective was to *preserve* traditions and *customs*.
這項目標是為了保存傳統與習俗。

respect a custom 尊重習俗

We must *respect* Western *customs* as well as Oriental ones.
我們必須尊重西方和東方的習俗。

become a fashion (trend) 成為潮流

The actress's accessories *became a fashion trend*.
那位女演員的配飾成為了一種流行趨勢。

follow a fashion (trend) 跟隨潮流

Let's *follow* street *fashion* in our next designs.
讓我們下次的設計來跟隨街頭潮流吧。

introduce a fashion (trend) 介紹／引入潮流

Do you know any good magazines which *introduce* the latest *fashions*?
你知道有哪些介紹最新時尚的好雜誌嗎？

set a fashion (trend) 創造潮流

The designer *set a fashion trend* for long skirts.
那位設計師創造了一股穿長裙的潮流。

acquire a habit 養成習慣

It is hard to *acquire a* good *habit*.
養成一個好習慣並不容易。

break a habit 改掉習慣

It's difficult to *break a* bad *habit*.
改掉壞習慣很困難。

develop a habit 養成習慣

I *developed an* odd *habit*.
我養成了一個奇怪的習慣。

make a habit 成為習慣

Don't *make* smoking *a habit*.
不要讓抽菸成為一種習慣。

adopt a practice 採納做法

We need to *adopt a* good *practice*.
我們必須採納良好的習慣做法。

follow a practice 遵循做法

If you *follow* the standard *practices*, everything will be fine.
如果你遵循標準做法，一切都會順利進行。

prohibit a practice 禁止做法

We *prohibit* religious *practices* on the premises.
我們禁止在場內進行宗教行為。

break (with) (a) routine 打破常規

How could she *break with* the old *routine* without permission?
她怎麼能在未經允許的情況下打破舊有常規呢？

change a routine 改變常規

Having *changed a* fixed *routine* worked.
改變了固定的常規後，效果不錯。

establish a routine 建立常規

At the early stage, somebody has to *establish a routine*.
在初期階段，必須有人來建立一個常規。

follow a routine 遵循常規

Our products are made by *following a* strict *routine*.
我們的產品是按照一個嚴格的常規製作的。

challenge a stereotype 挑戰刻板印象

The book *challenges a stereotype* of gender roles.
這本書挑戰了性別角色的刻板印象。

create a stereotype 建立刻板印象

Why do you guys *create a stereotype* based on rumors?
為什麼你各位要根據謠言來打造刻板印象？

reinforce a stereotype 強化刻板印象

Some actions *reinforce* bad *stereotypes*.
某些行為會強化不良的刻板印象。

reject a stereotype 拒絕刻板印象

The activist helped *reject a* negative *stereotype* for African-Americans.
這位社運人士幫助推翻了針對非裔美國人的負面刻板印象。

cherish a tradition 珍惜傳統

Most girls *cherish the tradition* of their fathers walking them down the aisle on their wedding day.
大多數女孩都珍惜父親在她們婚禮當天牽著她們走紅毯的傳統。

establish a tradition 建立傳統

He *established* 19th-century *traditions* in art.
他建立了 19 世紀藝術領域的傳統。

Customs and Habits   239

follow a tradition 遵循傳統

They got married *following* Catholic *traditions*.
他們按照天主教傳統舉行婚禮。

maintain a tradition 保有傳統

The actor chose to *maintain* Korean *traditions* rather than adopt Western cultural ideas.
那位演員選擇保有韓國傳統，而不是採納西方文化觀念。

Collocation Exercises

A 請將 List 1 的動詞與 List 2 的名詞做適當的連結，且符合完整句意。

List 1	List 2
broke with	social conventions
fostering	the culture
introducing	Russian fashion
observe	the prevalent practice
following	the routine

1. He refuses to _____ _____ and tries to set his own standards. Sometimes it hurts other people.

2. She made a lot of money by _____ _____ to South Korea. After her death, all her property was donated to establish a fashion academy.

3. Some men have been _____ _____ of spousal abuse, and it is increasing year by year.

DAY 40

4. The activist dedicated herself to _____ _____ of peace. She thought that peace was the very solution to violent and irrational times.

5. He _____ _____ of using exclusive spaces for VIPs. In his opinion, everyone deserved a chance to get a front row seat.

B 在以下句子空格處中選出適當的字詞。

6. We do not have to _____ the Western custom of wearing a suit and tie.
   (a) ban   (b) give
   (c) make   (d) observe

7. Some couples repeatedly _____ the stereotype of independent men and dependent women.
   (a) give off   (b) perform
   (c) prevent   (d) reinforce

8. We inherit customs from people older than us, but we can also ____ _____ new traditions.
   (a) donate   (b) establish
   (c) follow   (d) preserve

9. I've treated people who have _____ an addiction to cocaine that has turned their life upside down.
   (a) taken   (b) done
   (c) had   (d) used

10. The campaign to _____ the white stereotype of black has achieved some success.
    (a) endure   (b) provide
    (c) try   (d) challenge

C 請將以下句子翻譯為英文。

11. 父母應該幫助孩子養成寫日誌的習慣。

12. 你需要專家的幫助來克服網路成癮症。

13. 我們必須在珍惜優良傳統的同時,發展新的價值觀。

14. 我養成了一個月閱讀兩本書的習慣。

15. 穿高領衫在 80 年代成為一種流行趨勢。

Collocations on

DAY 41

Day-41.mp3

War and Peace

今天要針對 ally（盟友）、enemy（敵人）、negotiation（談判）、treaty（條約）… 等與戰爭、和平有關的核心字彙及搭配詞組進行探討與學習。例如：get/lose an ally、defeat/face an enemy、open/break off a negotiation、conclude/ratify a treaty… 等，現在就來深入學習 38 個關鍵的表達用語。

Collocation at a Glance

Verb + Noun	Meaning	Verb + Noun	Meaning
gain an ally	爭取盟友	make an enemy	樹立敵人
get an ally	得到盟友	cease fire	停止射擊
have an ally	擁有盟友	draw fire	引來（批評）砲火
lose an ally	失去盟友	hold fire	停止射擊
bear arms	攜帶武器	open fire	開火
lay down arms	放下武器	be armed with a missile	配備導彈
take up arms	拿起武器	deploy a missile	部署導彈
defeat an enemy	擊敗敵人	fire a missile	發射導彈
deter an enemy	嚇阻敵人	shoot down a missile	擊落導彈
face an enemy	面對敵人	break off a negotiation	中止協商／談判

War and Peace 243

enter into a negotiation	進行協商／談判	become a soldier	成為軍人，從軍
open a negotiation	展開協商／談判	accept a treaty	接受條約
resume a negotiation	重啟協商／談判	agree on/to a treaty	同意條約
bring about peace	促成和平	conclude a treaty	締結條約
keep the peace	維持和平	ratify a treaty	批准條約
make peace	達成和平／和解	be in a war	處於戰爭狀態
enlist as a soldier	入伍從軍	be ravaged by war	遭受戰爭的摧殘
play a soldier	扮演軍人角色	declare war	宣戰
serve as a soldier	服兵役	wage war	發動戰爭

Collocation in Use

gain an ally 爭取盟友

It's hard to *gain a* reliable *ally* in the war.
在戰爭中要爭取到一個可靠的盟友很難。

get an ally 得到盟友

The Democrats have *got* a lot of *allies* for the election.
民主黨在這次選舉中得到了許多盟友。

have an ally 擁有盟友

He *has* no *ally* and fights for himself.
他沒有盟友，且獨自奮戰。

lose an ally 失去盟友

She *lost* all *allies*.
她失去了所有盟友。

bear arms 攜帶武器

They are not allowed to *bear arms* in front of the king.
他們不被允許在國王面前攜帶武器。

lay down arms 放下武器

The police ordered the burglars to *lay down* their *arms*.
警方命令竊賊放下他們的武器。

take up arms 拿起武器

Take up arms and start shooting!
拿起武器，開始射擊！

defeat an enemy 擊敗敵人

The platoon failed in *defeating an enemy* by surprise.
這支小隊在奇襲敵軍的行動中失敗了。

deter an enemy 嚇阻敵人

We must desperately *deter the enemy* from proceeding.
我們必須拼命阻止敵軍前進。

face an enemy 面對敵人

Face your *enemy*!
面對你的敵人吧！

make an enemy 樹立敵人

Of all things, we need to try not to *make an enemy*.
無論如何，我們必須試圖避免樹立敵人。

cease fire 停止射擊

The commander ordered soldiers to *cease fire*.
指揮官命令士兵停止射擊。

draw fire 引來（批評）砲火

The arrogant writer *drew* the *fire* of critics.
這名傲慢的作家引來批評家的砲火

hold fire 停止射擊

They *held* their *fire* to cover their platoon.
他們停止射擊，以掩護他們的小隊。

open fire 開火

Opening fire means war here.
開火意味著就此開戰。

be armed with a missile 配備導彈

The U.S. is to *be armed with* intercontinental *missiles*.
美國將備妥洲際飛彈的軍力。

deploy a missile 部署導彈

They insisted that South Korea *deploy missiles* for strategic reasons.
他們堅持南韓應基於戰略因素部署導彈。

fire a missile 發射導彈

The commander orderd the crew to *fire the missiles* when the target came into view.
指揮官命令部隊，當目標出現在視線範圍內時即發射導彈。

shoot down a missile 擊落導彈

The soldier succeeded in *shooting down a missile* by chance.
那名士兵意外地成功擊落一枚導彈。

break off a negotiation 中止協商／談判

They *broke off* trade *negotiations* in the end.
他們到最後中止了貿易協商。

enter into a negotiation 進行談判

The company has to sincerely *enter into a negotiation* with the labor union.
公司必須誠懇地與工會進行談判。

open a negotiation 展開協商／談判

The agreement on *opening a* multilateral *negotiation* is the best outcome of this meeting.
本次會議的最佳成果是同意展開多方協商。

resume a negotiation 重啟協商／談判

The two Koreas agreed to *resume the negotiations*.
兩韓同意重啟協商。

bring about peace 促成和平

It takes considerable efforts to *bring about peace*.
促成和平需要付出相當大的努力。

keep the peace 維持和平

Japan sent troops to *keep the peace* in the region.
日本派遣部隊前往該地區維持和平。

make peace 達成和平／和解

Make peace rather than wait for it.
主動製造和平，而不是坐等和平到來。

enlist as a soldier 入伍從軍

His sister *enlisted as a solider*.
他的妹妹已入伍從軍。

play a soldier 扮演軍人角色

When we were kids, *playing soldiers* was fun.
我們小時候，扮演軍人是一件很有趣的事。

serve as a soldier 服兵役

Korean men must *serve as a soldier* for 2 years.
韓國男性必須服兩年的兵役。

become a soldier 成為軍人，從軍

He *became a soldier* to make money.
他為了賺錢而從軍。

accept a treaty 接受條約

The National Assembly refused to *accept the treaty*.
國會拒絕接受這項條約。

agree on/to a treaty 同意條約

The EU member states *agreed* unanimously *to the treaty*.
歐盟成員國一致同意這項條約。

conclude a treaty 締結條約

The two nations *concluded a treaty* and established an organization to enforce it.
兩國締結了條約，並成立了一個機構來執行此條約。

ratify a treaty 批准條約

The treaty should be *ratified* within this year.
這項條約應在今年內獲得批准。

be in a war 處於戰爭狀態

That country *is in a* serious *war* against drugs.
該國正處於一場嚴肅的毒品戰爭中。

be ravaged by war 遭受戰爭的摧殘

It is children and women who *were* most *ravaged by* the brutal *war*.
在那場殘酷的戰爭中，受害最深的是婦女和兒童。

declare war 宣戰

The allied nations attacked the country without *declaring war*.
盟國在未宣戰的情況下攻擊了那個國家。

wage war 發動戰爭

The company is ready to *wage* an economic *war*.
該公司準備發動一場經濟戰爭。

DAY 41

Collocation Exercises

A 請將 List 1 的動詞與 List 2 的名詞做適當的連結，且符合完整句意。

List 1	List 2
bear	reliable allies
gained	arms
ratified	trade negotiations
resume	a spiritual war
wage	the treaty

1. "We have to _____ _____ in this age of chaos," said the minister. Listeners nodded their heads in agreement.

2. It doesn't seem that they will _____ _____ any time soon. Their views have no common ground.

3. It is our right to _____ _____ . If the criminals have them, so should we.

4. The United States thought that they _____ a lot of _____ at the initial stage of the war. But the number gradually decreased.

5. The South Korean government _____ _____ two years ago. However, no organization has been established to enforce it.

War and Peace

B 在以下句子空格處中選出適當的字詞。

6. Her friends couldn't believe the news that she decided to quit graduate school to _____ as a soldier.
   (a) become (b) command
   (c) enlist (d) play

7. The enemy was armed with cutting-edge _____ while we had a few old rifles.
   (a) allies (b) missiles
   (c) strategies (d) summits

8. I can't forget the moment the troops started to _____ fire on us. It was the beginning of tragedy in Gwangju.
   (a) allow (b) cease
   (c) open (d) start

9. James, who's the host of a prime-time show, is _____ fire for using gay stereotypes on his show.
   (a) ceasing (b) drawing
   (c) blowing (d) catching

10. Don't start or _____ into any negotiation where there is any possibility of losing money rather than making it.
    (a) enter (b) begin
    (c) access (d) carry

C 請將以下句子翻譯為英文。

11. 維持和平比製造和平更加困難。

12. 我們總是在思考如何成為優秀的戰士。但我們真正需要學習的是如何避免樹敵。

13. 他們一展開談判，就開始互相叫罵。

14. 我們在選舉中失去了一個重要盟友。這場選戰將比我們想像中更加艱難。

15. 由於政府拒絕同意該條約，大多數非政府組織（NGO）都表達了他們的遺憾。

Collocations on Politics and Institution

DAY 42
Day-42.mp3

今天我們將探討與政治和制度相關的重要字彙及其搭配用語，例如 policy（政策）、affair（事務）、campaign（運動／活動）、address（演講）等。重點學習 36 個核心搭配詞語，包括 introduce/operate a policy、manage/settle an affair、organize/run a campaign，以及 deliver/give an address…等，請仔細掌握這些用語。

Collocation at a Glance

Verb + Noun	Meaning	Verb + Noun	Meaning
adopt a policy	採納／接受政策	take a vote	進行表決
develop a policy	制定／發展政策	launch a campaign	發起活動
introduce a policy	推出／引進政策	lead a campaign	領導活動
operate a policy	執行政策	organize a campaign	組織活動
administer an affair	掌管事務	run a campaign	推行活動
manage an affair	管理事務	appoint a committee	任命委員會
settle an affair	解決事務	chair a committee	擔任委員會主席
cast a vote	投票	create a committee	成立委員會
count a vote	計票	establish a committee	設立委員會
gain a vote	獲得選票	form a committee	成立委員會

face pressure	面對壓力	reveal a scandal	揭露醜聞
place pressure	施加壓力	spread a scandal	散佈醜聞
put pressure	施加壓力	betray a pledge	背棄誓言
resist pressure	抵抗壓力	fulfill a pledge	實現誓言
fight (in) an election	投入選戰	make a pledge	作出承諾
hold an election	舉行選舉	deliver an address	發表演講／演說
win an election	贏得一場選舉	give an address	發表演講／演說
cause a scandal	引發醜聞	make an address	發表演講／演說

Collocation in Use

adopt a policy 採納／接受政策

For our children, we should *adopt an* anti-drug *policy*.
為了我們的孩子，我們應該採納反毒品政策。

develop a policy 制定／發展政策

The government *developed an* effective *policy* to address the real estate problems.
政府制定了一項有效的政策來解決房地產的問題。

introduce a policy 推出／引進政策

The ruling party should *introduce a* strong *policy* against prostitution.
執政黨應該推出一項打擊賣淫的強硬政策。

operate a policy 執行政策

Operating a policy is as important as introducing one.
執行政策和推出政策是同等的重要。

administer an affair 掌管事務

He is to *administer* international *affairs* in the department.
他將掌管該部門的國際事務。

manage an affair 管理事務

He *managed a* laborious *affair* of providing food to 1,500 people from all over the world.
他負責管理一項艱鉅的事務 — 為全球各地 1,500 人提供食物。

settle an affair 解決事務

Settling a military *affair* requires different types of experiences.
解決軍事事務需要不同類型的經驗。

cast a vote 投票

I *cast a vote* against the Republican candidate.
我對那名共和黨候選人投下反對票。

count a vote 計票

Canvassers *counted votes* again to confirm his victory.
點票員為確認他的勝選而重新計票。

gain a vote 獲得選票

He *gained* most of the black *votes* in that state.
他在該州拿下多數非裔選票。

take a vote 進行表決

The UN *took a vote* on North Korea's nuclear issue.
聯合國就北韓的核問題進行表決。

launch a campaign 發起活動

The congressman illegally *launched an* election *campaign*.
那名國會議員非法發起一場選戰活動。

lead a campaign 領導活動

You might lose your health while *leading an* election *campaign*.
你在帶領選戰活動時，可能傷及自己的健康。

organize a campaign 組織活動

This new representative seems to have no experience in *organizing a campaign*.
這位新任代表似乎沒有組織活動的經驗。

run a campaign 推行活動

It is very challenging to *run an* anti-globalization *campaign*.
推行一場反全球化活動非常具有挑戰性。

appoint a committee 任命委員會

The CEO *appointed a committee* made up of marketing professionals.
這位執行長任命了一個由行銷專家組成的委員會。

chair a committee 擔任委員會主席

It is becoming more common for a woman to *chair an* executive *committee*.
女性擔任執行委員會主席的情況越來越普遍。

create a committee 成立委員會

After a long struggle, the African American activist made the federal government *create a committee* to settle racial conflicts.
經過長期奮鬥，那位非裔美國社運人士促使聯邦政府成立了一個委員會來解決種族衝突。

establish a committee 設立委員會

The Foreign Ministry announced that it would *establish an* international *committee* for peacemaking.
外交部宣布將設立一個促進和平的國際委員會。

form a committee 成立委員會

They voted eight to one to *form a* special *committee* to carry out the investigation.
他們以八比一的票數表決，成立了一個特別委員會來進行調查。

face pressure 面對壓力

Face both internal and external *pressure* to achieve your dream!
要實現夢想，就必須面對內部和外部的壓力！

place pressure 施加壓力

Place pressure on the newspaper by sending a lot of protest e-mails.
透過寄送大量抗議電子郵件來向該報社施壓。

put pressure 施加壓力

Don't *put* too much *pressure* on him.
別給他太大的壓力。

resist pressure 抵抗壓力

The machine was able to *resist* tons of *pressure*.
那台機器能承受數噸的壓力。

fight (in) an election 投入選戰

All of the parties are prepared to *fight in* the presidential *election*.
所有政黨都準備投入總統大選。

hold an election 舉行選舉

Iraq *held an election* to organize an interim government.
伊拉克舉行了一場組建臨時政府的選舉。

win an election 贏得一場選舉

In my local constituency, I *won an election* by only 7 votes.
在我的地方選區，我僅以 7 票之差贏得選舉。

cause a scandal 引發醜聞

His reckless behavior *caused a scandal*.
他的魯莽行為引發了一件醜聞。

reveal a scandal 揭露醜聞

The reporter disappeared after *revealing* the sex *scandal*.
那位記者在揭露這樁性醜聞之後便失蹤了。

spread a scandal 散佈醜聞

People will *spread a scandal*.
人們會讓醜聞散佈開來。

betray a pledge 背棄誓言

He is the last person to *betray a pledge*.
他是最不可能背棄誓言的人。

fulfill a pledge 實現誓言

Do your best to *fulfill your pledge*.
盡你所能去實現你的誓言。

make a pledge 作出承諾

Never *make a pledge* in front of too many people.
絕不要在太多人面前作出承諾。

deliver an address 發表演講/演說

I have never *delivered an address* during my college years.
我在上大學時從未發表過演講。

give an address 發表演講/演說

Lincoln *gave* one of the most famous *addresses* in the world in Gettysburg.
林肯在葛底斯堡發表了世界最著名的演說之一。

make an address 發表演講/演說

The scientist *made a* shocking *address* on the existence of UFOs.
那位科學家發表了一場有關不明飛行物存在的驚人演說。

Politics and Institution

Collocation Exercises

A 請將 List 1 的動詞與 List 2 的名詞做適當的連結，且符合完整句意。

List 1	List 2
won	foreign and international affairs
made	the second election
caused	a bribery scandal
launched	an election pledge
manages	an anti-drug campaign

1. He _____ _____ that he would make everybody happy. But his behavior as a governor made everybody unhappy.

2. The President usually _____ _____ while the vice president handles domestic ones.

3. Clinton _____ _____ and served for a total of 8 years.

4. It is an irony that he _____ _____ last month. He used to be a drug dealer!

5. His greed for money _____ _____ . He took about 1 million dollars from the businessman.

B 在以下句子空格處中選出適當的字詞。

6. I want to deliver _____ like Lincoln or Martin Luther King Jr.
   (a) a great address
   (b) a fierce attack
   (c) accurate judgments
   (d) a formal verdict

7. The prime minister faced _____ from NGOs for his corruption scandal.
   (a) stiff competition
   (b) a severe depression
   (c) a fundamental dilemma
   (d) strong pressure

8. I _____ a vote against the arrogant candidate.
   (a) cast
   (b) had
   (c) obtained
   (d) took

9. When the government has _____ a new policy which raised the cost of power, many people remained skeptical.
   (a) cancelled
   (b) done
   (c) introduced
   (d) told

10. I had to wait until 1960 to _____ an election, which I won by 52 percent.
    (a) vote
    (b) fight
    (c) call
    (d) hold

C 請將以下句子翻譯為英文。

11. 他們成立了一個因應青少年吸菸問題的聯合委員會。

12. 我們必須開發一項嚴格的環保政策。

13. 他違背了承諾且加入了另一方陣營。

14. 他與一名少女約會的事件引發一樁全國性的醜聞。

15. 總統在經濟合作與發展組織（OECD）年度會議上發表了一場專題演講。

Collocations on Liberty and Responsibility

DAY 43

Day-43.mp3

今天我們來探討與自由和責任相關的重要字彙及其搭配用語，例如 obligation（義務）、charges（責任）、blame（指責）、burden（負擔）…等。我們將仔細探討關鍵的 38 個表達用語，包括 fulfill/impose an obligation、admit/deny charges、lay/take blame、remove/place a burden…等搭配詞彙。

Collocation at a Glance

Verb + Noun	Meaning	Verb + Noun	Meaning
have **will**	擁有意志	deny **charges**	否認指控
lack **will**	意志力不足	accept **responsibility**	接受責任
lose **will**	失去意志	take **responsibility**	承擔責任
impose one's **will**	強加意志	deny **responsibility**	否認責任
fulfill **an obligation**	履行義務	place **responsibility**	施加責任
impose **an obligation**	施加義務	assert **a claim**	主張權利（或請求權）
owe **an obligation**	負有義務	lay **a claim**	提出權利主張
bring **charges**	提出指控，追究責任	prove **a claim**	證明權利（或請求權）
press **charges**	提起控訴	withdraw **a claim**	撤回請求權
admit **charges**	承認指控	enjoy **freedom**	享有自由（權）

gain **freedom**	獲得自由（權）	shift **blame**	轉嫁責任
maintain one's **freedom**	保障自由（權）	take **blame**	承擔責任
lose one's **freedom**	失去自由	enjoy **independence**	享受獨立（自主）
deny **an allegation**	否認指控	gain **independence**	獲得獨立（權）
dismiss **an allegation**	駁斥指控	lack **independence**	缺乏獨立性
make **an allegation**	提出指控	carry **a burden**	承受負擔
prove **an allegation**	證實指控	place **a burden**	施加負擔
lay **blame**	歸咎責任	remove **a burden**	解除負擔
put **blame**	施加責任	shift **a burden**	轉嫁負擔

Collocation in Use

have will 擁有意志

See if they *have the will*.
看看他們是否有此意志力。

lack will 意志力不足

He *lacks the will* to do the right thing.
他欠缺做對的事情的意志力。

lose will 失去意志

If I lose my girlfriend, I will *lose* the *will* for life.
如果我失去我的女友,我會失去求生的意志。

impose one's will 強加意志

To win this game, you have to try to *impose your will* on your opponent.
為贏得比賽,你必須試著讓你的意志力強過你的對手。

fulfill an obligation 履行義務

To enter adulthood means to *fulfill* family *obligations*.
進入成年期意味著要去履行家庭的義務。

impose an obligation 施加義務

The regional court *imposed an obligation* to the company to obey the labor law.
地方法院對這家公司施加遵守勞動法令的義務

owe an obligation 負有義務

The multinational company has *owed an obligation* to society to make a donation with no strings attached.
該跨國公司對這社會負有無附帶條件捐獻的義務。

bring charges 提出指控，追究責任

Prosecutors decided to *bring charges* of money laundering against the politician.
檢察官決定起訴該名涉及洗錢案的政客。

press charges 提起控訴

I don't care whether you will *press charges* against me or not.
我不在乎你會不會對我提起控訴。

admit charges 承認指控

After the investigators pressed hard on him, he *admitted* all *charges* of sexual abuse in the end.
在調查人員嚴厲逼問下，他最終承認了所有性侵指控。

deny charges 否認指控

The suspects *denied charges* of racism.
這些疑犯否認種族歧視的指控。

accept responsibility 接受責任

I will *accept* full *responsibility* for any consequences.
我會為一切後果承擔全部責任。

take responsibility 承擔責任

I'll *take responsibility* for my actions.
我會為自己的行為負責。

deny responsibility 否認責任

The leader of the student organization continued to *deny responsibility* for the riot.
學生組織領袖繼續否認應對暴動事件負責。

place responsibility 施加責任

He always *places* his *responsibility* on the shoulders of other people.
他總是將自己的責任施加到他人身上。

assert a claim 主張權利（或請求權）

He *asserted a claim* for damages under the Securities Act.
他根據《證券法》提出了損害賠償要求。

lay a claim 提出權利主張

He *lays* first *claim* to the land which has been wasted until now.
他第一個主張擁有那塊已被荒廢的土地之權利。

prove a claim 證明權利（或請求權）

The evidence appears to *prove* your *claims* at the trial!
證據似乎在審判中證明你的主張是對的！

withdraw a claim 撤回請求權

As the company replaced the defective phone with a new one, she *withdrew the claim* for a refund.
由於公司用新手機取代這款有瑕疵的手機，她撤回了退費的請求。

enjoy freedom 享有自由（權）

All people have the right to *enjoy* religious and political *freedom*.
所有人都有享受宗教和政治自由的權利。

gain freedom 獲得自由（權）

Even if we arrested the terrorist, we wouldn't *gain freedom* from fear of terror.
即使我們逮捕了恐怖分子，也無法擺脫對於恐怖行動的恐懼。

maintain one's freedom 保障自由（權）

This act can't *maintain women's freedom* of choice.
這項法案無法保障女性的選擇自由。

lose one's freedom 失去自由

If you lose trust from others, you will also *lose the freedom* to do whatever you want.
如果你失去了他人的信任，也將失去隨心所欲行事的自由。

deny an allegation 否認指控

Defendants *denied the allegations*.
被告否認了這些指控。

dismiss an allegation 駁斥指控

The politician *dismissed allegations* of corruption as baseless and untrue.
這名政客駁斥貪腐的指控，稱其毫無根據且非事實。

make an allegation 提出指控

The accused *made allegations* of misconduct with regrets.
被告後悔（自己）提出了不當行為的指控。

prove an allegation 證實指控

The investigation has failed to *prove allegations* over his business dealings.
這項調查未能證實他在商業交易中的相關指控。

lay blame 歸咎責任

We should not *lay the blame* on a dead man.
我們不該把責任推到已故之人身上。

put blame 施加責任

Let us *put the blame* where it belongs.
讓我們將責任歸咎於真正該負責的人身上。

shift blame 轉嫁責任

It is completely unethical to *shift blame* to someone else.
將責任轉嫁給他人完全是不道德的事。

take blame 承擔責任

I have the guts to *take the blame*.
我有勇氣承擔這個責任。

enjoy independence 享受獨立（自主）

Under any condition, *enjoy independence* throughout life.
在任何情況下，都要享受獨立自主的人生。

gain independence 獲得獨立（權）

The colonies *gained independence* from the empire.
這些殖民地脫離了這個帝國而取得獨立權。

lack independence 缺乏獨立性

The auditors seemed to *lack independence*.
審計人員似乎缺乏獨立性。

carry a burden 承受負擔

The weakest man *carries* the heaviest *burden*.
最脆弱的人往往肩負著最沉重的負擔。

place a burden 施加負擔

The CEO *placed an* unfair *burden* on his employees.
執行長將不公平的負擔加諸在他的員工身上。

remove a burden 解除負擔

The main economic policy of the Socialist Party in the election is to *remove the burden* of debt from the poor.
社會黨在選舉中的主要經濟政策是解除窮人的債務負擔。

DAY 43

shift a burden 轉嫁負擔

The US, which had rejected the Kyoto Protocol, had the intention to *shift* environmental *burdens* to other countries.
拒絕簽署《京都議定書》的美國意圖將環境負擔轉嫁給其他國家。

Collocation Exercises

A 請將 List 1 的動詞與 List 2 的名詞做適當的連結，且符合完整句意。

List 1	List 2
lay	the allegation
gain	independence
prove	no responsibility
accepted	a claim
impose	his or her will

1. He _____ _____ for that affair. He washed his hands and had nothing to do with it anymore.

2. Demonstrators accused the police of violence and harassment. However, they had no evidence to _____ _____ .

3. In the end, he had no choice but to move away from home in order to _____ _____ from his parents.

4. Nobody can _____ _____ on other people against their wishes.

5. You can _____ _____ to the property. To own it, however, you will have to prove your right in a court of law.

B 在以下句子空格處中選出適當的字詞。

6. We are holding an open debate where you can _____ complete freedom of expression.
   (a) allow
   (b) cost
   (c) enjoy
   (d) reduce

7. "Some people have all the luck," he murmured, _____ the blame for his failure on someone else.
   (a) accepting
   (b) getting
   (c) putting
   (d) escaping

8. Charges have been _____ against the suspects and they will be on trial for drug smuggling.
   (a) brought
   (b) removed
   (c) shared
   (d) shifted

9. I'm not giving up on him, but James doesn't seem to _____ a living will.
   (a) have
   (b) lose
   (c) make
   (d) impose

10. I knew it was me that broke the contract, but I had no courage to _____ full responsibility as well.
    (a) call
    (b) hold
    (c) take
    (d) make

C 請將以下句子翻譯為英文。

11. 母親們總是必須承擔照顧孩子的重擔。她們應該與其丈夫共同承擔才是。

　

12. 那名士兵試圖將責任推到別人身上。

　

13. 你不一定非得參與這場環保運動。我只是為了履行自己的道德義務才這麼做的。

　

14. 約翰強烈否認進口非法藥品的指控。

　

15. 公共衛生管理部門將「解決愛滋病問題的責任」歸於個人，而非政府。

Collocations on

DAY 44

Day-44.mp3

Law

今天要探討的是與法律有關的重要字彙及其常見搭配用法,例如,accusation(指控)、crime(犯罪)、sentence(判決)、witness(目擊)⋯等。搭配詞的部分,我們將深入學習 36 個核心表達用語,幫助您理解與應用,像是 make/face an accusation、commit/report a crime、pass/face a sentence、trace/present a witness⋯等。

Collocation at a Glance

Verb + Noun	Meaning	Verb + Noun	Meaning
establish an alibi	編造不在場證明	drop a case	撤銷案件
have an alibi	有不在場證明	appear before a court	出庭受審
supply an alibi	提供不在場證明	go to court	上法院
deny an accusation	否認指控	preside over a court	主持審判
face an accusation	面對指控	carry out a crime	犯下罪行
level an accusation	提出指控	commit a crime	犯罪
make an accusation	提起控告	report a crime	報案
adjourn a case	延後審理	tackle a crime	調查犯罪
highlight a case	使某案受到矚目	charge a defendant	起訴被告
illustrate a case	解說案例	defend a defendant	為被告辯護

DAY 44

release a defendant	釋放被告	pass a sentence	做出判決
sue a defendant	起訴被告	attend a trial	出席審判
become (a) law	成為法律	halt a trial	中止審判
enforce a law	執行法律	stand trial	受到審判
obey the law	遵守法律	call someone to be a witness	傳喚某人出庭作證
violate a law	違反法律	find a witness	找到目擊證人
appeal against a sentence	對判決提起上訴	trace a witness	追查證人／證物
face a sentence	面對判決	present a witness	出示證物，呈堂供證

Collocation in Use

establish an alibi 編造不在場證明

The accused failed in *establishing an alibi*.
被告無法編造不在場證明。

have an alibi 有不在場證明

I *have an alibi* for his whereabouts.
對於他案發時的所在位置，我有不在場證明。

supply an alibi 提供不在場證明

The lawyer was asked before the trial to *supply a* false *alibi* for the defendant.
律師被要求於審判前為被告提供虛假的不在場證明。

deny an accusation 否認指控

Far from expectations, Mary *denied the accusation* in court.
出乎意料之外的是，瑪麗在法庭上否認了這項指控。

face an accusation 面對指控

The CEO said that he would resign rather than *face an accusation*.
執行長表示，他寧願辭職也不願面對指控。

level an accusation 提出指控

The vice-president strategically *leveled an accusation* at his political enemy.
副總統策略性地對他的政敵提出指控。

make an accusation 提起控告

The civil organization *made an accusation* against a dishonest officer.
這個民間組織對一名不誠實的官員提出控訴。

adjourn a case 延後審理

It is impossible to *adjourn the case*.
這個案件不可能延期審理。

highlight a case 使某案受到矚目

The case was highlighted for its uniqueness.
該案件因其特殊性而受到矚目。

illustrate a case 解說案例

In the meeting, she *illustrated a case* to explain the importance of civil rights.
在會議上，她解說案例來說明公民權的重要性。

drop a case 撤銷案件

He got some pressure from his family members to *drop the case*.
他受到其家人要他撤案的一些壓力。

appear before a court 出庭受審

The defendant *appeared before the court*.
被告出庭受審。

go to court 上法院

I had to *go to court* for a traffic ticket.
我因為一張交通罰單而必須上法庭。

preside over a court 主持審判

Who will *preside over the court*?
誰將主持審判（＝審判長是誰）？

carry out a crime 犯下罪行

The teenagers *carried out a* terrible *crime*.
這群青少年犯下了一起可怕的罪行。

commit a crime 犯罪

He says he didn't *commit a crime*.
他表示自己並未犯罪。

report a crime 報案

The judges are reviewing *reported crimes*.
法官們正在受理已通報的犯罪案件。

tackle a crime 調查犯罪

The police are to *tackle the crime* of an illegal use of another's name on the Internet.
警方將調查網路上非法盜用他人名義的犯罪行為。

charge a defendant 起訴被告

The prosecutor *charged a defendant* with murder in the first degree.
檢察官以一級謀殺的罪名起訴了一名被告。

defend a defendant 為被告辯護

Some states have established a public defender's office, in which lawyers are paid by the state to *defend* poor *defendants*.
某些州設立了公共辯護律師處，律師由國家支付薪資，為貧困被告提供辯護。

release a defendant 釋放被告

The judge *released the defendant* for lack of evidence.
法官因證據不足而釋放了被告。

sue a defendant 起訴被告

The defendant being *sued* was her husband.
遭到起訴的被告是她的丈夫。

become (a) law 成為法律

The custom *became a law*.
這項習俗（後來）成了一條法律。

enforce a law 執行法律

The role of judicature is to *enforce laws* for public safety.
司法機構的角色在於執行法律，維護公共安全。

obey the law 遵守法律

Why do we have to *obey the law*?
為什麼我們必須遵守法律？

violate a law 違反法律

John *violated the law* intentionally because he thought that it favored only employers.
約翰故意違法犯紀，因為他認為這條法律偏袒僱主。

appeal against a sentence 對判決提起上訴

He *appealed against* his two month jail *sentence* for an offense of cruelty to animals.
他對自己因虐待動物罪被判兩個月監禁的判決提起上訴。

face a sentence 面對判決

The man who had killed his parents *faced the sentence* of life in prison.
殺害其雙親的那名男子面臨終身監禁的判決。

pass a sentence 做出判決

The judge is to *pass a sentence* upon the defendant tomorrow.
法官將於明天對被告做出判決。

attend a trial 出席審判

His family *attended his trial*.
他的家人出席了他的審判。

halt a trial 中止審判

The commotion *halted the trial* for a while.
這起騷動事件使得審判中止了一段時間。

stand trial 受到審判

He *stood trial* at the age of 104.
他在 104 歲時受到了審判。

call someone to be a witness 傳喚某人出庭作證

The counsel for the plaintiff *called a boy to be a witness*.
原告律師傳喚了一名男孩出庭作證。

find a witness 找到目擊證人

We were not able to *find a witness*.
我們無法找到目擊證人。

trace a witness 追查證人／證物

The investigator found an unexpected clue while *tracing a witness*.
調查員在追查證人時發現了一個意想不到的線索。

present a witness 出示證物，呈堂供證

A witness was *presented* for the defense.
辯方出示了一件證物。

Collocation Exercises

A 請將 List 1 的動詞與 List 2 的名詞做適當的連結，且符合完整句意。

List 1	List 2
appealed against	the public accusation
charged	the court
faced	juvenile crimes
presided over	the defendant
tackle	the sentence

1. The police are trying to _____ _____ , but they are increasing dramatically.

2. She _____ _____ of life imprisonment. She kept insisting that she was under the influence of drugs when she committed the murder.

3. Judge Kim, who is famous for his progressive view of labor and capital, _____ _____ . People expected a judgment of acquittal on the labor leader.

4. The man _____ _____ of bribery. He handed $20,000 to the lawmaker.

5. The prosecutor _____ _____ with bribery. He denied all the allegations.

B 在以下句子空格處中選出適當的字詞。

6. The prosecution decided to _____ the case for lack of evidence.
   (a) advance   (b) drop
   (c) show   (d) take

7. The case was adjourned to give the investigators more time to _____ a witness.
   (a) catch   (b) make
   (c) see   (d) find

8. The Attorney General said that he would _____ the law at any cost at his inauguration.
   (a) enforce   (b) impose
   (c) require   (d) violate

9. I'm not _____ an accusation, but you should know that I'm not going to let you get my father in trouble.
   (a) taking   (b) making
   (c) saying   (d) putting

10. Mr. Park showed mercy on the criminal, who otherwise would have _____ a life sentence.
    (a) passed   (b) got away from
    (c) pronounced   (d) faced

C 請將以下句子翻譯為英文。

11. 律師無法為被告提出不在場證明。

    _____

12. 就在其中一名證人企圖自殺時，法官中止了這場審判。

13. 他自 14 歲起便犯下了一連串令人髮指的罪行。

14. 我們不希望訴諸法院來解決這個勞資問題。

15. 法官應該對被告做出判決。

Collocations on

DAY 45

Day-45.mp3

Food

今天將學習與食物相關的重要字彙及其搭配用法,例如 drink(飲料)、vegetable（蔬菜）、meat（肉類）、ingredient（食材）…等。我們將深入探討 44 個最常用到的搭配用語,像是 sip/pour a drink、chop/peel a vegetable、grill/roast meat、add/mix an ingredient…等。

Collocation at a Glance

Verb + Noun	Meaning	Verb + Noun	Meaning
slice **cheese**	將起司切成薄片	take **a drink**	喝杯飲料
grate **cheese**	（用磨碎器）磨碎起司	sip **a drink**	小口啜飲
sprinkle (with) **cheese**	撒上起司	pour **a drink**	倒杯飲料
top with **cheese**	在上面放起司	serve **a drink**	提供飲料
clean **fish**	清理魚（去鱗、去腮等）	boil **a vegetable**	煮（或燙）蔬菜
fillet **fish**	將魚肉去骨切片	steam **a vegetable**	蒸青菜
gut **fish**	去除魚內臟	parboil **a vegetable**	將青菜稍微燙一下
grill **fish**	將魚放在烤架上烤	chop **a vegetable**	將蔬菜切碎
steam **fish**	蒸魚	peel **a vegetable**	削蔬菜皮
bake **fish**	烤魚	toss **a salad**	拌沙拉

Food

dress a salad	為沙拉添加醬料	pour an ingredient	倒入食材
serve something with a salad	將某物與沙拉一起端上桌	blend an ingredient	攪拌食材
fry an egg	煎蛋	mix an ingredient	混合食材
boil an egg	煮蛋	stir in an ingredient	將食材放入並攪拌
scramble an egg	煮炒蛋	turn up/down heat	提高／降低火力
beat an egg	將一顆蛋打散	lower heat	將火調小
consume meat	食用肉類	remove something from heat	將某物從火上移開
grill meat	（在烤架上）烤肉	return heat	將火調回（特定程度）
roast meat	（直接在火上）烤肉	adjust heat	調節火侯
stew meat	用小火燉肉	skip a meal	省略一餐
tenderize meat	軟化肉質	serve a meal	提供一餐
add an ingredient	添加食材	snap up a meal	迅速吃完一餐

Collocation in Use

slice cheese 將起司切成薄片

Mom *sliced* a piece of *cheese*.
媽媽切了一片起司。

grate cheese （用磨碎器）磨碎起司

It's time to *grate* some *cheese* for the salad.
該為沙拉磨些起司來用了。

sprinkle (with) cheese 撒上起司

Sprinkle with cheese and if desired, salt.
撒上起司，並視個人口味加些鹽巴。

top with cheese 在上面放起司

Top with cheese to taste.
在上面放些起司嚐看看。

clean fish 清理魚（去鱗、去腮等）

Many people ask her about the best way to *clean fish* with a knife.
很多人問她用刀清理魚的最佳方法。

fillet fish 將魚肉去骨切片

My mother demonstrated to me how to *fillet fish*.
我母親向我示範如何將魚肉去骨切片

gut fish 去除魚內臟

She is *gutting fish* at the sink.
她正在水槽處清除魚內臟。

grill fish 將魚放在烤架上烤

It's hard to *grill fish* outside.
在外面烤魚很困難。

steam fish 蒸魚

For *steaming fish*, turn the heat to medium high.
蒸魚時，將火侯調至中高溫。

bake fish 烤魚

Bake the fish until it's cooked.
將魚烤至熟透為止。

take a drink 喝杯飲料

After a hard workout, he *took a* long *drink* of water.
經過一場激烈的運動後，他喝了很大一口水。

sip a drink 小口啜飲

Mike sits at a bar and *sips a drink* every night.
麥克每天晚上都在酒吧裡坐著，慢慢喝著飲料。

pour a drink 倒杯飲料

After he lost his job, he *poured a drink* as he laughed to himself.
失業後，他一邊倒著酒，一邊自嘲地笑著。

serve a drink 提供飲料

Just *serve* me *a drink*!
給我一杯飲料就好！

boil a vegetable 煮（或燙）蔬菜

Boil a pot of *vegetables*.
煮一鍋蔬菜。

steam a vegetable 蒸青菜

You can also *steam vegetables* in a microwave oven.
你也可以用微波爐蒸煮蔬菜。

parboil a vegetable 將青菜稍微燙一下

Parboil the vegetables and keep aside.
將蔬菜略微燙熟，然後放在一旁備用。

chop a vegetable 將蔬菜切碎

I am busy *chopping vegetables* for dinner.
我正忙著將晚餐要用的蔬菜切碎。

peel a vegetable 削蔬菜皮

Could you *peel the vegetables* as thinly as possible?
你能把蔬菜的皮盡可能削薄些嗎？

toss a salad 拌沙拉

Toss the salad with dressing.
把沙拉和醬料拌在一起。

dress a salad 為沙拉添加醬料

Lightly *dress* each *salad*.
為每一份沙拉加一點點醬料。

serve something with a salad 將某物與沙拉一起端上桌

My parents *served* wine *with a salad* for my fiancé.
我父母為我的未婚夫端上一份搭配沙拉的酒。

fry an egg 煎蛋

She's at the stove, *frying eggs*.
她在爐子前煎蛋。

boil an egg 煮蛋

You couldn't *boil an egg*.
你連蛋都煮不好。

scramble an egg 煮炒蛋

First, *scramble eggs* with smoked bacon.
首先,用煙燻培根來煮炒蛋。

beat an egg 將一顆蛋打散

Beat in the *eggs*, a little at a time.
逐次慢慢地加入蛋液並攪拌均勻。(beat in the eggs 是「把蛋分次加入並攪拌混合」)

consume meat 食用肉類

The French *consume* the *meat* of horses.
法國人會吃馬肉。

grill meat (在烤架上)烤肉

Grill meat over the fire. That's the Korean food, bulgogi.
將肉放在烤架上火烤。那就叫「韓國烤肉(불고기)」。

roast meat (直接在火上)烤肉

Roast the meat for 10 minutes on each side.
將肉的每個面烤 10 分鐘。

stew meat 用小火燉肉

I *stewed meat* with vegetables for a long time.
我將肉和蔬菜一起燉煮了很長一段時間。

tenderize meat 軟化肉質

It's necessary to *tenderize the meat* before cooking it.
在煮肉之前,要先將它弄軟些。

add an ingredient 添加食材

Just *add* the three essential *ingredients*.
只需加入這三樣基本食材即可。

pour an ingredient 倒入食材

I *poured* all the *ingredients* into a blender to mix them.
我把所有食材倒進果汁機中混合。

blend an ingredient 攪拌食材

The cook *blended the ingredients* with ice.
廚師將食材與冰塊一起攪拌。

mix an ingredient 混合食材

The witch is *mixing ingredients* in a cauldron.
女巫正在用一個大鍋子中混合各種食材。

stir in an ingredient 將食材放入並攪拌

Stir in all the *ingredients* except sugar.
除了糖以外,將所有食材攪拌在一起。

turn up/down heat 提高／降低火力

Would you mind if I *turn the heat down*?
你介意我把火調小嗎?

lower heat 將火調小

Lower the heat another 10 degrees before the meat is burned completely.
請將火再調低 10 度,不然肉要完全燒焦了。

remove something from heat 將某物從火上移開

Would you *remove* the pan *from the heat*, and set it aside?
請把平底鍋從火上移開,然後放在一旁好嗎?

return heat 將火調回(特定程度)

Didn't I tell you to *return the heat* to medium?
我不是告訴過你要把火侯調回中度嗎?

DAY 45

adjust heat 調節火侯

Adjust the heat if the pan seems too hot.
如果平底鍋溫度過高，就要調整火侯。

skip a meal 省略一餐

Never *skip a meal*.
千萬不要有一餐沒吃。

serve a meal 省略一餐

Get ready to *serve* your first *meal*.
已準備好要端上您的第一餐了。

snap up a meal 迅速吃完一餐

I was so hungry that I *snapped up a meal* during the intermission of the musical.
我餓壞了，於是在音樂劇的中場休息時很快地吃完一頓飯。

Collocation Exercises

A 請將 List 1 的動詞與 List 2 的名詞做適當的連結，且符合完整句意。

List 1	List 2
blend	cheese
consume	her drink
sipped	all ingredients
skip	meat
sprinkle	your meals

1. The recipe says you have to _____ _____ or any favorite toppings over the salad.

2. Some radical environmentalists rarely _____ _____ . They think eating animals is one of the main causes for pollution.

3. After she _____ _____ , she began to worry about driving. Finally, she called a taxi and went home safely.

4. Don't _____ _____ . Making a presentation is quite energy-consuming and you'll be exhausted very soon.

5. "We don't _____ _____ in this bowl. We need another bowl here," said the cook.

B 在以下句子空格處中選出適當的字詞。

6. According to my experience, _____ the heat is very important in cooking good noodles.
   (a) adjusting   (b) consuming
   (c) making   (d) serving

7. Remember to just _____ the vegetable because boiling them fully can destroy nutrition.
   (a) add   (b) grill
   (c) hold   (d) parboil

8. In this seafood restaurant, we can see the cook _____ and grill the fish in front of us.
   (a) concoct   (b) fillet
   (c) store   (d) weave

9. I was going to _____ the salad without onions, but my mom insisted that I mix it together.
   (a) cook (b) make
   (c) set (d) toss

10. Make sure you don't _____ the eggs too long. I don't like them hard-boiled and rubbery.
    (a) boil (b) burn
    (c) foil (d) warm

C 請將以下句子翻譯為英文。

11. 我要煎蛋還是煮蛋？

12. 他用酒來軟化肉質。

13. 她調拌了沙拉，並為朋友們準備了一些酒。

14. 加些鹹味配料到火雞上。它嘗起來有點無味。

15. 將蔬菜切碎，然後倒入正在沸騰的燉湯中。

Collocations on Health

DAY 46

Day-46.mp3

今天我們要來學習與「健康」有關的重要字彙及其搭配用法，例如 recovery（恢復）、operation（手術）、symptom（症狀）、treatment（治療）…等。我們也將深入探討 34 個基本的表達用語，像是 make/hamper a recovery、have/undergo an operation、exhibit/identify a symptom、have/prescribe a treatment…等相關搭配詞。

Collocation at a Glance

Verb + Noun	Meaning	Verb + Noun	Meaning
give a donation	給予捐贈	develop (an) immunity	產生免疫力
make a donation	進行捐贈	lower (an) immunity	降低免疫力
depend on a donation	仰賴捐贈	make a recovery	恢復，康復
lose blood	失血	speed (up) a recovery	加快復原
shed blood	流血	hamper a recovery	妨礙恢復
smear blood	沾了血	have an operation	接受手術
donate blood	捐血	undergo an operation	進行手術
have (an) immunity	具有免疫力	carry out an operation	動手術
lack (an) immunity	缺乏免疫力	take antibiotics	服用抗生素
build up (an) immunity	建立免疫力	prescribe antibiotics	開立抗生素（處方）

suffer from **cancer**	承受癌症之苦	exhibit **a symptom**	顯現症狀
contract **cancer**	罹癌	aggravate **a symptom**	症狀惡化
diagnose **cancer**	診斷出癌症	identify **a symptom**	辨識症狀
inflict **pain**	施加痛苦	develop **a symptom**	出現症狀
alleviate **pain**	減輕痛苦	have **a treatment**	接受治療
endure **pain**	忍受痛苦	administer **a treatment**	進行治療
groan with **pain**	因痛苦而呻吟	prescribe **a treatment**	開立治療方案

Collocation in Use

give a donation 給予捐贈

Give a donation to victims.
向受害者施予捐贈。

make a donation 進行捐贈

The self-made man *made a donation* to the charity.
這位白手起家的男子向慈善機構做了一點捐贈。

depend on a donation 仰賴捐贈

The asylum for the aged has *depended upon donations* for its operation.
這間老人收容所的運作一直仰賴捐獻。

lose blood 失血

He has *lost* too much *blood*.
他失血過多。

shed blood 流血

Whoever *sheds* a man's *blood* must be punished.
凡殺人者皆須受到懲罰。

smear blood 沾了血

His face was *smeared* with *blood*.
他的臉上沾滿了血跡。

donate blood 捐血

I saw the subtitle on TV reading "Blood type Rh-B is needed." At once, I ran to the hospital to *donate blood*.
我在電視上看到字幕寫著「需 Rh-B 型血」。我立刻跑到醫院去捐血。

have (an) immunity 具有免疫力

They *have* no *immunity* to European diseases.
他們對歐洲疾病沒有免疫力。

lack (an) immunity 缺乏免疫力

The babies *lack immunity* to common illness.
這些嬰兒缺乏一般疾病的免疫力。

build up (an) immunity 建立免疫力

It takes a long time to *build up immunity* after a transplant operation.
在進行器官移植後，需要很長的時間才能建立免疫力。

develop (an) immunity 產生免疫力

You can't *develop an immunity* to food poisoning.
你無法對食物中毒產生免疫力。

lower (an) immunity 降低免疫力

Don't take medications that *lower immunity*.
不要服用會降低免疫力的藥物。

make a recovery 恢復，康復

He is expected to *make a* full *recovery*.
他有望完全康復。

speed (up) a recovery 加快復原

You need more oxygen to *speed up* your *recovery*.
你需要更多氧氣來加速康復。

DAY 46

hamper a recovery 妨礙恢復

The market continues to *hamper an* economic *recovery*.
市場狀況持續阻礙經濟復甦。

have an operation 接受手術

You have to *have an operation* in another country.
你必須到別的國家進行手術。

undergo an operation 進行手術

To survive, he needs to *undergo an operation* within 2 hours.
為了活下去,他必須在兩個小時內進行手術。

carry out an operation 動手術

We *carry out* all *operations* in our building.
我們所有的手術都在我們這大樓內進行。

take antibiotics 服用抗生素

To block this bacteria's reproduction, the infected people need to *take* the strongest *antibiotics*.
為了阻止這種細菌的繁殖,感染者必須服用最強效的抗生素。

prescribe antibiotics 開立抗生素(處方)

The doctor *prescribed* him a shot of *antibiotics*.
醫生給他開了一針抗生素注射劑。

suffer from cancer 承受癌症之苦

She's been *suffering from cancer* for two years.
她已有兩年的癌症病史了。

contract cancer 罹癌

The charitable doctor provided free treatment for the poor who *contracted cancer*.
這位慈善醫生為罹癌的貧困者提供免費治療。

diagnose cancer 診斷出癌症

She was *diagnosed* with breast *cancer*.
她被診斷出罹患乳癌。

inflict pain 施加痛苦

The rascal asked "How can I *inflict* on people as much *pain* as possible?"
那個無賴問道:「我要怎麼樣才能給人們帶來最多痛苦?」

alleviate pain 減輕痛苦

To sleep is the only way to *alleviate* my *pain* and stress.
睡覺是唯一能緩解我疼痛和壓力的方法。

endure pain 忍受痛苦

My ability to *endure pain* reached the limit.
我忍受疼痛的能力已達到極限。

groan with pain 因痛苦而呻吟

While delivering her baby, she yelled and *groaned with pain*.
在分娩過程中,她痛苦地大叫及呻吟。

exhibit a symptom 顯現症狀

They are sick although they may not *exhibit symptoms*.
即使他們可能沒有顯現症狀,但其實還是得病了。

aggravate a symptom 症狀惡化

Stress can *aggravate a symptom*.
壓力會讓症狀更加惡化。

identify a symptom 辨識症狀

The dermatologist *identified the symptoms* of food allergies with a cutting-edge medical appliance.
皮膚科醫生利用最先進的醫療設備辨識出食物過敏的症狀。

develop a symptom 出現症狀

Patients have *developed symptoms*.
患者們已經出現症狀了。

have a treatment 接受治療

I haven't *had a treatment* this year.
我今年還沒有接受過治療。

administer a treatment 進行治療

Physicians *administer treatments* to patients.
醫生為病人進行治療。

prescribe a treatment 開立治療方案

I did my best to *prescribe* the most beneficial *treatments* for you.
我盡力為你開出最有利的治療方案。

Collocation Exercises

A 請將 List 1 的動詞與 List 2 的名詞做適當的連結，且符合完整句意。

List 1	List 2
prescribed	emotional pain
made	a twelve hour operation
contracted	an effective treatment
underwent	lung cancer
inflict	a substantial donation

1. He _____ _____ of 2 million dollars to the charity last year. However, he proved to be a thief last week.

Health   293

2. He knew he had _____ _____ after three years. It was too late.

3. Please keep in mind that your selfish action may _____ _____ on others.

4. The doctor _____ _____ to reduce my smoking. Now I rarely smoke except when I drink.

5. She successfully _____ _____ without any complications. It was truly a miracle.

B 在以下句子空格處中選出適當的字詞。

6. The doctor _____ the symptom as athlete's foot.
   (a) aggravated   (b) developed
   (c) endured   (d) identified

7. Many parents try to protect their children from physical diseases. But I think they should consider it more important that our children develop _____ to immoral behaviors.
   (a) an ailment   (b) a donation
   (c) an immunity   (d) a treatment

8. Brown seaweed is believed to help women to make _____ after deliveries.
   (a) extreme pains   (b) dark bruises
   (c) fast recoveries   (d) inadequate nutrition

9. If you _____ antibiotics improperly, your body will develop antibiotic resistance.
   (a) digest   (b) eat
   (c) prescribe   (d) take

10. I found myself unable to _____ blood due to low blood pressure.
    (a) donate
    (b) give
    (c) offer
    (d) provide

C 請將以下句子翻譯為英文。

11. 每當他服用他的抗生素時，就會變得心情鬱悶。

12. 他救不活了。他失血過多。

13. 過多的壓力會降低你的流感免疫力。

14. 這種藥能加速你康復。但一天不得服用超過兩顆。

15. 我無法相信我的女兒曾接受過毒癮的藥物治療。

Collocations on

DAY 47

Day-47.mp3

Clothing

今天我們來學習與服裝相關的重要字彙及其搭配用法，例如 coat（外套）、shoes（鞋子）、style（風格）、glasses（眼鏡）…等。另外，我們也將深入學習如 button/hang up a coat、lace up/polish shoes、have/prefer a style、put on/adjust glasses …等 42 個最常見的表達用語。

Collocation at a Glance

Verb + Noun	Meaning	Verb + Noun	Meaning
put on **clothes**	穿上衣服	straighten **a skirt**	將裙子拉直
wear **clothes**	穿著衣服	put on **a skirt**	穿上裙子
take off **clothes**	脫下衣服	wear **a skirt**	穿裙子
dry **clothes**	將衣物曬乾／烘乾	lace up **shoes**	綁鞋帶
iron **clothes**	燙衣服	break in **shoes**	讓鞋子合腳
button **a coat**	扣上外套鈕扣	repair **shoes**	修理鞋子
hang up **a coat**	將外套掛起來	resole **shoes**	換鞋底
pull (on) **a coat**	拉緊外套（的衣領）	polish **shoes**	擦亮鞋子
pull down **a skirt**	將裙子往下拉	roll up/down **a sleeve**	捲起／放下袖子
smooth (down) **a skirt**	撫平裙子（的皺摺）	tug at **a sleeve**	拉／扯袖子

DAY 47

have (a) style	有（某種）風格	adjust glasses	調整眼鏡
prefer a style	偏好某種風格	clean glasses	清潔眼鏡
evolve a style	發展某種風格	peer over glasses	透過眼鏡上方凝視
tailor a style	訂製特定風格（的衣服）	don a hat	戴上帽子
copy a style	模仿某種風格	place a hat	放下帽子
drape a cloak	披上披風	tip a hat	舉帽致意
toss a cloak	（輕輕地）甩掉披風	wear a hat	戴著帽子
throw a cloak	拋起披風	fasten a button	扣上鈕扣
wrap a cloak	裹上披風	do up a button	扣好鈕扣
put on glasses	戴上眼鏡	undo a button	解開鈕扣
wear glasses	戴著眼鏡	lose a button	鈕扣掉了

Collocation in Use

put on clothes 穿上衣服

Go *put on* some *clothes*.
去把衣服穿上。

wear clothes 穿著衣服

I *wore* the same *clothes* for two days in a row.
我連續兩天都穿著同樣的衣服。

take off clothes 脫下衣服

Take off your wet *clothes* quickly. You might catch a cold.
快把你濕了的衣服脫掉。你可能會感冒。

dry clothes 將衣物曬乾／烘乾

This house has a yard for *drying clothes*. Let's look around it.
這房子有個曬衣服的院子。我們去看看吧。

iron clothes 燙衣服

My father is *ironing clothes* on the dining table.
我爸爸正在餐桌上燙衣服。

button a coat 扣上外套鈕扣

Today is quite freezing. Don't forget to *button* your *coat* completely before you go out.
今天很冷。出門前別忘了把外套的扣子全都扣好。

hang up a coat 將外套掛起來

The waiter *hung up* the guests' *coats* in the closet.
服務生把客人的外套掛在衣櫃裡。

pull (on) a coat 拉緊外套（的衣領）

With the wind blowing strongly, she *pulled* her *coat* tighter around her.
風吹得很猛,她把外套拉緊裹住自己。

pull down a skirt 將裙子往下拉

She *pulled* her *skirt down* to cover her knees.
她把裙子往下拉,遮住膝蓋。

smooth (down) a skirt 撫平裙子（的皺摺）

Right before the job interview, she *smoothed* her *skirt down* to remove the wrinkles.
就在面試前,她撫平裙子以去除皺摺。

straighten a skirt 將裙子拉直

She stood and *straightened* her *skirt*.
她站了起來,並將裙子拉直。

put on a skirt 穿上裙子

She *put on* the tightest and shortest *skirt*. All the men kept their eyes on her.
她穿上最緊最短的裙子。所有男人都盯著她看。

wear a skirt 穿裙子

She got her brother to *wear a skirt* for fun.
她為了好玩讓她哥哥穿上了裙子。

lace up shoes 綁鞋帶

Lace up your *shoes* firmly.
把你的鞋帶綁緊。

break in shoes 讓鞋子合腳

What is the best way to *break* my *shoes in*?
讓我的鞋子穿得合腳的最好辦法是？

repair shoes 修理鞋子

The rich person hired a man to *repair* and shine his *shoes*.
那位富翁雇人來修補並擦亮他的鞋子。

resole shoes 換鞋底

These *shoes* badly need to be *resoled*.
這些鞋子急需換鞋底。

polish shoes 擦亮鞋子

Let him *polish* the captain's *shoes*.
讓他來擦亮船長的鞋子。

roll up/down a sleeve 捲起／放下袖子

Do you mind *rolling up* your *sleeves*?
你介意把袖子捲起來嗎？

tug at a sleeve 拉／扯袖子

I was aware that the dog was *tugging at* his *sleeve*.
我注意到那隻狗在扯他的袖子。

have (a) style 有（某種）風格

He *has a* completely different *style* of clothing than us.
他的穿衣風格和我們完全不同。

prefer a style 偏好某種風格

He *prefers* the new *styles* in life even if he's conservative in politics.
即使他在政治上是保守派，但在生活中仍偏好新潮的風格。

Clothing

evolve a style 發展某種風格

An artist has every right to *evolve* his *style*.
藝術家有絕對的權利發展自己的風格。

tailor a style 訂製特定風格（的衣服）

The CEO *tailored* his suit *style* to fit the business.
執行長根據商務上的需求訂製了他的西裝風格。

copy a style 模仿某種風格

She intentionally *copied the style* of Italian paintings to draw Europeans' attention.
她故意模仿義大利畫作的風格來吸引歐洲人的注意。

drape a cloak 披上披風

He suddenly appeared with the black *cloak draped* over his shoulders.
他肩上披著一件黑色的披風突然出現。

toss a cloak （輕輕地）甩掉披風

Zorro *tossed* off his *cloak* at the start of a fight.
佐羅在打鬥開始時將他的披風甩掉。

throw a cloak 拋起披風

Throw a cloak over your head before you go out in the snowfall.
外面在降雪，你出門前先將一件披風披在頭上吧。

wrap a cloak 裹上披風

Wrap your *cloak* about you.
用披風裹緊身體。

put on glasses 戴上眼鏡

Whenever reading a book, she *puts on* her *glasses*.
每次看書時，她都會戴上眼鏡。

wear glasses 戴著眼鏡

The minister *wears glasses* whenever he has his photos taken.
部長每次拍照時都戴著眼鏡。

adjust glasses 調整眼鏡

When his political opponent argued against him in the TV debate, he *adjusted* his *glasses* and frowned.
當他的政敵在電視辯論中反駁他時，他調整了一下眼鏡並皺起了眉頭。

clean glasses 清潔眼鏡

Use the red cloth to *clean glasses*. It's cotton flannel.
用那塊紅色布來清潔眼鏡。它是棉絨材質的。

peer over glasses 透過眼鏡上方凝視

He *peered over* his *glasses* and pursed his lips more tightly.
他透過眼鏡的上方凝視，嘴唇抿得更緊了。

don a hat 戴上帽子

All the people have *donned* ludicrous party *hats* and are dancing.
所有人都戴上滑稽的派對帽在跳舞。

place a hat 放下帽子

He *places* his *hat* on a nearby chair.
他把他的帽子放在附近的椅子上。

tip a hat 舉帽致意

He *tipped* his *hat* and smiled. That behavior looked cute to me.
他輕輕舉起帽子並微笑。那舉動在我看來挺可愛的。

wear a hat 戴著帽子

She *wears* straw *hats* in the summertime.
她在夏天會戴草帽。

fasten a button 扣上鈕扣

Fasten the top *button* of the shirt. Otherwise you will look untidy.
把襯衫的最上面那顆鈕扣扣上。否則你會看起來很邋遢。

do up a button 扣好鈕扣

He always straightens his coat and *does up* its *buttons* in front of a mirror before going to work.
他總會在鏡子前整理他的外套,並扣好鈕扣才去上班。

undo a button 解開鈕扣

Because it was so hot, students started *undoing the buttons* of their uniforms.
因為天氣太熱,學生們開始解開他們的制服鈕扣。

lose a button 鈕扣掉了

He *lost* three *buttons* of his vest.
他弄丟了背心上的三顆鈕扣。

Collocation Exercises

A 請將 List 1 的動詞與 List 2 的名詞做適當的連結,且符合完整句意。

List 1	List 2
smoothed down	clothes
drying	my coat
pull	his glasses
tailor	her skirt
peered over	his or her style

DAY 47

1. The wind made me _____ _____ tighter around me. I wished we could have made this trip in the summer instead of February.

2. Windy days are the best for _____ _____ but also a nuisance, as things get blown down onto the lawn.

3. His uncle stopped tapping on the computer keyboard and _____ _____ at me.

4. Although her boyfriend would not be back until this afternoon, she _____ _____ as she hurried out of the drawing room.

5. A good media spokesperson should _____ _____ and the content of his or her material for general audiences, as appropriate.

B 在以下句子空格處中選出適當的字詞。

6. One _____ his sleeves and showed me his number, which was tattooed on his arm.
   (a) placed
   (b) rolled down
   (c) rolled up
   (d) wore

7. As they got closer, one of the men _____ his hat, saying "Good morning."
   (a) draped
   (b) fastened
   (c) held
   (d) tipped

8. He _____ his cloak over his shoulder like a sack.
   (a) buttoned
   (b) laced up
   (c) put on
   (d) tossed

9. The child is now able to _____ buttons without his mother's assistance.
   (a) fasten
   (b) press
   (c) tie
   (d) wear

10. My father used to _____ his leather shoes on a daily basis.
    (a) clean and polish
    (b) paint and decorate
    (c) repair and resole
    (d) wash and dry

C 請將以下句子翻譯為英文。

11. 他解開了那四顆扣住襯衫的鈕扣。

12. 我應該到哪裡去更換我的鞋底？

13. 等我一下，我把濕衣服脫掉。

14. 幾個世紀以來，人們一直都知道不同文化有不同的服裝風格。

15. 照片的左側有一位戴著軟呢帽的貴族。

Collocations on

DAY 48

Day-48.mp3

Weather

今天要探討的是與天氣相關的重要字彙及其搭配詞，如 sun（太陽）、rain（雨）、wind（風）、snow（雪）…等。緊接著我們還要學習 38 個這個領域的搭配用語。例如，the sun rise/set、the rain fall/let up、the wind howl/roar、the snow swirl/thaw…等搭配詞。

Collocation at a Glance

Verb + Noun	Meaning	Verb + Noun	Meaning
sun rise	太陽升起；日出	**lightning** light (up)	閃電照亮
sun set	太陽落下；日落	**ice** form	結冰
sun shine	陽光照耀	**ice** crack	冰裂開
sun come out	太陽露臉	**ice** melt	冰融化
fog lie	霧籠罩	**rain** fall	降雨
fog come down	霧降下	**rain** pour down	傾盆大雨
fog lift	霧散去	**rain** drip down	雨滴落下
lightning flash	閃電閃爍	**rain** come	下雨了
lightning hit	閃電擊中	**rain** let up	雨停歇
lightning strike	閃電劈下	**wind** blow	風吹拂著

Weather

wind sweep	風掃過	**thunder** growl	雷聲低沉地響起
wind howl	風呼嘯	**thunder** shake	雷聲震動
wind roar	風怒吼	**thunder** roll	雷聲低沉地迴盪
wind die down	風平息	**frost** set in	霜降臨
cloud gather	雲聚集	**frost** form	霜形成
cloud break	雲散開	**snow** cover	雪覆蓋
cloud cover	雲遮蔽	**snow** pile up	雪堆積
cloud hang	雲懸掛	**snow** swirl	雪飛舞
thunder boom	雷聲轟鳴	**snow** thaw	雪融化

Collocation in Use

sun rise 太陽升起；日出

The *sun rises* over the river.
太陽在河面上升起。

sun set 太陽落下；日落

The *sun* is *setting* in fast motion.
太陽正快速地落下。

sun shine 陽光照耀

The *sun is shining* overhead.
陽光從頭頂灑下。

sun come out 太陽露臉

The *sun came* back *out*.
太陽又露臉了。

fog lie 霧籠罩

A white *fog lay* heavily on the earth this morning.
今天早上大地籠罩著厚重的白霧。

fog come down 霧降下

I saw the *fog coming down*.
我看到霧降下來了。

fog lift 霧散去

The *fog* has *lifted* and the runways have been cleared.
霧已經散去，跑道已清楚可見。

lightning flash 閃電閃爍

Lightning flashes in the sky.
閃電在天空中閃爍著。

lightning hit 閃電擊中

Lightning hit the nose of the plane.
閃電擊中了飛機的機頭。

lightning strike 閃電劈下

Lightning never *strikes* the same place twice.
閃電從不會在同一個地方劈兩次。

lightning light (up) 閃電照亮

A flash of *lightning lit up* the room.
一道閃電照亮了這房間。

ice form 結冰

In a few weeks *ice* will start to *form*.
幾週後冰就會開始結成。

ice crack 冰裂開

The *ice cracked* at the edge of the lake.
湖邊的冰裂開了。

ice melt 冰融化

The *ice* between them is starting to *melt*.
他們之間的冰點（隔閡）正開始融化了。

rain fall 降雨

When *rain falls*, lightning flashes at times.
下雨時，有時會伴隨著閃電。

rain pour down 傾盆大雨

Tropical *rain pours down*.
熱帶暴雨傾瀉而下。

rain drip down 雨滴落下

The *rain* water *was dripping down* onto the floor.
雨水滴落到地板上。

rain come 下雨了

The *rain came* down on the deck.
雨水打在甲板上。

rain let up 雨停歇

This *rain* is going to *let up* some time soon.
這場雨很快就會停了。

wind blow 風吹拂著

The *wind* is *blowing* our way.
風正朝我們的方向吹來。

wind sweep 風掃過

A cold *wind swept* down from the south.
一陣冷風從南方襲來。

wind howl 風呼嘯

The *wind* is *howling* outside. It's the sign of the tornado's coming.
外面的風呼嘯著。這是龍捲風即將來襲的徵兆。

wind roar 風怒吼

Violent *wind is roaring* through the bridge.
狂風在橋上呼嘯穿過。

wind die down 風平息

It seems like the *wind* has *died down*.
風似乎已經平息了。

cloud gather 雲聚集

Clouds gather in the canyon. It's a spectacle.
雲在峽谷中聚集。這景象真是壯觀。

cloud break 雲散開

The storm *clouds* are *breaking* up.
滾滾雷雲正在消散。

cloud cover 雲遮蔽

Clouds cover the area.
雲層覆蓋著這個地區。

cloud hang 雲懸掛

The *cloud* of smoke *hangs* in the air.
這一團煙霧懸在空中。

thunder boom 雷聲轟鳴

Look at the window as *thunder booms*.
你看窗外，雷聲轟鳴作響。

thunder growl 雷聲低沉地響起

There is *thunder growling*.
那邊傳來了陣陣的悶雷聲。

thunder shake 雷聲震動

Thunder shakes the ground.
雷聲震動了大地。

thunder roll 雷聲低沉地迴盪

Thunder rolls in the distance.
雷聲在遠處低沉地迴盪。

frost set in 霜降臨

The *frost set in* last night.
昨晚降霜了。

frost form 霜形成

Usually *frost forms* on clear, calm nights, especially during early autumn.
通常在晴朗、平靜的夜晚，尤其是初秋時節會出現霜。

snow cover 雪覆蓋

Snow and ice *cover* every surface of the polar region all year round.
雪和冰全年覆蓋著極地的每個角落。

snow pile up 雪堆積

Snow piled up around the houses.
雪堆積在房屋周圍。

snow swirl 雪飛舞

I saw the *snow swirling* around the parking lot.
我看到雪在停車場周圍飛舞著。

snow thaw 雪融化

The *snow thawed* around the edge of the trash can.
雪在垃圾桶邊緣四周融化了。

DAY 48

Collocation Exercises

A 請將 List 1 的動詞與 List 2 的名詞做適當的連結，且符合完整句意。

List 1	List 2
The dense fog	rolled
Frost	lifted
Rain	has formed
Snow	piled up
The thunder	was pouring down

1. _____ _____ half a meter. Children were delighted and grown-ups worried.

2. There is one thing in common about the three murders. _____ _____ when they occurred.

3. _____ _____ as soon as the sun rose. Our journey resumed.

4. _____ _____ . We started to tell every kind of scary ghost story.

5. _____ _____ on the windshield, so I need to scrape it off before I leave for work.

Weather   311

B 在以下句子空格處中選出適當的字詞。

6. I used to like watching the sun rise. But as I grew old, I preferred watching the sun _____ .
   (a) catch   (b) come up
   (c) set   (d) warm

7. The wind _____ and the biggest forest fire of the year stopped spreading.
   (a) blew   (b) died down
   (c) roared   (d) whistled

8. _____ below us began to crack. Everyone panicked.
   (a) The forked lightning   (b) The light frost
   (c) The thin ice   (d) The cold water

9. Today's weather report predicted that lightning might _____ on this area.
   (a) shake   (b) shape
   (c) strike   (d) swirl

10. _____ hang high over mountains.
    (a) Lightning sparks   (b) Roll of thunder
    (c) Storm clouds   (d) Strong winds

C 請將以下句子翻譯為英文。

11. 當閃電劃過窗外時,嬰兒開始哭泣。

12. 烏雲在我頭頂上方聚集了起來。

13. 早晨時,他發現他的後院已經結霜了。

14. 濃霧從山坡上瀰漫而下。我們只能看見自己的手腳。

15. 這場煩人的雨終於停了,且陽光開始灑落。一切彷彿重新復甦。

Collocations on Sports

DAY 49

Day-49.mp3

今天我們來學習與運動相關的關鍵字詞和搭配詞用語，如 opponent（對手）、contest（比賽）、record（紀錄）、score（分數）…等。接著我們將深入學習 28 個核心的表達用語，例如 defeat/face an opponent、hold/run a contest、set/break a record、get/level a score 等。

Collocation at a Glance

Verb + Noun	Meaning	Verb + Noun	Meaning
defeat an opponent	擊敗對手	hold a title	擁有（冠軍）頭銜
face an opponent	面對對手	enter a contest	參加比賽
outwit an opponent	智勝對手	hold a contest	舉辦比賽
play a game	進行比賽	run a contest	負責比賽的運作
win a game	贏得比賽	hold a record	保持紀錄
lose a game	輸掉比賽	set a record	創下紀錄
get a penalty	被判罰	break a record	打破紀錄
give a penalty	祭出懲罰	kick a goal	踢進一球
appeal for a penalty	要求判罰	score a goal	取得進球
defend a title	衛冕／保住（冠軍）頭銜	allow a goal	被對方進球

DAY 49

block a shot	封堵射門	level a score	追平比分
miss a shot	封堵射門失敗	bounce a ball	使球彈跳
get a score	得分	drop a ball	使球掉落
take score	（雙方）比分（是…）	kick a ball	踢球

Collocation in Use

defeat an opponent 擊敗對手

Card games usually require good memory skills to *defeat opponents*.
紙牌遊戲通常需要良好的記憶力才能擊敗對手。

face an opponent 面對對手

You may *face a* strong *opponent* in the coming match.
你可能在即將到來的對抗賽中面對一名強勁的對手。

outwit an opponent 智勝對手

This game requires players to cooperate with partners and *outwit opponents*.
這款遊戲要求玩家與隊友合作才能智勝對手。

play a game 進行比賽

Manchester United *plays a* home *game* this week.
本週曼聯在主場會有一場比賽。

win a game 贏得比賽

We finally *won a game* after long defeats.
在經歷多次失利後，我們終於贏得了一場比賽。

lose a game 輸掉比賽

We didn't *lose the game*; we just ran out of time.
我們並沒有輸掉比賽；我們只是時間不夠。

get a penalty 被判罰

The key player *got a penalty* in an opening match, which will affect the next game.
這名主力球員在首場比賽中被判罰，這將影響下一場比賽。

give a penalty 祭出懲罰

It's natural to *give a penalty* when a foul is committed.
當有犯規情事發生時，自然是要祭出懲罰的。

appeal for a penalty 要求判罰

No foul was called, but the goalkeeper *appealed for a penalty*.
裁判沒有吹哨犯規，但守門員向裁判要求判罰。

defend a title 衛冕／保住（冠軍）頭銜

The golfer *defended* his *title* in this tour.
這名高爾夫球選手在本次巡迴賽中成功衛冕。

hold a title 擁有（冠軍）頭銜

The team *held* the soccer championship *title* until last year.
這支球隊一直保有足球的冠軍頭銜直到去年。

enter a contest 參加比賽

I *enter a contest* not just for participation but for prizes.
我參加比賽不只是為了參與，更是為了贏得獎項。

hold a contest 舉辦比賽

The university *held a* math *contest* for high school students.
這所大學為高中生舉辦了一場數學對抗賽。

run a contest 負責比賽的運作

It requires passion and commitment to *run a contest* successfully.
賽事的運作需要熱情與投入。

hold a record 保持紀錄

In Asia, Lee *holds the record* for most homeruns.
在亞洲，李選手是全壘打紀錄的保持人。

set a record 創下紀錄

The athlete has just *set a* new world *record*.
這位運動員剛剛創下新的世界紀錄。

break a record 打破紀錄

She *broke* the Olympic *record* in the women's 110m hurdles.
她在女子 110 公尺跨欄比賽中打破了奧運紀錄。

kick a goal 踢進一球

He tried to *kick a goal*, but the ball went over the end line.
他試圖將球踢進，但球越過了邊線。

score a goal 取得進球

The hockey player *scored* the winning *goal* for his team.
這名冰球選手為球隊敲進了致勝的一球。

allow a goal 被對方進球

He knew he couldn't *allow* another *goal* for them to take the title.
他知道他不能讓他們再進球了，否則冠軍就沒了。

block a shot 封堵射門

After you *block a shot*, pass the ball immediately to your teammates.
在你封堵對手射門後，立即將球傳給你的隊友。

miss a shot 封堵射門失敗

In defense, he *missed the shot* and his team was allowed an equalizing goal.
在防守時，他沒有擋到一球射門，導致其球隊被攻入追平分。

get a score 得分

Kobe *got* the highest *score* in the game.
柯比在這場比賽中拿下了最高分。

take score （雙方）比分（是…）

His last goal *took* the final *score* to 3-2.
他的最後一球將最終比分定格在 3 比 2。

level a score 追平比分

Park's goal in the second half *leveled the score*.
朴選手在下半場的進球追平了比分。

bounce a ball 使球彈跳

The novice tennis player *bounced the ball* and hit it over the fence.
這位網球新手將球彈起後，一擊將球打出了圍欄。

drop a ball 使球掉落

The pitcher deliberately *dropped the ball* to set up a double-play.
投手故意讓球落地，以策劃一次雙殺守備。

kick a ball 踢球

Carlos *kicks a ball* high and far.
卡洛斯踢出一球又高又遠。

DAY 49

Collocation Exercises

A 請將 List 1 的動詞與 List 2 的名詞做適當的連結，且符合完整句意。

List 1	List 2
enter	a ball
broke	the regional contest
defended	main opponent
kick	the long-standing record
outwitted	title

1. She used to _____ _____ against my wall. She said she would like to be a player like Pele.

2. A total of 24 teams will _____ _____ . Two teams will have the chance to participate in the world match.

3. Michael _____ his _____ , but many people think that he deceived the world.

4. She _____ _____ in the Olympic games. Now she is the fastest woman in the world.

5. She _____ her _____ against her rival in the quiz show. Now, no one can stop her.

B 在以下句子空格處中選出適當的字詞。

6. He _____ the shot and lost the game. It was the most distressing moment in his career.
   (a) caught
   (b) blocked
   (c) missed
   (d) took

7. He _____ the score with his fantastic overhead kick.
   (a) drew
   (b) finished
   (c) leveled
   (d) stopped

8. The goal keeper _____ just 2 goals in 7 games.
   (a) allowed
   (b) hold
   (c) made
   (d) scored

9. The referee didn't give that player _____ despite his obvious foul.
   (a) a chance
   (b) a handicap
   (c) a penalty
   (d) a punishment

10. The national women's handball team fought desperately to _____ the final game but ended up losing it.
    (a) break
    (b) get
    (c) take
    (d) win

C 請將以下句子翻譯為英文。

11. 我的總教練請求判罰，但反而被送了一次犯規。

_____

12. 他輸掉了比賽，也失去了愛情。

13. 他的進球將比分改寫為 3 比 2。整個球場氣氛沸騰。

14. 他創下了韓國的紀錄。現在他的目標是世界紀錄。

15. 我們必須面對世上最難纏的對手 ─ 懶惰。

Collocations on
Travel and Transportation

DAY 50

Day-50.mp3

今天我們要來學習與旅行和交通相關的重要字詞與搭配詞,例如 plane(飛機)、ship(船)、taxi(計程車)、visa(簽證)…等。同時,我們將深入探討 board/get off a plane、ride/mount a bicycle、take/call a taxi、renew/issue a visa…等 34 個核心表達用語。

Collocation at a Glance

Verb + Noun	Meaning	Verb + Noun	Meaning
board a plane	登機	fall off a bicycle	跌落自行車
catch a plane	趕搭飛機	get on/off the bus	上/下公車
get off a plane	下飛機	miss the bus	錯過公車;錯失良機
board a ship	登船	rent a bus	租借公車
come/go aboard a ship	登船	have a stopover	轉機,短暫停留
launch a ship	開船,(使)船隻啟航	make a stopover	轉機,短暫停留
steer a ship	駕駛船隻	need a stopover	需要轉機,需短暫停留
ride a bicycle	騎自行車	go on a pilgrimage	踏上朝聖之旅
mount a bicycle	跨上自行車	make a pilgrimage	前往朝聖
pedal a bicycle	踩自行車踏板	go by taxi	搭計程車過去

DAY 50

take a taxi	搭計程車	use the subway	（常態性）搭地鐵
call a taxi	叫計程車	obtain a visa	取得簽證
get into/out of a taxi	上／下計程車	renew a visa	更新簽證
travel on a train	搭火車旅行	issue a visa	核發簽證
jump on/from a train	跳上／跳下火車	deny a visa	拒發簽證
derail a train	造成火車出軌	act as (a) guide	擔任導遊
take the subway	搭地鐵	be a guide	成為導遊

Collocation in Use

board a plane 登機

She *boarded the plane* for New York without any words.
她一句話也沒說就登上了飛往紐約的班機。

catch a plane 趕搭飛機

I have *a plane* to *catch*.
我得趕搭飛機。

get off a plane 下飛機

First, *get off the plane*, and then wait for the luggage.
首先，從飛機艙出來，然後等待行李。

board a ship 登船

He *boarded* the wrong *ship*.
他上錯了船。

come/go aboard a ship 登船

We finally *went aboard the ship*.
我們終於登上了船。

launch a ship 開船，（使）船隻啟航

The cargo *ship* was *launched* to the International Station.
這艘貨運飛船被送往國際太空站。

steer a ship 駕駛船隻

Anyone can *steer the ship* in calm waters.
任何人都能在風平浪靜的水域駕駛船隻。

ride a bicycle 騎自行車

He *rode the bicycle* to school.
他騎自行車上學。

mount a bicycle 跨上自行車

He *mounted a bicycle* and pedaled 10 kilometers to the airport.
他跨上自行車，騎了 10 公里到機場。

pedal a bicycle 踩自行車踏板

Pedal a bicycle as fast as possible to get there in time!
用最快的速度踩自行車踏板，才能準時到達！

fall off a bicycle 跌落自行車

Chris has *fallen off his bicycle*.
克里斯從他的自行車上跌了下來。

get on/off the bus 上／下公車

When you want to *get off the bus*, ring the bell located above the windows.
當你想下公車時，請按下窗戶上方的鈴。

miss the bus 錯過公車；錯失良機

We regret that there are no refunds for passengers who *miss the bus*.
很抱歉，沒趕上公車的乘客無法退款。

rent a bus 租借公車

How much would it cost to rent a bus for a day?
租一輛公車一天要多少錢？

have a stopover 轉機，短暫停留

I *had an* overnight *stopover* in Bangkok.
我在曼谷轉機時停留了一整夜。

make a stopover 轉機，短暫停留

What about *making a stopover* in Malaysia, then in Thailand?
我們先在馬來西亞轉機停留，然後再去泰國如何？

need a stopover 需要轉機，需短暫停留

Do you *need a stopover* in Hanoi?
你需要在河內轉機嗎？

go on a pilgrimage 踏上朝聖之旅

An array of people *go on a pilgrimage* to the Holy Land.
許多人踏上前往「聖地」的朝聖之旅。

make a pilgrimage 前往朝聖

I hope that I would have the chance to *make a pilgrimage* to Mecca.
我希望有機會去麥加朝聖。

go by taxi 搭計程車過去

It's faster to *go by taxi*.
搭計程車去會更快。

take a taxi 搭計程車

It's the best way to *take a taxi* to get to Central Park.
最好的辦法就是搭計程車去中央公園。

call a taxi 叫計程車

Call us *a taxi*.
幫我們叫一輛計程車。

get into/out of a taxi 上／下計程車

Late for the meeting, Edward *got out of a taxi* and ran across the road.
因為開會要遲到了，愛德華下了計程車後，用跑的穿越了馬路。

travel on a train 搭火車旅行

It's convenient to *travel on* underground *trains* in cities like Seoul.
像是首爾等這些城市裡,搭地鐵旅行很方便。

jump on/from a train 跳上／跳下火車

He *jumped on* the moving *train*, where his girlfriend was boarding.
他跳上了移動中的火車,而他的女友正登上這班列車。

derail a train 造成火車出軌

The 40-car freight *train* was *derailed* in northwest China.
這列由 40 節車廂組成的貨運列車在中國的西北部出軌了。

take the subway 搭地鐵

Traffic is so heavy at this time. Let's *take the subway*.
這個時間交通太壅塞了。我們搭地鐵吧。

use the subway （常態性）搭地鐵

Could you tell me how to *use the subway* in Seoul?
你可以告訴我在首爾要怎麼搭地鐵嗎?

obtain a visa 取得簽證

There are two options to *obtain a* visitor *visa*.
取得觀光客簽證有兩種選擇。

renew a visa 更新簽證

You must *renew* your *visa* every 90 days.
你的簽證必須每 90 天更新一次。

issue a visa 核發簽證

We changed the regulation into *issuing a visa* to a person from India.
我們將規定修改為:可以核發簽證給來自印度的人。

deny a visa 拒發簽證

For national security, we should *deny visas* to the terrorists.
為了國家安全,我們應該拒發簽證給恐怖分子。

act as (a) guide 擔任導遊

She *acted as* his *guide* when he visited New York.
她在他到訪紐約時擔任他的導遊。

be a guide 成為導遊

She *was* his *guide* and helper.
她是他的導遊及助手。

Collocation Exercises

A 請將 List 1 的動詞與 List 2 的名詞做適當的連結，且符合完整句意。

List 1	List 2
acted as	his bicycle
deny	our tour guide
going on	a pilgrimage
pedal	a ship
steer	visas

1. As far as I know, US visa offices in Canada don't _____ _____ to Canadians unless they have some compelling reason to do so.

2. He _____ _____ , but all he did was to provide us with a lot of rip-offs.

3. Studying abroad is like _____ _____ ; it requires great perseverance and a clear objective.

4. To manage a company is to _____ _____ ; you need a lot of experience and wisdom as well as technique.

5. My brother waved to us and started to _____ _____ up the hill.

B 在以下句子空格處中選出適當的字詞。

6. We were thinking about _____ a taxi, but the millionaire rented a helicopter for us.
   (a) boarding   (b) making
   (c) mounting   (d) taking

7. He _____ the train for Nonsan. Praying for his health, his parents saw him off in tears.
   (a) derailed   (b) jumped on
   (c) met off   (d) traced

8. They say, " _____ the subway," but it is very difficult for the disabled to use it.
   (a) Have   (b) Launch
   (c) Make   (d) Use

9. As soon as he heard that his grandfather had passed away, he _____ the first plane home.
   (a) caught   (b) hijacked
   (c) picked up   (d) rode

10. Is there a direct flight? Or does the plane make _____ somewhere?
    (a) a shortcut   (b) a stop
    (c) a stopover   (d) a suspension

C 請將以下句子翻譯為英文。

11. 當警方開始行動時,他們早已登機了。
    _____

12. 我搭地鐵而不搭公車,因為地鐵比較快。
    _____

13. 我們在香港轉機。
    _____

14. 我們今年去日本短期旅行不需要辦簽證。
    _____

15. 我忘不了她說「我想成為你一輩子嚮導」的那一刻。
    _____

Collocations on

DAY 51

Day-51.mp3

Language

今天我們來學習與語言相關的核心字彙及搭配詞，例如 conversation（對話）、comment（評論）、term（術語）、tone（語氣，語調）…等。我們將深入學習 make/open a conversation、have/receive a comment、coin/define a term、take/soften a tone…等 48 個關鍵表達用語。

Collocation at a Glance

Verb + Noun	Meaning	Verb + Noun	Meaning
make (a) conversation	製造對話	understand (a) language	理解某種語言
have a conversation	進行對話，談談	use (a) language	使用某種語言
hold a conversation	維持對話	learn (a) language	學習某種語言
open a conversation	開啟對話	master (a) language	精通某種語言
begin a conversation	開始對話	use a term	使用術語
have a comment	發表評論	define a term	定義術語
draw a comment	引來評論	explain a term	解釋術語
attract a comment	吸引評論	coin a term	創造新術語
receive a comment	收到評論	say a word	說話
speak (a) language	說某種語言	use a word	使用詞語

DAY 51

pronounce a word	發出某字的音	withdraw a statement	撤回聲明
spell a word	拼字	have an accent	（說話）帶有口音
find a word	找字	acquire an accent	習得口音
coin a word	造字（詞）	lose an accent	改掉／矯正口音
deserve a mention	值得提名／表揚	draft a memo	草擬備忘錄
get a mention	獲得提名／表揚	write a memo	撰寫備忘錄
hear a mention	聽說被提及	send (out) a memo	發送備忘錄
make a mention	提及，陳述	receive a memo	收到備忘錄
receive a mention	被提及，受到關注	sign a memo	在備忘錄上簽名
make a statement	發表聲明	adopt a tone	採用某種語氣
issue a statement	發出聲明	take a tone	用某種語氣說話
release a statement	發布聲明	soften one's tone	緩和語氣
give a statement	提供陳述	change one's tone	改變語氣
deny a statement	否認聲明	lower one's tone	降低聲調

Collocation in Use

make (a) conversation 製造對話

The government tried to *make conversation* with the political activists.
政府試圖去製造與政治行動者之間的對話。

have a conversation 進行對話，談談

The movie star *had a* private *conversation* with one of her friends.
那位電影明星與她一位朋友私底下聊了一會兒。

hold a conversation 維持對話

The coach and the players *held a* whispered *conversation* during time-out.
教練和球員在暫停期間低聲交談。

open a conversation 開啟對話

Before *opening a* new line of *conversation*, the discussion panels asked for a break.
在開啟新的討論話題之前，討論會小組們要求休息一下。

begin a conversation 開始對話

Do you always *begin conversations* this way?
你們總是這樣開始對話的嗎？

have a comment 發表評論

We *have* no *comment*.
我們不予置評。

draw a comment 引來評論

The author's novels rarely fail to *draw a comment*.
這位作家的小說幾乎都能引起討論。

attract a comment 吸引評論

In this class, you will meet with controversial topics that may *attract* various *comments*.
在這堂課上，你將接觸到可能吸引各種評論的爭議性話題。

receive a comment 收到評論

Her presentation *received* a sarcastic *comment*.
她的報告收到了一則帶有諷刺意味的評論。

speak a language 說某種語言

I wish you *spoke* my *language*.
我希望你會說我的語言。

understand a language 理解某種語言

Nobody can *understand* every *language* ever spoken.
沒有人能懂所有存在過的語言。

use a language 使用某種語言

Don't ever *use* that kind of *language* again.
別再用那種語言了！

learn a language 學習某種語言

Practice and *learn* foreign *languages* with native speakers via e-mail, text chat or voice chat. We show you how.
透過電子郵件、文字訊息或語音聊天的等方式，與母語人士練習及學習外語。我們會告訴您如何進行。

master a language 精通某種語言

I can *master* any *language* after a matter of days.
我可以在短短幾天之後精通任何語言。

use a term 使用術語

Make sure not to *use* key *terms* loosely, or your paper will sound ambiguous.
務必謹慎使用關鍵術語，否則你的論文會顯得模糊不清。

define a term 定義術語

This news article *defined* sociological *terms* in a broad sense.
這篇新聞報導以廣義的角度定義社會學術語。

explain a term 解釋術語

Did you *explain* that medical *term*?
你解釋過那個醫學術語了嗎？

coin a term 創造新術語

Marx *coined the term* "class struggle."
馬克思創造了「階級鬥爭」這個新詞。

say a word 說話

Don't *say a word*!
別說話！

use a word 使用詞語

Try not to *use* those *words* if possible.
盡量不要使用那些詞語。

pronounce a word 發出某字的音

The baby has just *pronounced the word* "Mom."
那個嬰兒剛剛發出了「媽」這字的音。

spell a word 拼字

Unscramble the letters to *spell a word* using the hint and definition on the right.
利用右側的提示和定義，重新排列字母來拼出一個單字。

find a word 找字

I couldn't *find the word* anywhere!
我怎麼也找不到那個字！

coin a word 造字（詞）

Internet users *coin* a lot of new *words*.
網路使用者創造了許多新的詞彙。

deserve a mention 值得提名／表揚

This creative essay *deserves an* honorable *mention*.
這篇創意論文值得獲榮譽提名。

get a mention 獲得提名／表揚

The college's new scholarship policy *got a* very favorable *mention*.
這所大學新的獎學金規範獲得極高的評價。

hear a mention 聽說被提及

I have never *heard* any *mention* of this matter.
我從未聽說這件事被提到過。

make a mention 提及,陳述

The boy *made* no *mention* of bullying at school and kept silent to his parents.
那個男孩沒有提及在學校遭霸凌,且在他父母面前也保持沉默。

receive a mention 被提及,受到關注

Ten years ago such an incident might have *received a mention* in the newspaper.
十年前,這樣的事件可能會被刊登在報紙上。

make a statement 發表聲明

He is about to *make a statement*.
他即將發表一項聲明。

issue a statement 發出聲明

The health organization recently *issued a* public *statement* on epidemic influenza.
衛生組織最近發布了一則關於流行性感冒的公開聲明。

release a statement 發布聲明

The university officials *released a* confirming *statement* that there would be a tuition increase by 10% next year.
校方代表發布了一項確認聲明,指出明年學費將上漲 10%。

give a statement 提供陳述

The suspects *gave a* prepared *statement* to the police.
嫌疑人向警方提供了一份事先準備好的陳述書。

deny a statement 否認聲明

The scientist *denied the statement* that he manipulated his research.
這名科學家對於他被指操控其研究成果的這項聲明予以否認。

withdraw a statement 撤回聲明

The committee was forced to *withdraw the statement* because of UN opposition.
由於聯合國的反對，該委員會被迫撤回聲明。

have an accent （說話）帶有口音

She *has a* Spanish *accent*.
她說話帶有西班牙口音。

acquire an accent 習得口音

Is it possible to *acquire an* American *accent* with training?
有可能透過訓練來養成美式道地口音嗎？

lose an accent 改掉／矯正口音

Would you like to *lose* your *accent*?
你想矯正你的口音嗎？

draft a memo 草擬備忘錄

Draft a memo to the president.
擬一份給總裁的備忘錄吧。

write a memo 撰寫備忘錄

The poet *writes a memo* as soon as ideas come up.
這位詩人一有靈感就會寫下備忘錄。

send (out) a memo 發送備忘錄

Will you *send out* some *memos* to the personnel division?
你能發送幾份備忘錄給人事部門嗎？

receive a memo 收到備忘錄

I've just *received* your *memo*.
我剛剛收到你的備忘錄。

sign a memo 在備忘錄上簽名

Write, *sign*, and post *the memo*.
撰寫、簽署然後將這份備忘錄發布出去。

adopt a tone 採用某種語氣

He shakes his head and *adopts a* cooler *tone*.
他搖了搖頭，語氣變得冷淡些。

take a tone 用某種語氣說話

Don't *take* that *tone* with me.
別用那種語氣對我說話。

soften one's tone 緩和語氣

He *softens his tone* now.
現在他緩和一下他的語氣。

change one's tone 改變語氣

For a harmonious social relationship, learn to *change your tone*.
為了維持和諧的人際關係，學著改變自己說話的口氣。

lower one's tone 降低聲調

When he has complaints, he *lowers his tone* to a murmur.
當他有抱怨時，他會壓低自己的聲調，然後喃喃自語。

Collocation Exercises

A 請將 List 1 的動詞與 List 2 的名詞做適當的連結，且符合完整句意。

List 1	List 2
acquired	highly critical comments
attracted	her strong accent
coined	a serious conversation
lowered	the term
opened	the tone

1. "This is strictly between you and me." Then, she _____ _____ of the conversation.

2. There was some preliminary small talk about the weather before the executives _____ _____ .

3. The foreigner _____ _____ after moving to the southwest. I found it very difficult to understand.

4. _____ "Neocon" was _____ to refer to a "new-wave" of conservative thought.

5. The event attracted wide press coverage. At the same time, it also _____ _____ from the public.

DAY 51

B 在以下句子空格處中選出適當的字詞。

6. The old man has issued _____ through his attorney, protesting his innocence.
   (a) an alert
   (b) an apology
   (c) a statement
   (d) a threat

7. Humans seem to have inherited the linguistic ability to _____ language.
   (a) add and provide
   (b) avoid and prevent
   (c) conduct and evaluate
   (d) understand and use

8. The principal sent _____ to all teachers saying there would be minor changes in curriculum.
   (a) congratulations
   (b) a memo
   (c) a petition
   (d) a signal

9. I couldn't find any right _____ to say for such a stunning occasion.
   (a) speech
   (b) turn-taking
   (c) utterances
   (d) words

10. Leonardo da Vinci _____ special mention for his contribution to the Renaissance.
    (a) conserves
    (b) deserves
    (c) preserves
    (d) reserves

C 請將以下句子翻譯為英文。

11. 我厭倦了總是得試著找合適的話討好她這件事。

12. 你有聽到任何關於這件事的消息嗎？

13. 我收到教授對我研究論文所給的詳細評語了。

14. 面試時，放鬆自己，並將說話語氣柔化些。

15. 這個中心是學習手語的好地方。

Collocations on Study and Academic Work

DAY 52

Day-52.mp3

今天我們來看看與學習及學術工作相關的核心字詞及其搭配用法，例如 composition（作文）、class（課程）、subject（科目）、degree（學位）…等。接下來我們要認真學習 do/write an essay、drop/take a class、pass/take a subject、gain/receive a degree…等 34 個核心表達用語。

Collocation at a Glance

Verb + Noun	Meaning	Verb + Noun	Meaning
do a composition	做作文作業	read literature	閱讀文學作品
write a composition	寫作文	study literature	研究文學
accept criticism	接受批評	gain a degree	獲得學位
express criticism	表達批評	have a degree	擁有學位
level criticism	猛烈批評	obtain a degree	取得學位
make (a) criticism	發表批評言論	receive a degree	獲頒學位
provoke criticism	引來批評	do an essay	完成論文寫作
do an M.A. /a Ph.D. dissertation	進行碩士／博士論文研究	hand in an essay	繳交論文／作文
prepare an M.A. /a Ph.D. dissertation	準備碩士／博士論文	turn in an essay	繳交論文／作文
write an M.A. /a Ph.D. dissertation	撰寫碩士／博士論文	write an essay	撰寫論文／作文

Study and Academic Work

fail a subject	當掉科目	offer a class	提供課程
pass a subject	通過科目	register for a class	註冊課程
take a subject	修習科目	take a class	修習課程
do (some) writing	做（些）寫作作業	censor a book	審查書籍
improve writing	提升寫作能力	co-author a book	合著書籍
practice writing	練習寫作	plagiarize a book	抄襲書籍
drop a class	退選課程	revise a book	修訂書籍

Collocation in Use

do a composition 做作文作業

I've *done compositions* on such topics as family, work experience, etc.
我做過關於家庭、工作經驗…等主題的作文。

write a composition 寫作文

Applicants for this college have to *write a composition* in entrance examination.
申請這所大學的考生必須在入學考試中寫一篇作文。

accept criticism 接受批評

It is very hard to *accept criticism* from one's own students.
要接受自己學生的批評是件非常困難的事。

express criticism 表達批評

Major world religions *express criticism* at the "money-is-everything" attitude.
世界主要宗教都對「金錢至上」的態度表達批判之意。

level criticism 猛烈批評

National media watchdog groups *leveled criticism* at the yellow journalism of the popular tabloid newspaper.
全國媒體監督組織猛烈批評這家知名小報的黃色新聞。

make (a) criticism 發表批評言論

The minority party has *made* harsh *criticism* at the economic policies of the current regime.
少數黨對現任政權的經濟政策發表了嚴厲的批評。

provoke criticism 引來批評

Socially and environmentally irresponsible business practices worldwide have *provoked* increasing *criticism* for multinational corporations.
全世界關於社會與環境的不負責任商業行為,引來對跨國公司越來越多的批評。

do an M.A. /a Ph.D. dissertation 進行碩士／博士論文研究

She *did* her *Ph.D. dissertation* while doing a part-time job and raising two children.
她在進行博士論文研究的同時,還兼職工作並撫養兩個孩子。

prepare an M.A. /a Ph.D. dissertation 準備碩士／博士論文

He has *prepared* his *M.A. dissertation* for 2 years.
他準備碩士論文已經兩年了。

write an M.A. /a Ph.D. dissertation 撰寫碩士／博士論文

I dare say *writing a dissertation* is as painstaking as giving birth to a child.
我敢說,寫論文的辛苦程度如同生孩子一般。

read literature 閱讀文學作品

They *read* English *literature*. But they don't know anything about Korean literature.
他們讀英國文學。但他們對韓國文學一無所知。

study literature 研究文學

Studying literature is studying human nature.
研究文學就是研究人性。

gain a degree 獲得學位

Is it better to *gain a degree* than to have experiences in teaching?
獲得學位比擁有教學經驗更好嗎？

have a degree 擁有學位

He *has* two *degrees*; one in engineering and the other in physics.
他擁有兩個學位，一個是工程學，另一個是物理學。

obtain a degree 取得學位

It took seven years for me to *obtain* my Ph.D. *degree*.
我花了七年才取得博士學位。

receive a degree 獲頒學位

She *received* her *degree* in Russia.
她在俄羅斯獲頒了學位。

do an essay 完成論文寫作

You should *do an essay* over and over again to be a good writer.
要成為一位優秀的作家，你應該反覆去完成一篇篇的論文寫作。

hand in an essay 繳交論文／作文

College professors have observed growing number of instancesin which students were found to *hand in* ready-made *essays* purchased on-line.
大學教授觀察到，越來越多的學生被發現上網購買現成的論文來繳交。

turn in an essay 繳交論文／作文

Did you *turn in* the mid-term *essay*? It's due today!
你提交期中論文了嗎？今天是截止日期！

write an essay 撰寫論文／作文

I've decided to *write* my final *essay* on global warming and its consequences.
我決定撰寫關於全球暖化及其影響的期末論文。

fail a subject 當掉科目

He could not graduate because he *failed* two *subjects*.
他因為兩門科目被當掉而無法畢業。

pass a subject 通過科目

He *passed* just one *subject* while failing seven subjects.
他只過了一門科目,但卻有七科不及格。

take a subject 修習科目

The maximum number of *subjects* I can *take* this semester is seven.
這個學期我最多能修七個科目。

do (some) writing 做(些)寫作作業

He *does some writing* while listening to the radio.
他一邊聽廣播,一邊做寫作。

improve writing 提升寫作能力

If you want to *improve* your *writing*, write, write, and write again.
如果你想提升寫作能力,就寫、寫、一直寫!

practice writing 練習寫作

The experienced young writer once *practiced* her *writing* by improvising a story into different genres.
這位經驗老道的年輕作家曾藉由將即興故事改編成不同文體的方式來練習寫作。

drop a class 退選課程

He seldom *dropped* his *classes*.
他很少將其選過的課程退掉。

offer a class 提供課程

The company will *offer* some *classes* on auditing and finance.
這家公司將提供一些關於審計與財務的課程。

register for a class 註冊課程

To register for a class, fill out the form below and submit.
如要註冊上課，請填寫下方表格後提交。

take a class 修習課程

Alarge number of students *took a* history *class* covering the Korean War.
許多學生選修了一門涵蓋韓戰的歷史課程。

censor a book 審查書籍

They used to *censor books* in the 70's and 80's.
在 1970 和 1980 年代，他們曾經對書籍進行審查。

co-author a book 合著書籍

Two scientists *co-authored a book* on humor and health.
兩位科學家合著了一本關於幽默與健康的書籍。

plagiarize a book 抄襲書籍

The professor is suspected to have *plagiarized a* Japanese *book*.
這位教授被懷疑抄襲了一本日本書籍。

revise a book 修訂書籍

We will *revise the book* some time soon.
我們計劃近期對這本書進行修訂。

DAY 52

Collocation Exercises

A 請將 List 1 的動詞與 List 2 的名詞做適當的連結，且符合完整句意。

List 1	List 2
dropped	an MA degree
got	bitter criticism
leveled	the class
practiced	doctoral dissertation
prepare	writing

1. I _____ _____ . All the lecturer did was to tell boring and obscene jokes.

2. He was a full-time student in a Ph.D. course. However, because of financial difficulties, he had no choice but to _____ his _____ while making money as a train worker.

3. People _____ _____ at the National Assembly but the stupid politicians were proud of what they did.

4. He's not qualified for this position. He _____ _____ in economics. But we need a person with a Ph.D. in public administration.

5. She _____ _____ every day to be a persuasive writer.

B 在以下句子空格處中選出適當的字詞。

6. They _____ an introductory book for leadership. One explained principles of leadership and the other showed practical examples.
   (a) co-authored　　　　　(b) co-hosted
   (c) combined　　　　　　(d) cooperated

7. Students refused to _____ essays to the professor who had taken the bribe.
   (a) turn out　　　　　　(b) turn in
   (c) turn off　　　　　　(d) turn on

8. You have to write _____ to enter the college of humanity.
   (a) a business contract　　(b) a literary composition
   (c) a political announcement　(d) a technical manual

9. This class helps students _____ from many different genres in a critical manner.
   (a) do research　　　　　(b) make proposals
   (c) read literature　　　　(d) set agendas

10. I _____ the subject by a narrow margin.
    (a) entered　　　　　　(b) instructed
    (c) passed　　　　　　(d) succeded

C 請將以下句子翻譯為英文。

11. 你必須每天練習寫作，才能成為一位具原創性的作家。

_____

12. 他在寫完博士論文後改變了他的主修科系。

13. 我將那門課退掉了，因為它要求太嚴苛了。

14. 聚焦於同性主題的電影很可能會引來保守派影評人的嚴厲批評。

15. 請將你的期末論文繳交至系辦公室。

Collocations on

DAY 53

Day-53.mp3

Art

今天要來看看與藝術相關的核心詞彙與搭配用法，例如 craft（工藝）、artist（藝術家）、painting（繪畫）、sculpture（雕塑）…等。接著我們將深入學習 learn/master a craft、commission/feature an artist、do/hang a painting、create/display a sculpture …等 30 個核心表達用語。

Collocation at a Glance

Verb + Noun	Meaning	Verb + Noun	Meaning
commission **an artist**	委託藝術家（訂製作品）	learn **a craft**	學習手藝
feature **an artist**	以藝術家為主題，專題介紹藝術家	master **a craft**	精通手藝
apply with **a brush**	用畫筆塗抹	perfect **a craft**	使工藝技術完善
use **a brush**	使用畫筆	perform **a dance**	表演舞蹈
wield **a brush**	揮動畫筆	have **a dance**	來跳支舞
be cast in **bronze**	以青銅鑄造	sit out **a dance**	坐著不跳舞
be made in **bronze**	用青銅製作	compose **music**	作曲
mold **clay**	捏塑黏土	listen to **music**	聽音樂
shape **clay**	用黏土塑形	put on **music**	播放音樂
fire **clay**	燒製黏土	put something to **music**	將某事物譜成音樂

DAY 53

do **painting**	畫畫	learn **poetry/a poem** by heart	背誦詩歌
work on **a painting**	繪製一幅畫	memorize **poetry/a poem**	背下詩歌
hang **a painting**	掛上一幅畫	create **a sculpture**	創作雕塑
compose **poetry/a poem**	寫詩，作詩	display **a sculpture**	陳列雕塑
recite **poetry/a poem**	朗誦詩歌	exhibit **a sculpture**	展出雕塑

Collocation in Use

commission an artist 委託藝術家（訂製作品）

The wealthy patron of the art college *commissioned an artist* to draw his portrait.
那位很有錢的藝術學院贊助人委託一位藝術家為他畫肖像。

feature an artist 以藝術家為主題，專題介紹藝術家

The gallery is going to host an exhibition *featuring* major impressionist *artists*.
畫廊即將舉辦一場展覽，主題是介紹重要的印象派藝術家。

apply with a brush 用畫筆塗抹

Only those with a practiced eye can see the painting skill *applied* to the canvas *with* a thin *brush*.
只有具備訓練有素的眼光者，才能看出用細筆在畫布上展現出的繪畫技巧。

use a brush 使用畫筆

He can *use a brush* as skillfully as he uses a pen.
他用畫筆的技巧和用鋼筆一樣純熟。

wield a brush 揮動畫筆

The final step is to *wield a brush* to finish this painting.
最後一步是揮動畫筆完成這幅畫。

be cast in bronze 以青銅鑄造

Today the sculptures of Auguste Rodin have a limited number of replicas *recast in bronze*.
如今奧古斯特・羅丹的雕塑僅有少數以青銅重新鑄造的複製品。

be made in bronze 用青銅製作

In front of the building, there stood a statue *made in bronze*.
在這棟建築物前矗立著一座青銅製成的雕像。

mold clay 捏塑黏土

Children like to *mold clay* and make something unusual.
孩子們喜歡捏黏土,做出一些不尋常的東西。

shape clay 用黏土塑形

Shape clay into anything you want.
把黏土塑造成你想要的任何形狀。

fire clay 燒製黏土

Her hobby is to *fire clay* to make a mug.
她的嗜好是燒製黏土做成馬克杯。

learn a craft 學習手藝

Mom opened a place to *learn a* sewing *craft*.
媽媽開了一個可以學習縫紉手藝的地方。

master a craft 精通手藝

The chef apprentice *mastered* the cooking *craft* in the long run.
那位廚師學徒最終掌握了烹飪手藝。

perfect a craft 使工藝技術完善

I tried hard to *perfect* the wood carving *craft* under the direction of my teacher.
在我的老師指導下,我努力將木雕工藝學得完善。

perform a dance 表演舞蹈

The dancing circle will *perform a* traditional *dance* for the school festival.
舞蹈社將在校慶中表演一段傳統舞蹈。

have a dance 來跳支舞

We *had a* joyful *dance* at the graduation party.
我們在畢業派對上開心地跳了一支舞。

sit out a dance 坐著不跳舞

She was so shy that she *sat out the dance*.
她太害羞了，選擇坐在一旁呆坐著不跳舞。

compose music 作曲

He first attempted to *compose* church *music*, but was not successful.
他第一次嘗試編寫教會音樂，但沒有成功。

listen to music 聽音樂

I tend to *listen to* all kinds of *music* rather than listen selectively.
我傾向於什麼音樂都聽，而不是只挑某一類來聽。

put on music 播放音樂

My brother always *puts on music* when he's alone.
我弟弟一個人的時候總是會放音樂來聽。

put something to music 將某事物譜成音樂

He has talent for *putting* his sentiment *to* jazz *music*.
他具有將其情感融入爵士音樂的天賦。

do painting 畫畫

I *did* some *painting* at home with my family last Sunday.
上週日我和家人在家裡一起畫了些畫。

work on a painting 繪製一幅畫

He has been *working on a painting* for more than 5 years.
他一直在繪製一幅畫作，已經超過五年了。

hang a painting 掛上一幅畫

When seeking a good place to *hang* your *paintings* at home, it's best to avoid humidity and direct sunlight.
在家裡找掛畫的位置時，最好避開潮濕和陽光直射的地方。

compose poetry/a poem 寫詩，作詩

He *composed* a love *poem* for his girlfriend.
他為他的女友作了一首情詩。

recite poetry/a poem 朗誦詩歌

It is worth reading and *reciting* some of the modern *poems*.
有一些現代詩作值得一讀以及朗誦。

learn poetry/a poem by heart 背誦詩歌

It takes too much time to *learn* 19th-century English *poetry by heart*.
背誦 19 世紀的英文詩作太花時間了。

memorize poetry/a poem 背下詩歌

One of my friends *memorizes* hundreds of *poems* from five different countries.
我有個朋友將五個不同國家的數百首詩都背起來了。

create a sculpture 創作雕塑

Her first artwork was *a sculpture created* out of recycled materials.
她的第一件藝術作品是一件用回收材料創作的雕塑。

display a sculpture 陳列雕塑

Several stores in the street *display* huge wood *sculptures* of jang-seung.
那條街上有幾家店面陳列了巨大的木製長生柱雕塑。

DAY 53

exhibit a sculpture 展出雕塑

The curator has planned to *exhibit* a collection of the Renaissance *sculptures*.
策展人已規劃好展出一系列文藝復興時期的雕塑作品。

Collocation Exercises

A 請將 List 1 的動詞與 List 2 的名詞做適當的連結,且符合完整句意。

List 1	List 2
creates	the clay
molded	the traditional dance
put on	sweet music
performed	several paintings
work on	monumental sculptures

1. She _____ _____ for me. It was reminiscent of my childhood.

2. She _____ _____ while her husband played the drums. Their perfect harmony caught many passengers' attention.

3. He is going to _____ _____ of mothers with babies. He has been interested in expressing maternal love.

4. She _____ _____ into the shape of a boy. In fact, she had lost her only son in a tragic car accident.

5. The artist _____ _____ out of recycled materials and discarded electronic goods.

B 在以下句子空格處中選出適當的字詞。

6. She has baked pottery for more than 7 years to _____ the craft.
   (a) acquire   (b) master
   (c) skip   (d) transfer

7. The exhibition _____ various artists from art photographers to action artists.
   (a) commissions   (b) carries
   (c) features   (d) proposes

8. He _____ the oil paint with a Korean traditional brush usually used for calligraphy.
   (a) applied   (b) enameled
   (c) plastered   (d) varnished

9. The king ordered to have his statues _____ bronze.
   (a) applied to   (b) cast in
   (c) founded in   (d) minted in

10. The course requirement includes _____ a poem in front of the class.
    (a) reciting   (b) recollecting
    (c) reflecting   (d) resolving

C 請將以下句子翻譯為英文。

11. 那座士兵雕像是以青銅鑄造而成,高度約為十公尺。

12. 卡蘿畫了幾幅她自己的肖像。每一幅都展現了她身分的不同面向。

13. 那位老師希望學生能背誦詩作,因為他相信文學能帶來快樂與性情的穩定。

14. 越來越多人選擇學習書籍工藝,既作為興趣,也具實用目的。

15. 我寧可用滾筒來粉刷牆壁,而不用刷子。

Collocations on Feelings

DAY 54

Day-54.mp3

今天要來學習與情感相關的核心字詞及其搭配用語，例如 anger（憤怒）、embarrassment（尷尬）、surprise（驚訝）、hatred（憎恨）…等。我們將進一步學習像是 control/fuel one's anger、cover/relieve one's embarrassment、have/show surprise、bring/find happiness…等 38 個核心的表達用語。

Collocation at a Glance

Verb + Noun	Meaning	Verb + Noun	Meaning
control one's **anger**	控制某人的憤怒	overcome **fear**	克服恐懼
fuel someone's **anger**	激起某人的怒火	be filled with **happiness**	充滿幸福感
show one's **anger**	表現出憤怒	bring **happiness**	帶來快樂
tremble with **anger**	氣得發抖	cry with **happiness**	高興地流下眼淚
blush with **embarrassment**	因尷尬而臉紅	find **happiness**	找到幸福
cover one's **embarrassment**	掩飾尷尬	seek **happiness**	追求幸福
relieve someone's **embarrassment**	減輕某人的尷尬	be filled with **hatred**	充滿憎恨
save oneself from **embarrassment**	讓自己避免尷尬	burn with **hatred**	怒火中燒
experience **fear**	經歷恐懼	arouse **jealousy**	引起嫉妒
instill **fear**	激起恐懼	cause **jealousy**	導致嫉妒

DAY 54

feel **jealousy**	感到嫉妒	take **pride**	感到驕傲
declare one's **love**	宣示愛意	be tinged with **sadness**	帶著一絲哀傷
fall in **love**	墜入愛河	bring **sadness**	帶來悲傷
feel **love**	感受到愛	feel **sadness**	感受到悲傷
return **love**	回應愛意	show **sadness**	表現出哀傷
seek **love**	尋求愛	feign **surprise**	假裝驚訝
hurt someone's **pride**	傷害某人的自尊	have **surprise**	感到驚訝
restore (one's) **pride**	重拾榮耀	hide **surprise**	隱藏驚訝
swell with **pride**	充滿自豪	show **surprise**	表現出驚訝

Collocation in Use

control one's anger 控制某人的憤怒

Though the boys kept on making fun of her appearance, she managed to *control her anger*.
儘管那些男孩不停地取笑她的外貌，她仍設法控制自己的憤怒。

fuel someone's anger 激起某人的怒火

It's not a good idea to *fuel Daddy's anger* by telling a lie.
說謊會激起爸爸的怒火，這不是個好主意。

show one's anger 表現出憤怒

He *showed his anger* with his writing.
他用寫的來表達他的憤怒。

tremble with anger 氣得發抖

When she came to know that her husband had been murdered, she *trembled with* bitter *anger* and sorrow all day long.
當她得知丈夫早已被謀殺時，她一整天都在極度憤怒與悲傷中顫抖著。

blush with embarrassment 因尷尬而臉紅

When asked to sing a song, the shy guy *blushed with embarrassment* and hesitated for a moment.

當被要求唱一首歌時，那害羞的男生因為尷尬而臉紅，並猶豫了一下。

cover one's embarrassment 掩飾尷尬

I noticed that he tried to *cover his embarrassment* by coughing.
我注意到他試圖以咳嗽來掩飾自己的尷尬。

relieve someone's embarrassment 減輕某人的尷尬

His appearance *relieved my embarrassment*.
他的出現緩解了我的尷尬。

save oneself from embarrassment 讓自己避免尷尬

She *saved herself from embarrassment* by cracking jokes.
她以說笑話的方式來化解自己的尷尬。

experience fear 經歷恐懼

The only survivor from the coal mine collapse last Monday *experienced* terrible *fear* in the darkness.
上週煤礦坍塌事故中的唯一倖存者在黑暗中經歷了極度的恐懼。

instill fear 激起恐懼

Hackneyed horror movie techniques are hardly successful *to instill fear*.
老套的恐怖電影手法幾乎無法成功地激起觀眾的恐懼感。

overcome fear 克服恐懼

She *overcame fear* with faith in God.
她憑藉對上帝的信仰戰勝了恐懼。

be filled with happiness 充滿幸福感

Newly-married couples always seem to *be filled with happiness* and joy.
新婚夫婦似乎總是洋溢著幸福與喜悅。

bring happiness 帶來快樂

The baby's birth *brought* great *happiness* to him.
寶寶的誕生給他帶來了極大的快樂。

DAY 54

cry with happiness 高興地流下眼淚

The moment firefighters rescued the baby, the entire family started to *cry with happiness* and relief.
當消防員救出嬰兒的那一刻，所有家人開始流下幸福與安心的淚水。

find happiness 找到幸福

Modern people busy with their work hardly *find happiness* in a simple life.
現代人忙於工作，很難在簡單生活中找到幸福。

seek happiness 追求幸福

If you *seek happiness* for yourself, it will always elude you. If you *seek happiness* for others, you will find it for yourself.
如果你只為了自己追求幸福，它將永遠與你擦肩而過。如果你為他人尋求幸福，你也會因此獲得幸福。

be filled with hatred 充滿憎恨

During the revolution the city *was filled with hatred* and hostility, which led to the bloody massacre by police against civilians.
革命期間，這城市充滿了仇恨與敵意，同時導致警方對平民的血腥鎮壓。

burn with hatred 怒火中燒

When he found his daughter kidnapped, he *burned with hatred* and started to scream.
當發現女兒被綁架時，他怒火中燒並開始尖叫。

arouse jealousy 引起嫉妒

Her new boyfriend *aroused jealousy* in her ex-boyfriend.
她的新男友引起了她前男友的嫉妒。

cause jealousy 導致嫉妒

Jealousy between siblings is often *caused* by parents' partiality for one child over another.
兄弟姊妹之間的嫉妒往往肇因於父母偏愛某個孩子甚過另一個。

feel jealousy 感到嫉妒

True friends *feel* no *jealousy* towards each other.
真正的朋友彼此之間不會有嫉妒心。

declare one's love 宣示愛意

The Hollywood movie star openly *declared his love* for a young actress.
那位好萊塢電影明星公開宣示他對一位年輕女演員的愛意。

fall in love 墜入愛河

How dare she *fall in love* with a millionaire, who always keeps talking about true love?
她如何敢愛上一個老是談論真愛的富翁？

feel love 感受到愛

Who on earth will *feel* warm *love* beyond his cold appearance?
究竟會有誰能感受到他冷漠外表下那溫暖的愛呢？

return love 回應愛意

She broke up with me over the phone and I got depressed. I don't know how to *return* her *love*.
她在電話中和我分手，讓我感到很沮喪。我不知道該如何回應她這份愛。

seek love 尋求愛

Seek love and peace, not hatred and competition.
尋求愛與和平，而非仇恨與競爭。

hurt someone's pride 傷害某人的自尊

She looked down on me and treated me badly. That really *hurt my pride*.
她瞧不起我，並且對我態度惡劣。那真的傷了我的自尊。

restore (one's) pride 重拾榮耀

The National Soccer team seeks to *restore its pride* with Saturday's game against Japan.
國家足球隊希望透過週六對日本的比賽來重拾榮耀。

swell with pride 充滿自豪

Her heart *swelled with pride* while watching her son's piano concert.
在觀看兒子的鋼琴演奏會時,她的內心充滿了自豪感。

take pride 感到驕傲

Parents need to encourage their children to *take pride* in themselves and to focus on their success rather than failure.
父母應鼓勵孩子為自己感到驕傲,並將重點擺在成功,而非失敗的事。

be tinged with sadness 帶著一絲哀傷

The final lecture *was tinged with sadness*, but the professor asked his students to go on learning.
最後一堂課雖然帶著些許哀傷,但教授仍要求其學生繼續學習。

bring sadness 帶來悲傷

His death *brought* deep *sadness* to her.
他的去世給她帶來深切的悲傷。

feel sadness 感受到悲傷

They could *feel the sadness* his illness brought to the family.
他們能感受到他生病所帶給這個家庭的悲傷。

show sadness 表現出哀傷

The movie *shows the sadness* of unrequited love.
這部電影呈現出單戀的哀傷。

feign surprise 假裝驚訝

The man *feigned surprise* and shock at the police investigation and said that he had known nothing about the crime.
那名男子在警方調查時裝作驚訝與震驚的樣子,並聲稱他對這起犯罪案件一無所知。

have surprise 感到驚訝

I *had* a lovely *surprise* this morning when I received the admission notice from the medical school.
今天早上我收到醫學院的錄取通知，這讓我感到非常驚喜。

hide surprise 隱藏驚訝

My mother *hid* her *surprise* at my strong response.
媽媽隱藏了她對我強烈反應的驚訝。

show surprise 表現出驚訝

My girlfriend *showed* a pleasant *surprise* to the birthday gift.
我的女友對這份生日禮物面露驚喜。

Collocation Exercises

A 請將 List 1 的動詞與 List 2 的名詞做適當的連結，且符合完整句意。

List 1	List 2
cried with	the anger
was filled with	happiness
feigned	hatred
fueled	surprise
was tinged with	sadness

1. The city pushed ahead with the plan to demolish the old buildings, and it _____ _____ of the villagers.

2. The boy _____ _____ when he found the gift under the Christmas tree. In fact, he saw his parents put it there secretly last night.

DAY 54

3. She _____ _____ when she was declared innocent. Seven years had passed since her case started.

4. He _____ _____ for organized crimes. But he couldn't do anything about it.

5. Our party _____ _____. We won the championship but two of our players were seriously hurt.

B 在以下句子空格處中選出適當的字詞。

6. I don't feel _____ for rich people. However, I really envy intelligent people.
   (a) accomplishment (b) curiosity
   (c) jealousy (d) self-respect

7. She _____ with embarrassment when asked to sing a song in front of her congratulators.
   (a) blushed (b) cried
   (c) swelled (d) trembled

8. The memory of the accident _____ a deep fear of being alone in his mind.
   (a) disappeared (b) instilled
   (c) sat (d) survived

9. The president revealed that he _____ love with a famous fashion model. The next concern of the people was whether or not he would marry her.
   (a) brought (b) caused
   (d) declared (d) fell in

10. In spite of the recent fact that English is widely spread and used in France, French people have _____ pride in their national language, French.
    (a) made   (b) hurt
    (c) restored   (d) taken

C 請將以下句子翻譯為英文。

11. 她想從他身上找到愛，然而他給她的卻只有痛苦與遺憾。

12. 當那位女演員獲得「年度最佳女演員」獎時，她內心充滿了自豪。

13. 雖然他怒火中燒，但他說話的語氣卻低沉緩慢。

14. 這場災難的倖存者聚在一起共同克服對死亡的恐懼。

15. 那幅將穆罕默德先知描繪成恐怖分子的丹麥漫畫，引發了穆斯林世界遍野的怒潮。

Collocations on Interest and Concern

DAY 55

Day-55.mp3

今天我們將探討與興趣及關注事項有關的核心字彙，例如 attention（注意）、concern（關心、憂慮）、curiosity（好奇心）、expectation（期待）…等，以及它們的搭配用語。我們將仔細學習如 pay/draw attention、have/raise a concern、meet/realize expectations …等 36 個核心表達方式。

Collocation at a Glance

Verb + Noun	Meaning	Verb + Noun	Meaning
show **interest**	表現出興趣	disturb someone's **concentration**	干擾某人的專注力
take **interest**	有興趣	have (an) **appeal**	具有吸引力
lose **interest**	失去興趣	lose (an) **appeal**	失去吸引力
arouse **interest**	引起興趣	make (an) **appeal**	提出呼籲／上訴
have an **awareness**	有認知	widen (an) **appeal**	擴大呼籲／吸引力
increase **awareness**	提升認知	have **curiosity**	有好奇心
heighten **awareness**	加深認知	arouse someone's **curiosity**	激起某人的好奇心
require **concentration**	需要專注	satisfy someone's **curiosity**	滿足某人的好奇心
lose one's **concentration**	失去專注力	pay **attention**	注意
break someone's **concentration**	打斷某人的專注力	draw **attention**	吸引注意

require **attention**	要求注意，需要關注	realize **expectations**	實現期待
get **attention**	獲得關注	have **regard**	懷有顧念
have a **concern**	有點擔心	pay **regard**	給予關注
show **concern**	表現出憂慮／關懷	give **regard**	給予關注／問候
raise a **concern**	引起疑慮	take **care**	照顧
appreciate someone's **concern**	感謝某人的關心	provide **care**	提供照護
have **expectations**	有期待	need **care**	需要照護
meet **expectations**	達成期待	receive **care**	接受照護

Collocation in Use

show interest 表現出興趣

She's never *shown* any *interest* in you.
她從未對你表現出任何興趣。

take interest 有興趣

Why do we *take* so much *interest* in celebrities' lives?
為什麼我們對名人的生活這麼感興趣？

lose interest 失去興趣

He'll *lose interest* in a day or two.
他過一兩天就沒興趣了。

arouse interest 引起興趣

The TV lottery show for the biggest jackpot prize ever *aroused* national *interest*.
這個有史以來最大獎金的電視樂透節目引起了全國人民的關注。

have an awareness 有認知

The newly elected leader of the country seems to *have* greater *awareness* of religious conflicts between Islam and Christianity.
這位新當選的國家領導人似乎對伊斯蘭教與基督教之間的宗教衝突有更深的認識。

increase awareness 提升認知

The government aims to *increase* public *awareness* about the new disability employment policy.
政府致力於提升民眾對於這項新的殘障人士就業政策的認知。

heighten awareness 加深認知

African countries have made attempts to *heighten* HIV/AIDS *awareness* among young people.
非洲國家一直試圖提高年輕人對愛滋病的認知。

require concentration 需要專注

Test-taking *requires* a great deal of *concentration*.
考試時需要高度的專注力。

lose one's concentration 失去專注力

The pretty girl made him *lose his concentration* for a moment.
那位漂亮的女孩讓他一時失去了專注力。

break someone's concentration 打斷某人的專注力

The loud laughter *broke* the silence and *everyone's concentration*.
這大聲的一笑打破了寂靜，也打斷了大家的專注力。

disturb someone's concentration 干擾某人的專注力

A painful emotion may *disturb your concentration*.
痛苦的情緒可能會干擾你的專注力。

have (an) appeal 具有吸引力

The efforts may *have* some *appeal* after all.
這些努力或許最終能展現些許的吸引力。

lose (an) appeal 失去吸引力

The politician *lost* his popular *appeal* to middle-class working families because he failed to address the needs and concerns of them.
這位政治人物因未能解決中產階級勞工家庭的需求與關切，失去了在他們心中的魅力。

make (an) appeal 提出呼籲／上訴

Several religious leaders *made appeals* to the court on behalf of their religious organization to ban the development and destruction of human embryos for medical research.
幾位宗教領袖代表其宗教組織呼籲法院應禁止為醫學研究而開發與銷毀人類胚胎。

widen (an) appeal 擴大呼籲／吸引力

The rural areas that suffered severe devastation from heavy snows this winter *widened appeal* to the public for help.
今年冬天因暴雪遭重創的鄉村地區擴大呼籲民眾給予協助。

have curiosity 有好奇心

This cat appears to *have* no *curiosity* about things around it.
這隻貓對周遭事物似乎沒有好奇心。

arouse someone's curiosity 激起某人的好奇心

Mother's pregnancy often *arouses a child's* excessive *curiosity*.
母親懷孕常會引起孩子過度的好奇。

satisfy someone's curiosity 滿足某人的好奇心

The answer did not *satisfy my curiosity*.
這個答案無法滿足我的好奇心。

pay attention 注意

You'd better *pay attention* to more urgent matters.
你最好把注意力放在更緊急的事情上。

draw attention 吸引注意

The noise *drew the attention* of the soldiers.
那噪音吸引了士兵們的注意。

require attention 要求注意，需要關注

Handling employee conflicts is a matter *requiring* full *attention*.
處理員工之間的衝突是一件需要全神貫注的事情。

DAY 55

get attention 獲得關注

As he came to be known as a prince of a small country, he *got* unwanted *attention*.
當他被認為是某個小國的王子時,引來了他不想要的關注。

have a concern 有點擔心

I *have a concern* about the plane.
我對這架飛機有些擔心。

show concern 表現出憂慮/關懷

Her eyes *showed* deep *concern* for the hungry child.
她的眼神流露出對那個飢餓孩子深切的關懷。

raise a concern 引起疑慮

An acute problem of computer systems *raised* safety *concerns*.
一個電腦方面的嚴重問題引發了安全上的疑慮。

appreciate someone's concern 感謝某人的關心

I *appreciate your concern*.
我很感謝你的關心。

have expectations 有期待

He *has* high *expectations* of himself.
他對自己有很高的期望。

meet expectations 達成期待

I guess I couldn't *meet* their *expectations*.
我想我沒辦法達到他們的期望。

realize expectations 實現期待

She at last *realized* her father's *expectation*, but it was far different from what she was thinking about.
她最後終於實現了她父親的期望,但那與她原本所想的有很大不同。

have regard 懷有顧念

She *has* no *regard* for anyone else.
她對任何人毫無顧念。

pay regard 給予關注

He never *pays regard* to another's need other than his own family.
他從不顧及別人的需要,除了自己家人之外。

give regard 給予關注／問候

Please *give* him my best *regards*.
請代我向他致上最誠摯的問候。

take care 照顧

I'll give you tips that help *take care* of your skin and keep it clean.
我會給你一些肌膚保養及保持潔淨的小秘訣。

provide care 提供照護

This nursing home *provides* long-term *care* for elderly people.
這間護理之家為年長者提供長期照護。

need care 需要照護

Sick newborn babies *need* intensive *care*.
生病的新生兒需要加強照顧。

receive care 接受照護

Patients should *receive* appropriate *care* while in the hospital.
病人在住院期間應受到適當的照護。

DAY 55

Collocation Exercises

A 請將 List 1 的動詞與 List 2 的名詞做適當的連結，且符合完整句意。

List 1	List 2
aroused	awareness
increased	its appeal
raising	excessive care
take	public concern
widened	my curiosity

1. His restless behavior just _____ _____.

2. The conflict over territories has _____ _____ of the issue in both countries.

3. The website has _____ _____ due to its successful makeover of design and layout last year.

4. The union of pilots will begin a general strike after the government takes action, _____ _____ of an unprecedented major transportation disruption.

5. According to a survey, teenagers tend to _____ _____ of their appearance.

B 在以下句子空格處中選出適當的字詞。

6. Teachers often worry about their lack of experience in making students _____ more attention to the class.
   (a) consume
   (b) hold
   (c) pay
   (d) show

7. I _____ your concern and effort to talk about the issue of war with children.
   (a) appreciate
   (b) feel
   (c) have
   (d) win

8. Public welfare policies should _____ proper regard to the needs of social minorities.
   (a) meet
   (b) pay
   (c) satisfy
   (d) seek

9. My teacher's monotonous voice made me _____ my concentration and fall asleep.
   (a) break
   (b) disturb
   (c) lose
   (d) require

10. Those who _____ high expectations of a business boom tend to invest their money into stocks.
    (a) have
    (b) meet
    (c) take
    (d) watch

C 請將以下句子翻譯為英文。

11. 當年幼的孩童在看電視時,他們會對廣告表現極大的興趣。

12. 駕車時需要高度的專注力,尤其在天候不佳時。

13. 儘管他極盡努力,仍未能達到所有人的期望。

14. 傳統的英語教室致力於提升學生的文法以及英語精確用法的認知。

15. 年幼的孩童通常一次只能專注於一件事情。

Collocations on

DAY 56

Day-56.mp3

Values and Ideals

今天我們來看看與價值及理想有關的核心字彙與搭配詞，例如 fame（名聲）、justice（正義）、honor（榮譽）、ideal（理想）…等。我們將仔細學習 achieve/enjoy fame、do/get justice、have/defend honor、achieve/attain ideal …等 44 個核心表達用語。

Collocation at a Glance

Verb + Noun	Meaning	Verb + Noun	Meaning
achieve **fame**	獲得名聲	bring **shame**	帶來恥辱
enjoy **fame**	享有名聲	cause **shame**	造成羞愧
seek **fame**	追求名聲	feel **shame**	感到羞愧
win **fame**	贏得名聲	earn **respect**	贏得尊敬
do **justice**	公平對待，如實呈現	feel **respect**	（在心中）滿懷敬意
get **justice**	受到公正對待	gain **respect**	獲得尊重
want **justice**	想要公平正義	have **respect**	心存敬意
defend one's **honor**	捍衛名譽	hold **respect**	抱持著敬意
have **honor**	擁有榮譽，感到光榮	lose **respect**	失去尊重
restore one's **honor**	挽回名譽	win **respect**	贏得尊重

DAY 56

abandon **an ideal**	放棄理想	state **a belief**	陳述信念
achieve **an ideal**	實現理想	break **a promise**	違背承諾
attain **an ideal**	達成理想	fulfill **a promise**	實現承諾
betray **an ideal**	背叛理想	keep **a promise**	遵守承諾
pursue **an ideal**	追求理想	make **a promise**	做出承諾
support **an ideal**	支持理想	deserve **credit**	值得稱讚，值得信賴
assert **a belief**	主張信仰	get **credit**	獲得讚譽
express **a belief**	表達信念	give **credit**	給予信譽，標示出處
follow **a belief**	奉行信念／信仰	take **credit**	攬下功勞
have **a belief**	擁有信念／信仰	follow **an example**	效法榜樣
hold **a belief**	堅守信念／信仰	set **an example**	樹立典範
share **a belief**	共有信念／信仰	show **an example**	以身作則

Collocation in Use

achieve fame 獲得名聲

The historian *achieved fame* and recognition in his field.
這位歷史學家在其領域中獲得了名聲與肯定。

enjoy fame 享有名聲

Shakespeare's plays and poems *enjoy* lasting *fame*.
莎士比亞的戲劇與詩作享有不朽之盛名。

seek fame 追求名聲

He would feel empty if he stops *seeking fame* and fortune.
如果他停止追求名利，會感到空虛。

win fame 贏得名聲

The Eagles *won fame* and rose to the status of national celebrity as their hit single "Hotel California" achieved nationwide success.
老鷹合唱團憑藉暢銷單曲《Hotel California》在全國大獲成功，贏得了名聲並晉升至國家級名人的地位。

do justice 公平對待,如實呈現

Words don't *do justice* — you have to see it to believe it.
光靠言語無法說得清楚 —— 你必須親眼看到才會相信。

get justice 受到公正對待

I'm not leaving until I *get justice*.
在我獲得公道之前,我不會離開。

want justice 想要公平正義

I asked the client whether he really *wanted justice*, or he wanted mercy and grace.
我問了那位當事人,他是真的想要公平正義,還是渴望寬恕與仁慈。

defend one's honor 捍衛名譽

Martyrdom is an act of sacrifice to *defend the honor* of a religion and its teachings.
殉道是一種為了捍衛宗教名譽及其教義而犧牲的行為。

have honor 擁有榮譽,感到光榮

We *have* your *honor*.
我們以你為榮。

restore one's honor 挽回名譽

By killing the villain, he *restored his honor*.
他殺了那名惡棍之後,挽回了自己的名譽。

bring shame 帶來恥辱

The gross misconduct of the man *brought shame* upon the entire community.
那名男子嚴重的不當行為讓整個社區的人以他為恥。

cause shame 造成羞愧

Love should *cause* us no *shame*.
愛不應該讓我們感到羞愧。

feel shame 感到羞愧

I *felt shame* at my stupid mistake.
我對自己愚蠢的錯誤感到羞愧。

earn respect 贏得尊敬

You don't need to *earn* my *respect*.
你不需要贏得我的尊敬。

feel respect （在心中）滿懷敬意

Our heart *feels respect* for the officer that died.
我們對那位殉職的警官滿懷敬意。

gain respect 獲得尊重

The stepfather is looking for a way to *gain respect* from his children.
繼父正在尋找一個獲得他孩子們尊重的方法。

have respect 心存敬意

The politician *has respect* for diversity and struggles for racial equality.
那位政治人物尊重多元化，且一直為種族平等而奔波努力。

hold respect 抱持著敬意

The scientists *hold* a great deal of *respect* for technological advance in artificial intelligence.
這些科學家對於人工智慧技術的進步抱持著極大的敬意。

lose respect 失去尊重

Do you want me to *lose respect* for you?
你希望我失去對你的尊重嗎？

win respect 贏得尊重

The factory manager tried to build a good working environmentand. By doing so, he *won respect* from his coworkers.
廠長努力打造良好的工作環境。因此，他贏得他同事們的尊重。

abandon an ideal 放棄理想

He *abandoned* the unattainable *ideal* and determined to focus on what he could reach.
他放棄了那個遙不可及的理想,並決定致力於自己能實現的目標。

achieve an ideal 實現理想

Intellectuals during the Joseon Dynasty strived to *achieve* the Confucius moral *ideal*.
朝鮮時代的知識分子努力實現儒家的道德理想。

attain an ideal 達成理想

Emphasis on health and physical attractiveness drives people totry hard to *attain* the slim body *ideal*.
人們對於健康與外表吸引力的重視,使得他們拼命去達成纖瘦體態的理想。

betray an ideal 背叛理想

The dictator *betrayed* our democratic *ideal* of political freedom and equality.
這名獨裁者背叛了我們政治自由與平等的民主理想。

pursue an ideal 追求理想

Puritans *pursued* high ethical and religious *ideals* as Christians.
清教徒和基督徒一樣都追求高尚的道德與宗教理想。

support an ideal 支持理想

It's hard to convince people to *support a* particular *ideal*.
要說服人們支持特定的理想是很困難的。

assert a belief 主張信仰

In modern democratic societies, citizens are relatively free to *assert* their *beliefs*.
在現代民主社會中,公民有相當的自由來主張他們的信仰。

express a belief 表達信念

Galileo *expressed* his *belief* in the Copernican theory, which aroused fierce opposition and anger from the Roman Catholic Church.
伽利略表示他相信哥白尼式的理論，此舉引發了羅馬天主教會的強烈反對與憤怒。

follow a belief 奉行信念／信仰

He *follows* the *belief* that "Time is money."
他奉行「時間就是金錢」的信念。

have a belief 擁有信念／信仰

Korean independence activists during the colonial times *had a* deep *belief* in the importance of formal education.
殖民時期的韓國獨立社運人士深信正規教育的重要性。

hold a belief 堅守信念／信仰

Do you still *hold* no *belief* in God?
你仍然不信上帝嗎？

share a belief 共有信念／信仰

We *shared* similar *beliefs*.
我們擁有相似的信仰。

state a belief 陳述信念

He was merely *stating a belief*.
他只是陳述了一種信念。

break a promise 違背承諾

I never *break a promise*.
我從不違背承諾。

fulfill a promise 實現承諾

I'm afraid that I am unable to *fulfill the promise* I made to you.
我怕我沒辦法實現對你做出的承諾。

keep a promise 遵守承諾

You'd better *keep* your *promises*.
你最好遵守你的承諾。

make a promise 做出承諾

The presidential candidate *made a* bold *promise* to cut taxes for low earners.
這位總統候選人大膽承諾要為低收入者減稅。

deserve credit 值得稱讚，值得信賴

You *deserve* as much *credit* as I do.
你應得到和我一樣多的讚譽。

get credit 獲得讚譽

The mayor *got credit* for his efforts to improve the housing condition of low-income residents.
市長因致力於改善低收入居民的居住條件而獲得讚譽。

give credit 給予信譽，標示出處

In order not to commit deliberate or accidental plagiarism, don't forget to *give credit* to sources of information you used or borrowed.
為了避免蓄意或無意的抄襲，別忘了標明你所使用或借用的資料來源。

take credit 攬下功勞

What should you do when others *take credit* for your work?
當別人攬下你工作的功勞時，你該怎麼辦？

follow an example 效法榜樣

Let us *follow* his *example*.
讓我們追隨他的榜樣。

set an example 樹立典範

The peaceful regime change in the country *set a* good *example* for those countries looking forward to a free, fair election.
該國的和平政權更替為那些期盼自由、公平選舉的國家樹立了良好典範。

DAY 56

show an example 以身作則

Adults often *show* bad *examples* to the younger generation.
大人們常給了年輕一代做了不良的示範。

Collocation Exercises

A 請將 List 1 的動詞與 List 2 的名詞做適當的連結,且符合完整句意。

List 1	List 2
betraying	fame
bring	honor
enjoy	ideal
have	respect
won	great shame

1. The multi-millionaire singer said he would never make another album for sale in record shops because he did not need the cash and does not _____ _____ in San Francisco.

2. Can you _____ _____ and act dishonestly? Remember that honor and honesty are closely related.

3. That person has excluded himself, "spiritually" speaking, from the fellowship of his people by _____ his _____ of holiness.

4. Both of the scandals would _____ _____ to the nation and symbolize the continuing lack of moral behavior within the political and business sectors.

5. Critics of her early works said that she couldn't act but she gradually _____ their _____.

B 在以下句子空格處中選出適當的字詞。

6. She doesn't really understand the importance of _____ respect for each and every person.
   (a) doing			(b) having
   (c) pursuing		(d) winning

7. At least _____ him credit for trying even if he's not successful.
   (a) buy			(b) deserve
   (c) give			(d) hold

8. We _____ a strong belief that the Korean market will come back.
   (a) defend		(b) enjoy
   (c) hold			(d) set

9. In 1968, the young around the world who _____ social justice tried to remove unfair political restriction.
   (a) did			(b) got
   (c) had			(d) wanted

10. Korean MP3 industries don't have to follow iPOD _____ of the innovative design and the user-friendly interface.
    (a) examples		(b) fame
    (c) love			(d) respect

C 請將以下句子翻譯為英文。

11. 這張照片無法呈現她的真正風格！

12. 她就是背棄了她對我許下過的每一個承諾。

13. 要為孩子樹立好榜樣，而不是讓他們跟著壞榜樣走。

14. 我相信自己是一位優秀的英文學習者。

15. 那些缺乏自信的人，即使犯了一點小錯也會感到極大的羞愧。

Collocations on Signs and Symbols

DAY 57

Day-57.mp3

今天要來學習的是與標誌及象徵有關的核心字彙，例如 symbol（象徵）、pattern（類型）、flag（旗幟）、mark（標記）…等，以及它們常見的搭配用語，像是 bear/display a symbol、have/design a pattern、fly/wave a flag、get/leave a mark …等共 36 個核心的表達用語。

Collocation at a Glance

Verb + Noun	Meaning	Verb + Noun	Meaning
give **color**	增添色彩	bear **a logo**	印有商標
join the **colors**	入伍	carry **a logo**	帶有商標
show one's (true) **colors**	表明自身立場，展現自我本性	unveil **a logo**	公開商標
fly **a flag**	使旗幟飄揚	get **a mark**	有個印記
hang out **a flag**	懸掛旗幟	leave **a mark**	留下記號
lower **a flag**	降下旗幟	make **a mark**	做記號，成名
wave **a flag**	揮舞旗幟	take off **a mark**	去除記號
alter **form**	修改表格	have **a pattern**	具有某種模式／圖樣
change **form**	改變形狀	design **a pattern**	設計圖樣
take on **(a) form**	呈現某種形態	weave **a pattern**	編織圖樣

DAY 57

print a pattern	印上圖樣	have a sign	有標誌
get a notice	收到通知	exhibit a sign	有個標示可見
issue a notice	發出通知	recognize a sign	辨認標示
post a notice	張貼公告	show a sign	顯示跡象
sound a warning	發出警報／警告	bear a symbol	帶有象徵
give a warning	給予警告	display a symbol	展示象徵物
disregard a warning	無視警告	decipher a symbol	解讀象徵符號
bear a sign	帶有徵兆	interpret a symbol	分析象徵符號

Collocation in Use

give color 增添色彩

Effective use of collocations can *give color* to your writing or speaking.
有效運用搭配詞組能為你的寫作或口說增添色彩。

join the colors 入伍

After he returned from a journey around the world, he immediately *joined the colors*.
他環遊世界歸來後隨即入伍服役。

show one's (true) colors 表明自身立場，展現自我本性

Many students *show their colors* with tattoos.
許多學生以刺青來展現自己的本性。

fly a flag 使旗幟飄揚

The public square *flies a flag* high in the sky all through the year.
這個公共廣場一整年都有一面旗幟高高飄揚著。

hang out a flag 懸掛旗幟

A group of people *hung out a flag* to celebrate the festival.
一群人懸掛著旗幟來慶祝這個節日。

lower a flag 降下旗幟

The national *flag* was *lowered* when the annual memorial ceremony for the war dead was over.
當年度的戰亡者追悼儀式結束的同時，國旗也被降了下來。

wave a flag 揮舞旗幟

Spectators from different countries in the ski jumping stadium *waved* their own national *flags* to cheer up their national representatives.
在滑雪跳台上，來自不同國家的觀眾揮舞著自己國家的國旗，為其國家代表加油。

alter form 修改表格

Get this free legal *form*, and you may *alter* this to fit your business needs.
請下載這份免費的法律文件表格，你可以依照自己的商業需求做修改。

change form 改變形狀

The moon *changes* its *form* gradually.
月亮會逐漸改變它的形狀。

take on (a) form 呈現某種形態

A chameleon *takes on* different *forms* in different surroundings.
變色龍在不同的周遭環境中會呈現不同的形態。

bear a logo 印有商標

People prefer products *bearing a* famous *logo*.
人們偏好知名品牌的商品。

carry a logo 帶有商標

The advertisement still *carried* the previous *logo* of the company.
這則廣告仍帶有該公司先前的 LOGO（商標）。

unveil a logo 公開商標

The cosmetics company *unveiled* its new *logo* at the department store.
該化妝品公司在百貨公司公開了它新的 LOGO。

get a mark 有個印記

I don't know where I *got* this *mark*.
我不知道這個印記是從哪來的。

leave a mark 留下記號

Ancient people *left* a number of abstract, geometrical *marks* on stones or in the caves.
古人曾在石頭上或洞穴裡留下許多抽象性的幾何學記號。

make a mark 做記號,成名

The scientific expedition team *made* several distinguishing *marks* on its routes in case of emergency.
探勘隊沿路上做了幾個明顯的標記,以因應緊急狀況。

take off a mark 去除記號

The clerk *took* the brand *mark off* the shirt, as soon as I paid the bill for it.
我結帳後,店員馬上把襯衫上的品牌標籤拿掉了。

have a pattern 具有某種模式/圖樣

Each individual person *has* his or her own particular *pattern* of habits and behaviors.
每個人都有自己特有的習慣與行為模式。

design a pattern 設計圖樣

She *designed a* vintage, denim fabric *pattern*.
她設計了一款復古的牛仔布料圖樣。

weave a pattern 編織圖樣

The girl *weaved a* fish *pattern* on her jumper.
那女孩在她的套頭衫上織出了一個魚形圖樣。

Signs and Symbols 389

print a pattern 印上圖樣

The young artist *printed an* exquisite *pattern* on the paper by silkscreen technique.
這位年輕藝術家以絲網印刷技術在紙上印出一個精緻的圖樣。

get a notice 收到通知

The illegal immigrants *got a notice* from the Immigration office.
這些非法移民收到了移民局的通知。

issue a notice 發出通知

The college entrance exam board *issued an* important *notice* to test takers.
大學入學考試委員會向考生發佈了一項重要通知。

post a notice 張貼公告

The school official has *posted a notice* about the school's upcoming annual reunion on the bulletin board.
校方在佈告欄上張貼了一項即將舉行的年度校友會通知。

sound a warning 發出警報／警告

The riot police *sounded a warning* to protesters to disperse immediately and began to break up the crowd.
防暴警察對抗議者發出立即解散的警告，並隨即展開驅散人群的行動。

give a warning 給予警告

The evening weather report *gave a warning* of potential hazard from falling temperatures to campers on the mountain.
晚間氣象報導給了山區露營者一個警告：氣溫驟降可能帶來危險。

disregard a warning 無視警告

Only an idiot would *disregard a* tornado *warning*.
只有傻瓜才會無視龍捲風警報。

bear a sign 帶有徵兆

Atmospheric change such as global warming and ozone layerdepletion *bears a sign* of environmental crisis.
像全球暖化與臭氧層破壞等大氣變化是環境危機的徵兆。

have a sign 有標誌

The construction place *has a* caution *sign* to warn passers-by and drivers.
施工現場設有警戒標誌，以警告行人與駕駛注意安全。

exhibit a sign 有個標示可見

The entrance door *exhibits a sign* that says "Staff Only."
入口門上可見到一個「僅限員工進入」的標示。

recognize a sign 辨認標示

It's somewhat difficult to *recognize the sign*.
這個標示有點難以辨認。

show a sign 顯示跡象

The abandoned house *shows* no *sign* of life.
那棟廢棄的房子內沒有任何生命跡象。

bear a symbol 帶有象徵

According to The Da Vinci Code written by Dan Brown, artworks of Leonardo Da Vinci *bear* pagan *symbols* quite a lot.
根據丹‧布朗所撰寫的《達文西密碼》，達文西的藝術作品中包含大量異教象徵。

display a symbol 展示象徵物

The museum *displays* Nazi *symbols* to evoke in people's minds the danger of political extremism.
博物館展出納粹的象徵符號，提醒人們政治極端主義的危險。

decipher a symbol 解讀象徵符號

Not until the Rossetta stone came to light did scholars find a way to *decipher* ancient Egyptian *symbols*.
直到羅塞塔石碑出土後，學者們才找到解讀古埃及象徵符號的方法。

interpret a symbol 分析象徵符號

It is hard to *interpret* this *symbol*.
這個象徵符號實在難以分析。

Collocation Exercises

A 請將 List 1 的動詞與 List 2 的名詞做適當的連結，且符合完整句意。

List 1	List 2
left	a big mark
sounded	a geometric pattern
took on	human form
unveiled	the new logo
wove	the warning

1. The company _____ _____ on the anniversary of their founding.

2. The red ink _____ _____ on my best shirt, but I don't know where the nearest washroom is.

3. The goddess fell in love with the man. She _____ _____ to approach him.

4. The police _____ _____ to the demonstrators in front of the National Assembly Building.

5. She _____ _____ on her jumper. It looked something like a gigantic ear.

B 在以下句子空格處中選出適當的字詞。

6. In Egypt, many items _____ the dung beetle as a religious symbol. It represents the Sun God rolling the ball of the sun.
   (a) bear (b) care
   (c) draw (d) imagine

7. People _____ flags of different colors as the World Cup soccer team was passing by.
   (a) carried (b) posted
   (c) chose (d) waved

8. When I asked how to defeat Dracula, she _____ me the sign of a cross.
   (a) caught (b) changed
   (c) imagined (d) showed

9. The scientists group released the research that gives _____ to the controversy of evolution theory.
   (a) color (b) form
   (c) hands (d) marks

10. The Maritime Police _____ a formal notice warning ships to stay nearby in harbors.
    (a) applied (b) issued
    (c) got (d) told

C 請將以下句子翻譯為英文。

11. 我喜歡這條裙子，因為它上面有花卉圖樣。

12. 他把寫有「禁止吸菸」的告示貼在牆上。

13. 他已準備好在世界盃中嶄露頭角。

14. 我的醫生警告我過度運動的後果。

15. 每面國旗都展現了該國所屬的象徵。

Collocations on Direction and Movement

DAY 58

Day-58.mp3

今天要來學習的是與方向及移動相關的核心字彙及其搭配詞用法,像是 route(路線)、departure(出發)、advance(進展)、direction(方向)…等。另外,我們將深入探討 42 個相關的搭配詞組,例如:follow/take a route、make/hasten a departure、make/halt an advance、show/change direction …等。

Collocation at a Glance

Verb + Noun	Meaning	Verb + Noun	Meaning
take a direction	朝著某方向(邁進)	make progress	取得進展
change direction	改變方向	slow progress	拖慢進度
show direction	指引方向	accelerate progress	加快進展
face in a direction	面向某個方向	monitor progress	監視進度
lack direction	缺乏方向感	chart progress	繪製進度圖
follow a route	沿著路線走	gather pace	加快腳步/速度
take a route	走某路線	increase pace	提高速度
choose a route	選擇路線	quicken pace	加快步伐
turn off a route	駛離某路線	maintain pace	保持步伐
plan a route	規劃路線	make a retreat	進行撤退

cover a retreat	掩護撤退	stop an advance	阻止進展
lead a retreat	帶領撤退	find one's way	找到路
order a retreat	下令撤退	lose one's way	迷路
block a retreat	擋住退路	ask about the way	問路
change course	改變路線	point the way	指路
set a course	設定路線	make a departure	出發，離開
follow a course	沿著某路線走	hasten a departure	加快出發／離開
take a course	走某路線，上某堂課	delay departure	延後出發
make an advance	前進，逼近	make one's return	返回
halt an advance	停止推進	delay one's return	延後回程
resist an advance	阻擋推進	await someone's return	等待某人歸來

Collocation in Use

take a direction 朝著某方向（邁進）

The telephone company's rate plan *took a* new *direction* for better customer oriented service.
電話公司的費率方案朝著更以顧客服務為導向的新方向邁進。

change direction 改變方向

He found a perfect fishing spot where the river *changed direction*.
他找到一處絕佳的釣魚點，它位於河流改變流向的地方。

show direction 指引方向

They only *show* us which *direction* we need to go.
他們只是告訴我們應該往哪個方向走。

face in a direction 面向某個方向

She *faces in the direction* of the violinist.
她面向這位小提琴手的方向。

lack direction 缺乏方向感

You're talented, but you *lack direction*.
你很有天賦,但是你缺乏方向感。

follow a route 沿著路線走

The bus *followed a route* down the highway.
這輛公車沿著高速公路的路線行駛。

take a route 走某路線

I suggest we *take* another *route*.
我建議我們走另一條路線。

choose a route 選擇路線

Update your car navigation system and *choose* the shortest *route* possible.
更新你的車用導航系統,並盡量選擇最短路徑。

turn off a route 駛離某路線

Turn off route 30 in downtown, and drive south toward the general hospital.
在市中心離開 30 號公路,然後往南開往綜合醫院。

plan a route 規劃路線

The thief carefully *planned* his escape *route*.
那名竊賊仔細規劃過他的逃跑路線。

make progress 取得進展

Are you *making* any *progress* at all?
你有任何進展嗎?

slow progress 拖慢進度

It may have *slowed* his *progress* down.
這可能已拖慢了他的進度。

accelerate progress 加快進展

The purpose of the workshop is to *accelerate progress*.
這場研討會的目的是加快進展的速度。

monitor progress 監視進度

I've been *monitoring* your *progress*.
我一直在監視著你的進度。

chart progress 繪製進度圖

The school committee created an assessment model to *chart progress* on students' achievement.
學校委員會創建了一套評量模型,用來記錄學生學業的進步情形。

gather pace 加快腳步／速度

Scientific research in this field is likely to *gather pace* in the near future.
這個領域的科學研究很可能在不久的將來加速發展。

increase pace 提高速度

She *increasesd* her *pace* and started walking rapidly.
她加快了她的步伐,開始走得迅速。

quicken pace 加快步伐

I *quickened* my *pace*.
我加快了我的腳步。

maintain pace 保持步伐

The top five marathon runners *maintained* a fast *pace* from the start.
前五名馬拉松選手從一開始就保持著快速的步伐。

make a retreat 進行撤退

The runaway soldiers *made a* hasty *retreat* to the exit.
那些逃兵們匆忙地撤退到出口處。

cover a retreat 掩護撤退

The police shot bullets to *cover* their *retreat*.
警方開槍掩護他們撤退。

lead a retreat 帶領撤退

The lieutenant *led a* quick *retreat* from the front line.
那位中尉迅速帶領部隊從前線撤退。

order a retreat 下令撤退

He was forced to *order a retreat*.
他被迫下令撤退。

block a retreat 擋住退路

A tall warrior *blocked* their *retreat*.
一位高大的戰士擋住了他們的退路。

change course 改變路線

On receiving the scout's report about obstacles on the road, the commander ordered his troops to immediately *change course*.
在接獲偵查兵通報道路上有障礙物之後,指揮官命令其部隊即刻改變行進路線。

set a course 設定路線

The nation's economy policy *set a* new *course* to promote mutual cooperation with the EU.
該國的經濟政策設定了一個新的路線,即促進與歐盟的互惠合作。

follow a course 沿著某路線走

The motorcycle race *follows a course* up the hill.
這場機車賽的路線是沿著山坡的賽道行進。

take a course 走某路線,上某堂課

The baby swallowed a button, but the doctor told the mother, "just let nature *take its course*."
嬰兒誤吞了一顆鈕扣,但醫生告訴母親「那就順其自然吧。」

make an advance 前進，逼近

The fierce dog *made advances* towards him.
那隻兇猛的狗朝他逼近。

halt an advance 停止推進

This new vaccine is expected to *halt advances* of the flu virus.
這款新的疫苗預計能阻止流感病毒的進一步擴散。

resist an advance 阻擋推進

The heavy bombardment on the battlefield couldn't *resist the advance* of enemy troops.
戰場上的猛烈砲擊仍無法阻擋敵軍的推進。

stop an advance 阻止進展

The UN has taken measures to *stop* the scientific *advance* of the country towards creating a nuclear bomb.
聯合國已採取措施，阻止該國在製造核彈上的科學進展。

find one's way 找到路

They easily *found their way* to the museum.
他們輕鬆找到了前往博物館的路。

lose one's way 迷路

If I *lost my way*, would you stand with me?
如果我迷了路，你願意跟我站在一起嗎？

ask about the way 問路

I *asked about the* quickest *way* to the pub.
我問過通往酒吧最快的路（怎麼走）。

point the way 指路

The road sign *points the way* to the stadium.
這路標指向體育館的方向。

make a departure 出發，離開

A group of horses, with their riders on their backs, *made a* noisy *departure*.
一群馬匹，還有牠們背上的騎士，一起喧鬧地離開。

hasten a departure 加快出發／離開

She *hastened* her *departure* from the hotel despite bad weather conditions.
儘管天氣狀況惡劣，她還是匆忙離開了旅館。

delay departure 延後出發

We will *delay departure* of the cargo for a week due to technical problems.
因為技術問題，我們將出貨的時間延後一週。

make one's return 返回

After long-term treatment for a car accident injury, I *made my return* to work.
在經過長期治療車禍傷勢後，我回到了工作崗位。

delay one's return 延後回程

His fiancee *delayed her return* without a word.
他的未婚妻默默地延後了回程時間。

await someone's return 等待某人歸來

The parents patiently *awaited the return of their son*.
父母耐心等待他們兒子的歸來。

Direction and Movement

Collocation Exercises

A 請將 List 1 的動詞與 List 2 的名詞做適當的連結，且符合完整句意。

List 1	List 2
delay	big advances
taken	the course
gather	departure
made	pace
monitor	the progress

1. Planes aren't allowed to land there before 6:00 am, which forced us to _____ our _____ from San Francisco.

2. The late 1940s saw the beginnings of recovery, which slowly began to _____ _____ into the next decade.

3. Students who have _____ _____ of Spoken English and have attained the required level are also admitted.

4. The School Board will _____ _____ of all schools and will hold them to similar exacting standards of performance.

5. Thanks to lower labor costs and improved production techniques, many Asian countries had _____ _____.

B 在以下句子空格處中選出適當的字詞。

6. Jack's family _____ the return of his two sons.
   (a) awaited
   (b) changed
   (c) thought
   (d) made

7. Because his tour guide deceived him, he _____ his way at some point.
   (a) asked
   (b) followed
   (c) lost
   (d) set

8. The General was shot and severely injured, but he _____ the advance to continue.
   (a) made
   (b) stopped
   (c) planned
   (d) took

9. Unexpected inflation made markets _____ direction and stock investors became rattled.
   (a) lack
   (b) set
   (c) show
   (d) take

10. Though he loses his way, the male does not like to be advised of which _____ he should take.
    (a) arrival
    (b) departure
    (c) fact
    (d) route

C 請將以下句子翻譯為英文。

11. 我們也有可能沒有朝著正確的方向。

_____

12. 他突然從 50 號公路出口駛出，然後開始往北行駛。

13. 他成功地掩護了俄軍的撤退。

14. 老師監督著他學生的學習進度，並建立每個學生的檔案。

15. 一般來說，高溫會加快化學反應的速度。

Collocations on

DAY 59

Day-59.mp3

Danger

今天我們要來看看與危險事件有關的核心字彙及其搭配用語，例如 accident（意外）、caution（謹慎）、threat（威脅）、crisis（危機）…等。另外我們要深入探討 32 個最常見的表達方式，例如 cause/prevent an accident、advise/exercise caution、make/pose a threat、face/overcome a crisis …等等。

Collocation at a Glance

Verb + Noun	Meaning	Verb + Noun	Meaning
cause an accident	引起意外事故	face a crisis	面臨危機
prevent an accident	防止意外	overcome a crisis	克服危機
survive an accident	在意外中倖存	face danger	面對危險
cause (an) alarm	帶來警訊	pose danger	構成危險
raise (an) alarm	發出警報	see danger	了解危險（性）
sound an alarm	發出警報聲	bring (a) disaster	帶來災難
advise caution	提出警告	cause (a) disaster	造成災難
exercise caution	謹慎行事	avoid (a) disaster	避開災難
urge caution	呼籲提高警覺	survive (a) disaster	在災難中倖存
create a crisis	製造危機（事件）	give protection	給予保護

Danger   405

offer **protection**	提供保護	need **shelter**	需要庇護（所）
provide **protection**	提供保護	offer **shelter**	提供庇護（所）
ensure **safety**	確保安全	seek **shelter**	尋求避難所
guarantee **safety**	保證安全	make **a threat**	施以威脅／恐嚇手段
increase **safety**	提升安全	pose **a threat**	構成威脅／恐嚇
improve **safety**	改善安全	receive **a threat**	受到威脅／恐嚇

Collocation in Use

cause an accident 引起意外事故

High winds and heavy rains can *cause accidents*.
強風和豪雨可能會引起意外事故。

prevent an accident 防止意外

Find methods to *prevent an accident* from happening.
尋找防止意外發生的方法。

survive an accident 在意外中倖存

The family *survived a* fatal *accident*.
這家庭在一場致命的意外事件中倖存了下來。

cause (an) alarm 帶來警訊

Demographic changes *cause alarm* in Korea.
韓國的人口變化令人憂慮。

raise (an) alarm 發出警報

Scientists *raised alarm* about the cleanliness of the oceans.
科學家對海洋的潔淨度發出警報。

sound an alarm 發出警報聲

When a smoke detector *sounds an alarm*, sprinklers will operate.
當煙霧探測器發出警報聲時，灑水器會（自動）啟動。

advise caution 提出警告

Experts *advise caution* in using the tools.
專家警告小心使用這些工具。

exercise caution 謹慎行事

The movie director *exercised* great *caution* when handling controversial issues not to evoke harsh criticism.
這位電影導演在處理爭議性議題時格外謹慎,以免引來嚴苛的批評。

urge caution 呼籲提高警覺

Officials *urged caution* on unexpected roadway hazards.
官員們呼籲謹慎面對突發的道路危險。

create a crisis 製造危機(事件)

The internet can *create a crisis* through cyber-terrorism.
網際網路可能透過網路恐攻來製造危機事件。

face a crisis 面臨危機

No business wants to *face a crisis* in finance.
沒有任何企業希望面臨財務危機。

overcome a crisis 克服危機

Countries with few natural resources require measures to *overcome* potential oil *crisis*.
天然資源稀少的國家需要有克服潛在石油危機的措施。

face danger 面對危險

Keep contact with the emergency center in case you *face* some kind of *danger* on the job.
請與緊急應變中心保持聯繫,以防在工作中遇到某種危險。

pose danger 構成危險

Wildfires *posed danger* across the area.
野火構成了整個地區的危險。

see danger 了解危險（性）

Those who suffered severe side effects from the medication can *see the danger* of overdosing on medicines.
曾因藥物產生嚴重副作用的人能理解藥物過量的危險性。

bring (a) disaster 帶來災難

War will *bring disaster*.
戰爭將帶來災難。

cause (a) disaster 造成災難

A virus may *cause a* worldwide *disaster*.
病毒可能造成全球性的災難。

avoid (a) disaster 避開災難

He managed to *avoid disaster* while traveling.
他在旅途中成功避開了災難。

survive (a) disaster 在災難中倖存

Preparing today could help you *survive a disaster* tomorrow.
今日的準備能幫助你在明日的災難中倖存下來。

give protection 給予保護

Keeping clean *gives* a person *protection* against all sorts of diseases.
保持清潔能夠讓人免於各種疾病的侵害。

offer protection 提供保護

The security solutions *offer protection* from ID theft.
這些安全解決方案能防止個人資料遭竊。

provide protection 提供保護

Improvement of construction site safety policies can *provide protection* for all workers and prevent accidents.
改善工地安全政策能保護所有工人並防止事故發生。

ensure safety 確保安全

The coalition force made an official announcement to *ensure* the *safety* of civilians.
聯軍發表一份確保平民安全的正式聲明。

guarantee safety 保證安全

The parents association urged manufacturers to take measures to *guarantee* the *safety* of toy guns.
家長協會呼籲製造商採取保障玩具槍安全性的措施。

increase safety 提升安全

The newly set up surveillance cameras are expected to *increase* the *safety* of pedestrians on dark, narrow streets.
新設置的監視器預期能提升昏暗、狹窄街道上的行人安全。

improve safety 改善安全

They have embarked a new research in automotive design to *improve safety* and comfort for pregnant women.
他們著手展開汽車設計的新研究,以提升孕婦乘客的安全與舒適度。

need shelter 需要庇護(所)

Everyone *needs shelter* to provide them with rest, warmth, and protection from harsh weather.
每個人都需要庇護所,為他們提供休息、溫暖和抵禦惡劣的天候。

offer shelter 提供庇護(所)

The ecological preservation area *offers shelter* for birds during the coldest months.
這個生態保護區在最寒冷的月份為鳥類提供庇護所。

seek shelter 尋求避難所

The homeless *seek shelter* from hurricanes at this time of year.
每年颶風來襲的這個時候,無家可歸的人們會去尋求避難所。

Danger

make a threat 施以威脅／恐嚇手段

The husband habitually *makes threats* of violence against his wife.
這位丈夫經常對他的妻子施以暴力威脅手段。

pose a threat 構成威脅／恐嚇

The emission of toxic pollutants into the air and river can *pose a serious threat* to public health and the environment.
有毒污染物排放到空氣與河川中時，可能對公共健康與環境構成嚴重威脅。

receive a threat 受到威脅／恐嚇

The prosecutor handling a corruption case *received* personal *threats* by telephone.
負責偵辦貪污案的檢察官接到恐嚇電話。

Collocation Exercises

A 請將 List 1 的動詞與 List 2 的名詞做適當的連結，且符合完整句意。

List 1	List 2
face	a death-threat
offered	a temporary emergency shelter
provides	the best protection
received	the alarm
sounded	the worst crisis

1. The activist recently _____ _____ from an extremist group, but she continued building up the movement.

2. The flood victims were _____ _____ and a small amount of relief supplies.

3. This sunblock cream _____ you _____ against sun damage while you're doing outdoor activities.

4. As soon as the security system _____ _____, the bank robbers tried to run away, but, they were arrested by the police.

5. Lifeguards are trained to take immediate steps even when they _____ _____. They are considered professionals.

B 在以下句子空格處中選出適當的字詞。

6. The regular repair and maintenance of the building can guarantee and improve its _____.
   (a) chance (b) life
   (c) safety (d) warning

7. People all over the world are well aware of _____ posed by the arms race.
   (a) the coziness (b) the dangers
   (c) the intimacies (d) the lessons

8. The press reported that it was miraculous that anyone could _____ the terrible air disaster.
   (a) face (b) run
   (c) suffer (d) survive

9. The district public office introduced speed bumps on several points on the roads to _____ fatal car accidents.
   (a) cause (b) follow
   (c) prevent (d) urge

10. Diabetics should _____ extreme caution on diet; especially, they need to avoid sugar-rich food.
    (a) commit (b) exercise
    (c) express (d) want

Danger   411

C 請將以下句子翻譯為英文。

11. 許多事故是因為駕駛人愛睏及酒醉所引起的。

12. 我們呼籲在緊急情況下謹慎使用此救生衣。

13. 恐怖主義對國家安全構成嚴重威脅。

14. 此設備提供免於遭受潛在危險的保護。

15. 政府正在考慮這些針對信用卡公司財務危機的解決方案。

Collocations on Aid and Cooperation

DAY 60

Day-60.mp3

最後，我們將探討與援助及合作相關的核心詞彙，例如 support（支援）、coalition（聯合）、cooperation（合作）、encouragement（鼓勵）…等，以及它們的搭配用語，我們將深入探討像是 draw/receive support、create/join a coalition、demand/promote cooperation、offer/need encouragement…等 42 個最常用的表達用語。

Collocation at a Glance

Verb + Noun	Meaning	Verb + Noun	Meaning
draw support	取得支持	draw comfort	取得安慰
find support	找到支持	seek comfort	尋求安慰
receive support	接獲支持／支援	take comfort	得到安慰
cut support	中斷支持	have a partnership	擁有夥伴關係
offer assistance	提供協助	enter into a partnership	進入合作關係
need assistance	需要協助	establish a partnership	建立夥伴關係
require assistance	需要協助	form a partnership	形成夥伴關係
expect assistance	期待協助	create a coalition	建立聯盟
seek assistance	尋求協助	form a coalition	組成聯盟
bring comfort	帶來安慰	join a coalition	加入聯盟

Aid and Cooperation

lead a **coalition**	領導聯盟	seek a **sponsor**	尋求贊助商
promote **cooperation**	促進合作	attract a **sponsor**	吸引贊助者
need **cooperation**	需要合作	get a **sponsor**	找到贊助商
require **cooperation**	需要合作	ask (for) **advice**	詢問建議
demand **cooperation**	要求合作	accept **advice**	接受建議
offer **encouragement**	給予鼓勵	follow **advice**	遵從建議
need **encouragement**	需要鼓勵	ignore **advice**	無視建議
require **encouragement**	需要鼓勵	offer **guidance**	提供指引
draw **encouragement**	獲得鼓勵	provide **guidance**	提供指導
receive **encouragement**	受到鼓勵	need **guidance**	需要指導
collect a **sponsor**	招募贊助商	seek **guidance**	尋求指導

Collocation in Use

draw support 取得支持

Family and friends are two main sources where we can *draw* wholehearted *support*.
家人和朋友是我們可以取得真誠支持的兩大來源。

find support 找到支持

The anti-globalization protest *found* little *support* for its effort at home.
反全球化抗議活動在國內幾乎得不到什麼支持。

receive support 接獲支持／支援

Please contact us if you want to *receive* technical *support*.
若您想要獲得技術支援,請與我們聯絡。

cut support 中斷支持

There is a growing voice to urge the government to *cut support* for military solutions to political conflict.
要求政府停止支持以軍事手段解決政治衝突的呼聲日益高漲。

offer assistance 提供協助

Occasionally, you can help someone to achieve something higher than he or she initially expected, without any intention of *offering assistance* at all.
有時候，你即使在完全沒有打算提供幫助的情況下，也可能幫助他人達成超出他們原先預期的成就。

need assistance 需要協助

I *need assistance* finding a wealthy husband. I am in search of a man to support me financially.
我需要有人幫我找到一個有錢的老公。我正在尋找能一個在財務上支援我的男人。

require assistance 需要協助

Elderly persons *require assistance* with daily living.
年長者需要日常生活上的協助。

expect assistance 期待協助

The town, devastated from a big flood, is *expecting* emergency *assistance* from outside communities.
遭受大洪水重創的這座小鎮，正期待著外界社區的緊急援助。

seek assistance 尋求協助

The police are *seeking assistance* in solving a serial murder case.
警方為偵破一連串謀殺案件正尋求協助中。

bring comfort 帶來安慰

I must *bring comfort* to her.
我必須給她帶來安慰。

draw comfort 取得安慰

He *draws comfort* from his lover's affection when he feels deep sorrow.
每當他感到深切悲傷時，總是能夠從他戀人的愛中獲得安慰。

seek comfort 尋求安慰

I assume that she'd *seek* your *comfort*.
我想她會尋求你的安慰。

take comfort 得到安慰

When you're just doing things wrong, you can *take comfort* in the thoughts that you can use your mistakes to work not againstyou, but for you.
當你做錯事情時,你可以這麼想來安慰自己:我可以將這些錯誤轉化為幫助自己而非阻礙自己的力量。

have a partnership 擁有夥伴關係

In today's competitive business environment, it's tough for a corporation to survive unless it *has a* strategic *partnership* with its business rivals.
在當今競爭激烈的商業環境中,公司若沒有與競爭對手建立策略性合作關係,將難以生存。

enter into a partnership 進入合作關係

The company announced today it has *entered into a* strategic *partnership* with its biggest rival.
這家公司今天宣布,已與其最大競爭對手進入策略性的合作關係。

establish a partnership 建立夥伴關係

Major banks *established* mutual *partnerships* to improve profits.
數家大型銀行建立互惠合作關係以提升利潤。

form a partnership 形成夥伴關係

The owner of the shop wants *a partnership formed* by two or more persons with stable financial status.
店家老闆希望與兩位或以上財務穩定的人形成夥伴關係。

create a coalition 建立聯盟

A group of congressmen has *created a* conservative *coalition*.
一群國會議員建立了一個保守派聯盟。

form a coalition 組成聯盟

The member states of the UN security council agreed to *form a* broad military *coalition* that can be sent immediately into conflict areas.
聯合國安理會成員國同意組建一支可即刻派遣至衝突地區的聯合軍事部隊。

join a coalition 加入聯盟

Join the National *Coalition* for sexual freedom!
加入這個標榜性自由的全國聯盟吧！

lead a coalition 領導聯盟

The cross-party *coalition led* by the Progressive party launchedan election campaign primarily focused on domestic issues.
由進步黨領導的跨黨派聯盟發起了一場以國內議題為主的選舉活動。

promote cooperation 促進合作

Advocates of the screen quota system in Korea will host a meeting to *promote cooperation* in films.
韓國電影配額制度的支持者將舉辦一場會議，以促進電影業的合作。

need cooperation 需要合作

I don't *need* your *cooperation*.
我不需要你的合作。

require cooperation 需要合作

Peacekeeping operations *require cooperation* between countries in a particular region.
維和行動需要特定區域內各國的合作。

demand cooperation 要求合作

Prompt decision-making in a business *demands cooperation* among the unit.
企業的迅速決策仰賴單位內的合作。

offer encouragement 給予鼓勵

Linda *offered* him her support and *encouragement*.
琳達給予他支持與鼓勵。

need encouragement 需要鼓勵

To grow up into maturity, we all *need encouragement*.
為了能夠成長進入成熟階段,我們每個人都需要鼓勵。

require encouragement 需要鼓勵

Many Korean students *require encouragement* and practice to hone their English-language facility.
許多韓國學生需要鼓勵與練習來磨練他們的英文能力。

draw encouragement 獲得鼓勵

Religious people tend to *draw encouragement* from prayer to God.
宗教人士往往會藉由向上帝祈禱來獲得鼓勵。

receive encouragement 受到鼓勵

From the teacher's compliments and positive feedback, the students *received encouragement*.
學生們從老師的讚美與正向回饋中受到鼓勵。

collect a sponsor 招募贊助商

The sports club *collected* enough *sponsors* for its sports events.
這個運動俱樂部已招募到足夠的贊助商來支持其運動賽事。

seek a sponsor 尋求贊助商

We're *seeking sponsors* for our baseball team.
我們正為我們的棒球隊尋求贊助商。

attract a sponsor 吸引贊助者

The oil exploration project has failed to *attract sponsors* to fund it.
這項石油探勘計畫未能吸引贊助商來挹注資金。

get a sponsor 找到贊助商

Didn't you *get a sponsor* yet?
你還沒找到贊助商嗎?

ask (for) advice 詢問建議

Tim went to him to *ask for* his *advice*.
提姆去找他詢問他的建議。

accept advice 接受建議

You are too proud to *accept advice*.
你太驕傲,不願接受建議。

follow advice 遵從建議

Follow your manager's *advice*.
照著你經理的建議去做吧。

ignore advice 無視建議

Those who *ignore advice* from other people and do things as they please are likely to make trouble when they need to do aparticular group work.
那些無視他人建議、我行我素的人,在他們必須進行團隊合作時可能會製造麻煩。

offer guidance 提供指引

This book *offers* moral *guidance*.
這本書提供道德方面的指南。

provide guidance 提供指導

I need someone who can *provide guidance* and feedback for me.
我需要一位能給我指導與回饋的人。

need guidance 需要指導

She *needs* spiritual *guidance*.
她需要精神方面的引導。

seek guidance 尋求指導

I came here to *seek* practical *guidance* on this course.
我來這裡上這堂課是為了尋求實務上的指南。

Collocation Exercises

A 請將 List 1 的動詞與 List 2 的名詞做適當的連結，且符合完整句意。

List 1	List 2
brought	the doctor's advice
receive	the cooperation
needs	great comfort
follow	little encouragement
promote	assistance

1. Whatever the cost, the patient was determined to _____ _____ .

2. I have suffered a huge financial loss and had a tough time lately. However, her encouragement _____ me _____ from all the difficulties.

3. The aim of the meeting is to _____ _____ between the two parties and to attract a huge following in the next election.

4. My brother had surgery last week; he still _____ _____ from physicians when moving.

5. Students who _____ _____ from their teachers are likely to show poor performance.

DAY 60

B 在以下句子空格處中選出適當的字詞。

6. Korea and Japan _____ a partnership to hold the 2002 World Cup and had remarkable success.
   (a) allied   (b) broke
   (c) established   (d) took

7. Don't ask me to take your side. You won't be able to _____ any support from your friends for such an absurd claim.
   (a) assist   (b) find
   (c) need   (d) offer

8. The "Stop the War" coalition _____ by an anti-war organization provides information on peace events and related issues.
   (a) discussed   (b) led
   (c) presented   (d) restricted

9. The following website offers more detailed _____ on maintaining this laptop.
   (a) exception   (b) experiments
   (c) guidance   (d) safety

10. After exposing bribes of the media conglomerate for politicians, the newspaper had difficulty in _____ sponsors for financial aid.
    (a) attracting   (b) borrowing
    (c) providing   (d) showing

C 請將以下句子翻譯為英文。

11. 學生會正在為下個月的慈善拍賣活動招募贊助商。

12. 在你下任何結論之前,應該先針對此問題向專家尋求指導意見。

13. 我的意見得到我同事們的大力支持。

14. 他無視同事們的建議,結果把事情搞砸了。

15. 兒童的性格發展需要他們父母長期的鼓勵。

Days 31-60

Final Check-up

（1-5）請從方框中選出可共同填入下列括號中的動詞。

do(did)	get(got)	show(showed)	find(found)
give(gave)	make(made)	hold(held)	keep(kept)
take(took)	have(had)		

1 Some people _____ a bias for lawyers.

We gathered here to _____ international solidarity against racism.

They _____ their anger with their writing.

2 The state will _____ an election to organize an interim government.

The Lions _____ the soccer championship title.

We _____ a strong belief that the Korean market will come back.

3 It is a good habit to _____ a journal every day.

We should send troops to _____ the peace in the region.

You'd better _____ your promises.

4 His last goal _____ the final score to 3-2.

I _____ the maximum number of subjects last semester.

She showed me photos of all the children that she _____ care of.

5 He _____ me a promise when he was in the hospital that he would regain his health.

The anti-war movement _____ enemies of conservative groups.

Thanks to lower labor costs and improved production techniques, many Asian countries had _____ big advances.

(6-10) 請將 (A) 和 (B) 正確連接，以完成句子。

(A)	(B)
6. I couldn't make him 7. I have to 8. Shy people are reluctant to 9. Not a few women have been working to 10. Lifeguards are trained to take immediate steps even when they	(a) express their opinion in public. However, some of them are really good at private communication. (b) download the program. I cannot watch the video clip on my computer. (c) face the worst crisis. They are considered professional. (d) stop the prevalent practice of family violence, but it is increasing year by year. (e) understand the bottom line. He was a complete idiot when it came to accounting.

(11-15) 請從以下方框中找出適當的表達用語填入句子中，並使其語意通順完整。

> inflict emotional pain
>
> gain independence
>
> promote the cooperation
>
> prepare his doctoral dissertation
>
> have honor

Final Check-up 425

11. The aim of the meeting is to _____ _____ between the two parties and to attract a huge following in the next election.

12. Can you _____ _____ and act dishonestly? Remember that honor and honesty are closely related.

13. He was a full-time student in a Ph.D. course. However, because of financial difficulties, he had no choice but to _____ _____ while making money as a train worker.

14. Please keep in mind that your selfish action may _____ _____ on others.

15. In the end, he had no choice but to move away from home in order to _____ _____ from his parents.

（16-20）請根以下列翻譯內容，用適當的搭配詞填入空格。

16. He _____ _____ _____ after his girlfriend got fired from the bank.（他在女朋友被銀行解僱後，終止了自己的帳戶。）

17. Only the intelligence source has the program to _____ _____ _____ .（只有情報來源有解開這個密碼的程式。）

18. They _____ _____ _____ against the Mafia, but the Mafia didn't care what they did at all.（他們組成了個對抗黑手黨的聯盟，但黑手黨對他們所做的事毫不在意。）

19. His goal _____ _____ _____ to 3-2. The stadium was filled with excitement.（他的進球使比分變為 3 比 2。整個體育場陷入一片沸騰的情緒中。）

20. He _____ _____ _____ after he wrote his doctoral dissertation.（他在撰寫完博士論文後轉變了自己的主修科系。）

解答篇

DAY 01　DO ①

1. **business**, 愛德華是最不值得一起做生意的人。他的店已破產 3 次了。
2. **overtime**, 那位護士一個星期幾乎要加 3 個小時的班。她回到家時總是筋疲力盡。
3. **research**, 他正在進行跨國企業的研究。他說自己的發現將讓世人驚訝。
4. **job**, 儘管她身體孱弱，她仍然完成了一件了不起的工作。我們真的深受感動。
5. **activities**, 在一些學校裡，學生們必須參加課外活動才能畢業。
6. **experiment**, 即使已經與同學一起做了實驗，你們也必須提交用自己的話所撰寫的個人報告。
7. **service**, 目前，僅男性必須服兵役。然而，女性正主張平等，這麼說來，女性也該服兵役嗎？
8. **assignment**, 你不要自己寫作業。那不是你的作業 — 那是你孩子的作業。
9. **trade**, 研究全球經濟是一回事。實際從事貿易工作又是另一回事。
10. **work**, 他們正在尋找承包新購物商場建設工程的一些公司。
11. We are doing research on Korean traditional dance.
12. He did his assignment while smoking.
13. The state requires all men to do three years' military service.
14. I don't think he did a great job. He was just lucky.
15. You would rather focus on one thing than do a lot of businesses at one time.

DAY 02　DO ②

1. **exercise**, 除了瑜伽之外，做做其他運動也不錯。
2. **drugs**, 對於毒癮者來說戒毒的最佳方法之一就是尋求諮詢與治療。
3. **food**, 我們為了做派對的餐點，打電話聯絡了餐飲供應商。
4. **article**, 我計劃撰寫一篇關於韓國文化的論文。
5. **nails**, 如果想讓自己看起來更有時尚感，就把指甲塗成紅色吧。
6. **something**, 父親總是做出讓我感到心煩的事情。
7. **hair**, 我喜歡她修剪頭髮的方式，因為這些髮型總是相當獨特。

解答篇

DAY 01　DO ①

1. **business**, 愛德華是最不值得一起做生意的人。他的店已破產 3 次了。
2. **overtime**, 那位護士一個星期幾乎要加 3 個小時的班。她回到家時總是筋疲力盡。
3. **research**, 他正在進行跨國企業的研究。他說自己的發現將讓世人驚訝。
4. **job**, 儘管她身體孱弱，她仍然完成了一件了不起的工作。我們真的深受感動。
5. **activities**, 在一些學校裡，學生們必須參加課外活動才能畢業。
6. **experiment**, 即使已經與同學一起做了實驗，你們也必須提交用自己的話所撰寫的個人報告。
7. **service**, 目前，僅男性必須服兵役。然而，女性正主張平等，這麼說來，女性也該服兵役嗎？
8. **assignment**, 你不要自己寫作業。那不是你的作業 — 那是你孩子的作業。
9. **trade**, 研究全球經濟是一回事。實際從事貿易工作又是另一回事。
10. **work**, 他們正在尋找承包新購物商場建設工程的一些公司。
11. We are doing research on Korean traditional dance.
12. He did his assignment while smoking.
13. The state requires all men to do three years' military service.
14. I don't think he did a great job. He was just lucky.
15. You would rather focus on one thing than do a lot of businesses at one time.

DAY 02　DO ②

1. **exercise**, 除了瑜伽之外，做做其他運動也不錯。
2. **drugs**, 對於毒癮者來說戒毒的最佳方法之一就是尋求諮詢與治療。
3. **food**, 我們為了做派對的餐點，打電話聯絡了餐飲供應商。
4. **article**, 我計劃撰寫一篇關於韓國文化的論文。
5. **nails**, 如果想讓自己看起來更有時尚感，就把指甲塗成紅色吧。
6. **something**, 父親總是做出讓我感到心煩的事情。
7. **hair**, 我喜歡她修剪頭髮的方式，因為這些髮型總是相當獨特。

Answer Key 427

8. laundry, 她在洗衣服時可能會忘了放肥皂。
9. favor, 我不知道該怎麼感謝他。他在我需要幫助的時候對我伸出了極大的援手。
10. dishes, 他幫我們做了餐點，所以我自願去洗碗。因為我非常不擅長做菜，所以這樣的「分工合作」挺不錯的。
11. Do your nails before and after the trip.
12. I love the way he does things in a calm way.
13. If you want to express yourself, try doing an article.
14. He started doing drugs after his two sons died in a tragic car accident.
15. Many husbands say that they "help their wives do the laundry." But it is their own job.

DAY 03　DO ③

1. honor, 能夠邀請總統蒞臨我們的畢業典禮，對我們來說是莫大的榮耀。
2. reverse, 先從第一扇門進去，接著再進入第二扇門。離開時請反過來即可。
3. injustice, 將文化與教育分離，對少數民族來說是不公平的事。
4. translation, 我的一位朋友以法文翻譯英文為其職業。
5. sum, 你能用心算解決這個嗎？我要你將 1 到 100 的所有數字加總起來。
6. trick, 若你想贏得這場比賽，只是進行攻擊是不會成功的。
7. evil, 如果你對別人做壞事，終會受到報應的。
8. arrangement, 我們也可以幫您將我們為您製作的音樂進行編曲。
9. thinking, 他問我是否能讓學生做思辨能力的訓練。他一直關注學生是否能夠不只是接受所提供的內容，而是能從多元觀點進行思考。
10. calculation, 他雖然不太擅長計算，但卻是個數學方面的天才兒童。
11. I can do evil either with my head or my heart.
12. It is a teacher's duty to encourage students to do the thinking and talking.
13. If you want to run faster than your brother, this book might do the trick.
14. Many institutions still do injustice to people with disabilities.
15. Why don't you try doing the reverse? I guess the problem will be more easily resolved.

DAY 04 FIND ①

1. **mate**, 他當時三十三歲，且認為以自己的年紀應該要找個靈魂伴侶了。
2. **alternative**, 我們現在就得找出一個替代方案，否則我們就別無選擇，只能聽從老闆的指示。
3. **ally**, 聽好！你的周圍有太多的敵人了。如果無法找到一位盟友，你就得自己創造一個。
4. **volunteer**, 我們在當地報紙上刊登了一份招募非政府組織活動志工的廣告。
5. **occupation**, 你必須展現出自己的能力才能夠在那家公司謀得一職。
6. **sponsor**, 那位畫家遇見了一位資產豐厚的贊助人，並且能夠在享有盛名的大都會博物館舉辦她個人的展覽。
7. **survivors**, 他們在火災中發現了二十名生還者。
8. **replacement**, 我們需要尋找可以代替他的人選，因為他預計下週離職。
9. **culprit**, 房間裡電話上的指紋成為警方找出犯人的關鍵線索。
10. **recruits**, 要招募能在特種部隊服役的新兵越來越困難。大多數年輕人寧願從事行政工作，也不願在野戰中服勤。
11. He had a Ph.D. in Natural Science, so he had no difficulty in finding an occupation in the research industry.
12. The president has to find a replacement for the Prime Minister by next week.
13. The company tried to find an alternative for the order to recall its cars.
14. The police failed in finding the culprit. In fact, he was hiding inside a toilet in the police station.
15. One of the most important roles of the personnel department is to find recruits.

DAY 05 FIND ②

1. **salvation**, 牧師說：「有些人似乎在金錢與名譽中找到了救贖。但人所造之物並不能拯救我們。」
2. **nerve**, 就在那一刻，大衛與歌利亞的故事掠過他的腦海。他鼓起勇氣，挺身對抗那些嘲笑他的高年級學生。結果呢？他被揍了一頓。
3. **happiness**, 各種福利政策的制定，旨在幫助人們找到幸福以及達成自我實現。
4. **satisfaction**, 他是那種要「做到完美」才感到滿足的人，而非只是「做得好」而已。
5. **comfort**, 每當我陷入困境時，總會在宗教信仰中找到慰藉。但她卻說，那不過是自我欺騙罷了。

6. courage, 克服恐懼的最佳方法是什麼？那就是從你內心找到勇氣。
7. relief, 她無法從看著兒子的照片而得到慰藉。他已經永遠離開了，沒有人能將他帶回來。
8. peace, 這個世界充滿了痛苦，但我們可以在冥想與靈性對話中尋得內心的平靜。
9. inspiration, 他從古老神話中找到了創作奇幻小說的靈感。
10. forgiveness, 加害者無法從死去的受害者那裡獲得原諒，這使他長期飽受罪惡感的折磨。
11. He used to find his musical inspiration from Korean art.
12. She couldn't find true happiness in making money.
13. The mother tried to find relief in looking at the picture of her dead daughter.
14. The man failed in finding the nerve to talk back to his boss.
15. It is better to find salvation in the lotto than in politics.

DAY 06　FIND ③

1. pretext, 州政府試圖找出可以搜查那棟房子的藉口，但那根本荒謬至極。
2. explanation, 即便是尖端科技，也無法對奇蹟似的埃及金字塔建築找到恰當的解釋。
3. discrepancy, 你能說明一下我找到的這兩份文件之間的差異嗎？兩者本該一模一樣，但卻有所不同。
4. flaw, 在未檢討自己的缺點前，別試圖去找別人的缺點。
5. precedent, 我們找不到這類專案的前例。那意味著我們得從零開始。
6. meaning, 你想尋找人生的意義嗎？那麼你必須多讀書、常旅行，並將激發你靈感的事付諸實行。
7. information, 那名間諜成功地從這個秘密組織中找到了機密資料。
8. clue, 那名竊賊極為縝密，導致刑警完全找不到他犯案的任何線索。
9. evidence, 那名博士生找出了可反駁其指導者提出的假說。然而，他並未將其發表。
10. relationship, 他的研究顯示，我們可以在一個人的文化背景與其在寫作中展開主題的方式之間，找到強有力的關聯性。
11. The hacker was not able to find any discrepancy between the two files.
12. People have tried to find the meaning of life in philosophy and religion for thousands of years.

13. The United States found what they believed to be a plausible pretext of WMD (weapons of mass destruction) for attacking Iraq.
14. He found an important clue in the book. Some of the letters had been highlighted.
15. As we couldn't find a similar precedent, we had to start from scratch.

DAY 07　GET ①

1. last word, 那個固執的人從不讓他人作出最終決定，因此爭論未能達成共識。
2. approval, 一旦我提交了齊全且正確的申請書，需要多久時間才會獲得核准呢？
3. apology, 死去男孩的父母接受了肇事駕駛的道歉。
4. chance, 你建立第一印象的機會只有一次。
5. benefit, 若你希望透過飲食節制的方法來減重，就必須確實了解自己食物中的成分。
6. access, 在管理者核准之前，你無法進入有限存取的網路社群。
7. sentence, 他因開槍傷人而被判處五年徒刑。
8. edge, 在經濟仍然嚴峻的情況下，越來越多求職者為了在職場競爭者當中取得優勢，轉而尋求整形外科醫師的幫助。
9. exposure, 你有必要廣泛閱讀各種文體的作品，才能夠成為一位優秀的作家。
10. guarantee, 在他獲得經理給予升遷保證後，決定繼續留在這家公司。
11. Currently, the terrorists' activities in the Middle East are getting a lot of exposure in the press.
12. Though you never get a guarantee to win, you should fight on the side of justice.
13. After a long period of war, the country got an edge over the enemy.
14. He gets access to the secret library, but he is illiterate.
15. He got an approval from his boss, but he couldn't go on a leave for he had no money.

DAY 08　GET ②

1. point, 很明顯你沒有抓到重點。理解最簡單的事情到底要花多久時間？
2. feeling, 當我第一次凝視著你的眼睛時，我立刻有一種我們似曾相識的感覺。
3. taste, 參與式觀察和細緻的對話分析，或許是最能真正體會民族與文化的方式。

Answer Key 431

4. joke, 大家都在大笑的時候，總有一個人聽不懂笑話。
5. idea, 你是在哪得知我很快要搬家呢？
6. answer, 我不認為你已經得到答案了。在妄下結論之前，先停下來再想想，這是否合乎情理。
7. impression, 一份乾淨且易讀的履歷，會讓雇主覺得你確實很認真在找工作。
8. hang, 我在十四歲時學會了彈貝斯時，就開始跟樂團在全國巡迴演出。
9. grasp, 他那閃爍其詞的回答讓人難以理解事情的情況。
10. perspective, 如果你從一個新的觀點來看你自己寫作的過程，就更容易能突破「作家關卡」了。
11. I found that this was an excellent book to get a good grasp of English.
12. When you reach maturity, you get a different perspective on life.
13. When I saw her for the first time, I got the impression that she was a kind person.
14. It is painful but pleasant to get the hang of playing drums.
15. He always says that he got the point but makes mistakes over and over again.

DAY 09 GET ③

1. hiccups, 有人把青蛙放進我的外套口袋裡。就在我發現時，我嚇得打了整整一個小時的嗝。
2. results, 我們為那個產品投入了許多努力，且最後獲得了好的成果。我們也賺了大錢。
3. shots, 當暴風朝他逼近時，他大膽地拿出相機且拍了幾張照片。
4. grades, 有些學生交出的作品明顯不如其他同學的，卻還是拿到了好成績。
5. job, 工作經驗、積極態度以及良好的溝通技巧，能夠讓你得到一份長久的正職工作。
6. leave, 你還有（特休）假嗎？那麼，要不要和我一起去釣魚旅行？
7. liking, 這次她真的開始對我有好感了。這禮物確實產生效果了。
8. promotion, 我和別人一樣努力工作，卻從來沒獲得升遷。我打算另尋工作了。
9. score, 若額外支付費用，可以讓您的寫作獲得評分數且會附上評論意見。
10. name, 這名政客很渴望上新聞。
11. The director got a good name for directing the hit movie.
12. He got the highest score on the test.
13. She refused to get a sick leave and went on working.

14. It is really embarrassing to get hiccups in front of the prime minister.
15. He got depressed because he didn't get a promotion.

DAY 10　GIVE ①

1. **look**, 這篇關於 1987 年大選的報導似乎引起了極大的關注，主要是因為它探討了過去幾乎不為人知的政治事件。
2. **chase**, 巡邏艇展開追擊，雙方展開了 3,000 公里的追逐，有時兩艘船的距離甚至不到 1,000 公尺。
3. **eye**, 那位美麗的女子在路人對她拋媚眼時，只是露齒微笑並揮揮手。
4. **cue**, 請使用夠亮的燈泡，好讓你可以念書。燈光明亮會提醒大腦「是時候醒來了」。
5. **hand**, 他們這個週六搬來的，所以去我打了個招呼並幫忙他們搬了一些大件的行李。
6. **details**, 這個頁面詳細介紹了我們所屬的羽毛球聯盟。
7. **ring**, 我回到辦公室後會打電話給你。
8. **birth**, 那名女子透過施打促進排卵的藥物，生下了五胞胎。
9. **boost**, 一個善行就能大大提升你的名聲。
10. **view**, 這款望遠鏡比任何其他望遠鏡都能讓你更清楚地看風景。
11. Since the American woman moved in, my husband has been giving her the eye.
12. The article seems to give women the cue that using a sperm bank is the best way to treat infertility problems.
13. A hapless young man gave chase after my beautiful but fickle granddaughter.
14. He gave a boost to the local community by establishing a village symphony.
15. He gave details on early language education based on his point of view on critical period.

DAY 11　GIVE ②

1. **account**, 一旦克拉克提出解釋就會暴露自己的秘密身分，所以他只能被迫暫時入獄，直到風波平息為止。
2. **alibi**, 這名被告理應提出不在場證明，但卻他保持緘默。
3. **odds**, 我甚至下了大約 20 賠 1 的賭注。換句話說，如果他留在辦公室，他們就輸 1 美元；如果他準時離開，我就要賠給他們 20 美元。

4. voice, 已經十年過去了。在那段時間裡,我始終無法鼓起勇氣說出埋藏在心底多年的那句話。
5. example, 他成為腦傷協會的成功典範——這個協會的多數成員都是腦傷患者及其家人。
6. comfort, 在將他安葬後,牧師向來賓們說了幾句安慰的話。
7. total, 根據 1900 到 1910 年的目錄總共記載了 302 個登記案件。
8. evidence, 國際特赦組織撰寫的這份報告,提供了國家安全法侵犯人權的證據。
9. instruction, 在駕訓期間,我被教導是要以穩定的速度行駛。
10. demonstration, 您可以示範一下這些東西要怎麼組裝嗎?
11. I couldn't even find the courage to give comfort to those with a brain injury.
12. Give me an account of why you were forced to give them 20 dollars.
13. She gave her students instructions to read the textbook aloud.
14. We should give voice to immigrant workers who are suffering from miserable conditions.
15. The boy gave an alibi that he had been studying at home, but his clothes were so dirty.

DAY 12　GIVE ③

1. party, 我想辦一場盛大的派對,並品嘗一些從前才吃得到的珍稀美食。
2. discount, 我們提供快速付款的優惠;若您在第一期付款截止日前或當日一次付清全額,我們將提供折扣。
3. way, 自上個世紀以來,美國電視新聞所自豪的傳統,已逐漸讓位給娛樂導向的產業。
4. access, 透過這個網站可進入國會圖書館,並可使用各種服務與資訊。
5. rebate, 污染問題嚴重的城市可以提供購買油電混合車並退還舊汽油車的居民一定金額的補助。
6. audition, 布萊恩問我是否願意將幾位配音員帶到我們其中一間錄音室試鏡。
7. first-aid, 儘管法律規定每個人都有義務給予傷者急救措施,但道路事故現場車輛完全不停地經過的情況,仍屢見不鮮。
8. wave, 當我看到他在車裡顯得非常慌張的模樣時,我忍不住放慢車速,朝他揮揮手並給他一個微笑。
9. start, 許多韓國人一致認為,從小學習英語能為孩子在學術與社交上帶來更有利的起跑點。
10. dimension, DVD 收錄的特別影片為電影欣賞開啟一個有趣且不同的新視角。

11. Once I take them to one of my studios, I am going to give a big party.
12. Thank you for giving me a start on translating the website.
13. When I passed him sitting in his car, he was giving way to another car.
14. She gave me a cheerful wave, but she was shedding tears.
15. The production gave an audition to 200 people but hired no one.

DAY 13 HAVE ①

1. agreement, 雙方就誰來支付法律費用達成了協議。
2. check-ups, 定期做健康檢查以確認身體是否健康，是照顧自己的一部分。
3. affair, 她的丈夫極力否認他與她一位朋友有婚外情這件事。
4. argument, 我不想和那些老是阻礙協商、不理性的對手爭辯。
5. baby, 我們已經有三個孩子了，但正試著再生一個。
6. go, 過來試試看吧！如果你能自己完成，一定會感到更驕傲的。
7. chat, 昨天我在辦公室和我老闆談到了那項計畫的推進情況。
8. check, 在做決定之前，要先大致檢查一下車輛，確認它是否是贓車或事故車。
9. arrangement, 那對夫妻雖然已離婚，但為了孩子仍會定期安排碰面。
10. abortions, 越來越多女性開始高談闊論自己曾墮胎的經驗，並在同溫層團體中分享自己的故事。
11. Management announced that it had an agreement with the unions to secure welfare services.
12. Some women go through emotional difficulties in deciding to have an abortion.
13. The discussion panelists had a long argument over the current nuclear issue.
14. The doctor advised him to have a physical check-up but he just ignored the advice.
15. They had just a short chat together but felt attracted to each other.

DAY 14 HAVE ②

1. attitude, 那位教授對社會環境不健康的風氣非常反感。
2. affection, 他顯然對他的寵物懷有深厚的感情。
3. bent, 當我在攝影比賽中得獎時，才意識到自己有藝術方面的才能。
4. choice, 當警方從四面八方同時展開圍捕時，那些罪犯只能選擇投降。

Answer Key   435

5. benefit, 那家購物中心在人口密集區獲得了龐大利益。
6. clue, 他們完全不知道哪裡可以找到辦法來處理這部中毒了的電腦。
7. assurance, 那個國家並未獲得任何可以確保其政權不受到任何攻擊的堅定保證。
8. advantage, 那家公司相較於其競爭對手更具有優勢。
9. addiction, 有些政治人物似乎有嚴重的權力成癮症。
10. access, 數百萬名貧困國家的愛滋患者仍無法取得可能拯救他們性命的藥物。
11. The business consulting firm has unique access to up-to-date financial information.
12. Once you have an addiction to the Internet, it will take over your life.
13. This website has the advantage of being accessible by any user.
14. She has more affection to her family than to her social activities.
15. Having a positive attitude is the key to success.

DAY 15 HAVE ③

1. insight, 若想與他人有效溝通，就必須洞悉他們的想法及感受。
2. effect, 《京都議定書》對全球暖化產生了深遠的影響。
3. credibility, 身為教師的你，若真想在年輕學子面前擁有信任度，關鍵在於你擁有他們需要、想要並且能夠運用的東西。
4. difficulties, 任何對於學校作業上感到吃力的學生，應該給予鼓勵，以免他們對學習失去興趣。
5. urge, 在我聽到一聲巨響後，我有一股想往窗外看看的強烈衝動。
6. cause, 沒有理由因為害怕而退縮。你正在做正確的事。
7. agenda, 工會已將醫療照護服務的使用問題列為討論議題。
8. connections, 被逮捕的男子們據稱與恐怖組織網絡有關聯。
9. comment, 警方不會有任何進一步的評論，直到他們完成所有文書作業時。
10. differences, 即使長得一模一樣的雙胞胎也可能存在身體上的差異；他們所處的環境可能不同。
11. Both players had a big difference of opinion, but they cooperated well with each other.
12. If you have any comments, please send an e-mail to this address.
13. I had an urge to hold her hand.

14. The meeting has too many agenda points so participants could not focus on one.
15. Simplicity and accessibility is one of the requirements for a website to have credibility.

DAY 16 HOLD ①

1. election, 該政權違背了舉行自由選舉的承諾，並鎮壓了反對獨裁的公民運動。
2. power, 即使在這項法律生效之後，它在三年內對我們仍無效力。
3. meeting, 委員會同意召開一場會議，以決定該問題的程序性事項。
4. balance, 少數政黨和無黨派政客在國會中仍握有維持權力平衡的實力。
5. key, 能將這個國家從經濟衰退中拉出來的關鍵政策是什麼？
6. talks, 那些國家就目前的核武威脅秘密召開了多方會談。
7. conference, 上週教育部宣布，將召開會議討論青少年的性教育問題。
8. reins, 你認為幾個掌握政權的政客將國家帶向戰爭的這件事可以合理化嗎？
9. auction, 「鯨魚朋友們」將舉辦一場募款拍賣會，屆時會有許多值得競標的好東西。
10. summit, 來自政府一份報告指出，南北韓雙方可能在兩個月內舉行一場高峰會。
11. When do you think the two Koreas will hold a summit again?
12. Once a year, the school holds an auction to raise money for its scholarship fund.
13. These days, many wives hold power over their husbands.
14. The NGO held a "green conference" to organize an environmental campaign.
15. Schools demand teachers (should) hold the balance between strictness and generosity.

DAY 17 HOLD ②

1. views, 對這些問題持不同意見的人必須有具說服力的論點來支持自己的觀點。
2. patent, 這些創作家主張自己擁有此技術的專利，而最後他們也獲得了這項權利。
3. position, 此教育座談會介紹了其四人小組，他們每一位都擁有「卓越教授」的職位。
4. office, 在韓國，總統任期為五年，且不得連選連任。

Answer Key   437

5. share, 為了在競爭日益激烈的市場中維持公司的市占率，必須進行更多投資。
6. promise, 新型油電混合車輛有望提升燃油效率。
7. inquiry, 軍方堅定拒絕對可疑的死亡案件展開調查。
8. values, 資本主義者除了追求利潤最大化之外，對其他事情並不重視。
9. rank, 所有用來製作香水的花朵之中，紅玫瑰一直被認為是最出色的。
10. record, 我想來介紹一位保持一個月賣出 125 輛車紀錄的超級業務員。
11. Who holds the world record for the 100m sprint?
12. The woman holds the position of spokesperson of the party.
13. This new learning strategy may hold promise for improving achievement.
14. The venture company holds the patent on the stem cell technology.
15. Some home-schooling supporters hold a critical view on school education.

DAY 18   HOLD ③

1. tongue, 無論看到或聽到什麼，都閉嘴。這個房間裡保持完全的安靜很重要。
2. fire, 警方接獲命令，在罪犯接近時不得開槍。
3. tune, 我們正在尋找一位有音樂才華、能搭配旋律的新團員加入我們的樂團。
4. moisture, 熱空氣會增加其水氣的容納量，並降低其相對濕度。
5. territory, 那個國家被質疑不是在推廣自由，而是在試圖掌握領土。
6. line, 麻煩請不要掛電話好嗎？我去看經理在不在。
7. attention, 那位演講者的宣告吸引了眾多觀眾超過 15 分鐘的注意。
8. hostage, 上週被暴民挾持為人質的八名工人已被釋放並回到其祖國的懷抱。
9. breath, 如果那隻怪物不自己出現的話怎麼辦？我們就只能這樣屏息等待嗎？
10. hands, 瑪麗向他伸出手時，他遲疑了一下，最後才脫下了手套。
11. We held our breath in fear.
12. After holding hands with his girlfriend, the young man wondered what was next.
13. The movie completely held the watchers' attention throughout two hours.
14. The first sergeant ordered his men to hold fire but no one could hear his voice.
15. The boy succeeded in holding the girl's attention by showing a magic trick.

DAY 19　KEEP ①

1. **files**, 總統以「愛國法」和反恐為手段，試圖合理化自己的行為，以及合法持有其人民的檔案資料。
2. **faith**, 無神論正擴散至全世界。因此，許多人在堅守對上帝的信仰上受到了挑戰。
3. **engagement**, 該公司為了履行約定付出了各種努力。不過，他們最終仍以失敗告終且宣告破產。
4. **value**, 耐用又設計良好的產品能保有其長久的價值。它不會被丟棄或被新品取代。
5. **statistics**, 若要掌握一個國家的人口成長情況，有必要對所有出生人數進行統計。
6. **diary**, 沒有規定要你每天或每週必須寫日記，但有些人知道那樣做是有用的。
7. **account**, 他應該要把所有的收據與支出登記入帳簿，並於每季末提出財務報告。
8. **record**, 無論使用的材料多麼少，製造商都會將所有材料供應商和進口商做紀錄。
9. **promise**, 我相信人們對民主的信念能促使特定政客信守自己的承諾。
10. **resolutions**, 雖然許多人無法堅持新年立下的運動計畫，但自己對自己許下的每一項承諾都是值得堅持的。
11. The president should keep his promise and release the imprisoned environmental activists.
12. Keeping a diary makes us reflect on everyday life.
13. He still keeps his resolution to stop smoking.
14. The pastor chose death as a reason to keep his faith as a Christian.
15. It is necessary to keep records for all the meetings for clear communication.

DAY 20　KEEP ②

1. **peace**, 聯合國在這個地區要做的事是維持已同意停火的衝突勢力之間的和平。他們應該透過對話而不是戰爭來解決分歧。
2. **distance**, 那位追緝謀殺犯的警探與他認定的主要嫌疑人 — 一名魅惑的女子 — 保持距離。
3. **control**, 施暴者之所以開始並持續施暴，是因為暴力被視為控制他人的有效手段。
4. **pace**, 公司企業必須與人口遷移與需求變化保持一致的步調。否則，他們無法生

Answer Key   439

存下去。
5. secret, 她像是再也無法保守秘密般，臉突然漲紅。她心中有一股要將一切全盤托出的衝動。
6. sight, 你必須鎖定好你的目標，並牢記，即使是漫長的旅程也都是從最初的一小步開始的。
7. perspective, 當我們回顧過去並且想從我們認為是陰暗面的事情中學習時，保持正確的觀點是很重要的。
8. balance, 保持環境中動植物的平衡是非常重要的。
9. shape, 你的襯衫看起來像新的一樣。它怎麼可能在車子的置物箱裡還能保持這麼平整？
10. eye, 別擔心。我在天花板裝了幾台攝影機，正 24 小時全天候監控顧客一舉一動。
11. The box was too weak to keep the shape of the cake.
12. The government keeps control of the stock market.
13. Will you keep an eye on my kids until I get back?
14. She kept her distance from the young boss to avoid co-workers' attention.
15. Keeping a secret is far more difficult than making one.

DAY 21　KEEP ③

1. temper, 他在討論時常常大聲說話，最後總是變成爭吵。他必須控制自己的脾氣。
2. hand, 他喜歡戲劇。儘管卡特是眾所皆知的企業執行長，他依然努力維持對表演藝術的關注。
3. company, 我們經常接觸的人或朋友會影響我們的人生。所以我們應該努力與他們維持良好關係。
4. track, 這是一個可以記錄收入、稅金和支出的免費試算表。
5. house, 「做家事是女性責任」的觀念正在改變。丈夫們若要建立真正平等的關係，就必須付出實際行動。
6. contact, 透過電腦和網路，我們可以輕鬆查閱新聞標題，也能與親友保持聯繫。
7. watch, 當孩子們靠近湍急的河流時，請務必時時刻刻顧好他們。
8. grip, 教育部長計畫對現職教師進行教育訓練，好讓他們能運用更多干預措施與策略來管理學生。
9. change, 我聽說在某些國家，不收找零是非常失禮的事，所以我通常都會收找零。

10. **pets**, 飼養寵物是侵犯動物的自由權嗎？還是剛好相反呢？
11. Keeping a pet can reduce the loneliness of the old.
12. In spite of studying abroad, he kept contact with friends in his homeland.
13. Here is 5000 won. Keep the change.
14. I think he needs to keep his temper under control. Don't you agree?
15. I feel it is difficult to keep company with alumni once they get married.

DAY 22 MAKE ①

1. **purchase**, 理查為了他的女朋友買了東西。但她對他所買的東西感到失望。
2. **improvement**, 儘管政府施以壓迫手段，人民仍奮力為民主的進步而努力。
3. **withdrawal**, 他應該先去從帳戶提領現金，以免假日時無法取得銀行的功能。
4. **offer**, 她總是對她的顧客提出適當的建議。他們也信任她的能力。
5. **investment**, 近日，這家電子公司的股價節節高升。人們應在股價上漲前趕緊投資。
6. **apology**, 如果他不犯那樣愚蠢的錯誤，我認為就不需要道歉。
7. **recommendation**, 在你的期末報告中，你可以根據你的分析與意見提出建議。
8. **profit**, 該公司允許人們銷售其免費的軟體並從中獲利，但不允許他人限制它的散佈權利。
9. **payment**, 這個網站不再只要求訪客以信用卡付款。你也可以從你的儲蓄帳戶進行轉帳。
10. **response**, 我們懇請您對於我們的信件不吝賜覆。如此，我們便能針對這個可能造成致命影響的問題，迅速做出決策。
11. He has to make a payment of the rent within a week.
12. She made no response to his proposal.
13. After becoming equipped with new facilities, the company made good profit.
14. He made a sincere apology to her, but she thought it was fake.
15. The photographer made recommendations for various digital cameras and lenses.

DAY 23 MAKE ②

1. **conversation**, 老師應該要富有熱忱，並具備與學生對話的能力。
2. **statement**, 政府宣布，總統是被一名對當前政治情勢極為不滿的高官所暗殺。

Answer Key   441

3. appointment, 為了安排合適的會面時間，請撥打下方的電話號碼與我們聯繫。否則，您亦可親自前來我們辦公室。
4. call, 如果您想撥打國際電話，在撥號前需要先按「0」。
5. mess, 清理我兒子弄亂的東西花了我兩個小時。我真的累壞了。
6. speech, 白宮表示，總統會在德州發表關於這場戰爭的演說。
7. noise, 除非你身陷一個特別糟糕的處境，否則你發一丁點噪音就會讓熊逃跑。
8. reference, 這名革命理論家引用馬克思的《共產黨宣言》來強調歷史的進展。
9. contact, 我很遺憾地要通知您，最好是聯絡一下其他能滿足您學術期待的大學。
10. reservation, 這間飯店建議提前預約。否則你可能得等上一段很長的時間，最糟的是，還得另尋其他飯店。
11. Please check the conference room schedule before making a reservation.
12. Students are required to make contact with their professor at the beginning of the course.
13. During the election campaign, the presidential candidate made a speech about reducing taxes.
14. The ASEAN leaders made a statement on the future of Asia.
15. The kid always made a mess of his room, but his parents thought it was a sign of his creativity.

DAY 24 MAKE ③

1. start, LCD 市場雖然在年初時有個好的開始，但從二月起價格開始下滑。
2. contributions, 所有人對於重建內戰期間被摧毀的小鎮都做出了貢獻。
3. difference, 我相信我的身體障礙對打破世界紀錄毫無影響。我不會像過去那樣感到挫敗。
4. visit, 若您希望來訪，請事先通知我們。如此，我們可以提供更好的諮詢服務。
5. point, 她用來指出重點的手勢有效吸引了聽眾們的注意。所有人都點了點頭。
6. error, 在面試期間，他過於緊張，以致於不自覺地犯了為自己錯誤辯解的錯。
7. discovery, 他正致力於幹細胞移植技術的突破性發現，未來有望為緩和重大疾病帶來希望。
8. assessment, 環保團體主張，在隧道工程開始前，應對國家公園進行大範圍的評估。
9. arrest, 警方逮捕了一名涉嫌在酒吧殺害一名年輕人的嫌疑犯。目擊者稱，他是在一場因被潑到飲料而起爭執時被刺傷的。

10. haste, 三星正加緊修復因停電導致的電器損壞。但目前仍未查明停電的起因。
11. The prosecutor made an arrest of the suspect right before he fled abroad.
12. The government asked the ambassador to make haste in the final negotiation.
13. It took her one week to make an assessment of all the students' essays.
14. What kind of job should I take to make a contribution to Korean society?
15. "Your attitude makes an action. Your action makes a difference," read the picket.

DAY 25　SHOW ①

1. goodwill, 據說羅馬人在戰爭中是殘暴的，但對於所有站在他們這邊的人展現善意。
2. profit, 在 1980 年代，電視網開始要求新聞部門創造收益，然此舉卻讓他們淪為廣告商的掌控。
3. ability, 首爾舉行的「古典音樂大賽」相當成功，而麥可大賽中的許多賓客面前展現了他演奏鋼琴的實力。
4. way, 棘手的是，沒有人能告訴你解決問題的方法。你必須自己想辦法。
5. door, 我們公司已決定請吸菸的員工走路，即使他們在自己空閒的時間抽菸。
6. film, 當我們參觀製片攝影棚時，他們用大螢幕上播放這部影片。
7. leadership, 州長持續展現他的領導力以及對我們社區的奉獻精神。
8. teeth, 那隻狗可能會低吼、露牙威脅，或是吠叫。
9. deference, 像中國、印度、美國這些東協地區強權參與該區域的論壇，以及對該組織表達敬意，這都證明東協仍然具有重要性。
10. passport, 海關人員會要求您出示護照，並掃描您的行李。
11. The hardest thing is that there is no one to show his or her leadership in pedagogical areas.
12. School authorities showed the door to the students who were protesting against the administration.
13. I am always asked to show my teeth when I smile.
14. She showed great ability in comedy and soon became a millionaire.
15. Showing deference to a national flag does not mean that we support the current government.

DAY 26　SHOW ②

1. **partiality**, 所有提交參賽的產品將由一群對所有品牌一視同仁的評審團進行品味評分。
2. **faith**, 你的父母一直都是信任你的。他們把新車交給你，代表他們認為你值得被賦予更多責任。
3. **unease**, 法院可以容忍和平且具溝通意願的示威抱持寬容，但當示威活動威脅到「秩序」時，則會表現出高度的不安。
4. **flair**, 這是一場包含拼圖題、時間一個鐘頭的選擇題筆試；然而，對於有數學天賦的學生來說是一種享受的過程。
5. **hand**, 他從不暴露他的底牌，因此他肯定是位擅長撲克的高手。他將情緒隱藏在表面之下，始終保持冷靜。
6. **diplomacy**, 請在聊天室中保持應有的分寸與禮貌。任何人若有粗口或無禮行為，將被請出聊天室。
7. **affection**, 當他站上舞台時，他向觀眾展現出的熱情與潛力讓我印象深刻。
8. **mercy**, 他願意向其他不值得同情的人展現慈悲。
9. **concern**, 「國家警察大隊」對近期謀殺、強暴與人口販運等惡性犯罪的增加表示擔憂。
10. **respect**, 一個女人需要一個與她對話或提到她時，能夠尊重她的丈夫 — 他應該總是在人前稱讚她且絕不會輕視她。
11. He made an impressive appeal to students who show a flair for puzzles.
12. Citizens showed their concern about the establishment of the new government.
13. You can't show your hand so soon, or you'll give away too much information.
14. The nurse showed the mercy of taking the beggar to her home and treating him.
15. Mother showed unease when her son said he would quit his job and start his own business.

DAY 27　SHOW ③

1. **promise**, 身為新人的他展現出了潛力，但他的潛能似乎尚未完全發揮，因為他的傷勢迫使他必須坐一段時間的冷板凳。
2. **bias**, 針對俄亥俄州工人家庭的最新調查顯示，對於黑人的偏見是存在的。
3. **approval**, 院長批准了以圖章取代簽名的新支付系統。
4. **tendency**, 該團體傾向於不被分割，而是作為整體行動。

5. sign, 可惜的是，我個人原本期望那位作家會展現出些許成熟感，但很快地在讀完第一段後，這個期望就沒了。
6. world, 現在正值聖誕季節，是個向全世界展現你有多慷慨的好機會。
7. change, 由曼德拉先生主導的愛滋研究顯示出人們性行為的變化。
8. proof, 請您注意，申請該大學入學許可時，需證明您的英文的語言能力。
9. pattern, 這部電影呈現出典型的精神分析模式。這位英雄的心理衝突與理想化行為源自於其幼年與父母的關係。
10. world, 朴智星在上一場對戰切爾西的比賽中攻入致勝一球，向全世界展示自己已完全從腿傷中恢復。
11. He showed the world that his potential can be fulfilled.
12. People sometimes show a bias against the elderly or the disabled.
13. His paintings show a pattern of distorting established "truths."
14. This statistics shows the tendency that young people are getting more and more uninterested in politics.
15. His statement shows the proof that he is one of the accomplices in the crime.

DAY 28　TAKE ①

1. day off, 超過 100 名工人將請假一天，他們要將其技能與時間奉獻給非營利組織。
2. message, 我會幫忙無法接電話或不在辦公室的人留言。
3. break, 你需要稍作休息、伸展身體讓血液循環。長時間久坐不休息是有害的。
4. pill, 我希望我的丈夫每天服藥後能逐漸恢復肝功能。
5. picture, 我用數位相機拍攝了校園周圍的風景。
6. course, 沒有修過經濟學概論的學生必須修這門課。
7. second, 我建議你在面試開始前花點時間整理一下思緒。
8. test, 若你無法在預定日期參加考試，你有責任提前安排一個補考日期。
9. chance, 他知道她可能會拒絕他的晚餐邀請，但他還是去試試看。
10. orders, 這家中式餐廳甚至還接受簡訊外送訂餐。
11. I took a chance and invited the prettiest and most popular girl to the dance.
12. During my absence, ask the secretary to take a message.
13. The waiter took our order, but never came back to deliver our food.
14. The doctor told my father to take the pill twice a day, but he just drank every day.

15. I took a day off as I had caught a cold. I slept all day long.

DAY 29 TAKE ②

1. trouble, 閱讀能力不足的人不願意花心思從內容中推敲作者的意圖。因此他們的閱讀能力測驗的分數往往低於預期。
2. delight, X 世代樂於打破舊有做事情的方式。前一代有時則無法理解他們的行為。
3. jump, 我認為一位有野心的女性能在這間公司中一舉躍昇至最高層級，只要她非常有能力且足夠聰明
4. look, 當我仔細檢視了我們公司的保安系統，發現了幾個缺點。
5. effort, 韓國人會努力以微妙的方式表他們的達情感。但美國人則較為直接，且會直接切入重點。
6. shape, 如果你將每個點連起來，最後會形成一條與圖七所示相同的線條，那應該是你熟悉的圖形。
7. breath, 當海豚需要呼吸時，會浮到水面上。
8. interest, 我希望全體國民能更關注環保運動。
9. note, 請注意，若想獲得更多資訊，必須先上網登記。
10. turns, 因為旅途遙遠，我們輪流開車。
11. He admitted that he failed to take note of recent advances in human rights.
12. This activity requires each student to take a turn as a class discussion leader.
13. After taking a deep breath, he ran to her.
14. I took delight in participating in the civil movement. However, my parents wanted me to make money.
15. My friend took the trouble to drive me to the station, and I made it home in time.

DAY 30 TAKE ③

1. place, 資訊與通信科技不僅取代了傳統教學方式，也正在改變師生之間的關係。
2. care, 人們認為國家提供他們終身的照顧與保障是合理的。
3. aim, 作者們鎖定幾個與統計有關的迷思，並於前言中加以說明。但若缺乏科學與社會背景知識，理解其內容並不容易。

4. action, 當機器出故障時，立即採取行動可能更有利。
5. charge, 以你的年紀，現在正是你該吃得更健康、多運動，對自己的健康負責的時候了。
6. issue, 若總統沒有這項計畫提出異議，你的提案應該就能通過。
7. point of view, 他們採納金融界經理人的觀點 — 他們想要與極有效率的資本市場互動。
8. risk, 工程師們往往不願冒險發展新科技，因為沒有人願意給予財務支援。
9. advantage, 學習英文詞彙時應充分利用字典。特別為第二語言學習者設計的字典會有幫助。
10. part, 共有 32 位學生參加了這場 MBA 寫作工作坊，其聚焦於論文寫作在 MBA 錄取過程中的重要性。
11. Once you enroll, you'll take advantage of e-learning.
12. Prominent scientists will take part in the conference and make speeches.
13. He took a big risk in trying to rescue her from the burning building.
14. The right-wing professor took issue with the government's socialist labor policy.
15. The local government should take immediate action for the increasing aging problems.

DAY 01-30　Final Check-up

1. do, 在我們英文課堂上有幾種活動是我們可以進行的。／她是最不值得一起做生意的人。／我們除了看電影之外，也可以透過運動來釋放壓力。／一個國家無權對另一國家做出不公不義的事。
2. hold, 該博物館預定在 3 月 1 日舉辦一場銷售藝術品的拍賣會。／那位獵人會在熊進入他的視線時才會開槍。／砂糖的水分含量不高。／這堂講座沒能吸引大多數學生的注意。
3. got, 我得到了與籃球隊教練見面的機會。／她透過在百老匯演唱而為自己建立了名聲。／我獲得晉升為我部門的組長。／我用我手機的相機拍了一張那位女演員的照片。
4. take, 你得休息一下。／所有員工在元旦這一天都會休假。／我常常在小事情中找樂趣。／我喜歡旅行，且我夠年輕，有冒險的本錢。
5. had, 我們彼此熱絡地閒聊著。／她除了接受邀請之外，別無選擇。／那項治療當然有效。／她知道自己是個殘疾人，但仍渴望看見這個世界。
6. (a), This page gives details of the badminton leagues we play in （這一頁詳細記載了我們加入的羽球聯盟內容。）

Answer Key 447

7. (d), The software company makes a huge profit from the new system（那家軟體公司藉由這個新的系統取得巨大的獲利。）
8. (e), The thief was so cautious that the detective could not find any clue that he committed the crime（那小偷相當小心謹慎，以至於刑警無法找到任何他犯案的線索。）
9. (c), The Prime Minister has yet to keep his promise to reduce taxes（首相至今尚未兌現他的減稅承諾。）
10. (b), A recent survey of working families in Ohio showed a bias against black people（最近一項針對俄亥俄州勞工家庭的調查顯示對於黑人的偏見是存在的。）
11. views, 對這些問題持不同觀點的人必須以有說服力的論點來支持他們的意見。
12. point, 你顯然沒有抓到重點。你要多久時間才能理解最簡單的事情？
13. track, 警方持續在追蹤 MP3 檔案的非法散播。但網路使用者不斷開發新的緊急措施來規避其監控。
14. effort, 會努力以微妙的方式表他們的達情感。但美國人則較為直接，且會直接切入重點。
15. share, 為了在競爭日益激烈的市場中維持公司的市占率，必須進行更多投資。
16. Who holds the world record for the 100m sprint?
17. Will you keep an eye on my kids until I get back?
18. It took her one week to make an assessment of all the students' essays.
19. During my absence, ask the secretary to take a message.
20. The president has to find a replacement for the prime minister by next week.

DAY 31　Business and Economy

1. plunged into a long recession, 您認為我們已陷入長期的經濟衰退嗎？我認為我們很快就會走出來。
2. launched a new product, 我們推出了一個新產品上市。令人傷心的是，似乎沒有人認可它。
3. reduce warfare expenditures, 那位高官同意裁減軍費的計畫。
4. exceeded our budget, 支出超出了預算。我們本來只有五百美元，但卻花了兩萬元。
5. maintain the insurance, 他想續保，但手頭上沒有錢。
6. (c), 政府對於那個問題的立場不一致。總理主張增加預算，而財經部長則認為應該減少。

7. (a), 每一位業務員都必須意識到競爭的存在。市場正逐漸因類似的產品所飽和。

8. (d), 為了逃避遺產稅，他把一半的財產轉到兒子名下。

9. (a), 你必須考慮發行新股所帶來的影響。它可能會對公司的投資人關係（IR）產生重大影響。

10. (c), 降價並不是解決銷售不佳的萬靈藥：這可能會讓顧客產生你的產品不具頂級品質的印象。

11. The NGO is trying to balance its budget without getting aid.

12. The company issued 2 classes of shares.

13. The DVD market has lost substantial revenue from widespread illegal copies.

14. The company went bankrupt as soon as my uncle acquired 3,000 shares.

15. The defrauder claimed the insurance. It turned out later that he hurt himself.

DAY 32　Finance

1. declared sudden bankruptcy, 我無法忘記我們執行長突然宣布公司破產的那一天。

2. qualify for disability payments, 您不符領取殘障人士津貼的資格。失眠不能視為殘疾。

3. opened a secret account, 那名貪腐官員為了隱藏自己的黑錢，在海外開設了秘密帳戶。

4. charge high fees, 不要用信用卡提現。銀行會收取高額手續費。

5. attract new investment, 他的商業計劃未能吸引新的投資，且他離開了公司。

6. (a), 若超過轉帳限額，您將得支付額外費用。

7. (b), 那名小偷在當地一家銀行申請貸款時被逮捕了。

8. (b), 她賺了很多錢。她每個月會將一萬五千美元存入自己的帳戶。

9. (b), 聯邦準備委員會（FRB）擁有調控利率的權限，以確保經濟保持穩定。

10. (c), 請注意若您沒有收據，您的電子產品將無法取得退款。

11. You need to submit your receipt to get a refund.

12. It seems that shopping is the aim of her life. She always wastes money.

13. He closed his account after his girlfriend got fired from the bank.

14. He draws his pension at the local welfare center.

15. We tried to escape from bankruptcy.

Answer Key   449

DAY 33 Work and Office

1. have a meeting, 首先，考慮一下是否真有必要開會。為開會而開會只會浪費時間與資源。
2. understand the bottom line, 我無法讓他理解重點。他在會計方面完全是個白癡。
3. win the construction contract, 那個團隊幾乎篤定能獲得建設合約。那份合約價達 20 億美元。
4. give a presentation, 我真的需要做簡報嗎？我覺得寫封非正式的電子郵件就可以了。
5. run the office, 他說他只靠電子郵件與遠端會議系統就能經營辦公室。但，管理辦公室還是需要面對面的接觸與個人的溝通。
6. (a), 那位獵才顧問向我提出了相當具有競爭力的年薪，但我並不喜歡那份工作。
7. (c), 兩家公司能夠透過簽訂排他性的合作備忘錄（MOU）完成那筆交易。
8. (d), 董事會將他晉升為行銷部門的高階經理。那意味著他現在要負責國內外的行銷工作。
9. (c), 觀光公司接待員向我確認可以搭乘這班飛。然而，航班因為大雪被取消了。
10. (c), 開公司只是個起點。經營又是另一回事了。
11. The president shut down the factory because of the workers' strike.
12. The boss gave me confirmation on the reservation.
13. The meeting was canceled and his salary was dramatically cut.
14. You must make a written contract and sign it.
15. I admit that she deserves the rapid promotion.

DAY 34 Information

1. respect my privacy, 她面露不耐地說，「我希望你別再干擾，且請尊重我的隱私。」
2. are denied access, 未持有效執照的記者不得查閱機密資訊。
3. save your document, 為了不丟失你目前寫好的東西，請盡可能頻繁地將你的文件存檔。
4. released its special report, 當局根據警方對那起犯罪事件的調查，發布其特別的報告。
5. take a safety tip, 請聽我說明一項安全守則；將這些化學物品放回架上並遠離它們。

6. (b), 這個入口網站會隨時更新正在進行的活動消息。
7. (b), 科學家們正在蒐集全球各地關於全球暖化跡象的資訊。
8. (c), 對事實的詮釋不同可能會導致截然不同的結論。
9. (c), 資安程式設計師在他們的加密技術被破解時會感到慚愧。另一方面，駭客則為入侵保安系統而感到自豪。
10. (b), 別再談抽象的主題了，我們來討論一些細節吧。
11. Only the intelligence source has the program to crack this code.
12. If you are interested in this proposal, I'll send you further details in a week.
13. The intelligence agency seriously violated privacy by wiretapping people.
14. The government will issue a report on the FTA negotiations.
15. He gave me some tips about how to increase the number of website visitors.

DAY 35　The Internet

1. surf the net, 他的興趣是上網。他知道所有好用的網站。
2. download the program, 我需要下載程式。我無法在我的電腦上觀看這個影片片段。
3. hacked the system, 系統有問題。一定是有人入侵了系統。
4. filter the spam mail, 最近垃圾郵件太多了。我們得購買軟體來過濾垃圾郵件。
5. scan for viruses, 他說明了防毒軟體在他們電腦中掃描病毒的運作方式。
6. (b), 可以請你把那封信轉寄給我嗎？我的郵件伺服器出現問題，收不到郵件。
7. (d), 我覺得自己很難建立部落格。我對電腦一竅不通。可以給我一些提示嗎？
8. (d), 請在「確認」文字框中再次輸入密碼。
9. (c), 我們不登入網站也可以在你的部落格留言嗎？
10. (d), 上網太久對你的健康不好。試著減少上網並增加戶外活動的時間吧。
11. How much time do you spend online a day?
12. You have to make it a habit to log out from a website.
13. I forgot my password so I was not able to access the website.
14. Instructions on how to uninstall this program are available.
15. Simply open the e-mail and read the message.

Answer Key   451

DAY 36 Press and Media

1. **pass religious censorship**, 很快地，埃及的電視節目將必須通過宗教審查。資訊部長下令，電視劇必須尊重埃及社會的價值觀。
2. **draw up the Communist Manifesto**, 馬克思與恩格斯決定草擬完成《共產黨宣言》，以向世界宣告他們的革命思想。
3. **grab headlines**, 當嚴重災難事故成為媒體頭條時，會有更多日常的氣候變化 — 比方說，對於靠天氣吃飯的行業構成威脅的天氣狀況 — 實際上會受到忽略。
4. **carries an editorial**, 《國際先驅論壇報》今天刊登了《紐約時報》的一篇社論，內容是關於俄羅斯聯邦正在上演的財政危機。
5. **convene a diplomatic conference**, 目前許多國家已要求署長召開外交大會，審議提出的修正案。
6. (d), 如果您想將報導投稿給我們，請點擊「特稿提交」按鈕。
7. (c), 他洩漏了公司即將在兩週內被收購的消息。
8. (d), 我曾經訂閱過幾本運動雜誌，但現在我把錢花在攝影相關的書籍上。
9. (b), 不說明資料來源而引用片段，這是典型的抄襲案件。
10. (c), 他主持那個節目已經 20 年了。現在他的播報風格自然地像是在酒吧裡和朋友聊天。
11. The magician hosted the magic show in his own house.
12. The reporter drank 3 bottles of soju and revealed the source of his scoop.
13. He really wanted to submit a scoop to the magazine and become famous.
14. I received the dramatic news that the tortoise beat the hare in the race.
15. They started to issue a magazine on how to make a lot of money.

DAY 37 Opinion

1. **voiced their opposition**, 學生們對校長的承諾表達了反對意見。他們也反對他在學校管理方面的保守觀念。
2. **handle students' diverse complaints**, 教師資格之一是處理學生對學校教育各種不滿的能力。
3. **express their opinion**, 害羞的人往往不敢在眾人面前表達自己的意見。然而，他們當中有些人非常擅長私下的溝通。
4. **reached a general consensus**, 他們似乎已達成整體的共識。然而，他們在細節方面仍有分歧。
5. **Defend your political position**, 捍衛你自己的政治立場，只要它站在捍衛人權的立場。與在當地運作的社運人士建立有效關係應該會有所幫助。

6. (c), 我們在一開始辯論時就得壓制住對手。
7. (d), 我們不支持你的政治觀點，但我們尊重你的言論自由。
8. (b), 文化教育在幫助孩子避免種族偏見方面扮演著非常重要的角色。
9. (d), 你怎麼能推翻那個決定？那可是雙方長時間協商的結果。
10. (c), 他似乎將撤回對工廠私有化的反對意見；他的策略顧問達成的結論是：他有必要支持新政府對私部門的政策。
11. Old people don't change their opinion. Young people don't have any opinion.
12. We need the chairman's confirmation to reverse the decision.
13. The party decided to withdraw the objection and support the candidate.
14. He seems to have corrected his bias towards black people.
15. The statesman declared his opposition to the party's economic policy.

DAY 38　Family and Social Relationships

1. build a long-term relationship, 我們必須與他們建立長期關係。他們對我們具有策略上的重要性。
2. seek a divorce, 不要把離婚當作逃離目前不快樂的出路。
3. have a childless marriage, 她希望過沒有孩子的婚姻生活，但她的丈夫一直堅稱有孩子才會讓他們的婚姻更快樂。
4. launch a multidisciplinary team, 那所大學的心理學家與神經科學家計畫成立一個跨領域的研究團隊，以探索語言習得的機制。
5. bring up a family of 6 boys, 我非常尊敬我的母親。她獨自撫養一個六個男孩的家庭，卻從未抱怨過一句話。
6. (b), 她沒有任何父母。她是個孤兒。
7. (d), 非政府組織與政府在處理全球暖化問題上展現出社會的團結。他們共同舉辦了一場集會。
8. (c), 他迅速躋升到高層了。他的人生唯一目標似乎就是成為那家公司的 CEO。
9. (a), 若你能戰勝慾望，你比那些攻擊敵人的人更加勇敢；因為最艱難的勝利是戰勝自我。
10. (c), 離婚的經歷如同「面對死亡」，因為所經歷的情緒與失去近親的感覺非常相似。
11. She asked her husband for a quick divorce but he refused.
12. The Iraq war promoted solidarity among Middle East countries.
13. They formed an alliance against the Mafia, but the Mafia didn't care what they did at all.

Answer Key 453

14. Students and teachers formed a project team to settle the problem.
15. Improve relationships with your peers and families.

DAY 39　Social Concerns

1. **overcome the unfair prejudice**, 要克服一些西方人對亞洲人不公平的偏見非常困難。
2. **gives equal opportunity**, 社會上普遍認為每個人都有平等的機會。但我認為這世界實在太不公平了。
3. **respects equal rights**, 女性主義教育並不只是關注女性權利的提升。它更是尊重男女的平等權利。
4. **reduce urban poverty**, 他提出減少都市貧窮問題的想法真是荒謬。他主張我們都必須搬回鄉下去。
5. **ensure national security**, 我們必須確保朝鮮半島的國家安全。那是統一的基礎。
6. (a), 國際紅十字會向聯合國請求緊急援助。
7. (d), 政府為應付這位總統來訪期間可能發生的危安事件而加強了安全措施。
8. (a), 全球石油供應問題有時會導致中東地區的軍事衝突。
9. (b), 美國為解決衝突所付出的努力，對我們在伊拉克目睹的局勢恐怕不會帶來太大改變。
10. (c), 任何有興趣上電視的人都可以報名參加這個比賽；所以把握機會在鏡頭前展現自己吧！
11. They launched a local campaign to promote child welfare.
12. Some ambassadors abuse the diplomatic privilege they have.
13. They approached the problem in a new way.
14. We should protect human rights anytime, anywhere.
15. The queen granted enormous privileges to the knight.

DAY 40　Customs and Habits

1. **observe social conventions**, 他拒絕遵守社會規範，試圖建立自己的標準。有時候那會傷害到別人。
2. **introducing Russian fashion**, 她將俄羅斯時尚引進南韓並賺進大筆財富。她去世後，所有財產都捐贈來創辦一所時尚學校。

3. **following the prevalent practice,** 有些男性對伴侶有持續性的暴力行為，且這樣的案例逐年上升。
4. **fostering the culture,** 那位社運人士致力於培養和平文化。她認為，和平就是暴力與非理性時代的解決方案。
5. **broke with the routine,** 他打破了專為 VIP 設置的專用空間之慣例。他認為，每個人都應該有機會坐到前排。
6. (d)，我們沒有必要遵循西方穿西裝打領帶的習俗。
7. (d)，有些夫婦不斷地在強化「獨立的男性與依賴的女性」這種刻板印象。
8. (b)，我們繼承來自長輩的傳統，但我們也可以建立新的傳統。
9. (c)，我一直在治療那些因古柯鹼成癮而毀掉人生的人。
10. (d)，打擊白人對黑人刻板印象的運動獲得了一定的成功。
11. Parents should help their children acquire the habit of keeping a journal.
12. You need the help of experts to overcome Internet addiction.
13. We have to develop new values while cherishing good traditions.
14. I make a habit of reading 2 books a month.
15. Wearing turtleneck shirts became a fashion trend in the 80's.

DAY 41　War and Peace

1. **wage a spiritual war,** 牧師表示，「我們必須在這混亂的時代中發動一場心靈的戰爭。」聽眾們點頭表示認同。
2. **resume trade negotiations,** 他們似乎不太可能很快重啟貿易談判。他們的觀點缺乏共識。
3. **bear arms,** 擁有武器是我們的權利。如果罪犯都有武器，那我們也應該擁有。
4. **gained, reliable allies,** 美國在這場戰爭初期認為他們有許多可靠的盟友。但後來數量逐漸減少了。
5. **ratified the treaty,** 南韓政府在兩年前批准了那項條約。然而，至今尚未設立任何執行該條約的組織。
6. (c)，她的朋友們無法相信她為了從軍而決定放棄研究所的消息。
7. (b)，我們手上只有幾把老舊的手槍，而敵人卻武裝著最新型的飛彈。
8. (c)，我永遠無法忘記軍隊開始對我們開火的那一刻。那正是光州悲劇的開始。
9. (b)，黃金時段節目主持人詹姆斯，因在自己的節目中利用同性戀的刻板印象而遭到炮火批評。
10. (a)，如果一場談判有可能賠錢而不是賺錢，那就不要開始或參與。

11. Keeping the peace is more difficult than making peace.
12. We always think about how to be good fighters. But what we have to learn is how not to make enemies.
13. As soon as they opened the negotiations, they started shouting at each other.
14. We lost an important ally in the election. The campaign will be tougher than we thought.
15. As the government refused to agree on the treaty, most of the NGOs expressed their regret.

DAY 42　Politics and Institution

1. made an election pledge, 他在選舉時曾承諾要讓所有人都幸福。但他身為一位州長的行為卻讓所有人不悅。
2. manages foreign and international affairs, 總統通常負責外國與國際事務，而副總統則處理國內問題。
3. won the second election, 柯林頓贏得了第二任期的選舉，且合計任職了八年。
4. launched an anti-drug campaign, 上個月他發起了一個反毒運動，這真是個諷刺。他曾經是毒販！
5. caused a bribery scandal, 他對金錢的貪慾造成了一件賄賂醜聞。他從那名商人手上拿了近百萬美元。
6. (a), 我想發表一場偉大的演說，就像林肯或馬丁‧路德‧金恩那樣。
7. (d), 總理因其貪腐醜聞面臨非政府組織的強大壓力。
8. (a), 我對這名傲慢的候選人投了反對票。
9. (c), 當政府推出一項提高電力成本的新政策時，許多人持懷疑態度。
10. (b), 我必須等到 1960 年才能打一場選戰，當時我以 52% 的支持度當選。
11. They formed a joint committee to fight against juvenile smoking.
12. We need to develop a strict policy for environmental protection.
13. He betrayed his pledge and joined the other team.
14. His date with a teenage girl caused a national scandal.
15. The President gave a keynote address at the OECD annual conference.

DAY 43　Liberty and Responsibility

1. accepted no responsibility, 他並未承擔那件事的責任。他撇清了關係，表示自

己與那件事無任何瓜葛。

2. prove the allegation, 示威者控訴警方施暴與騷擾。然而。他們並無證據證明這項指控。
3. gain independence, 最後，為了不再依賴他的父母，他沒有選擇只能離開家裡。
4. impose his or her will, 沒有人可以強迫他人接受自己的意志。
5. lay a claim, 你可以主張對財產的所有權。然而，若要實際持有，你必須在法庭上證明自己的權利。
6. (c), 我們將舉辦一場公開辯論會，屆時你可以享有完全的表達自由。
7. (c),「有些人運氣實在太好了。」他喃喃自語著，將自己的失敗歸咎於他人。
8. (a), 疑犯已被起訴，且他們將被以毒品走私罪刑審判。
9. (a), 我不會放棄詹姆斯，但他彷彿已經沒有求生意志了。
10. (c), 我知道是我違反了合約，但我也沒有勇氣承擔全部責任。
11. Mothers always have to carry the burden of childcare. They need to share it with their husbands.
12. The soldier tried to shift the blame onto someone else.
13. It is not necessary for you to take part in this environmental movement. I only did so to fulfill my moral obligation.
14. John vehemently denied charges of importing illegal medication.
15. The public health administration placed the responsibility of addressing AIDS issues on individuals rather than on the government.

DAY 44　Law

1. tackle juvenile crimes, 雖然警方正努力處理青少年犯罪問題，但案件仍急劇增加中。
2. appealed against the sentence, 她對無期徒刑的判決提出上訴。她一直堅稱她受藥物影響才犯下謀殺罪。
3. presided over the court, 金法官 — 以對勞動與資本持進步觀點聞名 — 是這場審判的主審。人民期待他對那名工會領導人作出無罪判決。
4. faced the public accusation, 那名男子面臨社會大眾對其收賄行為的指控。他曾給了那名國會議員兩萬美元。
5. charged the defendant, 檢察官以收賄罪起訴被告。他否認了所有指控。
6. (b), 由於證據不足，檢方決定予以不起訴。
7. (d), 這案件暫時休庭了，好讓調查人員有時間尋找目擊證人。

Answer Key 457

8. (a), 檢察總長在他的就職典禮上表示，無論如何他都會依法辦事。
9. (b), 我不是在責怪你，但你要知道，我不會坐視你讓我父親陷入困境。
10. (d), 朴先生對犯人展現寬容，否則犯人會被判無期徒刑。
11. The lawyer failed to supply alibis for the defendant.
12. The judge halted the trial when one of the witnesses tried to commit suicide.
13. He has committed a series of heinous crimes since he was 14 years old.
14. We don't want to go to court to solve this labor issue.
15. The judge was supposed to pass a sentence on the accused.

DAY 45 Food

1. sprinkle cheese, 食譜上寫著可以在沙拉上灑起司或任何你喜歡的配料。
2. consume meat, 有些激進的環保人士幾乎不吃肉。他們認為吃動物的肉是造成環境污染的主要原因之一。
3. sipped her drink, 她啜飲了些酒後，開始擔心自己還得開車。最後，她叫了計程車並平安地回到了家。
4. skip your meals, 不要略過任何一餐。發表報告是相當消耗精力的，你很快就會感到疲憊。
5. blend all ingredients,「我們不會將所有食材都混在這碗裡。我們這還需要一個碗，」廚師如此說道。
6. (a), 根據我的經驗，要做出美味的麵條，調整火候非常重要。
7. (d), 記得蔬菜要稍微燙一下就好，因為完全煮沸的話可能破壞掉營養素。
8. (b), 在這間海鮮餐廳，可以看到廚師在我們面前將魚去骨切片並烤給你吃。
9. (d), 我本來想不加洋蔥來拌沙拉，但媽媽堅持我要把洋蔥也一起拌進去。
10. (a), 請你務必不要將雞蛋煮太久。我不喜歡煮得太熟、變得很硬的那種。
11. Shall I fry or boil the egg?
12. He uses wine to tenderize meat.
13. She dressed the salad and prepared some wine for her friends.
14. Add some salty ingredients to the turkey. It tastes bland.
15. Chop the vegetables and pour them into the boiling stew.

DAY 46　Health

1. **made a substantial donation**, 他去年捐給慈善機構一筆兩百萬美元的巨款。然而，上星期卻證實他是一名小偷。
2. **contracted lung cancer**, 他在三年後才知道自己罹患了肺癌。一切都太遲了。
3. **inflict emotional pain**, 請記住，你自私的行為可能會對他人造成情感上的痛苦。
4. **prescribed an effective treatment**, 那位醫生給了我一個有效的療法，讓我減少抽菸。現在除了喝酒的時候，我幾乎不抽菸了。
5. **underwent a twelve hour operation**, 她成功地接受了長達 12 小時的手術，且毫無併發症。那真是一項奇蹟。
6. (d), 醫生們確認那是香港腳的症狀。
7. (c), 許多父母努力讓孩子避免罹患身體疾病。但我認為，他們更應該重視孩子是否具備抵抗不道德行為的免疫力。
8. (c), 海帶被認為有助於女性在產後迅速恢復健康。
9. (d), 如果你不當服用抗生素，你的身體將對抗生素產生抗藥性。
10. (a), 我發現自己有低血壓而無法捐血。
11. He gets gloomy whenever he takes his antibiotics.
12. There was no way to save him. He lost too much blood.
13. Too much stress lowers your immunity to the flu.
14. This medicine will speed your recovery. But don't take more than 2 pills a day.
15. I cannot believe that my daughter has had medical treatment for a drug addiction.

DAY 47　Clothing

1. **pull my coat**, 因為風太大，我將身上的大衣拉得更緊些。我真希望這次旅行是在夏天不是在二月。
2. **drying clothes**, 有風的日子最適合晾衣服，但同時也很惱人，因為一些東西會被風吹到草地上去。
3. **peered over his glasses**, 他的叔叔停下敲打電腦鍵盤的動作，用眼鏡上方的視線看著我。
4. **smoothed down her skirt**, 儘管她男朋友要到今天下午才會回來，她還是匆忙地從客廳出來，並整理著自己的裙子。
5. **tailor his or her style**, 一位優秀的媒體發言人應該能夠適當地調整自己的說話風格以及題材內容，以迎合大眾。

Answer Key

6. (c), 有個人捲起他的袖子，讓我看看他的號碼，那個號碼刺在他的手臂上。
7. (d), 他們接近時，其中一名男子微微將帽子往上一抬並致意說：「早安。」
8. (d), 他像扛袋子一樣，把自己的斗篷披在肩上。
9. (a), 那孩子現在已經可以自己扣上鈕扣，不用媽媽幫忙了。
10. (a), 我父親過去每天都會把自己的皮鞋擦得乾乾淨淨。
11. He undid the four buttons that held the shirt together.
12. Where should I get my shoes resoled?
13. Just wait a second while I take these wet clothes off.
14. It has been known for centuries that different cultures have different styles of clothes.
15. At the left side of the picture is a nobleman donning a fedora hat.

DAY 48　Weather

1. Snow piled up, 積雪厚達半公尺。孩子們感到開心，而大人們則感到擔憂。
2. Rain was pouring down, 那三起謀殺案之間有一個共通點。案發時都下著傾盆大雨。
3. The dense fog lifted, 濃霧在太陽升起後立刻散去，我們重新踏上了旅程。
4. The thunder rolled, 雷聲轟隆。我們開始講起各種可怕的鬼故事。
5. Frost has formed, 汽車前擋風玻璃結了霜，所以我在出門上班前得把它刮乾淨。
6. (c), 我曾經喜歡看日出。但當我長大後，我較喜歡看日落。
7. (b), 風勢漸緩，而那年最大的森林火災也不再擴散。
8. (c), 在我們腳底下的那層薄冰開始出現裂痕。所有人都陷入了恐慌。
9. (c), 今天的天氣預報說這個地區可能會打雷。
10. (c), 烏雲高掛在山巔上方。
11. As lightning flashed outside the window, the baby started to cry.
12. Dark clouds were gathering right over my head.
13. In the morning, he found frost had set in in his back yard.
14. Thick fog came down the hill. We could only see our own hands and feet.
15. The boring rain finally let up and the sun began to shine. All things seemed to revive.

DAY 49 Sports

1. kick a ball, 她曾對著我家的牆踢球。她說她想成為像比利一樣的球員。
2. enter the regional contest, 總共有 24 支隊伍將打進區賽。有兩支隊伍將獲得進軍世界大賽的機會。
3. outwitted, main opponent, 麥可雖然智取了他的主要對手，但許多人認為他欺騙了全世界。
4. broke the long-standing record, 她打破了長年未被打破的奧運紀錄。現在她是全世界跑得最快的女人。
5. defended, title, 她在益智問答節目中擊敗了對手，成功保住了自己的頭銜。現在已經沒有人能擋得住她了。
6. (c), 他錯失了那一擊並輸掉了比賽。那是他職業生涯中最懊惱的時刻。
7. (c), 他用一記精彩的倒掛金鉤將比分扳平。
8. (a), 那位守門員在七場比賽中只讓對手進了兩球。
9. (c), 儘管那個選手明顯犯規，裁判卻沒有對他做出任何處罰。
10. (d), 女子國家手球代表隊在決賽中拼盡全力想贏得比賽，但最終還是落敗了。
11. My head coach appealed for the penalty kick, but rather was awarded a penalty.
12. He lost the game and lost his love.
13. His goal took the score to 3-2. The stadium was filled with excitement.
14. He set the Korean record. Now his target is the world record.
15. We have to face the toughest opponent on earth, laziness.

DAY 50 Travel and Transportation

1. deny visas, 據我所知，駐加拿大的美國簽證辦事處並不會在沒有令人信服的理由下拒絕發簽證給加拿大人。
2. acted as our tour guide, 他曾擔任我們的導遊，但他做的唯一一件事就是經常對我們敲竹槓。
3. going on a pilgrimage, 留學就像是一場朝聖之旅；它要求的是極大的毅力和明確的目標。
4. steer a ship, 經營公司就像掌舵一艘船；你需要豐富的經驗與智慧，還要有技術。
5. pedal his bicycle, 我弟弟朝我們揮了揮手，然後開始踩著腳踏車往山坡上騎去。
6. (d), 我們打算搭計程車，但那位百萬富翁給我們租了一架直升機。

7. (b), 他登上了開往論山的列車。他的父母含著淚為他送行,並祈求他身體健康。
8. (d), 他們説「請搭乘地鐵」,但對行動不便者而言是非常困難的。
9. (a), 他一聽到爺爺去世的消息時,立刻搭上返家的第一班飛機。
10. (c), 有直飛的航班嗎?還是這班飛機中途會在哪裡停留?
11. When the police started to move, they had already boarded the plane.
12. I take the subway rather than the bus because it is faster.
13. We had a stopover in Hong Kong.
14. This year we don't need to be issued a visa for a short trip to Japan.
15. I can't forget the moment when she said, "I want to be your guide for all of your life."

DAY 51　Language

1. **lowered the tone**, 「嚴格來説,這是你我之間的祕密。」説完,她將交談的語調壓低。
2. **opened a serious conversation**, 高層主管們在開始嚴肅的對話之前,先聊了幾句關於天氣的小話題。
3. **acquired her strong accent**, 那位外國人移居到西南部地區後,口音變得更重了。我發現很難聽懂他説的話。
4. **The term, coined**, 「新保守派」(Neocon)這個詞是為了指稱保守思想的「新潮流」而創造出來的。
5. **attracted highly critical comments**, 那起事件吸引了媒體的大肆報導。同時,它也引來社會大眾強烈的批評。
6. (c), 那位老人透過他的律師發出一份聲明,主張自己是清白的。
7. (d), 人類似乎與生俱來就具備理解並運用語言的語言能力。
8. (b), 校長發送一份備忘錄給所有教師,通知課程將會有些微調整。
9. (d), 在那種令人驚奇的場合中,我無法找到合適的話來説。
10. (b), 李奧納多・達文西,因為他對文藝復興時期的貢獻而應該特別提及。
11. I'm getting sick of trying to find the right words to make her feel better.
12. Have you heard any mention of the affair?
13. I have received detailed comments from the professor on my research paper.
14. In a job interview, relax yourself and soften your tone.
15. This center is a good place to learn sign language.

DAY 52　Study and Academic Work

1. **dropped the class,** 我將那門課退掉了。那名講師只會講些無聊又不入流的笑話。
2. **prepare, doctoral dissertation,** 他是博士班的全職學生。然而,因為財務上的困難,他別無選擇,只能一邊準備博士論文,一邊做鐵路工賺錢。
3. **leveled bitter criticism,** 人們對國會提出強烈批評,但那些愚蠢的政客卻對他們所做所為感到自豪。
4. **got an MA degree,** 他不適合擔任這個職位。他擁有經濟學碩士學位。但我們需要的是擁有公共政策博士學位的人。
5. **practiced writing,** 她每天都練習寫作就為了成為一位有說服力的作家。
6. **(a),** 他們合著了一本關於領袖特質的概論書。一位作者解釋了領導力的原則,另一位則展示了實際的例子。
7. **(b),** 學生們拒絕將論文交給那名收賄的教授。
8. **(b),** 你必須撰寫文學性的文章才能進入人文學院。
9. **(c),** 這門課引導學生以批判性的方式閱讀各種文類的作品。
10. **(c),** 我勉強通過了那一科。
11. You have to practice writing every day to be an original writer.
12. He changed his major after he wrote his doctoral dissertation.
13. I dropped the class because it was too demanding.
14. Movies focusing on same-sex themes are likely to provoke harsh criticism from conservative critics.
15. Please hand in your final essay to the department office.

DAY 53　Art

1. **put on sweet music,** 她為我播放了甜美的音樂。它讓我想起我的童年時光。
2. **performed the traditional dance,** 她丈夫在打鼓時,她則表演傳統舞蹈。他們完美的默契吸引了許多乘客的目光。
3. **work on several paintings,** 他打算創作幾幅描繪母親與嬰兒的畫作。他一直對表現母愛很有興趣。
4. **molded the clay,** 她用黏土捏製出一個男孩的模樣。事實上,她曾在一場悲慘的車禍中失去了她的獨子。
5. **creates monumental sculptures,** 那位藝術家用回收材料與廢棄電子產品創作了具有紀念價值的雕刻品。

Answer Key 463

6. (b), 她為了精進陶藝，已經燒製陶器超過七年了。
7. (c), 那場展覽以各種藝術家為特色，從藝術攝影師到行為藝術家都有。
8. (a), 他將通常用於書法的韓國傳統筆刷技術運用於油畫上。
9. (b), 國王下令鑄造自己的銅像。
10. (a), 該課程的要求之一是要在全班同學面前背誦一首詩。
11. The statue of soldiers was cast in bronze, which was about 10 meters high.
12. Kahlo did some paintings of her own image. Each painting shows different aspects of her identity.
13. The teacher wanted his students to learn poetry by heart because he believed that literature makes people happy as well as stable.
14. More and more people choose to learn bookcrafts for hobby and practical purposes.
15. I'd rather use a roller than a brush to paint the wall.

DAY 54　Feelings

1. fueled the anger, 市府推動拆除老舊建築的計畫，而此舉引發了村民的怒火。
2. feigned surprise, 男孩在聖誕樹下發現禮物時假裝驚訝。其實，他前一晚就看到父母悄悄把禮物放在那裡了。
3. cried with happiness, 當被宣判無罪時，她喜極而泣。她的案件開始至今已歷時七年了。
4. was filled with hatred, 他對組織犯罪有滿腔的憤怒。但他卻沒有能力做什麼。
5. was tinged with sadness, 我們的派對夾雜著一絲悲傷。雖然我們贏得了冠軍，但我們有兩位球員受了重傷。
6. (c), 我並不嫉妒有錢人。然而，我真的很羨慕有智慧的人。
7. (a), 當她被要求在前來恭賀的賓客面前唱首歌時，她尷尬得滿臉通紅。
8. (b), 這起事故的記憶在他心中已滲入一種對孤獨的深深恐懼。
9. (d), 總裁透漏自己愛上了一位知名的時尚模特兒。接下來人們最關注的就是他是否會與她結婚。
10. (d), 儘管英文在法國普遍使用已是近年來的事實，但法國人仍對他們母語法語感到自豪。
11. She sought love from him, but all he gave her was pain and regrets.
12. The actress swelled with pride as she won the award of "Actress of the Year."
13. He was burning with hatred, but his voice was deep and slow.

14. The survivors of the disaster gathered together to overcome the fear of death.
15. The Danish cartoon depicting the Prophet Mohammad as a terrorist fueled widespread Muslim anger.

DAY 55 Interest and Concern

1. aroused my curiosity, 就是他的不安舉止引起了我的好奇心。
2. increased awareness, 領土的爭端已升高了兩國對該問題的關注度了。
3. widened its appeal, 因為那個網站去年成功更換了設計與版面配置，變得更加受歡迎了。
4. raising public concern, 飛行員工會在政府採取行動之後發動總罷工，這引發了民眾對於可能出現前所未有的交通大亂感到不安。
5. take excessive care, 根據一項調查，青少年往往過度在意自己的外貌。
6. (c), 教師們經常擔心他們缺乏讓學生更專心於課堂的經驗。
7. (a), 我感謝您出於關心與努力，與孩子們談論戰爭議題。
8. (b), 公共福利政策應當對社會弱勢群體的需求給予應有的關注。
9. (c), 我老師單調的聲音使我失去專注力且讓我睡著了。
10. (a), 對於經濟景氣回升有高度期望的人們傾向於將其資金投入股市。
11. As young children watch TV, they show great interest in commercials.
12. Driving requires great concentration, especially when the weather is not in good condition.
13. Despite his desperate effort, he failed to meet everybody's expectations.
14. Traditional English classrooms attempted to heighten students' awareness on grammar and accurate use of English.
15. Young children usually pay attention to one thing at a time.

DAY 56 Values and Ideals

1. enjoy fame, 那位億萬富翁歌手表示，絕不會在唱片市場再推出另一張專輯，因為他既不需要錢，也無意在舊金山享有名聲。
2. have honor, 你能夠在保有名聲的同時行為不檢點嗎？請記住，名聲與誠實是息息相關的。
3. betraying, ideal, 就「精神層面」而言，那個人因背棄自己靈性神聖的理想，已經與自己的族群疏離了。

Answer Key

4. **bring great shame,** 這兩起醜聞都將給國家帶來巨大的恥辱,並象徵著在政治與商業領域中,道德行為一直是欠缺的。
5. **won, respect,** 她早期作品的批評家表示,雖然她演技拙劣,但她已逐漸贏得了他們的尊敬。
6. **(b),** 她並沒有真正了解尊重每一個人的重要性。
7. **(c),** 就算他不會成功,但至少在嘗試這一點上,應給予肯定。
8. **(c),** 我們堅信韓國市場將會復甦。
9. **(d),** 1968年時,世界各地渴望社會正義的年輕人試圖廢除不公正的政治限制。
10. **(a),** 韓國的MP3產業無需追隨創新設計與好用介面為特色的iPod典範。
11. The picture does not do her justice!
12. She simply broke every single promise she ever made me.
13. Set a good example for children rather than make them follow a bad one.
14. I have a belief in myself that I am a good English learner.
15. Those who have low self-confidence feel great shame at a little mistake.

DAY 57 Signs and Symbols

1. **unveiled the new logo,** 該公司在他們的創立週年日中揭示了公司的新logo。
2. **left a big mark,** 我最好的襯衫上留下一大片紅色墨水漬,但我不知道最近的洗手間在哪裡。
3. **took on human form,** 女神愛上了那名男子。為了接近他,她化身為人類的模樣。
4. **sounded the warning,** 警方對國會大廈前的示威者發出警告。
5. **wove a geometric pattern,** 她在夾克上縫了一個幾何圖案。那看起來像一個巨大的耳朵。
6. **(a),** 在埃及,許多物品上會以聖甲蟲作為宗教象徵。它代表著滾動太陽這顆球的太陽神。
7. **(d),** 人們在這支世界盃足球隊經過時,揮舞著五顏六色的旗幟。
8. **(d),** 當我問她該怎麼打敗德古拉時,她向我比劃了一個十字架的符號。
9. **(a),** 科學家團體公開了一項讓具爭議的進化論變有趣的學術研究。
10. **(b),** 海巡警隊發出一項正式通知,警告船隻停泊在附近港口。
11. I like the skirt because it has a floral pattern on it.
12. He posted the notice reading "NO SMOKING" on the wall.
13. He is ready to make his mark at World Cup.

14. My doctor gave me a warning about the consequences of excessive exercising.
15. Each national flag displays the nation's own symbols.

DAY 58　Direction and Movement

1. delay, departure, 由於凌晨六點以前不允許飛機降落，我們只好延後離開舊金山的時間。
2. gather pace, 在 1940 年代末期開始復甦，並於下個十年（1950 年代）加快了速度。
3. taken the course, 修完口說英語課程並取得必要等級的學生，也可取得入學資格。
4. monitor the progress, 學校委員會將監督所有學校的進展，並將確保其表現維持類似的嚴格水準。
5. made big advances, 多虧了低廉的人力成本及生產技術的提升，許多亞洲國家有了巨大的進步。
6. (a), 傑克的家人們等待著他兩個兒子的歸來。
7. (c), 因為他的導遊欺騙了他，他在某個地方迷了路。
8. (a), 將軍雖然中槍且受中傷，但仍繼續向前推進。
9. (a), 預期之外的通膨使得市場無所適從，股市投資人也變得不安。
10. (d), 即使這名男子迷了路，他也不喜歡被指點該走哪條路。
11. We also might not be facing in the right direction.
12. He suddenly turned off at the route 50 exit and began traveling north.
13. He covered the retreat of the Russian army successfully.
14. The teacher monitors his students' progress in learning and builds up a profile of each student.
15. Generally, high temperatures quicken the pace of a chemical reaction.

DAY 59　Danger

1. received a death-threat, 這名社運人士最近收到激進分子的死亡威脅，但她仍不斷推進這項運動。
2. offered a temporary emergency shelter, 洪水災民獲得了臨時緊急避難所與少量的救援物資。

Answer Key 467

3. provides, the best protection, 這款防曬乳液是你從事戶外活動時防止皮膚曬傷的最佳保養品。
4. sounded the alarm, 保安系統警報聲一響起時，銀行搶匪試圖逃跑，但，他們最終還是被警方逮捕了。
5. face the worst crisis, 救生員已被訓練到即使在面對最糟的危機時，也能立刻採取行動。他們被視為專業人士。
6. (c), 建築物定期的修繕與維護可以保證並提升其安全性。
7. (b), 全世界的人們都清楚軍備擴張競賽帶來的危險。
8. (d), 媒體報導指出，若有人可以在那場可怕的空難中生還，那簡直是奇蹟。
9. (c), 區公所為了防止致命的車禍，在各處道路設置了減速丘。
10. (b), 糖尿病患者必須格外注意飲食，他們尤其必須避開高糖分的食物。
11. A lot of accidents are caused by sleepy and drunken drivers.
12. We urge caution in the use of this life jacket in case of emergency.
13. Terrorism poses a serious threat to national security.
14. This equipment provides protection from potential hazards.
15. The government is considering the proposals to overcome the financial crisis of credit card companies.

DAY 60 Aid and Cooperation

1. follow the doctor's advice, 不管要花掉多少錢，這名病患決心遵從醫生的忠告。
2. brought, great comfort, 最近我遭遇了巨大的財務損失且生活過得艱難。然而，她的鼓勵讓我在所有困境中獲得了莫大的安慰。
3. promote the cooperation, 會談的目的是促進兩黨之間的合作，並在下次選舉中爭取到廣大的支持。
4. needs assistance, 我哥哥在上週動了手術；他現在移動時仍需要醫生們的協助。
5. receive little encouragement, 幾乎得不到老師稱讚的學生，其成績可能不會太好。
6. (c), 韓國和日本建立起一個夥伴聯盟來舉辦 2002 世界盃足球賽，並取得了巨大的成功。
7. (b), 別要求我站在你這邊。你提出那種荒謬的要求也無法從你的朋友們那裡得到任何支持。
8. (b), 由一個反戰組織主導的「停戰聯盟」提供和平運動以及相關議題的資訊。
9. (c), 下列網站提供了關於維護筆記型電腦更詳細的指南。

10. (a), 該報社在揭露某媒體大亨對政治人物行賄的事件後，很難再吸引能提供財務支持的贊助者。
11. The student association is collecting sponsors for next month's charity auction.
12. You should seek guidance from an expert on this matter before you jump to any conclusions.
13. My opinion received strong support from my colleagues.
14. He ignored his colleagues' advice, and then he made a mess of things.
15. Personality development of children requires long-term encouragement from their parents.

DAY 31-60　FinalCheck-up

1. show, 有些人對律師心存偏見。／我們聚在這裡是為了展現反對種族主義的國際團結。／他們用寫的來表達憤怒。

2. hold, 那個國家將舉辦一場選舉來組織臨時政府。／獅子隊保有足球冠軍的頭銜。／我們對韓國市場的復甦有強烈的信心。

3. keep, 每天寫日誌是一個很好的習慣。／為了維持該地區的和平，我們應派遣軍隊。／你最好遵守你的承諾。

4. took, 他最後一記進球讓最終比分變成 3 比 2。／我上學期選修的課程最多。／她給我看了她照顧的所有孩子的照片。

5. made, 他住院時向我承諾，他一定會恢復健康。／那場反戰運動讓保守派團體成了全民公敵。／由於低工資和生產技術的提升，許多亞洲國家已有了相當的成長。

6. (e), I couldn't make him understand the bottom line. He was a complete idiot when it came to accounting.（我無法讓他搞懂最基本的損益。一提到會計，他簡直就是個十足的白痴。）

7. (b), I have to download the program. I cannot watch the video clip on my computer.（我得下載那個程式。我沒辦法用我的電腦觀看這影集片段。）

8. (a), Shy people are reluctant to express their opinion in public. However, some of them are really good at private communication.（害羞的人通常不願在眾人面前發表意見。但，其中有些人非常善於私底下的溝通。）

9. (d), Not a few women have been working to stop the prevalent practice of family violence, but it is increasing year by year.（不少女性一直在努力制止普遍存在的家庭暴力，但這類事件仍逐年增加。）

Answer Key   469

10. (c), Lifeguards are trained to take immediate steps even when they face the worst crisis. They are considered professionals.（救生員已被訓練到即使在面對最糟的危機時，也能立刻採取行動。他們被視為專業人士。）

11. promote the cooperation, 會談的目的是促進兩黨之間的合作，並在下次選舉中吸引廣大的支持。

12. have honor, 你能夠在保有名聲的同時行為不檢點嗎？請記住，名聲與誠實是息息相關的。

13. prepare his doctoral dissertation, 他是博士班的全職學生。然而，因為財務上的困難，他別無選擇，只能一邊準備博士論文，一邊做鐵路工人賺錢。

14. inflict emotional pain, 請記住，你自私的行為可能會對他人造成情感上的痛苦。

15. gain independence, 最後，為了不再依賴他的父母，他不得不離開家裡。

16. He closed his account after his girlfriend got fired from the bank. 在他女朋友被銀行解雇後，他關閉了自己的帳戶。

17. Only the intelligence source has the program to crack this code. 只有情報來源有解開這個密碼的程式。

18. They formed an alliance against the Mafia, but the Mafia didn't care what they did at all. 他們組成了一個對抗黑手黨的聯盟，但黑手黨對他們所做的事毫不在意。

19. His goal took the score to 3-2. The stadium was filled with excitement. 他的進球使比分變為 3 比 2。整個體育場陷入一片沸騰的情緒中。

20. He changed his major after he wrote his doctoral dissertation. 他在撰寫完博士論文後轉變了自己的主修科系。

搭配詞索引

A

abandon an ideal	379
abolish censorship	202
abuse a privilege	229
accelerate progress	397
accept a fact	185
accept a treaty	246
accept advice	418
accept criticism	341
accept responsibility	262
access information	181
access the net	192
achieve a consensus	209
achieve an ideal	379
achieve fame	376
acquire a habit	237
acquire an accent	335
acquire an asset	158
acquire shares	156
act as (a) guide	326
add an ingredient	283
adjourn a case	271
adjust glasses	300
adjust heat	284
administer a treatment	292
administer an affair	252
admit charges	262
adopt a policy	252
adopt a position	212
adopt a practice	237
adopt a tone	336
advise caution	406
aggravate a symptom	291
agree on a treaty	247
agree to a treaty	247
alleviate pain	291
alleviate poverty	229
allow a goal	316
alter form	387
announce a decision	208
announce news	198
annul a marriage	221
appeal against a sentence	273
appeal for a penalty	315
appear before a court	271
apply for a loan	165
apply with a brush	350
appoint a committee	254
appreciate someone's concern	370
approach a problem	230

Index 471

approve a budget	157	be armed with a missile	245
arouse interest	367	be cast in bronze	351
arouse jealousy	360	be filled with happiness	359
arouse someone's curiosity	369	be filled with hatred	360
arrange a loan	165	be in a war	247
ask about the way	399	be made in bronze	351
ask for a confirmation	173	be ravaged by war	247
ask for a divorce	219	be tinged with sadness	362
ask (for) advice	418	bear a logo	387
assert a belief	380	bear a sign	390
assert a claim	263	bear a symbol	390
assist a manager	173	bear arms	243
attack an enemy	217	beat a recession	156
attain an ideal	379	beat an egg	282
attend a conference	202	become (a) law	273
attend a meeting	172	become a fashion (trend)	236
attend a presentation	176	become a soldier	246
attend a trial	274	begin a conversation	331
attract a comment	331	betray a pledge	256
attract a sponsor	417	betray an ideal	379
attract investment	167	blend an ingredient	283
avoid a bias	209	block a retreat	398
avoid (a) disaster	407	block a shot	316
await someone's return	400	blush with embarrassment	358
		board a plane	322
B		board a ship	322
bake fish	280	boil a vegetable	281
balance a budget	157	boil an egg	282
be a guide	326	boot a system	191

Index

bounce a ball	317	call a meeting	172
break a code	183	call a taxi	324
break a consensus	209	call for aid	226
break a habit	237	call someone to be a witness	174
break a promise	380	cancel a meeting	172
break a record	316	carry a burden	265
break down (a) prejudice	227	carry a headline	200
break in shoes	298	carry a logo	387
break off a negotiation	245	carry an editorial	201
break (off) an alliance	219	carry out a crime	272
break someone's concentration	368	carry out an operation	290
break (with) (a) routine	237	cast a vote	253
break with convention	235	catch a plane	322
bring (a) disaster	407	cause (a) conflict	227
bring about peace	246	cause (a) disaster	407
bring charges	262	cause a problem	230
bring comfort	414	cause a recession	156
bring happiness	359	cause a scandal	255
bring sadness	364	cause an accident	405
bring shame	377	cause (an) addiction	234
bring up a family	218	cause (an) alarm	405
build a relationship	221	cause jealousy	360
build a team	220	cause shame	377
build up (an) immunity	289	cease fire	244
burn with hatred	360	censor a book	345
button a coat	297	chair a committee	254
		challenge a stereotype	238
C		challenge views	211
call a conference	202	change a routine	237

Index

change an opinion	210	collect a sponsor	417
change course	398	come aboard a ship	322
change direction	395	commission an artist	350
change form	387	commit a crime	272
change one's position	212	compose a poem	353
change one's tone	336	compose music	352
charge a defendant	272	compose poetry	353
charge a fee	164	compromise security	228
charge interest	166	conclude a treaty	247
chart progress	397	confirm opposition	208
check details	184	consume meat	282
cherish a tradition	238	contract cancer	290
choose a route	396	control interest	166
chop a vegetable	281	control one's anger	358
cite a source	201	control spam (mail)	192
claim a pension	166	convene a conference	202
claim insurance	158	copy a style	299
claim right(s)	228	correct a bias	210
clean fish	280	count a vote	253
clean glasses	300	cover a fee	164
clean viruses	190	cover a retreat	398
close an account	163	cover one's embarrassment	359
cloud break	308	crack a code	183
cloud cover	308	create a blog (of one's own)	192
cloud gather	308	create a coalition	415
cloud hang	308	create a committee	254
co-author a book	345	create a crisis	406
coin a term	332	create (a) culture	235
coin a word	333	create a document	182

Index

create a hierarchy	218	demand cooperation	416
create a sculpture	353	demonstrate solidarity	220
create a stereotype	238	deny a statement	334
cry with happiness	360	deny a visa	325
cure (an) addiction	234	deny access	184
cut a budget	157	deny an accusation	270
cut a price	157	deny an allegation	264
cut support	413	deny charges	262
		deny responsibility	263
		depend on a donation	288

D

damage a relationship	221	deploy a missile	245
decipher a symbol	391	deposit money	165
declare bankruptcy	164	derail a train	325
declare one's love	361	deserve a mention	333
declare opposition	208	deserve a promotion	174
declare war	247	deserve credit	381
decrease a salary	176	design a pattern	388
defeat an enemy	218, 244	destroy a relationship	221
defeat an opponent	314	deter an enemy	244
defend a defendant	272	develop (a) culture	235
defend a position	212	develop a habit	237
defend a title	315	develop a policy	252
defend one's honor	377	develop a product	155
define a term	332	develop a relationship	221
delay departure	400	develop a symptom	292
delay one's return	400	develop (an) immunity	289
delete an e-mail	193	diagnose cancer	291
deliver an address	256	discuss details	184
demand a refund	164	dismiss an allegation	264

display a bias	209	do nails	20
display a sculpture	353	do overtime	15
display a symbol	390	do painting	352
disregard a warning	389	do research	16
disturb privacy	183	do reverse	23
disturb someone's concentration	368	do service	15
do a calculation	23	do (some) writing	344
do a composition	341	do something	20
do a favor	19	do sum	23
do a job	15	do the dishes	18
do a Ph.D. dissertation	342	do the laundry	19
do a trade	15	do the trick	24
do an activity	14	do thinking	24
do an article	18	do translation	24
do an assignment	14	do up a button	301
do an essay	343	do work	15
do an experiment	15	don a hat	300
do an M.A. dissertation	342	donate blood	289
do anything	20	download a program	193
do arrangement	22	draft a manifesto	200
do business	15	draft a memo	335
do drugs	19	drape a cloak	299
do evil	23	draw a comment	331
do exercise	19	draw a pension	166
do food	19	draw attention	369
do hair	19	draw comfort	414
do honor	23	draw encouragement	417
do injustice	23	draw fire	244
do justice	377	draw support	413

Index

draw up a manifesto	200	escape (from) bankruptcy	164
dress a salad	281	establish a committee	254
drop a ball	317	establish a hierarchy	218
drop a case	271	establish a partnership	415
drop a class	344	establish a routine	238
dry clothes	296	establish a tradition	238
		establish an alibi	270
E		evolve a style	299
earn a salary	176	exchange information	181
earn interest	166	exercise a privilege	229
earn respect	378	exercise caution	406
earn revenue	155	exhibit a sculpture	354
edit a document	182	exhibit a sign	390
eliminate poverty	229	exhibit a symptom	291
encourage a debate	207	expect assistance	414
encourage investment	167	experience fear	359
endure pain	291	explain a term	332
enforce a law	273	express a belief	380
enjoy fame	376	express an opinion	210
enjoy freedom	263	express criticism	341
enjoy independence	265	express opposition	209
enlist as a soldier	246	express solidarity	220
ensure safety	408	express views	211
ensure security	228		
enter a contest	315	**F**	
enter a password	191	face a crisis	406
enter into a negotiation	245	face a problem	230
enter into a partnership	415	face a sentence	273
eradicate poverty	229	face an accusation	270

Index

face an enemy	244	find a mate	28
face an opponent	314	find a precedent	36
face bankruptcy	165	find a pretext	36
face competition	156	find a recruit	28
face danger	406	find a relationship	37
face in a direction	395	find a replacement	28
face pressure	255	find a scoop	199
fail a subject	344	find a sponsor	28
fall in love	361	find a survivor	28
fall off a bicycle	323	find a volunteer	28
fasten a button	301	find a witness	274
feature an artist	350	find a word	333
feed a family	218	find an ally	27
feel jealousy	361	find an alternative	27
feel love	361	find an explanation	36
feel respect	378	find an occupation	28
feel sadness	364	find an opportunity	227
feel shame	378	find comfort	31
feign surprise	362	find courage	31
fight (against) an enemy	218	find evidence	36
fight (in) an election	255	find forgiveness	32
fight off competition	156	find happiness	32, 360
fight spam (mail)	192	find information	36
fillet fish	280	find inspiration	32
filter spam (mail)	192	find meaning	36
find (a) discrepancy	36	find one's way	399
find a clue	35	find peace	32
find a culprit	28	find relief	32
find a flaw	36	find salvation	32

Index

find satisfaction	32	frost set in	309
find support	413	fry an egg	282
find the nerve	32	fuel someone's anger	358
fire a missile	245	fulfill a pledge	256
fire clay	351	fulfill a promise	380
fly a flag	386	fulfill an obligation	262
fog come down	306		
fog lie	305	**G**	
fog lift	306	gain a degree	343
follow a belief	380	gain a vote	253
follow a course	398	gain access	184
follow a custom	235	gain an ally	243
follow a fashion (trend)	236	gain freedom	263
follow a practice	237	gain independence	265
follow a route	396	gain respect	378
follow a routine	238	gather information	181
follow a tradition	239	gather pace	397
follow advice	418	get a benefit	41
follow an example	381	get a chance	41
follow convention	235	get a confirmation	173
forget a password	191	get a grade	48
form a coalition	416	get a grasp	45
form a committee	254	get a guarantee	41
form a partnership	415	get a job	49
form a team	220	get a liking	49
form an alliance	219	get a mark	388
forward an e-mail	193	get a mention	333
foster (a) culture	235	get a name	49
frost form	309	get a notice	389

get a penalty	315	get off a plane	322
get a pension	166	get off the bus	323
get a perspective	45	get on the bus	323
get a point	45	get out of a taxi	324
get a promotion	49, 174	get passed over for a promotion	174
get a refund	164	get the bottom line	173
get a result	49	get the feeling	44
get a scoop	199	get the hang of	45
get a score	49, 317	get the joke	45
get a sentence	41	get the last word	41
get a shot	49	give a boost	53
get a sponsor	418	give a cue	53
get (a) taste	45	give a demonstration	58
get access	40	give (a) dimension	63
get an ally	243	give a discount	63
get an answer	44	give a donation	288
get an apology	40	give a hand	53
get (an) approval	41	give a look	53
get an edge	41	give a party	63
get an idea	45	give a penalty	315
get an impression	45	give a presentation	176
get an update	182	give a rebate	63
get attention	370	give a refund	163
get credit	381	give a ring	53
get exposure	41	give a start	63
get hiccups	48	give a statement	334
get into a taxi	324	give a tip	185
get justice	377	give a total of	59
get leave	49	give a view	54

Index

give a warning	389	go on a pilgrimage	324
give a wave	64	go online	190
give access	62	go through a divorce	219
give an account	58	go to a conference	202
give an address	256	go to court	271
give an alibi	57	grab a headline	200
give an audition	63	grant a privilege	230
give an example	58	grasp an opportunity	228
give an instruction	58	grate cheese	279
give an opportunity	228	grill fish	280
give an update	181	grill meat	282
give birth	52	groan with pain	291
give chase	53	guarantee safety	408
give color	386	gut fish	280
give comfort	58		
give credit	381	**H**	
give details	53	hack a system	191
give evidence	58	halt a trial	274
give first-aid	63	halt an advance	399
give odds	58	hamper a recovery	290
give protection	407	hand in an essay	343
give regard	371	handle a complaint	212
give someone a confirmation	173	handle (a) conflict	227
give the eye	53	hang a painting	353
give voice	59	hang out a flag	386
give way	64	hang up a coat	297
go aboard a ship	322	hasten a departure	400
go by taxi	324	have a baby	68
go into bankruptcy	165	have a belief	380

Index

have a benefit	72	have a stopover	324
have a bent	72	have (a) style	298
have a bias	209	have a tip	184
have a chat	68	have a treatment	292
have a check	68	have access	184
have a check-up	68	have affection	72
have a choice	72	have an abortion	67
have a clue	72	have an accent	335
have a comment	76, 331	have (an) access	71
have a complaint	212	have (an) addiction	71, 234
have a concern	370	have an advantage	72
have a confirmation	173	have an affair	67
have a connection	76	have an agenda	75
have a contract	175	have an agreement	68
have a conversation	330	have an alibi	270
have a dance	352	have an alliance	220
have a debate	207	have an ally	243
have a degree	343	have (an) appeal	368
have a difference	76	have an argument	68
have a difficulty	76	have an arrangement	68
have a family	219	have an asset	158
have a go	68	have (an) assurance	72
have a marriage	221	have an attitude	72
have a meeting	172	have an awareness	367
have a partnership	415	have an effect	76
have a pattern	388	have (an) immunity	289
have (a) prejudice	227	have an insight	76
have a scoop	199	have an operation	290
have a sign	390	have an opinion	210

Index

have an urge	76	hold a summit	80
have cause	75	hold a title	315
have credibility	76	hold a tune	89
have curiosity	369	hold a value	85
have expectations	370	hold a view	85
have honor	377	hold an account	163
have regard	371	hold an auction	79
have relatives	217	hold an election	80, 255
have respect	378	hold an inquiry	84
have surprise	363	hold an opinion	210
have views	210	hold attention	89
have will	261	hold fire	88, 244
hear a complaint	212	hold hands	89
hear a mention	333	hold hostage	89
hear news	198	hold line	89
heighten awareness	368	hold moisture	89
hide surprise	363	hold office	85
highlight a case	271	hold one's breath	88
hit a headline	200	hold power	81
hold a belief	380	hold promise	85
hold a conference	80	hold respect	378
hold a contest	315	hold shares	156
hold a conversation	330	hold talks	80
hold a meeting	80	hold territory	89
hold a patent	85	hold the balance	80
hold a position	85	hold the key	80
hold a rank	85	hold the reins	81
hold a record	85, 316	hold tongue	89
hold a share	85	hold views	210

Index

hook up to the net	193	install a system	191
host a show	201	instill fear	359
hurt someone's pride	361	interpret a fact	185
		interpret a symbol	391
I		introduce a fashion (trend)	236
ice crack	306	introduce a policy	252
ice form	306	invent a code	183
ice melt	306	iron clothes	296
identify a symptom	291	issue a journal	199
ignore advice	418	issue a magazine	199
illustrate a case	271	issue a notice	389
impose an obligation	261	issue a report	182
impose censorship	202	issue a statement	334
impose one's will	262	issue a visa	325
improve a relationship	222	issue shares	156
improve safety	408		
improve security	228	**J**	
improve welfare	226	join a coalition	416
improve writing	344	join the colors	386
increase a price	157	jump from a train	325
increase a salary	177	jump on a train	325
increase awareness	368		
increase pace	397	**K**	
increase revenue	155	keep a balance	96
increase safety	408	keep a diary	92
incur a fee	164	keep a distance	97
incur expenditure	158	keep a file	93
inflict pain	312	keep a grip	101
install a program	193	keep a pet	101

Index

keep a promise	93, 381	**L**	
keep a record	93	lace up shoes	298
keep a resolution	93	lack (an) immunity	289
keep a secret	97	lack direction	396
keep a shape	97	lack independence	265
keep (a) watch	102	lack will	261
keep an account	92	launch a campaign	253
keep an engagement	93	launch a manifesto	200
keep an eye	97	launch a product	155
keep change	100	launch a ship	322
keep company with	101	launch a team	220
keep contact with	101	lay a claim	263
keep control	96	lay blame	264
keep faith	93	lay down arms	244
keep house	101	lead a campaign	253
keep one's hand in	101	lead a coalition	416
keep one's temper	101	lead a retreat	398
keep pace	97	lead a team	221
keep peace	97	leak news	198
keep perspective	97	learn a craft	351
keep sight	97	learn a language	332
keep statistics	93	learn a poem by heart	353
keep the peace	246	learn poetry by heart	353
keep track of	101	leave a mark	388
keep value	93	level a score	317
kick a ball	317	level an accusation	271
kick a goal	316	level criticism	341
know a fact	185	lightning flash	306
		lightning hit	306

Index

lightning light (up)	306	maintain a tradition	239
lightning strike	306	maintain insurance	158
listen to music	352	maintain one's freedom	264
log in to a web site	190	maintain pace	397
log out from a web site	190	make a call	111
look after relatives	217	make a contribution	116
lose a button	301	make (a) conversation	111, 330
lose a contract	175	make (a) criticism	342
lose a debate	207	make a decision	208
lose a game	314	make a departure	400
lose an accent	335	make a deposit	106, 167
lose an ally	243	make a difference	116
lose (an) appeal	368	make a discovery	116
lose blood	288	make a donation	288
lose interest	367	make a habit	237
lose one's concentration	368	make a headline	200
lose one's freedom	264	make a mark	388
lose one's way	399	make a mention	334
lose relatives	217	make a mess	111
lose respect	378	make (a) noise	111
lose revenue	155	make (a) payment	106
lose will	261	make a pilgrimage	324
lower a flag	387	make a pledge	256
lower (an) immunity	289	make a point	116
lower heat	283	make a presentation	176
lower one's tone	336	make a profit	106
		make a promise	381
M		make a purchase	106
maintain a custom	236	make a recommendation	106

Index

make a recovery	289	make haste	116
make a reference	111	make interest	166
make a refund	163	make money	165
make a reservation	111	make one's return	400
make a response	107	make peace	246
make a retreat	397	make progress	396
make a speech	111	manage a factory	174
make a start	116	manage an affair	253
make a statement	112, 334	manage an office	175
make a stopover	324	master a craft	351
make a threat	409	master a language	332
make a visit	117	meet an objection	211
make a withdrawal	106	meet expectations	370
make an accusation	271	meet expenditure	158
make an address	256	memorize a poem	353
make an advance	399	memorize poetry	353
make an allegation	264	miss a shot	316
make an apology	105	miss the bus	323
make (an) appeal	369	mix an ingredient	283
make an appointment	110	mold clay	351
make an arrest	116	monitor progress	397
make an assessment	115	mount a bicycle	323
make an enemy	218, 244	move down a hierarchy	218
make an error	116	move up a hierarchy	218
make (an) improvement	106		
make an investment	106, 167	**N**	
make an objection	211	name a source	201
make an offer	106	need a confirmation	173
make contact	111	need a stopover	324

Index 487

need assistance	414	open fire	245
need care	371	operate a policy	252
need cooperation	416	order a retreat	398
need encouragement	417	organize a campaign	253
need guidance	418	organize a conference	202
need information	181	outwit an opponent	314
need shelter	408	overcome a crisis	406
negotiate a contract	176	overcome (a) prejudice	227
		overcome (an) addiction	234
O		overcome fear	359
obey the law	273	owe an obligation	262
observe a custom	236		
observe convention	235	**P**	
obtain a degree	343	parboil a vegetable	281
obtain a visa	325	pass a sentence	273
offer a class	344	pass a subject	344
offer a refund	164	pass censorship	203
offer assistance	414	patch a program	193
offer encouragement	417	pay a deposit	167
offer guidance	418	pay attention	369
offer protection	407	pay regard	371
offer shelter	408	pedal a bicycle	323
open a conversation	331	peel a vegetable	281
open a debate	207	peer over glasses	300
open a document	182	perfect a craft	351
open a factory	174	perform a dance	352
open a negotiation	245	place a burden	265
open an account	163	place a hat	300
open an e-mail	194	place pressure	255

place responsibility	263	prohibit a practice	237
plagiarize a book	345	promote a product	155
plan a route	396	promote cooperation	416
play a game	314	promote investment	167
play a soldier	246	promote solidarity	220
plunge into a recession	156	promote someone to manager	173
point the way	399	promote welfare	226
polish shoes	298	pronounce a word	333
pose a problem	230	propose a salary	177
pose a threat	409	propose marriage	221
pose danger	406	protect right(s)	229
post a notice	388	prove a claim	263
postpone a meeting	172	prove an allegation	264
pour a drink	280	provide aid	226
pour an ingredient	283	provide an update	182
practice writing	344	provide care	371
prefer a style	298	provide guidance	418
prepare a Ph.D. dissertation	342	provide insurance	157
prepare an M.A. dissertation	342	provide protection	407
prescribe a treatment	292	provoke (a) conflict	227
prescribe antibiotics	290	provoke criticism	342
present a report	182	publish a journal	199
present a witness	274	publish a magazine	199
preserve a custom	236	pull (on) a coat	297
preside over a court	272	pull down a skirt	297
press charges	262	pursue an ideal	379
prevent an accident	405	put blame	264
print a pattern	389	put on a skirt	297
produce (a) culture	235	put on clothes	296

put on glasses	299	receive a memo	335
put on music	352	receive a mention	334
put pressure	255	receive a salary	177
put something to music	352	receive a threat	409
		receive aid	226
Q		receive an e-mail	194
qualify for a pension	167	receive an update	182
quicken pace	397	receive care	371
quote a source	201	receive encouragement	417
		receive news	198
R		receive support	413
rain come	307	recite a poem	353
rain drip down	307	recite poetry	353
rain fall	307	recognize a sign	390
rain let up	307	reconsider a decision	208
rain pour down	307	reduce expenditure	158
raise (an) alarm	405	reduce poverty	229
raise a concern	370	register for a class	345
raise a family	219	reimburse a fee	164
raise an objection	211	reinforce a stereotype	238
ratify a treaty	247	reject a stereotype	238
reach a consensus	209	relax censorship	203
reach a decision	208	release a defendant	272
read a journal	199	release a report	183
read a magazine	199	release a statement	334
read literature	342	relieve someone's	
realize expectations	370	embarrassment	359
receive a comment	331	remove a burden	265
receive a degree	343	remove something from heat	283

Index

renew a visa	325	revise a book	345
rent a bus	323	ride a bicycle	323
repair shoes	298	roast meat	282
reply to an e-mail	194	roll down a sleeve	298
report a crime	272	roll up a sleeve	298
require assistance	414	run a campaign	253
require attention	369	run a contest	315
require concentration	368	run a factory	175
require cooperation	416	run an editorial	202
require encouragement	417	run an office	175
reset a password	192		
resist an advance	399	**S**	
resist pressure	255	satisfy someone's curiosity	369
resole shoes	298	save a document	182
resolve a complaint	212	save money	165
respect a custom	236	save oneself from	
respect privacy	183	embarrassment	359
respect right(s)	229	say a word	332
restore (one's) pride	362	scan a headline	200
restore one's honor	377	scan for viruses	191
restrict access	184	score a goal	316
resume a negotiation	246	scramble an egg	282
retain right(s)	229	see a show	201
return heat	283	see danger	407
return love	361	seek a divorce	219
retype a password	192	seek a sponsor	417
reveal a scandal	255	seek assistance	414
reveal a source	201	seek comfort	415
reverse a decision	208	seek fame	376

seek guidance	419	show (a) film	121
seek happiness	360	show a flair	126
seek love	361	show a passport	121
seek shelter	408	show a pattern	131
seize an opportunity	228	show a profit	121
select a fact	185	show a sign	131, 390
send (out) a memo	335	show a tendency	131
send an e-mail	194	show a vestige	132
send details	184	show ability	120
serve a drink	281	show affection	125
serve a meal	284	show an example	382
serve as a soldier	246	show approval	130
serve something with a salad	281	show concern	125, 370
set a course	398	show deference	121
set a fashion (trend)	236	show details	184
set a price	157	show diplomacy	126
set a record	316	show direction	395
set an example	381	show faith	126
set up a factory	175	show goodwill	121
settle (a) conflict	227	show hand	126
settle an affair	253	show interest	367
shape clay	351	show leadership	121
share a belief	380	show mercy	126
shed blood	288	show one's (true) colors	386
shift a burden	266	show one's anger	358
shift blame	265	show partiality	126
shoot down a missile	245	show promise	131
show a bias	131, 209	show proof	131
show (a) change	131	show respect	126

Index

show sadness	362	spell a word	333
show solidarity	230	spend time online	190
show surprise	363	spread a scandal	256
show teeth	122	spread viruses	191
show the door	121	sprinkle (with) cheese	279
show the way	122	stand trial	274
show the world	132	start a blog (of one's own)	192
show unease	127	state a belief	380
shut down a factory	175	state an objection	211
sign a contract	176	state an opinion	210
sign a manifesto	201	stay online	190
sign a memo	336	steam a vegetable	281
sip a drink	280	steam fish	280
sit out a dance	352	steer a ship	323
skip a meal	284	stew meat	282
slice cheese	279	stir in an ingredient	283
slow progress	396	stop an advance	399
smear blood	288	straighten a skirt	297
smooth (down) a skirt	297	study literature	342
snap up a meal	284	submit a scoop	199
snow cover	309	subscribe to a journal	199
snow pile up	309	subscribe to a magazine	199
snow swirl	309	sue a defendant	273
snow thaw	309	suffer from cancer	290
soften one's tone	336	sun come out	305
sound a warning	389	sun rise	305
sound an alarm	405	sun set	305
speak a language	331	sun shine	305
speed (up) a recovery	289	supervise an office	175

Index

supply an alibi	270	take a risk	145
support a manifesto	201	take a route	396
support an ideal	379	take a second	136
support relatives	217	take a shape	140
support views	211	take a subject	344
surf the net	193	take a taxi	324
survive (a) disaster	407	take a test	136
survive an accident	405	take a tip	185
swell with pride	362	take a tone	336
		take a turn	140

T

		take a vote	253
tackle a crime	272	take advantage of	144
tailor a style	299	take aim	144
take (an) action	143	take an interest in	140
take (an) issue	144	take an order	136
take a break	135	take antibiotics	290
take a breath	139	take blame	265
take a chance	135	take care	144, 371
take a class	345	take charge	144
take a course	136, 398	take comfort	415
take a direction	395	take credit	381
take a drink	280	take delight in	139
take a jump	140	take effort to	140
take a look	140	take interest	367
take a message	136	take note	140
take a picture	136	take off a mark	388
take a pill	136	take off clothes	296
take a point of view	144	take on (a) form	387
take a position	212	take out a loan	166

Index

take part in	144	turn in an essay	343
take pride	362	turn off a route	396
take responsibility	262	turn up heat	303
take score	317		
take the day off	136	**U**	
take the place of	144	undergo an operation	290
take the subway	325	understand a language	331
take the trouble to	140	understand the bottom line	174
take up arms	244	undo a button	301
tenderize meat	282	uninstall a program	193
throw a cloak	299	unveil a logo	387
thunder boom	308	upgrade a system	191
thunder growl	308	urge caution	406
thunder roll	309	use a brush	350
thunder shake	308	use a code	183
tighten (up) security	228	use a language	332
tighten censorship	203	use a term	332
tip a hat	300	use a tip	185
top with cheese	279	use a word	333
toss a cloak	299	use the subway	325
toss a salad	281		
trace a witness	274	**V**	
trade shares	157	violate a law	273
transfer an asset	158	violate privacy	183
travel on a train	325	voice a complaint	212
treat (an) addiction	235	voice opposition	208
tremble with anger	258		
tug at a sleeve	298	**W**	
turn down heat	283	wage war	247

Index 495

want a divorce	219	wind blow	307
want a promotion	174	wind die down	308
want justice	377	wind howl	307
waste money	165	wind roar	307
watch a show	201	wind sweep	307
wave a flag	387	withdraw a claim	263
wear a hat	300	withdraw a statement	335
wear a skirt	297	withdraw aid	226
wear clothes	296	withdraw an objection	211
wear glasses	300	withdraw money	165
weave a pattern	388	work on a painting	353
widen (an) appeal	369	work on a scoop	199
wield a brush	350	wrap a cloak	299
win a contract	176	write a composition	341
win a debate	216	write a memo	335
win a game	314	write a Ph.D. dissertation	342
win a promotion	174	write an editorial	202
win an election	255	write an essay	343
win fame	376	write an M.A. dissertation	342
win respect	378		

台灣廣廈 國際出版集團
Taiwan Mansion International Group

國家圖書館出版品預行編目（CIP）資料

分類主題 實用搭配詞：金星宇、李浚涉、李海彥、張仁喆 著. --
初版. -- 新北市：國際學村，2025.06
　　面；　公分
ISBN 978-986-454-423-3（平裝）
1.CST: 英語　2.CST: 詞彙

805.12　　　　　　　　　　　　　　　　　　114004632

國際學村

分類主題 實用搭配詞
10大核心動詞×30大情境主題，日常生活到職場商務，百倍提升英文表達力！

作　　　者／金星宇・李浚涉 　　　　　李海彥・張仁喆	編輯中心編輯長／伍峻宏・編輯／許加慶 封面設計／曾詩涵・內頁排版／菩薩蠻數位文化有限公司 製版・印刷・裝訂／皇甫・秉成

行企研發中心總監／陳冠蒨　　　　線上學習中心總監／陳冠蒨
媒體公關組／陳柔彣　　　　　　　企製開發組／張哲剛
綜合業務組／何欣穎

發　行　人／江媛珍
法　律　顧　問／第一國際法律事務所 余淑杏律師・北辰著作權事務所 蕭雄淋律師
出　　　版／國際學村
發　　　行／台灣廣廈有聲圖書有限公司
　　　　　　地址：新北市235中和區中山路二段359巷7號2樓
　　　　　　電話：(886) 2-2225-5777・傳真：(886) 2-2225-8052
讀者服務信箱／cs@booknews.com.tw

代理印務・全球總經銷／知遠文化事業有限公司
　　　　　　地址：新北市222深坑區北深路三段155巷25號5樓
　　　　　　電話：(886) 2-2664-8800・傳真：(886) 2-2664-8801
郵　政　劃　撥／劃撥帳號：18836722
　　　　　　劃撥戶名：知遠文化事業有限公司（※單次購書金額未達1000元，請另付70元郵資。）

■出版日期：2025年06月　　　　ISBN：978-986-454-423-3
　　　　　　　　　　　　　　　版權所有，未經同意不得重製、轉載、翻印。

결정적 어휘력 콜로케이션 붙어다니는 짝꿍단어 1500 [2판]

Copyright ©2022 by KIM SUNG WOO & LEE JUN SEOP & LEE HAE EON & JANG IN CHULL All rights reserved.
Original Korean edition published by Surprise Publishing.
Chinese(complex) Translation rights arranged with Surprise Publishing.
Chinese(complex) Translation Copyright ©2025 by Taiwan Mansion Publishing Co., Ltd. through M.J. Agency, in Taipei.